THE
WORM
IN
THE ROSE

THE
WORM

Also by Tom Stacey:

FICTION
The Brothers M
The Living and the Dying
The Pandemonium

NONFICTION
The Hostile Sun
Summons to Ruwenzori
Today's World

IN THE ROSE

TOM STACEY

STEIN AND DAY/*Publishers*/New York

First published in the United States of America in 1985.
Copyright © 1985 by Tom Stacey
All rights reserved, Stein and Day, Incorporated
Printed in the United States of America
STEIN AND DAY / *Publishers*
Scarborough House
Briarcliff Manor, N.Y. 10510

Library of Congress Cataloging-in-Publication Data

Stacey, Tom, 1930–
   The worm in the rose.

  I. Title.
PR6069.T18W67   1985   823'.914   85-40249
ISBN 0-8128-3049-0

Special thanks to R.J. and S.W.E.S.

In memory of Tom Milton

PART
ONE

1

One would be wrong to suppose when I learned of the sudden death of Saqr that I was consciously seeking a means of "rectifying the spirit", or whatever the term may be. But here was something I could do. It had been needling, oh, perhaps most of my life, from whenever the worm entered the rose, needling, intruding . . . my present companion had used the word "possession", laughingly claiming the role of exorcist: one could call "it" the worm itself.

I had plenty to do as it was. Making the farm pay. Providing for Sophia my lawful wife, rendering her due affection according to the vows given by the heart and also before God. Discharging troubled loyalties to our single offspring, Frances. Satisfying the expectations of employees and friends (whom Sophia divided into *mine* and *hers*). Generally to present a face to the world that was reasonably in keeping with my background, blah, blah, blah (I am one of those with a "background").

I had been out of the newspaper business too long to take an insider's interest in the demise of an unknown princeling from a part of the world I had no likelihood of going back to. So what made me act? The death of love? To be rid of the stink of an old corpse of love? To . . .

We – that is, Sophia and I – take three dailies, which I still regard as a minimum for keeping abreast of human affairs; and an account of the event is given in each. As normal, I have fetched the papers and the post from the drive gates after milking and bring them in to breakfast.

"Morning dog," I say. "Morning Sophia."

"Oh thank you," she replies, but I pretend not to hear, her intention being to complain that I greeted the labrador before I greeted her. Perhaps she is justified: it doesn't take all that much of a person to love a dog.

It is a stubbornly hopeful moment of day. The breakfast room, an annexe of the kitchen, is in yellow to which Sophia ascribes warmth. An hour in the milking sheds has sharpened the appetite. Clambering dreams – dead-end escapes – are obliterated by phoney solidities: our own yellow butter, a pot of coffee, the morning news. Sophia picks up the *Mail* first. They have made it the second lead – it is a thin day – and almost at once she mutters, "Your friend Timmy Lunt . . ."

"Yes?"

"This prince shot himself on Timmy Lunt's shoot."

"Did he?"

"Yes, in Wales."

Wales. I remember Wales. I have not been able to forget Wales.

The Times' account covers six inches below the fold on page one, and even the *FT* has given it two paragraphs inside. It hardly merited more: a straight shooting accident – climbing a fence without unloading, silly bugger. There would be the formality of an inquest. Unlucky for Timmy, a junior minister in the Foreign Office, that young Prince Saqr should have been his guest at the time. But the shaikhdom to which Saqr is heir is hardly significant even in Gulf politics.

"He shouldn't have taken him out," Sophia comments, cup in hand.

"If somebody wants to make a fool of himself . . ." I begin. "Timmy Lunt is hardly to blame."

I am accustomed to seeing Timmy's name in print, his face on the box. I didn't grudge him when his political career began to glimmer – I had my own spell of relative fame, as something of a star of Fleet Street, reporting from abroad the squalid dramas of contemporary history for a decade and more: at least one escaped in those days that condescending query *What d'you do with yourself these days, Anthony?* plus puzzled frown, as if one is temporarily out of prison. In my newspaper period people knew what I did – which was more than could then be said of Timmy Lunt, trailing his coat round the winnable Tory constituencies. He found a marginal, which he lost, but by the next General Election redistribution had awarded him a plump little majority.

By then I was almost through one career. It had dried up my family life, and as Britain's power shrivelled so – I assured myself – did the significance of the job. When Sophia's family

4

land came to her the decision to quit while I was still at the top did not seem difficult. But then – that was embedded in other, subtler decisions: to stay in a single place, put down roots, to discover my own child, to give love another chance. I used to set great store by loving.

Meanwhile, Timmy began to emerge. You can't always tell, can you, the qualities that are going to count. Nor what talent a party leader has access to in the elected House, or what caches of obligation can be built up on Back Bench committees by long hours or judicious toadying. Timmy always had a kind of sardonic drive . . . At any rate, when the electorate re-entrusted his lot with their traditional role, I observed that Timothy Percival Charles Lunt, who up to the age of fifteen went to bed in winter wearing his underclothes beneath his pyjamas, had achieved minor ministerial office in the Department of this or that. And lo and behold a Parliament or two later he was transferred to one of the Under-Secretaryships in that field where I could not help but still regard myself a professional, namely foreign affairs. It seemed natural that I should write to congratulate him, fully aware that I had more understanding of his subject in my little finger than he had in the whole of his (slightly deformed) body. I received back on House of Commons writing paper a typed note of puff-chested humility at the portentousness of his task in a troubled world, with a *Dear Anthony* and *Yours, Timmy* in that familiar hand which I had always guessed would never quite achieve an impression of maturity.

Should it be thought that my intervention into the bizarre affair of Saqr was inspired by jealousy, I will declare at once, *Yes*, there is a thread of it. Newspapermen often reckon that if chucked the desk keys of the politicians whose functions they cover, *they* would do a better job. Such conceit is part of their stock-in-trade. Often enough the reporter has been handling the subject a lot longer than the politician; yet it is on the other's half-truths and mealy compromises he must hang much of his copy. Were I still in the game, to be trailing after Timmy on some itinerary abroad, waiting to pick up piddling truisms or evasions as he steps onto a plane, rising to my feet with the proud-to-be-asked guests as he takes his place at an official banquet, watching him slide off in a limousine amid

5

outriders with my despatch still to file before going to bed, would give me the pip. But not more than the pip. To the journalistic profession high office has no awe. What might impress? The petty authority? The grandiose honours? The brief prominence? At such close quarters they are sounding brass and tinkling cymbals. You learn to judge the politicoes coldly for their worth, and one in ten might be worth one tenth of what is claimed for him or her. To say that is not jealousy, it's accuracy. Only if I were to find my colleagues taking Timmy at face value might that thread . . .

Perhaps it was never so much to do with Timmy himself as what I chose to make him stand for; even now, I can't unravel that. And in the end I could be tempted to pity him.

Sophia puts aside the paper and starts on the post. "If you're going to disappear for lunch," she says, reminding me of her domestic burden, "I hope you'll trouble to let me know."

"I always do." Which earns me no more than the tiniest of coughs, scarcely a clearing of the throat, registering my response as beneath contempt.

Sometimes my affairs bring me to London all on my little own for the day and sometimes a night as well. These affairs are not what Sophia, who is adept at inducing a sense of guilt under a general heading of indifference to others, can choose to hint. I don't know if she still cares if there are other women in my life or is, as usual, making what she has to put up with an object of reverence – a little fetish of hard wood in the corner of her hut. She will defend this ferociously. Then all at once it is no longer there: she will be confused, compliant, contrite, having made shapes out of mere shadows. For a moment (sometimes with tears) – but only for a moment – I will be reminded of the accessibility of happiness I have taken as for ever forfeited.

What in fact brings me to London is that I am still writing the occasional piece for friendly editors – an "op ed" twelve-hundred worder for my old "distinguished" daily, a couple of legs of solid print for one of the weeklies. That kind of thing. I like to keep in touch with Fleet Street. But the actualities of keeping the farm in the black make it difficult to find subjects to which I have still something worth adding . . . I could write about God – Sophia has taken to calling me a "spiritual dilettante", a term I happen to know she picked up from a clever neighbour which hurts because it fits. But who would want to read me on God with convictions forever fading and returning like the Cheshire cat? So I don't offer God.

If I stay away the night I put up innocently enough at one club, and usually dine at another, a Fleet Street coterie from which I have never persuaded myself to resign, and where the subject of young Prince Saqr's death comes up naturally enough a few evenings later. For that same afternoon the Foreign Secretary answered a Back Bencher's planted question by reiterating official grief, and painstakingly endorsing the findings of the coroner's inquest: a simple shooting accident. Nobody tried to score Party points. The Opposition spokesman wished to identify his side of the House with the Government's condolences to the old Shaikh, who is Saqr's father and the present Ruler of the Khor shaikhdom. Nobody put any supplementaries.

"Nor did they at the F.O. briefing for the foreign press this morning," the Diplomatic Correspondent of a national newspaper dining next to me says. He is a news-hardened Scot whose handkerchief flowering in his breast pocket establishes him as a character. "I'm afraid that's all it is, just any regular idiot climbing a fence without unloading."

"What d'you mean 'afraid'?" a man linked with the *Guardian* asks, a newcomer since my day, whom the Scot accords the merest frown of pity, adding that all the same the incident will have done Timothy Lunt no good.

"I don't agree." The editor of the national daily for which I used to work has intervened. "It won't affect him either way. He's handled it without getting the least rattled."

"He shouldn't have invited Saqr out shooting if the laddie didn't know his gun drill."

"That prince'd been out before on one of Lunt's shoots," the editor retorts. "Heavens alive, he'd been through Sandhurst. Nobody's going to blame Lunt."

"Not even in the Gulf?" The Dip Corr is still combative, but chastened. The editor has seen a lot, once briefly held Cabinet office. "The old Shaikh's dying. Saqr was his heir. He was rated high – one of our lads. Pro us."

"So what?"

"His death de-stabilizes the Shaikhdom."

7

"There'll be other sons."

"There is another son, yes," the Dip Corr says. He has his facts.

"There you are."

"He's a wreck."

"What d'you mean exactly?" the *Guardian* man asks but again gets no direct reaction beyond the Dip Corr reasserting that in the Gulf there would be whispering, Who was to blame? Was the death engineered? It's the most volatile area in the world, a third of the world's oil coming out of that bloody Gulf . . .

"Saqr's shaikhdom has no oil," I interpose, at which the Dip Corr asserts heavily, "Dominoes, dear boy."

Then the editor wonders aloud: Am I not an old school mate of Lunt? And I – just as if it were the most commonplace enquiry in the world – confirm that I was an exact contemporary: I knew him even before we were at school together, for my cousins lived not far from that very estate in North Wales where Saqr died. I visited the Lunt house as a small boy and shot a rabbit . . .

"And learned to unload climbing fences," the Dip Corr puts in, wiping his mouth with his linen flowers.

The editor pursues his own train of thought. "The Party still likes a few broad acres on the Front Bench. Ancestral pastures are in short supply in the House nowadays – one can have enough smarty-boot entrepreneurs and tricky lawyers."

"And bleeding-heart defectors from local government," the Dip Corr adds provocatively for the *Guardian* man.

The conversation swings elsewhere – there is no meat on the story. So that when, half an hour later crossing the street to see his early edition, the editor remarks, "So you know Lunt really well, then, Anthony?" I am surprised he should have mentioned Timmy again.

2

Whom do we ever know? We can become strangers to those who share our lives. Yet it isn't easy to believe we can ever be a stranger to those we once knew intimately as children. Nor, I suggest, to those with whom we have shared some great ordeal. Which is why I am confident in my knowledge of Billy French, though we shared scarcely a week of our lives.

I *knew* Billy French, and knowing him so well, so sharply, I have a clear enough view of Elaine his wife – that same afternoon Saqr died – coming out onto the veranda of their rather lowly bungalow overlooking the Gulf's straits to meet the Wali's clerk. She has heard his footsteps on the gravel and prefers him not to find her in the kitchen. Without her make-up she looks sallow and tight mouthed; two in the afternoon is an odd time for a caller.

As she takes the strip of white paper from the clerk's dark hand, what is in her mind, according to her own account later, is *How dare Billy give me a conscience about being in the kitchen? What else is there for me to do?* The other "Western" wives all have an occupation: one her weaving, one her Arab infants, one her archaeology. And they are younger than she.

Elaine's interests, not counting the care of Billy, are far from this heat-sieged bachelor bungalow where nothing belongs to them except Billy's leopard: they are back in Essex where six months of the year she escapes this wilderness of rock and water – back with the little granddaughter Sharon has given her (who could so easily have died), and her very own garden, her church.

She steps down from the veranda and crosses the gravel to the work-room Billy is pleased to call the "majlis". She lays the message on his trestle table without reading it since it is none of her business, although her eye involuntarily catches the IMMEDIATE on the top like a cockroach on the kitchen floor. There is nothing she can do: Billy is away somewhere with his beloved tribesmen and will return that night in his own good

9

time. He is as much married to his tribesmen as to her.

With a cook-houseboy, a shared driver, and a gardener, what indeed is left for her? . . . except every now and then to give substance to her shafts of love for Billy in little dishes meticulously prepared. How often would he contrive to blunt those shafts, being such a small eater, or late, or skipping his meals altogether.

"Go for a drive," Billy would suggest, half serious.

But they are at the end of the earth! The race of men that populates the globe eastwards from Casablanca ends here in nether Arabia, where gaunt mountains crumble into the sea in a confusion of fjords and bights and promontories and barren islets, a wilderness fit for its scattering of semi-savages. With her kind of visa, she can't even drive up the coast and across the frontier to the Shaikhdoms. Billy can . . . but Billy will go out of his way to avoid the bright lights.

Life is gay across the frontier. She can tell that from the *Gulf Times*, which reaches the *suk* by mid-morning these days; a different world – scuba clubs, tennis tournaments, whist drives, ice cream parlours, cinemas, five-star hotels, skating rinks, show business personalities from London . . . In the big towns over there they even have a Women's League of Health and Beauty. Sometimes she can hardly bear to look at the *Gulf Times*, except for the Stars. She is Virgo. (She was to tell me she fitted Virgo to a T – tender, compliant, thoughtful, loyal, careful.) No doubt she has read what is forecast for Virgo on the day I write of, although most of the things the Stars say cannot properly apply because every day is the same void: nothing to do, nowhere to go.

At night, when Billy is up in the mountains with his tribesmen, she watches the lights of the tankers passing through the middle of the strait, fifteen miles out. She marvels at the liberty of those ships like a prisoner watching birds in flight through the grill of a cell. If you average it out, so they say, one tanker goes through every twenty-eight minutes.

She watches them this particular night, waiting for Billy, with Mercy the cat (whom Billy will call Fido) in her arms.

The tankers, as it happens, do not berth at the first port – a hundred miles over the frontier from where Elaine French watches – because that neighbouring Shaikhdom, Saqr's, possesses no oil. But this self-same evening, the Wilkses are holding one of their musical evenings, and the Wilkses comprise a social presence sufficient to persuade friends to drive all the way from the big new towns further up the coast to demonstrate allegiance to the civilisation they subscribe to. Later, I came across the programme in Ismail Barzakh's flat: *A Musical Soirée of the xvi & xvii centuries.*

In the interval after the Byrd and the Thomas Tallis, Lucy Wilks – so appealing, so vital – does her hostess thing, bowling them into the food phase in the adjoining elegant upper chamber with carefree authority. Grover Wilks himself, it seems, briefly vanishes after the last applause – easily done in such complex Arab house. Ismail Barzakh reckons he alone among the guests perceives the restiveness in Grover Wilks, but of course Barzakh alone among the guests was to have cause to speculate on the events of that evening. Moreover, he is the only non-Westerner among the guests, the only one whose first language is also that of the servants. A different viewpoint.

Wilks' return a few minutes later calls for no more interruption in the chatter than passing acknowledgements. "Ah, the maestro!" "Have a drink, Amadeus," and certain guests whom Barzakh thinks ought to know better proffer him his own gin sling which their host declines with the diffident, buried wit that shields him so efficiently. Wilks does not drink. One of the ladies lightly catches his arm and assures him, *sotto voce*, how much she is looking forward to the Palestrina, she really is. She wants him to discern music in her background, but Wilks' "You *are?*" in his leisured New England tone delivered with a new-moon smile gives her no cue.

A difficult man to get close to, Grover Wilks; none would dispute that, not excepting Barzakh. His brilliance is widely recognised, and the fact he is so thoroughly in the know. Anyone would be glad of his trust, but no one gets it. "What I say about Grover," Ismail Barzakh declared emphatically when retailing to me the events of this particular evening, "is, he is always a step ahead. *Comprenez?*"

Wilks introduces Barzakh all round, his arm draped across his Arab friend, the shorter (and older) man: "Surely you know Ismail, the Jonathan Swift of the Lower Gulf?" And scolds them for not reading Arabic and so keeping up with "progressive thought" in the Gulf by taking the monthly journal Barzakh brings out in the shaikhdoms' federal capital.

Lucy Wilks, meanwhile, is informing each little cluster of guests in turn that there is "only moussaka, it's all you are getting," which is an understatement since the Eritrean maid and Adeni driver are gliding amongst the guests bearing trays not only of moussaka but an innovative salad of melon, celery and nuts, and after that a most delicious *mocca* gateau which Barzakh has to wolf to recapture his seat before the recital resumes.

It seems there are about thirty present this evening, nearly all driven down from the skyscraper shaikhdoms – bankers, engineers, oilmen; a species of businessman from London, another from Los Angeles; two diplomats (one American, one English – Nigel Fountain) and their wives; a popular young ex-Horse Guards officer who manages the old Shaikh's stables, and his sparkling little wife; the lower Gulf's rugged Cartier representative (formerly a mercenary in a shaikhly army) just returned from skiing with his "very very liberated" (Barzakh's view) young lady; a French architect completing the latest Méridien; and heads of the rival hospital management teams, American and British. That was all Barzakh could remember. But, "When the Wilkses give a party, Anthony, the people really worth knowing in the lower Gulf are likely to be there, even if only passing through. That is Madame Lucy's special gift."

As they file back into the long *majlis*, talk turns on the grave illness of the local Shaikh, an old man widely honoured. The stable manager saw him a month before, perky but frail and yellow. The disease is in the liver. Somebody asks why they didn't keep him at the Wellington, so Barzakh has to explain that if he died in a London hospital the tribes would suspect he was poisoned: Fountain nods sagely. Someone remarks that young Saqr has a lot of his dad in him, which is to say that the Shaikhdom would still be in good hands when the old man was called.

Yet, as I was to calculate later, even taking into account the time difference between the Gulf and Britain, Saqr is dead before Grover Wilks is into the Palestrina . . .

A *sssh* indicates that Wilks is about to address them from the raised portion under the arch where the harpsichord stands – a fragile figure in open-necked shirt and cotton trousers, waiting for the hubbub to subside. Barzakh, who never developed a taste for Western classical music, settles at the far end behind the rows of chairs, under one of the screened arches which in daytime admit the light. Wilks' introductory homily – how, singlehanded, by creative genius and political decisiveness at the Papal court, Palestrina released upon Europe the first flood of polyphony – is given with his hesitant blend of humour and intensity. Then he sits down to play with firm authority.

Brian Proctor, cellist, from the British Bank, turns the pages. On the walls behind the harpsichord, as I can now vouch, a prayer rug is suspended. Dried sunflowers stand on a period table across from the player and the plucked sounds ring clear and brilliant between the chequered marble of the floor and high ceiling as if offered anew to the glory of God.

13

3

"Darling" – in the metallic timbre I detect instantly the intended note of despair, though have I not shown often enough my imperviousness to her standard style of despair? – "Darling I simply want to know before I go shopping. That's all I'm asking. If you're not going to be around, there's hardly any point in my shopping at all. I've no desire to go shopping for myself."

I flick a glance at my trainee farm manager and point out calmly that I am trying to explain a matter of complexity and immediacy, and that I don't yet know what my plans are. I attempt to resume but will not be allowed to.

"You can bloody well do the shopping yourself." Her bunch of keys lands violently on the farm office desk. "Does it ever occur to you that other people have lives to live?" For a few years now she has preferred to generate her quarrels in the presence of third parties, having discovered that she can be as vehement as she pleases without fear of response in kind. Though my calm fuels her.

Quite often I have heard people call Sophia saintly on account of being married to me – and only half in jest. It may be true since saintliness has a random definition and none of us knows what others have to endure inside. Her selfless devotion, when she perceives a call for it, is certainly exemplary – as applied for instance to our daughter Frances or her mother or even me, though I am not so often in need of it. Her unselfishness comes in rages and can be often accompanied by a proportionate disgust at the selfishness or thoughtlessness of others peripherally involved such as, quite often, myself. Selfish sins of commission (like intemperate noise when Frances is said to be having a migraine) are much easier to avoid than sins of omission, which are seldom or never pointed out at the time but are left to go bad like poisoned mice under the floorboards until the house reeks of nameless accusation.

It is also a fact that Sophia can look saintly. She reached

14

adulthood with a purity of expression and cleanness of facial lineament that could be breathtaking. In Sophia you could believe it possible to love God and love a woman in the same person. At our rather fashionable wedding (St Paul's, Knights-bridge) not one but two female guests, both married them-selves, gave as their opinion that Sophia was really too lovely to be married – a pseudo-profundity which I suspect was doing the round at the reception (at the Berkeley). Had we not all just borne witness to God having joined us in holy matrimony? At least they had the courtesy to imply that whoever married Sophia – not specifically I – would be soiling her. Yet I was unmistakeably rakish beside her. And a journalist too. How much more suitable a well-laundered young diplomat or smug little merchant banker.

I myself noticed points of comparison between Sophia's face and the only authentic portrait of St Catherine of Genoa, on whom Friedrich von Hugel wrote his masterpiece on spirit-uality I was reading sometime around then. It seems that Catherine's saintliness was highlighted by her husband's reputation for neglect and wastrelly conduct. So far as outsiders were concerned my most obvious offence was to spend long periods abroad, usually in places unsuitable for a correspondent's wife to follow, especially after Frances arrived. That "neglect" alone was enough to endorse Sophia's reputation.

After several years, St Catherine's husband fell into line and buckled down alongside her in her charitable work until his early death, rather as I came back to run Sophia's family farm after her father died. But in our case I left it too late: too much had happened, and there was also the difference that it was I, not she, who had the interest in religion. I had a need for it, would be caught desolate without it, sensed it to be an ingredient in human affairs which, neglected, invited cata-strophe. This is not to suggest these recurring attempts to perceive and sometimes even to respond to the intentions of God made me a better person: the opposite could be true, because a propensity to recognise evil brings with it wonder at the properties of evil, especially as they may be manifest in oneself.

The contention this morning on the farm arises from young

Prince Saqr's sudden death. I have told Sophia that my former editor – still in the chair – expressed interest in my having known Lunt closely and that as a result an assignment is in the wind which after all these years would disrupt our routine of life. I suspect she has already sensed the truth (as she is quick to do) – that it is I who took the initiative. To try to explain why would be to lead her into an old minefield: even if she accepted that I alone could spot evidence of pure evil merely by glancing at a television interview, for me to act on such a hunch would demonstrate me as someone – as I mentioned before – "possessed".

The fact is, choosing my time carefully between the 11 a.m. editorial conference and lunch, I telephoned my old editor and put to him an idea concerning the death of Prince Saqr, and the editor said he would think it over and call me back. That was the day before yesterday. I mentioned nothing to him, either, about a television interview, and instead allowed him to suppose I am still in touch with my Middle Eastern contacts whose suspicions are aroused, not about Lunt's part in it, but by the death itself.

I detected from his tone a genuine interest. He asked me how I might tackle it – go to see Lunt himself, for example? "Not in the first instance," I replied. "What, then?" I said: "If it were anything other than an accident, there would be two aspects – a motive, and the mechanics of it."

"And a cover-up, I suppose." (I let him say it.)

"No need for any cover-up if the mechanics were clever enough."

"Nobody's even so much as hinted at a motive, Anthony."

This was a sort of caution. Editors these days are especially wary of being taken for a ride by plausible journalists who turn out more creative than investigative.

"I thought I might take a closer look at the mechanics first," I said.

"You mean, Wales," he answered, obviously relieved that I wasn't asking him to finance a trip to the Middle East on so slender a pretext.

"That's all," I assured him, before ringing off.

So it is no surprise when later in the morning on which I have my *contretemps* with Sophia I receive a call tantamount to approval to proceed. There is an unsatisfactory qualification: the paper will cover my expenses, but since the assignment has been my proposal rather than theirs, may we regard it as something less than a definite commission at this stage and agree a fee "on results"?

When I eventually tell Sophia – at dinner that evening, after more telephoning has intervened – that I will be away for a long weekend the next but one, the third in January, engaged in journalistic research, she asks in a pejorative tone if I have become a "crime reporter". I am curt and reticent. "I thought you had shaken that off by now," she says, as if it was a disease, and she seems so genuinely crestfallen, her fist clenched round her thumb on the tablecloth, that I feel caddish at not including her more fully in my life and for only seeing things from my point of view. Whatever "my life" may mean.

Later that night in the bed in my dressing room where I have taken to sleeping, I become grievously lonely. I keep seeing that little fist on the tablecloth, which she and Frances chose in a flurry of delight for the pretty way it blended with the dining room wallpaper. "Results!" – how dare they assess my worth by "results", a man of my experience! Sophia had never wanted "results" from me. Perhaps she now sought the opposite: an experience of failure that love could heal. The seeds we "innocents" once planted – could they have proved utterly barren? When I was blown, found to be not innocent, she masked her love: the mask was now grown into her face, and for a long time now I have not attempted to recognise beauty in her. Sometimes it still strikes me, this beauty, though I see it as the relic of beauty, like a widow's. That word came to me just recently – the exquisite lines of the face that had once impelled my heart to seek hers were of a bereaved woman . . .

In my single bed I long to go through to her but I know I will not, for fear of a sour reprimand for waking her. Sleep has grown to be sacrosanct to her just as it does to all those in whom joy has been obliged to die.

17

4

I am still capable of the imaginative effort of identifying with another. For example, Elaine French: I have no difficulty filling out the sketch she herself was to give me, during the intimacy of our shared grief. It is with Sophia that my talent for lively sympathy deserts me.

There is Elaine on her veranda at night, waiting for Billy's return, watching those tankers twisting through the straits round the apex of the peninsular enclave of her Arabian exile. I share her sense of isolation. I can smell the partly-cooked meal she fears re-heating will spoil, and I can hear the dying strains of *The Skater's Waltz* on her record player in the kitchen. I join in her worries about her little granddaughter as she weighs up Billy's argument that after Sharon's "boo-boo" – having her child out of wedlock – Sharon will never pick herself up and make a life of her own if she, Elaine, is "scurrying around providing for all her wants".

She must ask Sharon in her next letter whether the camellia has come out, as occasionally it does in mild Januaries in its protected spot by the back door. During her first full winter at home (whenever that may be) she will keep a diary of all the little changes day by day from October to May.

For Elaine French is beauty-starved. Here, nothing is beautiful in nature. Or almost nothing. When once she accompanied Billy into the *jebel*, she wandered off on her own when the tribesmen were at their *mahgreb* prayer and saw a fox asleep in a little hollow. The late evening sun caught its coat, turning it into a hundred glints of russet, tan, bronze. She stood for many minutes until the last of the sun was gone from it, praying it would not awaken and run off – a prayer answered! She thinks it is the only thing belonging here she has ever seen that is beautiful – a solitary hint that God has not overlooked this place utterly.

Yet she knows Billy rejoices in this posting for its remoteness and desolation. That is Billy's way. He is a remote man himself

18

– hardy not hard, not a cosy man at all but not cold – oh dear
no: why, the previous year, didn't he bring a little tribal child
down from the mountains, almost blind, to this very bungalow, making such an upheaval, tending her at all hours of day
and night as if she was his very own daughter? Elaine very
nearly grew jealous of her – she has admitted so to me. Billy
badgered and badgered the Wali, (who he said had promised),
to get her into the new eye hospital faraway in the capital,
refusing to let her take a bed at the peninsula's Health Centre
for fear it might be decided that local treatment would suffice.
He made such a nuisance of himself. *And* got his way. "Know
what your scripture says, Elly? 'Suffer little children and forbid
them not; for such is the kingdom of Oz.' "

Billy could be so perverse. She had never managed to get him
to church on home leave. He declared himself godless, but she
did wonder. He'd never forgotten his Testament from his days
in the funeral business and out would pop his quotations when
you'd least expect. Just the other day: " 'Everyone that
forsaketh houses or brethren or children, tiddly-pom, shall
receive a hundredfold.' Right?" – when she was confiding her
homesickness; and when she groused at the way he would pick
at his food: " 'Take no thought for your life, what to eat, what
to drink' " – pat, like that – " 'Is not life more than meat, and
the body more than raiment?' Eh, dear?" "But you don't
believe in Jesus, Billy." "Life's too short."

There was no fathoming him. Sometimes she thought he
didn't belong anywhere, he was a wanderer, needing no home,
no place to rest, no heritage or progeny of his own at all . . .

The crunch of Billy's Land Cruiser on the murram road wakes
her from her reverie. Mercy leaps from her arms and patting
her weak hair she is on the veranda steps to greet him, with her
cheek forward for a little kiss – "just a token" as she was to tell
me all those weeks later. Her life is like that of a prisoner upon
whom the smallest intervention tells.

Billy gathers his canvas waterbottle – his "chargol" – from
the wing-mirror, and his reading spectacles, map-case and
field-glasses from the front seat. He gleams with sweat from
the top of his bald brown head right down along his hairy
arms, for he perspires dreadfully. It soaks across the shoulders
of his shirt, over his belly and along the top of his trousers-

seat.

She would rather he sat down at once to eat but she tells him of the message having come for him from the Wali's office.

"Message from 'wof'?" he protests. "What they on about?"

She put it in the *majlis*, she says.

He chucks his things onto the bed and enters the kitchen to make tea for both of them. "I think it said 'immediate'," she says.

And again he protests. "Immediate, immediate. They put 'immediate' on everything they send anywhere. Nobody reads anything unless it's got 'immediate' all over it."

He brings the mugs down from their hooks and slings in two teabags with their labels over the edge. She doesn't really want to drink sweet tea just before their meal.

"Give a wog a word like 'immediate' and before you turn round he's devalued it."

"I'll fetch it, Billy." And when she comes back the kettle is boiling already: Calorgas produces a wonderfully hot flame. He fills both mugs and passes Elaine hers. Settling at the table he gently kneads the teabag with his spoon, then scoops it out and swaddles it in the spoon with its own string, to extract a few extra drops of essence of tea. (He is very skilled at this.) Then a spoon of sugar – no milk: he takes it as his tribesmen do. He draws the telex towards him.

"Elly, dear, my specs." And she fetches them from the bedroom. He reads slowly. He puts his mug down frowning. He whispers slowly under his breath.

"Christ Alfuckingmighty."

Now it is Elaine's turn to protest. "You sound horrid when you say that, Billy. I can't tell you how horrid you sound."

He does not seem to be aware of her, which she attributes – mistakenly she now thinks – to his having grown deaf, during all his years on the Paludrine.

And at the same time, perhaps the same hour, that same hundred miles up the coast across the frontier, other more dramatic exterior happenings intrude upon the domestic scene. For an account of these I am indebted to two sources, one of whom is Ismail Barzakh, seated under the window arch. The music party is still in progress, though Grover Wilks has concluded his Palestrina on the harpsichord. Rising from the

20

stool to acknowledge applause more dutiful than passionate, (they would have preferred Gershwin or Scott Joplin), he is instantly diffident and remote once more, the pouchy mouth twitching downwards in characteristic self-deprecation, the little bow obscuring his forehead with fine pale hair. He hastens to introduce a *Bourré* of Praetorius for recorder, violin, 'cello (Mr Proctor of the British Bank) and tabor (to wit, a tribal Arab hand-drum, boldly, by the lady from the Craft Centre). Since in this work he has no part, he settles among the audience at the end of the front row of chairs.

The strains of the *Bourré* are bright and primal and not quite so out of tune that the faint but persistent sounding of the gate bell goes unnoticed. The intrusion is accented by Ahmed entering to whisper to Lucy Wilks in the back row, whereupon the lady quits the *majlis* at once, only to reappear thirty or forty seconds later at the musicians' entrance beckoning to her husband. Wilks' frown induced by the performance deepens; he rises and slips out past the musicians, his wife at once resuming her place among her guests at the back. Only Barzakh, from his arched window, sees where Wilks emerges: at the illumined outer gate in the garden wall. Thus – if I may include, indirectly, our host himself – I have the privilege of a second angle on this strange scene.

A flowering creeper, a heavy scented oleander, overhangs the garden's small iron door. In an untidy double rank along the wall of the garden compound and on either side of his own car port are ranged the twenty or so vehicles of the guests. It was the Shaikh's wish for the town not to expand on this northern perimeter, where the *wadi* cuts through the soft rock. Barzakh from above can make out the movement of Lucy's mare on its tether, alerted by the shaft of light and the intrusion of strangers. Beyond the bay animal, and the two acacias under which it resides, is the darkness of the *wadi* cleft, and further – into the desert – the lights of the cement plant and quartz company.

Now the actors.

Of the two Arabs confronting Grover Wilks across the garden doorway, one is terribly disfigured. His face and hands are a violence of raw lesions and lumps, caked and oozing blood as if a leopard from the *jebel* had got at him. His garments are bored by burns and stained blood-brown. Ravaged legs are visible through the *dishdasha*. His chequered headcloth, holed and scorched, is clutched across his lower face by the torn claw of his hand; his lashless eyes like blisters turn towards the lights of the compound. That he stands at all – even with another's support – makes him seem a phantasm, vaguely grinning behind lips ballooned by depravity: a minatory victim conjured by dark powers. Yet the blood is certainly real, having marked his companion's garments.

A laconic interchange ensues. Barzakh notices the servant Ahmed hovering in the garden behind Wilks.

Wilks closes the iron door upon them. The outer light is extinguished. Wilks moves back through the garden and into the stone passageway to the forecourt on the town side – his floating walk, but fast now. He mounts the stairway and slips back into the *majlis*, where the audience has broken into inexplicably enthusiastic clapping. He reappears under the arch beside the performers. The audience is as pleased with its own clapping as with the music: two at the back sarcastically compete for an encore like dimwits outbidding one another at an auction. Wilks is trying to announce something.

"They say 'A woman's work is never done' " – shyly, self-mockingly offered. The words dance among the guests and are caught only in snatches. "And it could be said of an adviser on tribal affairs too. A message from on high," – forefinger pointing up, Shaikhwards – "a little errand will take me away right now. Brian Proctor where are you?" – he glances about for the banker cellist, standing to one side with an expectant, tortured smile – "Brian will introduce the next item since I think it's fair to say that Henry Purcell had his viola da gamba chiefly in mind when he wrote it. You'll all forgive me if I slip away." And, *glissando*, he does, to a scatter of applause which takes him out onto the inner balcony and thence by the stone stairway and passage to the garden compound, now dark. In the ground floor office a telephone rings unanswered; Ahmed still hovers at the iron door of the garden and receives a quick instruction.

Outside, just visible, the two Arabs are stock still among the guests' fat cars, like lovers uplifted. Wilks moves to his Range Rover under its plywood canopy.

The couple shuffling forward, not lovers now: something vile, double-headed, multi-limbed; something to be forgotten, to be expunged, fumbling into the vehicle. Two half-wild pye-dogs run out to bark at the Range Rover which moves away cautiously. An accident in the *jebel* with kerosene, Barzakh supposes. But the manner of Wilks' excusal prompts him not to refer to the incident when they next meet.

5

The ancestral estate of the Foreign Office minister with special responsibility for the Middle East is high in acreage but low in income. It occupies a region whose climate and terrain are deemed fit to support only a scattering of peasant farmers, innumerable mountain sheep and sufficient imported pheasants to provide sport for half a dozen organized shoots between October and January. But North Wales is an antique land whose bones show through its skin, and makes for sullen reverence among its Welsh-tongued natives.

I have visited this place before. I was eight years of age; Timothy Lunt six months older. It was a summer holidays, during a stay with neighbouring cousins long since departed – but not all of that holidays, surely: a few weeks of it at most. How often was I driven out here – three or four times? I remember nothing about the look of it except a mullioned grandeur. Was a handful of visits enough for Timmy to implant that magnetic dread, not so much of him, but of what he might find in me? Today his elderly mother presides with her "partners" – two corgies and a venerable labrador. I have no recollection of such a formidable lady and nothing, surely, will connect eight-year-old Anthony Guise with her present Let Shoot visitor, a Mr "Tony Goode", a London insurance man. Only the *numen* of the house stirs memories of a granite authority and, on entering, an odour – saddlesoap – and a resonance: the heavy front door shutting, and voices, barks, footsteps approaching from depths and wings.

The *grande dame* is explaining: the season's first three shoots are for friends and neighbours – "not necessarily the same thing, you'll understand that, Mr Goode." She peers challengingly across the lunch table at her other guest, a gaunt duenna of a mere seventy-two (ages pointedly stated) who needs a blackthorn to walk with. "The third shoot's New Year's Day, Bank Holiday, all that bilge: one of the New Year holiday days, anyway – who can tell the difference? Nobody

24

does any work nowadays. Timmy brings a rabble for New Year unless there's a crisis. This year we had our own crisis right here of course. Thank God the poor little Prince didn't shoot anyone else. Much more to pay out for you insurance chaps for a start. The next two are Let shoots. They're what matter – the only way you can make any loot. Then there's the Staff Shoot. My God," she exclaims, "that's the battle of the Somme. Never dare set foot outside the house during the Staff Shoot. Meant to be only a dozen guns per drive, but there's never less than thirty. Anything that moves gets shot into Kingdom Come. Charley called it Massacre of the Innocents. Charley's my late husband," she clarifies in an unsettling present tense. "Now Bea, for heaven's sake take a splodge of that and a splodge of the other, you'll break Jonesie's heart." She refers to the apple meringue and rice pudding on offer from a dumpy parlourmaid.

"Mr Goode, *you* won't let Jonesie down, I know. That's one advantage of your arriving so dreadfully early – you'll gladden Jonesie. She always cooks too much whoever I have to lunch, even though she knows Lady Wynn-Williams just picks at her food."

"I have a perfectly normal appetite, Trix. I just won't guzzle."

"Nobody asks you to *guzzle*, dear."

Lady Wynn-Williams shoots a wicked glance to secure my complicity. She is like an old kestrel.

"It's really only the grandchildren I can trust to eat up properly. They eat like Trojans – they're my daughter's children: Timmy doesn't breed. Timmy was a good eater when he was younger. Now he's got an ulcer – all you can expect from politics: can't eat this, can't eat that."

He was already a boarder, I still at my pre-prep, a mere day-boy, an ignoramus . . . I can pinpoint year and season – fat lambs on the sward in front. And dark woods, crawling on bare knees. "He likes his politics, though. I was never sure he enjoyed his childhood," she complains sharply, as if he had no right not to. Yet the boy I knew seemed so precocious, fearing no one, plausible among adults. I never thought of him as a "child" at all. He was a male person that much older, colder, more organised. It's true there was no light in him: he

25

absorbed light. If you were his friend – whatever the appropriate word is – it was reward enough to see your own light glint in him sometimes.

"His arm kept him off games," Lady Wynn-Williams says.

Mrs Lunt looks at her ferociously. Yet we all knew one arm was a little shorter than the other – some infantile mishap, perhaps congenital. It interfered with cricket and rowing, and rugby football. It marked him out early, then we forgot; nobody ragged him at the public school where I joined him at thirteen. But at this lunch table we have blundered on ancient privacy. And thus alarmed, the great bust under layers of beige cashmere, festooned with miniature jewjaws, the splodge of a face, like Jonesie's pudding, with its negligently stained hair dumped on top like a lawyer's wig, appear no longer genial, but dangerous.

"Timmy could shoot, fish, play tennis," she ticks them off for me, while the venom is directed at her companion. "All the normal things."

To compliment Mrs Jones, I am conducted via a green baize door down a stone corridor to a kitchen of majestic proportions, and announced as Mr Goode, come to say his piece: "not expected for lunch at all but now he's here we're making the best of him."

One of Mrs Jones' eyes is wildly askew. Dumpy and indulgent she tells me at once she has been working here thirty-eight years, come May: sheer continuity justifies existence. "It was different then, mind. We 'ad the meat 'angin' from the ceiling, salted or smoked. We 'ad to wear our caps, them maggots kept droppin' on us." The ranked hooks are still there. So are the bells, one for every room, two dozen or more, high on the wall.

I must have eaten her food before – cake at some long-forgotten tea-party for the young master.

"We 'ad three in the kitchen then, di'n' we, ma'am, and five in the 'ouse. Now it's just me and Evans, like. Except for 'ouse parties – you don't know what to expect, Mr Tim bringing these oriental potentates."

"They bring slaves in *droves*," Mrs Lunt declares. "One of them tried to get off with you Jonesie, didn't he."

"I wouldn't let 'im touch me." With a grotesque snarl Mrs

26

Jones raises a kitchen knife in stabbing readiness. "I don't care 'oo they are." The proposition is difficult to visualise. "Your dog's been cryin' for you, sir."

But first I am to tour the house. "Don't you come, Bea, for the love of Mike," she declares, "with your leg. You know it like the back of your hand." Lady Wynn-Williams insists that she wants to see "where everyone was". To which Mrs Lunt ripostes to me, "I don't know what she's talking about," in rather more than an undertone.

It is an ambulatory rite conducted at speed like a gabbled liturgy. No chamber is omitted though several are only to be glimpsed, so that repeatedly Mrs Lunt is sailing out in full commentary while I and Lady Wynn-Williams are bobbing in: scullery, pantry, silver room, boiler room . . . "We heat the whole caboosh on oil – costs an absolute fortune. Quite daft, whole place crammed with trees – you could heat it twice over with what falls down every winter" . . . larder, buttery, game larder, office . . . "told that little prince if he wanted to keep in with us, send us some oil but he honestly said he hadn't got any – can you believe it? Said it was all next door at Abby Dabby . . ." laundry, servants' hall, back parlour.

Then library, music room, drawing-room once more . . . " 'Course you're perfectly normal, Mr Goode – insurance people usually are. Some of the people one gets on Let weekends, you'd hardly believe! Would he, Bea? Yugoslavs, Dutchmen, Greeks, the whole book of Pentecost. Scrap metal men, building contractors. Nylon tweeds and brand new Purdies they can't fit together. And the Yanks! – the paraphernalia! . . ." dining room again, billiard room, writing room . . . "what I call the telly room. I won't have it in my drawing room, everyone just gawps . . ." And still no mementoes of her only son except, in "Charley's den", a photograph of Timmy with the Party leader wearing vast rosettes. Or is the baby Timmy in the locket round her neck? Through the hall, bobbing into the gun room, then up the great staircase, the practised corgies scampering ahead, and all the while the link eludes me: how the cold and secretive boy issued from this body, sucked there. What passes on, what is suppressed by parent in offspring? Timmy a foundling? Not legitimate? "That's my husband's grandfather, Mr Goode, he

27

built the place, year of the Great Exhibition. Mind you, the Wynn-Williamses wouldn't speak to us when we arrived, would you, Bea? Thought Charley's grandfather was a parvenu with more money than was good for him, all made out of sleepers."

"Sleepers?"

"Choo-choo-choo."

It is a sombre portrait in oils of a surprisingly young man with full brown whiskers, gun dog at his feet. Parkland (not precisely hereabouts) stretches beyond. Apart from a pair of canny eyes it gives no clue that he came from nowhere and planted himself here, a ready-made fief with regional vowels . . . And then I see, unmistakeably, the tell-tale Lunt mark that has refused to grow out, trace of a flaw which the sitter – like the painter – contrived to nestle among the whiskers: the Lunt mouth.

"And horror of horrors," the mother is pursuing, "he was a Whig."

We have reached a panelled smoking-room, lined with hunting trophies where the late Charles' father, conveyor of that stubborn oral gene, started each day by reciting prayers to the entire staff, ". . . sixty-five, Mr Goode, before the first War, when I used to come here as a girl . . ." after which he blew the hunting horn and work began. The year *1854 AD* is carved above the central panel. It all has an air of dilapidation, as if the house has been patched since, but not repaired.

"And here's the old night-nursery – where we put the little prince. I hope you're satisfied, Bea."

The bed is a four-poster. The high ceiling has a moulded frieze and on the walls of big blue roses hangs a full-length portrait in pastel of a swan-necked young woman in a high bodiced, brocaded evening dress, in a Victorian frame behind glass. All trace of the night-nursery is gone. "They buzzed about him like flies two solid days. Doctors, coroners, detectives. Secret service. Our Welsh police chief himself, the big panjandrum. 'Course, they had to pull out all the stops for Timmy – he's got power of life and death over the lot. There were all the little prince's entourage . . ."

I postulate airily: Doesn't she think anyone else could have possibly shot him?

"Oh Lor', no." I get the whole spiel. No one else anywhere

28

near. Timmy himself on the very next peg, other side of the trees. The little prince trying to climb the fence and never unloaded. The shot got him under the chin, straight up into his skull. You'd have thought he'd know — been out before, been *here*, year before last. He'd done the right things up till then — Timmy wouldn't have been fool enough to take him out otherwise. People do get sloppy, of course. Over-excited. Sometimes quite proper people, let alone little princes from the back of beyond. 'Course, you don't get fences in the desert . . .

"*I* wouldn't be at all surprised if the prince was murdered," Lady Wynn-Williams pipes up unexpectedly, throwing me one of her wicked glances.

"What the blazes are you yabbering about, Bea?"

"He's just the sort of person who would be."

"Why talk drivel, dear?" her hostess asks with heavy sweetness.

We have paused under the mullioned windows giving onto the lawn. Beyond the haha stretches the pasture, scattered with cedars that mount towards banks of rhododendrons and woods where the drive emerges.

"If anybody had wanted to kill him," I volunteer, "they wouldn't have known what peg he would be on at that stand, would they?"

I get a clownish look. "Lying in wait for him, you mean?"

"Something like that."

"He was shooting at number one," Lady Wynn-Williams puts in, not to be outdone. "Peg One."

"Everybody knows that, Bea. They were rotating the numbers quite normally."

"Two by two?" I suppose.

"There were eight guns, dear, weren't there?" Our hostess amends her sharpness, but with condescension. "If he was number One, he must have been number Seven for the last drive before lunch. He'd have drawn Three." Pigeons peck the lawn . . . The prince died on the first shoot after lunch: I know that. They did the draw before they set off in the morning.

"The funeral people practically mummified him," Mrs Lunt is saying, "for flying back to his Gulf. Patched him up better than new."

Lady Wynn-Williams protests, "*I* wouldn't sleep in that

29

bed."

"If they'd given him a special space at hospital in Wrexham, Bea, the unions'd have down-tooled. Timmy saw that immediately."

"I don't suppose your son wanted any fuss," I venture.

"Exactly. If you only knew how sensitive that Gulf is, the responsibility he carries . . ." Her pride is in the role. I have a sudden desire to declare myself, and by confessing her son's blight on me extract her own confession of why she blanks him out – then it's gone like a mistaken shaft of sun on a dark day. "Reporters were absolutely brazen as it was," she is saying, "driving up here as if they owned the place. I can't abide reporters. We had a police barrier at the lodge, and on the back drive. It was like the siege of Cawnpore, Mr Goode."

In the graceful assurance of the portrait in evening dress, something familiar holds my attention – the way the head is held on the long neck. "Do I recognise . . ." I begin, but feel my hostess wanting to move on, bundle us out.

"I was very young at the time," she answers snappishly, as if reprimanding life for its cruelty.

6

Billy French has come out of the hills and *wadis* at the tip of the peninsula unbidden. He drives himself by the coast road, through the primitive frontier posts that formally divide the two countries, with his canvas chargol swinging from his wing mirror. On one side stretches the opal sea, and on the other the wild mountains of the Emirate's peninsula soon give way to the scrub desert and plantations of the Shaikhdom's lowland tribes. He must see Grover Wilks in person. The catastrophe of the water party surely touches Wilks too. Instability is their common foe.

They see one another seldom, for they are employed by ancient enemies. Local elements both sides of the border would be quick to exploit any overt collusion between the two pale foreigners. But I am soon to learn how wholeheartedly French admires Wilks. He admires him for his political savvy and the disdainful humour that dissolves worry. Unlike his own stumbling Arabic and the tribal patois picked up these eleven years on the job, Wilks speaks and writes Arabic like an educated native. He is silky as a woman with his Shaikh and the family, and deciphers the crisscross factions, like the self-exiles from the Emirate, with the arcane assurance of a gypsy reading a palm. And he is committed to his Arabs: in French's eyes, that is the touchstone. Everyone knows Wilks gave up the fleshpots of the State Department to come out here.

As an American "Gulf hand" Wilks is a rare bird, but a welcome change from the toffee-nosed English expats in the Emirate's capital. It's Billy French's stated view the Whitehall types back home lost their nerve and walked out on their responsibilities in this part of the world. A photograph in his bungalow shows Curzon being carried ashore along this very coast – the Viceroy of India himself, the Emperor-King's accredited stand-in wearing spats and topee in an open palanquin, held high out of the waves by six grinning Lascars. Up the beach shaikhs and elders wait with their resplendent camels, one with a howdah on its hump to bear the great man to fort, feast and parley. That was when the British knew where they were going. Is not Billy French himself one of the last scions of that heritage?

When he goes, his post will be filled by a local. One of the new breed of layabouts from the capital will sit on his arse for thirty years pushing paper. French's contracts have got shorter and shorter: it's only a matter of two or three years, maybe less, before localization catches up and he gets his marching orders.

French, as I now know, arrives early for his meeting. Between themselves, Grover and Lucy Wilks have a nickname for him, "Wadi Fransi": he is for ever off "up the wadi" and Fransi is his name in Arabic. The supercilious Ahmed admits his Land Cruiser into the forecourt and the visitor is observed from above taking a swig of water from his chargol. He smoothes his Edwardian – or is it Mexican? – moustache in the wing mirror, and fluffs out the tufts on his cheek with forefinger. Then he gives his bald head a wipe with a spotted handkerchief from his bush jacket pocket. Ahmed leads him through the house by the arched passageway to the walled garden, and he is next seen in a high-backed basket chair in the shade of the house wall.

"Well, well, well, Billy!" The mobile grin, the easy charm, the touch of condolence: Wilks enters in sandals and an open shirt. "And how was the drive down?"

"Left oh-nine hundred on the nail. That Jap job goes like the clappers. Give me a long wheel-base every time, not these bloody dodgems."

"No trouble at the frontier post?"

"They know uncle Billy."

With a g and t in hand – Wilks on the tonic alone – French settles into his task like a man picking bandages from a wound. He shakes his head, the brown eyes grow with pain. "The whole bloody lot – *phut*! I thought of you at once, Grover. *You* know what that well-digging party was to my people. *You* know the situation. I've been pleading with the capital for years to do something about wells up in the *jebel*. I don't have pull with Water Resources. They've always got money enough for flooding their bloody flower-beds at a quid a gallon, but if

32

it's tribes three hundred miles off at the back of beyond and no road link, they don't want to know."

Wilks frowns for him. "Same for us all, Billy."

"The same? Your tribesmen along the border have had all sorts of wells dug for them."

"It's always a struggle," Wilks sighs.

"You don't know what the word means. You'll pardon me, Grover, I'm touched by your sympathy, but it's misplaced. All my tribesmen know there's more water on the Shaikhdom side. It's what your old man wants. You know that."

It is traditional mischief, suborning the Emirate's tribesmen. The Shaikh's claim to a slice of his neighbour's territory is a sacred heritage. Ten years ago a so-called independence movement broke surface in the Emirate, instantly endorsed by Soviet Russia and assisted privily by the Shaikhdom. A flurry of bombings spattered the port and, inland, mines were laid along vehicle tracks serving the highland villages: a "show of strength" by the semi-educated to awe the illiterate. But troops flew in from the capital and the rebels fled hot and proud to the Shaikhdom.

"It was just darned unlucky," Wilks ruminates solemnly. "An old mine, the finger of God. Tell me just what happened, Billy."

French peers hopelessly ahead. He tells how the Ministry at last relented – shipped in a water-drilling truck, brand new. Beautiful job. Bloody magic. Two engineers and a geologist chappie flew up. He found them a guide. It was just crawling up to the pass at the head of Wadi Gibra and *wump*! It could only have been a mine. Practically nothing left of it. All four found dead by his tribesmen.

"No one around, Billy? No follow-up? No one claiming?"

"It must have been an *old* mine . . . They'll never send another. It's put the kybosh on wells for my tribesmen. What they want now – some of them, anyway – is to come down across the border and see your Shaikh . . . see what *he* can do for them. I want you to see them first and stop them coming."

The wound is now fully exposed. Wilks makes no answer. His eyebrows arch. He recrosses his long legs.

French shakes his head again. "If your old man sees 'em, gives 'em comfort . . . God knows how my Emir would react.

33

It's the beginning of the end. 'The last state worse than the first,' right?"

"My old man's dying," Wilks says soothingly.

"If he's dying, he's got nothing to lose. He could renounce all the Shaikhdom's claims on Emirate territory."

"Oh, dear old Billy." Wilks turns his frown on his visitor as if to condole his sanity too. "Nobody can blame *you*."

"Me? Who cares about me? I'll be gone and forgotten in two shakes. That's not the point at all."

"I heard you had a turn, Billy. We were worried."

"What are you trying to tell me?"

"We were worried, Billy. That's all."

"About what?"

"Up in the *jebel*," Wilks says softly. "Didn't I hear? . . ."

"Dizzy spell. Nothing." He laid up all day in a tribal hut with pain grabbing at his chest. He did not even tell Elaine. Yet word of this brief, private portent has travelled a hundred miles through barren mountains and across a frontier to this very house.

"Worried, Billy. That's all."

"You needn't have wasted it."

"You don't want to fret about your elders coming to see H.H. I'll see to them. You want to take things easy."

"You can head 'em off, Grover?" He brightens hopelessly.

"We'll look after you."

"What d'you mean 'look after me'? It's not *me*, it's *them* — they're babes in the wilderness. They're children playing in a bomb factory. Right? They'll be the first to go up in a puff of smoke if they persuade your Shaikh to start operating across the border. And he could respond, your old man, I know he could. He's living in another age. The whole thing depends on you, Grover. You've got to persuade him to renounce the claims. You've said yourself. They follow strength, not goodness."

Wilks reaches across and lightly grips his arm — Wadi Fransi in his shorts and cheap yellow boots so bandy and hairy beside his own Yankee breeding. But the hand's touch does reassure: moisture clouds his eyes. "Count on me, Billy."

French brushes his nose with his knuckles. "It's just a job for me, of course. Like any other." Pockets of air in his cheeks

34

make the flesh twitch above his moustache. "I need you, though, Grover, as much as I've needed anybody."

"*Harambee*," Wilks says. "*Harambee*, pull together, the French-Wilks *entente cordiale*!"

"You talk to your old man . . ."

"He's lost interest in this world since Saqr died. Given up the fight. It was what we were afraid of, soon as we heard the news about Saqr. Lucy said, 'It'll kill the old man.' Well, it just about has."

"Nothing venture, nothing fucked."

"It's still only a few weeks since it happened. He hasn't left his room in the old palace since. He sees his *diwan*, sees his doctor. Once or twice he's actually seen Hamood. I'm told he's not eating. Kidneys packing up. He just wants to go and be done with it."

"I'd like to come with you," French says stubbornly.

"One must be realistic, Billy. It's Hamood now – the day-to-day business, the protocol stuff."

"H is bad news."

"We all have our weaknesses. We'll make something out of Hamood yet."

"A silk purse."

"Hamood would rather like to be a silk purse." Wilks breaks into a pouchy smile.

Ahmed hovers by the drinks. Paired bulbuls flash into the hibiscus. There is a sound of water, for Lucy has hidden a rock pond and cascade in a corner . . . elements of paradise, a garden to love in, to gain acquaintance with good and evil. Beyond the wall stretches the desert, and a scattering of anxious commercial projects.

"Incidentally, there *was* something."

"Something?" Wilks echoes.

"A *binte* saw two strangers."

"Where?"

"Five miles from where it went off. Day before."

"A *binte*, Billy?"

"A crone. Out collecting *arfaj*. Are the exiles by any chance up to anything?"

"The exiles care about the towns, not the tribes in the *jebel*. Don't imagine them as guerillas in the hills: they've lost the

35

mountain habit."

"Listen" – a slight fuzz in the voice now – "I want you to stop that delegation seeing anybody. Anybody that matters."

"Old friend, Grover Wilks will do his best, but don't overestimate him. I advise on tribal affairs, I'm court musician. I can see them of course. But they'll want a touch of royalty. Have a nut."

"I don't care a monkey's tit what they want."

"Look, old friend," Wilks expounds. "Every emir, sultan, malik, shaikh, in this part of the world since time began has claimed bits of his neighbour's territory. And the allegiance of his neighbour's tribes. It's the spice of life. They mayn't go galloping off on a *ghazura* any more, raiding palm groves, rustling camels. But nobody takes away their right to bicker over borders. Leave it to me to look after our common interests, Billy. What's the view of h.q., anyway?"

"You mean my capital?"

"Exactly. How've they reacted . . ."

"We've got a little detachment, of course. They don't go up the *jebel*. Rather stay in barracks wanking."

"But since that old mine went off?"

"A Minister flew in . . ."

"What flavour?"

"Oh, Public Works. Just for a day. All he wanted was to go fishing, except he called me every two hours on the radio. 'Mr Fransi,' – they all call me Fransi – 'I see one of the mosques is covered with graffiti. Have it painted.' 'Yes sir!' So I look around, and there's this shrine – somebody's bones in it – up on the promontory beyond the town – 'HMS Kilroy' daubed on it. Arabic this and that too. I march myself into the Wali and tell him: 'The Minister's commanded me to paint that shrine. You want me to take my bunch of infidels down there to paint it?' 'I'll kill you if you do,' he says, 'but I won't tell you not to.' 'Shrines don't go with Islam,' I remind him. 'Shouldn't venerate the dead.' So I call up the Minister on his boat and tell him, Does he really want me to have my Hindis painting the mosque which isn't a mosque . . . ? He says he'll think about it and let me know. He avoids me altogether after that."

The gin has loosened him, and here the lady enters in person, an arm extended to him rigid.

36

"Surprise, surprise," French says, and rising topples his wicker chair.

"Silly Hindi chairs," she scolds. Ahmed moves to restore it. She can see the sweat beading his baldness, and gives his hand an intimate little twist. "Haven't you and Grover settled the future of the world yet? Do sit, Billy. You'll stay for lunch? We've got Ismail coming, haven't we, Grover? Another place to lay, that's all."

"Don't eat lunch as a rule. These nuts are all I'll need."

"You can't eat just nuts for lunch," she laughs. "Nobody can." As he sips, his little finger crooks, she's such a handsome little thing, so compact a figure, soignée; quick and dainty. He is always uneasy with her – and vulgar and stupid. Her county way of speech reminds him of the types in the capital he avoids like the plague. He tugs at a tuft on his cheek. "All I need, honestly." He raises the little silver bowl, a fine sample of local craft already extinct. "I've got to get back up the wadis, anyway."

Her glance darts to her husband. "You must take lots of nuts with you, up the wadis. Ahmed," – catching at her breath – "find another tin of nuts for Sayyid Fransi, for up the wadis. Ooh *dear!*" She collapses into a chair, assailed by giggles. Her breath heaving, she dries her eyes with some material she carries. "I thought of something so funny."

"Evidently," her husband says drily.

French looks from one to the other, munching nuts carefully. The complicity between them eludes him: it was gone like a lizard as soon as one moved a hand, become a mere rustle. She wipes one eye for quite a long time, as if something had got in it, and the men wait. Still weak from the gust, she holds out two pieces of material for an opinion – a maroon damask and shot silk of a similar colour – turning brightly to each. For the new palace, Wilks explains. And French enquires, "For the curtains? Or the counterpanes?" But Lucy corrects him – "Not the 'counterpanes', Billy," making it sound the wrong word in any context – "the *walls*, the main *majlis* walls." "Cloth on the walls?" he queries. "Is that what they do nowadays? The 'in' thing, eh? He won't want to live in the old man's palace, then?"

"Impossible place to air-condition," she declares. "Almost

37

as bad as this." She gestures at the wind tower. Wilks explains. Hamood started on his new palace long before anyone realized the old man was on his last illness: if anyone was to live in the old palace it would have been Saqr.

French has heard they didn't get along – the old man and his surviving son.

"The generation gap," Wilks says.

"Bit of a piss-artist, one hears."

"None of us is perfect, Billy."

"What a tragedy, brother S going like that. What a bloomin' shame." It is not for him to bandy names in front of hood-eyed Ahmed, who has crept up with the drinks tray. French covers his empty glass, "B*sss* . . .", shaking his head. He doesn't want a giddy spell standing up. "The finger of God," Wilks is saying.

"It's going to change things here – right? – when the youngster takes over?"

"He's not such a youngster. Thirty-nine. He was older than Saqr . . . a few months. Different mum, of course. Most people don't realize."

"So they passed him over. Right?"

"The old man must have thought he wouldn't shape up. Mum went off the rails early: I don't suppose he had much of a chance."

"*Tout comprendre*," Lucy says lightly.

"But it'll change things," French says. "Right?" And Lucy sees his chin buckling, quelling a belch, and his fingers going out for nuts.

"It'll change the *rubato*," Wilks says, "when Hamood moves up." French is not going to ask what he means in front of the lady, and all at once he is standing, and Lucy is protesting brightly, "But you've come all this way . . . You haven't told us how Mrs French is."

"Elly doesn't like the hot weather. Pack her off home for the summer, soon."

"And haven't you a daughter? Surely?" – solicitous queries like paper darts, straight out of her nose.

French puts out a stiff hand and for a moment she acts as if hers is lost among the materials. When it comes free he shakes it so firmly she exclaims. "Oo, you are strong."

"Saw your nag. He's nice." Often, he notices, she seems to

38

miss his meaning straight off. He gestures beyond the garden wall. "Oh – oh, yes. My mare."

Wilks leads him through the dark arched corridor. In the shady forecourt they can smell the fish *suk* at the inlet head. A pair of helicopters head inland, supplying the *jebel*. Alone together, Wilks, taller, though slighter, drapes an arm across French's shoulder. "Don't lose sleep over the tribes, Billy. You know them well enough. These *jacqueries* never come to very much. Not without the towns." French is comforted by Wilks' comradeship but furrows for the significance of what is said: later he will unskein it from his memory. "Look at history, Billy. The towns can carry the peasantry, never the other way. Of course, it helps if the peasants are sympathetic."

"Helps what?"

"In a case of real trouble nothing stays the same, old friend – one can't expect that." French feels him to be confiding, but his eyes are directed at his naked head as if counting the surviving hairs. "Specially in our part of the world. The changes here have to be violent, because all government is rigid. One shouldn't delude oneself about permanence." Ahmed is hovering, an unopened can of nuts on a silver tray. "The scale of power around here is too small for the modern world. But the *leverage* – that's enormous."

"I really ought to be on my way, Grover."

The habitual teasing humour returns. "Up the *wadi*?" Wilks rarely grins, and when he does it makes him look daft.

"*Jebel*," French corrects, puzzled by the other's shifting demeanour. "I'm building cisterns in all the high villages. Carry all the stuff up by chopper. Westlands, we've got. Better than your Frog jobs." He climbs into his vehicle and starts up, backing cautiously: along the wall are ranged tall amphorae from a pre-Islamic culture, dredged from the sea mud.

"Tell you what, Billy." Wilks leans on the vehicle's open window. "How about I fly up to the *jebel* on our side – Bani Salimi area, say – we meet on the invisible line and you take me across your side to palaver with your tribesmen, then I slip back to my side. Just a coupla days."

Gratitude and relief floods out of French as if a boil has been lanced. Then they fix up the politically delicate assignation meticulously, like an illicit tryst.

A bell rings in the house, and Ahmed returns to let in a visitor. Wilks abruptly switches off their intimacy. "This'll be Ismail Barzakh. You know Ismail? Edits the *New Age*. You'd better say hallo." The iron gates admit an ill-used Corolla whose engine shudders on after it is switched off. Its driver has got out — a quick man, sallow, ageing, monkey-ish, under a mop of surprisingly rich brown hair. He declares dramatically, "The motor is overheating. So is the man. Grover, I have no a.c. I shall need a cold beer to get upstairs. Is someone trying to escape me?" His head darts round at the occupant of the Land Cruiser.

"Mr Billy French," Wilks announces, "is about to depart for the *wadis* of the Emirate."

"This then is Fransi of the tribes, of whom I hear tell?"

"You see, Billy, how famous you are."

"Nothing escapes the man of Reuters News Agency," Barzakh says.

"Former," Wilks corrects.

"Former," Barzakh concedes, and asks what brings French down here — to play the fiddle, or are he and Grover dividing the world between them?

"Mr French is the lead soprano in my new opera, Ismail." French tries to return Barzakh's compliment, saying he knows his magazine, it crosses the border, and Barzakh declares that he too must cross the border.

"Be my guest," French says. "I'd count it an honour. I've got to toddle now, though. A job to do."

"Toddle, toddle!" Barzakh grips French's hand. "Tell the Emirate the *New Age* is with them."

7

The three men, the woman. The dark servant . . . I try to lay it all forth in proper sequence. You may not do this as a newspaperman. You put the supposed culmination first – the tragedy, triumph, dénouement, revelation: you "put the cherry on the top", as my first proprietor would have it. The "cherry" seldom comprised the truth. One reason knowing folk complain that journalists "get it wrong" is that, while facts may be sacred, out of their unreportable context "facts" mislead. That's why I needed to give up reporting. Beneath the flux of events is another order which has no place in a newspaper. Man's isolation. His fear of nothingness. The elusiveness of love. That he shall not live by bread alone but by illusions of significance, by greed for power. Or by every word that proceedeth out of the mouth of God. Yet God said so much, or filled the world with his silence.

As it is, I stopped writing because I couldn't advance in my understanding and because whatever flashes of perception I once had had, lately recurred as flickers, impossible to act upon. Even now I am uncertain if this narrative tells of light shed or quenched.

An hour after my conducted tour of Timmy Lunt's family home, I am still in my tweeds, Game Book on knee, seated in a deep sofa of the oak-panelled drawing-room. Over the broad fireplace hangs a large, tatty seascape, with a naked young woman beached across the foreground, dead or dying. Now I recall this milk-white woman from my childhood visit, for she is the first nude I ever saw. Her son is present in the picture, a young contemporary – perhaps four. He had slipped my mind, though here he is now, feet apart, little hands gripping the hilt of his lost papa's massive Viking broadsword, too heavy for him to raise its point from the sand. Is this a child the infant Timmy identified with? Yet one of Timmy's arms is crippled.

Mrs Lunt has retired for an afternoon nap. Lady Wynn-Williams is still on hand, beyond the fire and the snoring

41

labrador, to provide an explanation of the unrepaired triangular rent in a corner of the canvas. Old Charley Lunt let the estate run down. Imagined he could live like a lord all his life on income from tenant farmers and the sheep on the hills but of course that isn't possible these days; he never had enough to look after the tenants properly and so forfeited their loyalty. The place was mortgaged. Timmy is always caught up with his politics – he must know what's what, but politicians live in a fool's paradise. Anyway Timmy can't reach his mother.

"Can't reach?"

"Exactly. He's always been a bit of a cold fish." She perches in her high-backed velvet chair, canny and ferocious, an old raptor on a high rock. "You understand, Mr Goode, when *my* husband died and the hearse came for him all the estate workers and all the tenants *and* their wives lined the drive by the lodge gates. There they all were, bare-headed, to see him off, a complete surprise as he came round the corner."

I nod my understanding – the squire amid his inheritance, duties among his rights. It had its bearing on eternity.

"When she goes" – the beak coming up dangling an entrail – "God forbid, but it comes to us all – she's as old as God – Timmy will have to sell up. Sometimes I think it's what she wants." She takes out a little white handkerchief and dabs the stains at each corner of her mouth. The eyes blink slowly. "It's not as if Timmy had a Welsh constituency." Generations of Wynn-Williamses have gone to English public schools and married into the English upper class. But the Welsh allegiance remained defiant. Whatever brigandage got it for them in the dark age, soul has become tenant of the land. "The staff are ripping her off."

"Really? – Old Jonesie?"

"Hardly Mrs Jones."

"Who else is there?"

"Well, one really can't go into details Mr Goode, it's none of our business."

"Keeper? Shepherd?"

"If no one can afford to look after them, you can't blame them – Welshmen don't come to terms with newcomers easily. Not your true Taffy." What was 1854 compared to the infinite Celtic ancestry of Wynns and Williamses?

42

"So the keeper connives with the poachers . . ." I speculate.

"If it was only that, my dear."

Only now do I lay the Game Book aside.

"You see, Mr Goode" – demi-tasse poised at her mouth in a be-ringed talon – "Dai Rhys-shepherd here is brother of Rhys the Game, our keeper. We wouldn't have Dai. We call him Dai Black-Sheep. There are three brothers and only one good one among them, he's our keeper, wonderful with his hands, made this stick," and she raises it to display the lovingly carved ram's-horn haft. "The point is, Mr Goode, nobody knows how many sheep belong to this estate except Dai Black-Sheep. Trix Lunt doesn't know, Timmy certainly doesn't. So when the third brother comes to market with all these sheep to sell, whose are they?" She looks at me as if she can spot mischief like a rabbit on a mountainside. "The third brother works at the chemicals factory at Ruabon and he's got a tenancy of sixty acres, according to our Rhys. You can't graze much of a flock on sixty acres."

"Two bad apples out of three . . ."

"There used to be a little girl. She was the eldest. When she died, the mother ceased to cope." She draws back her head, pursed and regretful, knowing so much.

"Have you suggested to Mrs Lunt that something's amiss?"

"We gave up years ago trying to tell the Lunts anything. We used to try. Charley was a proud man. He couldn't bear to think he wasn't in full control. Timmy's the same sort, you know. Too aloof for his own good."

"The other brother – the factory worker – is he close to Dai Black-Sheep?"

"Thick as thieves, those two. Always up here for the shoots, getting his whack as a beater. I don't know what they think at the factory – I suppose he just goes absent."

"What's his name?"

"Name?" she frowns, as if he hardly deserved one. "Alwyn." If I really want to know.

"Was he up here for the last shoot?"

"I really couldn't tell you, Mr Goode." Quite sharply. "You'll have to ask Mrs Lunt." Probably she has spoken far too much. A stranger – a gentleman perhaps, but a stranger.

I renew attention to the Game Book. The "Let Weekends"

43

are indicated by a "C" in the margin – this I deduce from Mrs Lunt's account of the annual pattern. "C" for Commercial. So far this season there have been no other Let shoots. Last season seven guns were present at the first Let shoot, eight at the second where the guns were out both the Friday and Saturday – time enough for a stranger to get to know the ground. Let week-end guns are listed by name, without addresses, up to two years previously with a steel pen in a cursive hand – the late Charley Lunt presumably, latterly with a ballpoint in the keeper's wary script: two Colonels, two Brigadiers, a Major-General; Captain St. J. Evans who could be naval; two Smiths and a Smythe; various double-barrels; an L. Willoughby; an Hon. E. Browne; a Prewitt (Dr. F.); a Schultz (American? German?); a P. Constantinidi (the Greek, presumably – the penman had trouble with that); an Abramson; a De Fries . . . Certain names occur from year to year. Mrs Lunt spoke of "regulars", and of others obtained through Lloyds', and an agency that "bleeds 'em white." I am at the window, Game Book under arm. A wintry sun has rinsed earth and sky alike. Cawing crows twist like kites on a string. I plan: "I think I'll take a wander," but Lady Wynn-Williams has dropped off, upright in her eyrie, hands on her tweed lap like bones.

In the hall my old gun-case, given me by Sophia, reposes in a corner. I leaf through the Visitors' Book on its marble table. The military men reside in Old Vicarages, Meads, Granges, Oast Houses; the Hon. E. Browne in a Kensington flat. Dr. Prewitt is to be found in Portman Square, Mr. Abramson at The Ritz; Schultz is indeed from New York, two give California. L. Willoughby hasn't bothered with an address. Under *Comments* some essay wit – "glorious eleventh!!" (a January 11 shoot) and "Borridar to our feathered friends"; others strain after appreciation – "sumptuous fare!" and "worth every penny" (the scrap merchant?); one mysterious poignancy – "just like old times" (Captain St. J. Evans). I take a notebook from my pocket and rapidly copy out names and addresses from the last four pages.

The cedars scattering the pasture in front – do I remember these? There is a darkness I recall, darkness and secrecy – a leafy, secret place, shrouded. Maybe a child's fear darkens the memory . . . The cedars are mature trees, widely spaced, bearing nothing malign. And were we not sealed from sight and sound of others? A question of crawling in, surely. Then opening out into a definable place, inaccessible to grown-ups, utterly and dreadfully secluded. But was it in front of the house, or behind? And was I already afraid or did the fear come later? Perhaps it was not yet fear but that thrill which portends the indelible . . .

I go down to the river, the banks cleared of trees for fly-fishing – no recollected darkness here. Then round the back through empty stables. As she recognises my footfall the tone of Gertie's bark alters: at the kennels I stroke her head until she restores to me her own conviction of the readiness of created things to love. Then past the garages and across the gravel to the back door. Mrs Jones has quit the kitchen. Beyond the larders the stone corridor runs to a little office, where leaving the door ajar, I settle into a swivel chair and open out a back number of *Estate Management* on the narrow desk.

The keeper is a methodical man. Under a glass paperweight containing a pheasant's plume I find my own hand-penned letter with its Lloyds' address and a batch of correspondence from my expected Let Shoot companions. In a pillar of the desk are letters from the agency and prospective visitors of recent years in elastic bands.

My skulking investigation is interrupted by the sound of wheels on gravel. I rapidly restore the desk to its former state. Footsteps in the corridor – brisk, youthful footsteps, approaching from the servants' hall – and I visualize Timmy's sardonic pity as I am released from the local police station through his personal intervention: "Dear lad, what in heaven's name could have reduced you to this?" – then the back door opens. Voices, wah-wah. A guest is led through to the front. The maid's steps recede into the servants' hall. I slip out with the magazine under my arm and the letters in the breast pocket of my shooting jacket.

8

When we married Sophia saw me as a certain person, perfect and complete, and when I failed to conform to this vision would not acknowledge me as recognisable – at least, not recognisably hers. She was always waiting for the real "man she married" to return: I suppose she has spent most of her life waiting for this return, and lives in hopeless disbelief of the stranger who shares her bed and board. On her dressing-table she keeps a photograph of us taken on the steps of St. Paul's, Knightsbridge, on our wedding-day; at some later time she tucked into the same frame a snapshot of me as a little boy frowning down upon an injured bird – a thrush, as I recall – cupped in my hands.

Far be it from me to dismiss her original vision as false, but I think what she saw was the light shining on me at a moment that belonged to our "first fine careless rapture". Her forlorn expectancy came to exasperate me and seal the corruption in me. Even at the time I was surprised by the primal innocence she resurrected in me more or less intact. I had forgotten it. For a short while I called her my "lucky fairy", which delighted her. Her purity astonished me, and conjured from me its lost counterpart. But as with things done by magic it was unreasonable to suppose it would endure. It did not allow for change, not even a change of light.

Sophia built up all manner of obstacles to my taking on this assignment. I was "letting down Frances" by being absent during the last days of the Christmas holidays. Only the previous week, she claimed, I had said that our trainee manager was nowhere near ready to look after the farm. (I had no recollection of expressing such an opinion.) Various negligible social commitments were presented as more or less obligatory. Then she produced a financial crisis – like a rabbit out of a hat – in Frances' presence: that goes without saying. In fact it was Frances who came to me in the farm office, whimpering, with a plea to know why I had refused to give

Mummy any money. I assured Frances as gently as I could that Mummy had mentioned nothing about needing any money over and above her regular allowance (paid automatically from the farm trustees' account). But of course Frances could hardly believe me. Why else should Mummy be rending herself with semi-private tears unless I was refusing her the money that alone would prevent her life becoming an impossible struggle? "How much d'you think Mummy needs?" I ask. The child is glum and hostile. I draw out my private account cheque book and there and then hand her a large cheque for Sophia. Maybe she had genuinely run short – I couldn't tell; she had made no explicit request although now I came to think about it I recognised recent innuendoes. These little financial tantrums had a certain pattern, for whenever I protested ignorance of her need I would receive a supplementary accusation, more bitter still – *did she always have to spell it out?* After a time I came to read in them a hidden protest at deeper deprivations which an impending absence sharpened.

Did she in turn perceive in this excursion to rural Wales symptoms of a different kind of departure?

Theoretically I could have brought Sophia with me. Wives accompany two of the seven guns. Their commodity broker husbands are pursued by professional anxieties into this wild countryside, and their need to telephone is like an affliction of incontinence. But after a wary dinner and Mrs Lunt's retirement, the two couples' long acquaintance turns from chaff and private jokes to horseplay, particularly at the expense of the brother to one of the wives who proves to be a little business in himself selling machinery to the Middle East. The commodity men have dubbed him Offshore Ollie, which sobriquet he takes as a compliment, finangling being the name of the game in the Square Mile. I ask him, What kind of machinery? "Agricultural, old chap," with an irrational wink. "Junk, and no mistake," a brother-in-law chaffs: "nothing grows out there anyway." "Absolute balls," Offshore Ollie grins. He has peakish eyes, a low, pink, naked head, and he roams the corridors with an inquisitive lope – (was this the way to the downstairs loo?) – charmed by everything, inexhaustibly appreciative. His ingratiation is distributed equally to all in layers of impervious banality. At table he tries Mrs Lunt out on

47

foreign policy – her son's political eminence is naturally being a *cachet* of this shoot – but her views prove comparable to Henry Ford's on history. "Foreign policy is codswallop, Mr Mullins."

"Do you really think so?"

"Certainly. That's why I said it. You've only got to read the morning paper. Have some more fruit."

"Could I be absolutely awful and take a tangerine?" The fruit bowl is put within his reach. "Are you quite shoo-er?" With a leer. "I've got an absolute passion for tangerines, haven't you? They're my favourite things," gobbling segments. "Is it absolutely awful of me?"

Any positive effect of Offshore Ollie's charm on the other three visiting guns, all lawyers from Liverpool, is offset by a vulgar exclamation from one of the wives over a transaction concerning cartridges, and the more or less instantaneous recognition that they were of Jewish extraction.

Our house party awakens that second morning to shrouded hills and at breakfast cold rain squalls at the windows. An hour later, with all of us assembled in the hall for the day's sport, Mrs Lunt descends in a knitted house-coat to rap the barometer with a yellowed talon and announce that it had clamped down for the duration.

On the doorstep everyone is indistinguishably waterproofed in mud-coloured Barbours, leggings, gumboots and tweed caps (the ladies' caps secured by scarves). Keeper and shepherd, waiting to conduct the draw, are identifiable from the others only because they carry sticks not shotguns. The keeper, Ivor, with a chrome whistle round his neck, is squat, bandy, rubicund. The shepherd – "Dai Black-Sheep" – is quite different: tall for a Welshman, dark-eyed, alternately senatorial and shifty.

Mrs Lunt herself emerges into the cold porch with a little silver box embossed with game birds. "Morning, Ivor. Morning, Dai." Two caps touched, and with a little plopping motion she presents the box to Ivor, who fishes a notebook from his pocket and passes the box to Dai. Dai opens the hinged lid and I am there to draw first, delicately. There are to be four drives, two before lunch and two after. I must pick the number four ivory tag, indeed I come up with number four,

48

having the previous evening visited the gun-room to lodge its tip between panels of the box. Amid comparisons with earlier years (the Liverpool circuit lawyers) and other shoots (the commodities men) we squeeze into the vehicles in dank stiff gear around the old labrador. A formidable voice summons the corgies to the porch.

By lunch, back at the house, Mrs Lunt presiding, we have bagged twenty-two brace. It has been a fractious morning, the birds reluctant to get up at all and then coming over fast and low. "At least you haven't shot each other," is our hostess' pointed comment. We are gathered by the log fire, under the stranded Viking-ess, in an attempt to dry off patches of clothing penetrated by rain. Drinks are on offer, Mrs Lunt dispensing.

"You shoo-er?" Offshore Ollie gropes for confirmation. "You absolutely shoo-er?" And a few minutes later is in pursuit once more — "Could I be absolutely awful," empty glass in hand, a forefinger poking towards the gin decanter. Mrs Lunt declares firmly we are all going into lunch and he recoils as if the decanter has struck him like an adder.

At table we agree the beaters have been Trojans. Eight of them have been working the woods, under Ivor's direction; the shepherd Dai Rhys stayed with the guns, distributing us to our pegs at each stand, quick to identify each of us despite our uniform disguise, to assess our sporting skill, casually speculating as to our professions and substance and chatting up the ladies at the stands, masculine confidence overriding difference of station. I alone leave him unsatisfied, for I am strangely contaminated, and he singled me out, ready with gratuitous information — that all the beaters were estate workers or tenants except for his own brother Alwyn.

What did Alwyn do? I asked him.

"Alwyn-bach is one of us, born and bred right here on the farm."

"So he's a farmer?"

" 'E's got a tenancy of sixty acres and 'is own sheep, that's very true, but not on the estate 'ere. And 'e's got his job at Ruabon, too, in the works."

"He can get off for the shoots?"

"Week-ends are 'is own, mind you. And they're down to

49

three days a week anyway, aren't they, terrible for industry. I don't suppose you're in industry, Mr Goode."

"I've got my own farm in the home counties."

"I'd 'ave mistaken you for a businessman." Has he already inspected my misleading letterhead? "Mixed farming, naturally . . ."

"Beef cattle and cereals."

"Then you don't get enough to shoot on a big farm like that?"

"I wouldn't mind some sheep, Mr Rhys. Lamb's been fetching good prices these last couple of years."

"Up one year, down the next."

"I'd like to talk to you about sheep, one of these days. You or Alwyn. Alwyn sounds like my scale of things. I can't turn over more than fifty or sixty acres to sheep. Would he give me the benefit of his advice?"

"No 'arm in askin' 'im, if that's what you'd like."

Alwyn bore a sharp resemblance to his brother: a stronger character, noticeable, his sideburns grown broad and bushy, a curve to the lower lip suggesting scorn or defiance. He was a spring of humour among his fellows but when all the guns were together at the end of a drive a specific derision for this ritual of killing held him back. I spotted him mockingly touching his forelock to Ivor when the keeper issued an instruction. The beaters spoke Welsh among each other, and when Dai or Ivor addressed the guns in English Alwyn would sometimes cap the announcement with his own Welsh wit, leaving us guns wondering . . .

"Cheer up, Mr Goode," Mrs Lunt instructs, as the apple charlotte approaches. "The Ty-Nant drive is best of all, but will you all be careful to unload crossing fences? Who's shooting number one?"

"I am."

"Especially you, Mr Goode."

As we disembark near the stand the rain buffets. Dai Rhys directs each gun to his peg. The shepherd insists on accompanying me down the slope towards my peg, beyond a tongue of trees. The shepherd breaks the silence, "I suppose you'll want to know 'ow it 'appened, eh?"

"The prince's death, you mean."

50

Wind and rain skirmish from the side: conversation isn't easy.

"Naturally," the shepherd says.

"How he was killed . . ."

"Killed himself."

"Of course."

"Some of the shot struck 'is jawbone, underneath, mind. 'Ere." He indicates the area under the throat with his thumb. "Shot penetrated right up under the skull. But it was drowning finished 'im. You read the autopsy report, Sir?"

"No."

"Never saw the autopsy?" (I leave my lie unrepeated.) " 'E toppled forward into the ditch, other side of the trees." We are just coming up to the trees which are making a racket in the high wind.

"Did they come out here?"

" 'Oo, then, Mr Goode?"

"Whoever did the autopsy. The coroner's men."

"Out 'ere? I should say. We 'ad the whole lot, all over the place. We thought you'd 'ave an interest. We 'ad the Detective Chief Superintendent 'imself, 'ead of North Wales. Two or three plain clothes men. Special Branch. One from MI5, so we heard. Their own radio van. They 'ad everybody in for questioning. One by one. You 'eard that I expect?"

We thought, *we* heard . . . In my dark room I sense something strange. "I hadn't imagined," I say.

"Oh yes. All the guns. All the beaters. Prince's own men – 'e 'ad two with 'im. They 'ad someone down from London to translate."

"What did they want to know from you?"

"You'd be amazed, Mr Goode. Or maybe you wouldn't."

And at this I am aware of a live thing disturbed in the blackness, a flitting of guilt.

"Well?"

"They 'ad this whole list of questions, the two of 'em, putting it all on a tape-recorder. What organisations we belonged to, or ever 'ad. Plaid Cymru, I told 'im, and Welsh Methodists, and the AAW. And 'ad I ever been in trouble? 'Ad I gun? – Of course I 'ad. 'Where's the certificate?' ''Ere it is.' Once I'd forgot to renew – I told 'im straight: young Pugh 'ad

51

come round on 'is bike, 'e's the constable, and give me forty-eight hours to renew or I'd be up at Wrexham for a fine. An' who did I know, who did I ever know, who 'ad any interest in Arabs, or international politics, or ever asked me 'ow these shoots were organised. 'You think it was a murder, eh?' I said and they said stranger things 'ave 'appened. So I said, 'Who'd want to?' an' they just looked at each other."

We are entering the tongue of woodland that separates off Peg One. The two labradors – my bitch and the Lunts' old dog – are obediently at heel, but presently Gertie finds a scent among the bracken and I have to summon her back. It is lumpy underfoot here: the strip of trees has grown up where ancient cultivators dumped the rocks from their hard-won pastures. " 'Oo'd want to?" the shepherd repeats. The gale is quelled here and conversation easier. "I expect you've an answer to that, sir. You're a man of the world."

"I thought you were convinced it was an accident." I catch the shepherd's glance for the first time: expecting wariness I find hostility.

"That's what the coroner found, right? 'Accidental death'. 'Ere 'e was exactly." We have halted at a three-strand fence and a half-rotten stile against a young hazel, the ditch just beyond. "'E was right there, 'ead down, but they'd pulled 'im out before I got up. I was in the middle of the beaters' line. Gwyn Evans found 'im first, 'e called, then Alwyn and Ivor run up. Mr Tim came running over – it was 'im running made me realize something weren't as it should be." The undergrowth is still trampled all round. "They searched 'ere all day," the shepherd persists. "Every inch of it. 'Ad it fenced off with white tape."

There is nothing now: mud, leaves, reeds agitated by the wind. Gurgle of the ditch audible between gusts. Old tyre marks further into the field, near the peg.

" 'E was a good little prince, I read. Poor little beggar."

"It was an accident of course," I say.

The shepherd shows no inclination to proceed or return. I make no move to climb the fence. He is webbed up in a species of guilt. But what species?

"You don't think so, do you, sir?"

I catch the tone – an accusation, with a thin coating of

humour or threat.

"What are you telling me, Mr Rhys?"

"You come early sir, you pick this peg. We don't know 'oo sent you. First you're a City man, next you're a farmer." Over the wind the keeper's distant whistle: the beaters have begun the drive. In a minute or two birds will be coming over. I regard him coldly, make no comment. But he has a little speech.

"We Welsh are an old people. All sorts come to Wales from outside. They come, they go. We 'ad the Romans once. We don't object to visitors, within reason. We don't take to intruders. We can always tell one from the other." He sounds like a man accustomed to his threats being heeded.

"Come now, Mr Rhys. Perhaps we should talk about sheep-farming."

"With intruders we clam up and clamp down. I don't know any more about this prince than you do, Mr Goode. And if I did, I wouldn't tell you."

From up the line the ragged firing of shotguns. The dogs have begun to whine. A single hen pheasant bolts over our treetops and across the unattended peg in the little field below.

"They'll need your dog up the line, Mr Rhys."

"I don't require your advice, sir." And turns, to move back up the line.

Pheasant are coming over in numbers now and Gertie has run ahead excitedly; the Liverpudlian lawyer on peg two will expect to hear firing, though he is out of sight.

Climbing the barbed fence by the stile, I try to re-enact precisely the prince's movements. A branch has been snapped off the hazel sapling at shoulder level. I study the lie of the ditch to judge the cover provided by the reeds and old bracken. If the shot entered his brain from under the chin, any killer must have fired from below as he scaled the fence, an awkward shot for a recumbent marksman with a shotgun. And where could he have run out to in that brief time between the fatal shot and the realisation up the line that no one was firing on Peg One? Unless . . . A cry behind me: I twist to see the shepherd several yards away facing me through the trees.

"What?"

"You called something, sir."

"I was calling the dog."

"My mistake." And he turns up the line.

9

On the telephone the editor made his position plain. "I know it's all the craze, 'investigative journalism', though I'm not sure what the term means. It never was a reporter's business to take things at face value. If it means one's got to assume that every official finding is a cover-up, that of course comes to be rather tedious and childish. A lot of people get upset and the paper finishes up with egg on its face."

"I couldn't agree more, Harry." He was a Privy Councillor as it was, yet why forfeit a knighthood or a life peerage for a layer of truth that is in the end unreportable?

"Parts of the profession have never quite got over Watergate. Anyway, you're far too experienced a chap to go rushing in. You mentioned you had a little lead on this story. I don't suppose you can be more specific?"

"Did I say 'lead'?" Perhaps I did. The appropriate word had proved slippery. "Hunch" would have raised suspicions about motive, a private vendetta; "tip-off" was too hard. Harry himself handled me like a gent, but if he pushed me across to the news editor, "tip-off" would provoke direct questions, Who? How? Where? When? It's a reporter's right to withhold his sources, but it's a news editor's right to avoid a *canard*.

"I think you did say 'little lead', Anthony. Something of the kind."

"It's got into the Arabs. I picked it up on the Arab net."

"You still keep in touch?"

"In touch."

"They're a fanciful bunch." Give a dog a bad name. "There's nothing like a solid fact, I suppose – nothing as rude as that?"

Ah – a fact. Is a demeanour a fact? A characteristic contortion around the mouth – no, less than a contortion: a twist, a pout, approximating to a flinch. Which bespeaks a state of mind. Is such "a fact"? I had hoped to graduate from *facts* . . .

"Something's bitten them in the tail," I said.

"Bitten who, exactly? The diplomats?"

One is thankful for the telephone. I never lose my nerve on the telephone. "More, the layabout aristocracy."

"The Gloucester Road lot, you mean. Ducking out of Ramadan."

"That's about it. Friends and relations."

"Would gossip be too harsh a word?"

"Not necessarily – that's what I reckon's worth establishing. Could be a will o' the wisp." Overstated, regrettably. I marked the little silence. "But *yet* . . ."

"Motive, though."

"I quite agree. That's obscure." Who'd want poor little Saqr dead?

"Well now, Anthony."

I didn't like the direction we were pointing for the summing up. I had been the paper's star man in the Third World once. But an aeon ago – nine years. Nine years half in the sticks, a freelance; a "bucolic spasmodic" an old colleague said. Harry was no fool. He had begun in newspapers, then politics, then back to Fleet Street. He knew what happened to journalists when the disciplines went. All sorts of bias, prejudice, private grievance can sprout when a man's released from the strictures of objectivity, attribution, *fact*. An ex-newsman, out to pasture, on the beer – sometimes there's nothing left but *folie de grandeur* and a blundering way with words. Even a newsman self-retired and in his mid-thirties, at the top of his skills . . . Or was I already over the top? They had entreated me not to quit. Harry himself had taken me out to lunch. But weren't the symptoms already evident? The tell-tale signals of decay? Were they not deducible from my very readiness to quit? – that the realities of hard news had become burdensome? that I was prematurely played out, must slide from participation to reminiscence, from events to reverie? Those previous months, when I had more or less decided to get out of Fleet Street, I was covering south Asia and tried to persuade Harry to let me live the life of a crippled beggar for a couple of months on the streets of Bombay, staining my skin and following as faithfully as I could a beggar's daily and nightly pattern of life. To write a piece, of course; a series of pieces.

Harry wouldn't wear it. I can still remember his humouring tone on the international phone . . . That was nine years ago.

"Can I put it like this, Anthony? You dig away among your Arab friends" – he didn't really believe they existed, and he was right, he was right – "and go back to Wales if you want to. But I think phase one ought to be Anthony Guise acting independently. D'you regard that as fearfully craven? I don't mind covering the petrol, the odd hotel bill – or maybe you've got your friends down in Wales still? But I think we ought not to make it an assignment from the paper as such. Not at this stage. Until you come up with something. Is that fair do's?'

It's not what I told Sophia. Not at all. I told Sophia Harry had urged me to take it on, *pressed* me. Though I never explained exactly what "it" was: for if it was anything at all, it concerned her, it concerned that estate of holy matrimony and a region where I must go alone – what one might call the "flip side" of all that the vicar of St. Paul's, Knightsbridge had so painstakingly prepared us for.

10

Grover Wilks' helicopter sets him down at one of the last villages on the Shaikhdom side of the frontier, at about four thousand feet. The crew make their own camp of tents and folding beds, but Wilks himself accepts the tribal headman's hospitality, and lodges that first evening in a stonebuilt hut from which children have been evicted, supping on the porridge of winter wheat and chicken, and probably glutinous date fudge, proffered by his host. They know him here, of course, this Wilikis, a sprite, demiurge, manifestation of an unprecedented epoch, flitting between continents, an Amriki more at ease in their second lingo Arabiyya than they themselves; limitlessly knowledgeable and indefinably influential – a genie of the Shaikh. Over the pale coffee and cardamom brew replenished by boys, late and long, the old men and young fathers and the youngsters on leave from the Shaikhdoms' federal army will be conversing with him, crosslegged on mats of woven grasses, upon the tragic death of Saqr; upon this final illness of the old Shaikh; upon the prospect of Saqr's brother, Hamood. Upon the explosion that smithereened the Emirate's water party; upon disaffection of Emirate kinsmen and disputes concerning the frontier. Upon the laborious approach of the road; upon the allocation of government land and crop subsidies and the outrageous profits of middlemen. Upon the pall of black oil smothering their fishing (for they migrate to the coast). And thence to the blind struggle at the head of the Gulf, and the President of Amrika whose men walk the moon and who yet declines to impose peace on the ignorant and fractious.

I suppose that, concerning Hamood, the villagers' curiosity is expressed by reticence, pools of silence round which the talk delicately steps. For years it has been permissible to retail scandalous hearsay and to cast Hamood in the role of the flawed relative, characteristic of aristocracies, who actually enhances the qualities of the one in principal authority. Now, by the quirkiness that is Allah's privilege Hamood is to become Shaikh and *ex officio* deserving of honour, beyond reproach of voice or even of heart, if simple tribesmen are to sleep untroubled . . . just so long as he is their statutory Shaikh, their pinnacle, tent-pole.

Surely the name of Billy French will have cropped up. Sayyid Fransi. Wadi Fransi. Invoking disgruntlement, and titters perhaps, at a wry silence from Wilikis. But also awe at Fransi's sacrificial energy and ubiquity on the other side of the grudgingly acknowledged frontier bisecting their tribal highlands.

Next morning it is hard for Wilks to prevent all the men of the village from accompanying him to the agreed rendezvous. Having no desire to upstage French, he reduces the cortège to a handful, plus donkey, and sets off through the barbarous and malevolent beauty; the air is still crisp and perilous tracks cling to their shadows. Wilks reaches the high pass first, and waits there under a rock overhang. French, with two tribesmen and no impedimenta, greets him within the hour with a *"Dr Livingstone I presume!"* He then conducts his visitors down into the wadi and up the other side through a jumble of tiny settlements and fragmented cultivation.

Here French, playing convivial host, proudly shows Wilks the cisterns he has had dug out of rock and lined with cement, to capture the mean rain. Would Grover visit the pass where the water party met its fate? "We found blood on a stone, thirty yards away." "Oh really, Billy? But I've done enough trekking this morning." "In a little pool. Dried up, naturally, It wasn't spattered." "One would expect blood." Blood appals Wilks.

In the evening the village rasheeds foregather, making quite a *"durbar"*, as Wilks puts it, being a student of British imperialism. From time to time French grows concerned at the cascade of supposed grievances tumbling at Wilks' feet. It is as if the American, above meaningless boundaries, can dispense equity from a point of transcendent detachment. Quite frequently French loses the drift of the Arabic interchange (he is on firmer ground with his self-taught tribal patois.) He cannot but admire how Grover handles them, crosslegged amidst a group of four or five headmen, catching the shifts and swerves of each man's opinion like swallows on the wing. French himself never likes to have more than one man speaking at once, would forbid it if he could, his hearing not as perfect as it was; it invites misunderstanding. Yet Grover seems untroubled, fielding a doubt here, a nuance there, scooping up a silence, like the mercurial cricketer French had known at school in Grantham who never missed a catch however thick and fast the balls came across the slip-catch. The skill is uncanny . . . and the trust he can repose in Grover is itself a source of pride.

When Wilks goes back next day by the same tracks to Shaikhdom territory and his attendant helicopter, French feels that his tribesmen are reassured, enjoined to patience. Wilks has promised the headmen he will return, which seems to French a surprising commitment (he learnt long ago the danger of carefree promises to simple people, who take one's word literally). Yet hasn't the visit eased the air of crisis left by the obliteration of the water party? One way or t'other, Grover has got them to set aside their humiliating decision to send a delegation to the old Shaikh. Thanks be, Grover Wilks.

As it turns out, by the time Wilks' helicopter returns to the Shaikhdom's diminutive capital, the old Shaikh has already died. Of cruel nature's causes.

59

11

By now my pursuit of buried truth has drawn me back to Wales, not precisely to the Lunt corner but to a lowland town the Dee skirts further downstream, some five miles from the depressed little industrial town of Ruabon and smack against another frontier, that with England.

Steep deposits of grey and yellow snow fill the corners of the market. I am here ostensibly to buy a pair of Welsh tups to breed from.

Most pens contain ewes with lambs at foot – "couples" on offer by those with insufficient grazing – as well as a few old rams and cast ewes for slaughter. The auctioneer in his white coat on his raised ramp between the pens resembles a cheap preacher, or a pardoner hawking indulgences. His little mob of cloth-capped sinners (local farmers and dealers) have stepped out of a Breughel, each man immemorially distinct, shrewd, hard-bitten, weathered, and sharp-coloured all except one: he is parchment-yellow and himself half-penned for slaughter of another kind. His protests will be no whit less futile than his lambs'. There in the jostle, just behind this dying man, the bushy sideburns of Alwyn Rhys; wearing a big dark duffle, half a head taller than most he has a look in the eye – cunning, humorous, wary – that is unmistakeably Welsh.

When he spots me through the cold rain surprise is lacking, and I can tell he knows my purpose is other than sheep. He edges towards me.

"A long way to come for a couple of tups, Mr Goode." The scorn habitual in the grin. " 'Oo wants Welsh rams bar a Welshman?" By afternoon I have bought neither tup nor ewe, but professing interest in his own flock I am invited to follow with my Land Rover behind his old A-40 van up to the cottage. He and brother Dai must have conferred: that was evident – a pair of peasants in a cramped world, cursed with intelligence. Maybe the eldest brother, Rhys the Game, Rhys good, is blessed with dull wits, a feeble curiosity . . .

We drive six or seven miles, uphill mostly, leaving tarmac for farm tracks. Rain falls as snow here, already an inch settled. The wind is up. Through two gates, across a sheep grid, we follow the poles that share the electric and telephone. Cottage and out-buildings are dumped there like a geological afterthought. A chained collie greets his master with one bark and warns of me with another: alarmed at one end, wagging the other. Ritual evergreens – holly and box – also guard the approach.

We stoop to enter the peeling green door, stamping our feet on slate flags. "Now you've come all this way back 'ere, Mr Goode," he begins, but then steps back: "I prefer the Welsh. You won't have Welsh, eh, a name like Goode? I 'ave it correct – Goode? Would that be an English name?"

"Saxon, I suppose."

"We Celts 'ad trouble with the Saxons. And the Normans."

We shed outer garments in a low living-room built for stubby Welshmen not this long-shanked strain. One wall is filled by a black cast-iron range with a patch of red embers which he stokes from a scuttle. Other walls are papered with damp-stained blooms, an approximation of blighted corn-flowers. The late February daylight funnelling through a small lattice-window in the wall two-foot-thick is supplemented by a single electric ceiling bulb in a dusty pink flounce. From a corner, a large television documents the paper industry in brilliant shifting colours but no sound. Beneath, an enamel hip-bath, quite new; alongside, on a small cheap table, a modern clock with brass mechanism gyrating behind glass stands on a doily. A telephone is attached to the wall, on which Alwyn now makes a call in the Welsh language, unintelligible to me. Books litter the lid of an ornate harmonium beside me, several stops missing and brass candle-holders tarnished; I can see Arthur Mee's *Children's Encyclopaedia*, a tattered *History of the World* by H. G. Wells, several copies of a journal named *World Trade Union Movement*, a Welsh songbook, and several pamphlets. Up a twist of narrow wooden stairs I can hear children caught up in a fantasy which demands intense concentration.

"I'd be glad to see your ewes before dark," I prompt. "Just how you manage single-handed with so many sheep, and the job, too."

"The wife's 'ere." The slovenliness and stale air give no hint that a woman cares for the low room we big men cramp so. "Or Dai can drive over. The eldest – she's nine – she's big enough to 'elp."

Now Mrs Rhys is entering with tea and factory-made jam tarts on a plastic tray. She fills the pot from the kettle on the range.

"You'll not be joining us then, Megan?" Alwyn says in English, mixing charm with a challenge to me; I am waiting for privacy. She is as wanly listless as he muscularly is vigorous. "This gentleman is a Mr Goode from England." As if England was not ten minutes down the road.

She offers a worn, red hand and a tired smile. An affliction of the skin has crept along her forearm, and out of sight. When she is gone we sit drinking tea in silence. The milk jug has "Rhyl" across it.

"You're a cautious man, Mr Goode, I wouldn't doubt. Coming up 'ere, looking into everything ever so closely."

"I don't want to rush it." Buying rams, that is. "Do my sums. If I'm to see your flock . . ."

"I've to go out in any case. There's ewes lambing already." Two exquisite children are gazing sullenly from the bottom stair – a girl of nine, a boy of six. "Say 'ow-d'you-do to Mr Goode, Myfanwy." The girl neither moves nor speaks. Their eyes go from me to a great tree toppling silently towards the camera, then back to me. We men don our coats and caps, and go out into the dervish snow and dwindling light. Alwyn carries a paraffin lamp. He releases the dog. We each take a straw bale in both hands, and Alwyn carries a fork as well.

"You can do your sums," he comments, "but you won't get 'em right. Common Market won't let you. So why not come to the point, Mr Goode?" I am instantly aware of flitting again, of the alarmed bat in my own darkness. *Guilt.*

We have gone over the brow behind the building and are among sheep, alerted by the dog.

"The point?"

"You were interested in that prince," Alwyn says.

"That's what your brother Dai thought."

"Dai can read a man."

"It was an interesting occurrence," I concede.

"Occurrence," he echoes. "That's the word. Why bother me?"

"I haven't."

"But you intend to."

One ewe is lying awkwardly on her side by a knuckle of rock, with several others in discreet attendance. Alwyn sends the dog to block retreat. The ewe gets to her feet, but dog and men close on her. The shepherd catches her with his crook and tips her up. She surrenders at once and his hands probe her swollen belly through the matted fleece. She pants lightly. We place bales windward of her in an open pentagon and tramp downhill now, towards the darkness of trees and ripple of a stream. Three or four ewes have already lambed and they and their offspring have bunched under the lee of sycamores and oaks. A stack of hay shoulder-high stands under a tarpaulin, which we unpeg, and Alwyn deposits forkfuls in the snow round about. We move on to two more fields and do likewise, Alwyn carrying fork, lamp and crook, I nothing. In the whirl of snow I lose sense of direction, and our footmarks are soon covered. We speak little. Daylight has gone now and Alwyn's lamp rings us. He brings out an oilskin pouch and rolls a cigarette, offering it to me – though a non-smoker, I accept, in hope of a thin, brief delusion of shared security. We pause there, in our tiny rondel of light. "I thought you might know something," I say.

"What is your interest, Mr Goode?"

"I happen to know that the prince's death was not an accident."

"What was it then?"

"It was murder."

"And 'oo might be tellin' you that, like?" He has raised the lamp to scrutinize. He sees a lean face, a narrow gaze, grey-eyed, probably a glint of fear. Fear is on standby, both sides.

"The prince's friends. Private friends."

"Private bloody friends," the sing-song making the words spring. "I could leave you 'ere, in a 'eap, 'oo's to bloody tell, Mr 'Oo-ever you are." He still has the fork.

"I'd very soon be traced," I reply coldly. "You too."

He sets up off the incline, I alongside – same side as the fork,

63

the safer side. I think: Let him speak next, anything he wants.

"Supposin' it wasn't himself killed 'im, it wasn't me either. Is that what you want to know, eh?"

"I don't doubt," I offer meekly, and provoke vehemence.

"*Don't* you? It couldn't 'ave been. You don't know a bloody thing. You wouldn't be wasting your time. They've been into all that. A to Z, Timothy's English rabble. You're not Special Branch, I can tell that. You're not Foreign Office. You want to ask them. They're satisfied." He stops. "Why should I care?"

We almost trample an angle of bleating flesh, a few minutes old; it is on its knees, unable to get up, its mother to one side with a stronger twin. Alwyn puts down lamp and fork to gather the weakling. He nuzzles its cold fur, shiny from the womb, against his cheek. A ragged umbilicus hangs from its belly and bits of cowl cling to it. The ewe has not even licked it clean.

"Put 'im under your coat. Cover 'im 'ead and all."

We go on up through an open gateway into a field, precarious life at my chest. Is that the light of the cottage some distance on? Then I realize it is another lantern, carried by hand. Our lights approach. It is not one newcomer but two. At a few yards I recognise Dai Rhys, and a companion, same build, same cast of face – the third brother, the gamekeeper.

They have been summoned; they know whom to expect; their perfunctory greeting is in a speech that shuts me out.

Alwyn conducts us to where the ewe lies in faulty labour between our straw bales. Dai-shepherd kneels to feel her, then the gamekeeper inspects her and gives an opinion. Alwyn hands the lamp across, takes off his overcoat and pushes up the sleeve of sweater and shirt. He slings his coat round him like a cloak. Lamplight catches the bulging eye of the ewe, who makes a fretful token butting. Kneeling, Alwyn slips his narrowed hand and – swiftly – all of his thick forearm through the cervix of the ewe, now quite still and abandoned to ultimate forces. The experienced hand works within her, the other hand upon the belly, face and head right down into her flank. We three others stand silently above this primal crib. A single syllable of provisional accomplishment escapes Alwyn, and the ewe groans. Gradually the arm withdraws, now wrist, the upper hand – the other hand pressing the belly from

64

outside, kneading urgently, in a slow rhythm. The lamb's head, still in its cowl membrane and its forefeet with it, emerges in a casque of human fingers; the two forelegs are drawn out wholly, and then – swiftly, sliding out in one brief spasm – the entire immaculate living organism. Alwyn clears the mouth with a quick scoop of his forefinger. A tiny bleat escapes, to be answered at once by the ewe. Holding the lamb in one hand, Alwyn gently drags it over the ewe's back, marking her with the blood, and lays her lamb, its back to her, on a patch of straw which Dai has pulled from the bale. From each teat Alwyn squeezes a tiny yellow jet, to unclog the source of life; then straightening up, he takes the lamp from his brother's hand. The four of us in a ragged circle wait without speech in the middle of this white pasture, inaugurating a birth; a minute or two later the lamb staggers to its feet, and its miniature face probing its mother's underbelly, releases us to our *post mortem*.

12

And here, to keep the equilibrium of this tally of the good and the bad that wrack us, I must interpolate an encounter three thousand miles away, where the solid iron gates of Shaikh Hamood's new palace are being opened to Grover and Lucy Wilks. She carries a sketch pad. I make no claim to mastering the distinction between what is good and what bad, for both are shot through with sadness and pain, and both, too, with freedom and joy. But I do claim the distinction exists, and that it is man's honour and curse to wrestle all his life to interpret it.

The hour is already nearly 11 p.m. Hamood is eccentric as to the common proprieties of shaikhly conduct. He holds intimate audiences late at night. He even admits a lady of the expatriate community into his presence – properly scarved and long-skirted and accompanied by her husband.

Wilks sheds his sandals, his wife her espadrilles, alongside other footwear: one pair three-ply garish wedge sandals, one pair Italian down-at-heels. They approach the little group across the astroturf. The Shaikh is settled cross-legged among rugs laid out beside a floodlit garden wall. Random teeth missing from the lower jaw and two central teeth from the upper make him – as my informant has it – "a leering Othello".

He greets them expansively from ground level, "Amriki Grover Wilikis and the Madam Lucy Wilikis Inglisi well come. Sit. Take whisky." Cushions are plumped and assembled. "Madam Lucy, the decorator appointed!" He presents her to his companions – a youth in Arab attire and a lugubrious Lebanese contractor already known to the Wilkses, evidently the residue of a larger gathering.

An outsize bottle of Red Label Johnny Walker is steered towards them on a tin tray like a doomed ship, an empty lies wrecked on the astroturf amid flotsam of tumblers and thick plastic sack containing ice.

The host endorses the newcomers. "Most Amriki are fucky

bastards, but Mister Grover Wilikis is my friend and okay. Also Lucy, his Madam who makes my palace as beautiful as she." He raises his glass stiffly, in a military way: she smiles and bobs her trim figure. English is one of Hamood's accomplishments, but now he confirms in Arabic that Wilikis is famous for being "okay" right along the coast and, moreover, knows the President of the United States. The Lebanese is despairingly impressed, perceiving a once-for-all opportunity to apply for salvation that will surely be lost, and Wilks' airy disclaimer in Arabic that "His Highness exaggerates" brings no relief.

This Lebanese has had the misfortune of winning the tender to build the palace. Although partially occupied it is still unfinished, dogged by Hamood's capricious shifts of mood which have long ago swallowed the profit envisioned in the original specification. The edifice which began as a pastiche of the White House (itself a pastiche) is now islamicised by turrets and arches. Yet no Shaikhly signature accommodates the catastrophic additional cost to this contractor, who is a good Muslim, dislikes drunkenness, longs for his chubby wife and fat children in tormented Beirut.

The Shaikh has returned to a familiar jest. "You know what, Grover? They can plant the hair like the grass!" He sticks all his fingers into the tight black curls of his oddly square head. "Shall I give to Faraj a lot of beautiful hair like mine?" The contractor morosely feigns enchantment: being very bald, he has conducted timorous strands from the rim of his scalp across the desert of his pate. Shaikh Hamood grins and widens his eyes – the traditional Shakespearean Moor, sallow rather than black, Mediterranean Africa in his lips and curls and obsession in the protruding eyes, the jet irises entirely ringed by white. Fur sprouts in tufts on his upper and lower lips; elsewhere shaving has been more recently neglected. "Or maybe he likes Wilikis' hair?" – and he mimes, with his fingers, Grover's fine pale hair flying in the wind.

The slender young Arab drops his gaze, dreading to be drawn into the jape. The description I have is of a doe-eyed youth in a chequered headcloth, folded to form a broad peak like the cloth cap of a golfer in an old-time comedy; he flicks at it skilfully to make it fall just right at the back. Massive gold cufflinks secure his sleeves.

"How was the *jebel*, Grover Wilks?" the Shaikh demands suddenly. "You saw Fransi? He is a fool."

"I have a little report, Highness." The two men engage in a staring match which ends in a draw, the Shaikh spontaneously launching into an account of a previous civilisation that once mastered the lower Gulf. This civilisation exploded an atomic bomb that opened the straits, thus creating the waterway by which it grew rich. Proof exists in the presence of identical species of wild animals on both sides of the straits. The civilisation flourished 48,000 years ago. (He would always produce exact figures.) When the Koreans were excavating for sewers up the creek they broke into an underground chamber of huge dimensions where they found 119 clay idols in the form of life-size men. "I saw them with my own eyes" – he points to his manic eyes – "but my father made the Koreans to cover the excavation for fear of the religious authorities."

A well-known outcrop of rock up the coast, he explains, was built as a citadel by this lost civilisation. He draws at his whisky, swilling it in his mouth. The Wilkses have heard much of it before, but the fantasy gathers its own random accretions.

"I shall make it tested," he declares. "Okay? They can test how old is anything. You know that Grover? My friend will take the contract. He told me about this testing how old."

"Which friend?" they enquire.

"He is a duke. He has a tribe in Scotland." And fumbling in a pocket extracts an address book, rolling over to reach a shaft of light so that an obscene rump obscures the dusty flowers along the wall like twin plump stormclouds. A white cat observes from the top of the wall.

Then he rolls back and begins to punch a number but fails repeatedly to obtain a connection. Wilks intervenes, "What are you dialling, Highness?"

"The Duke of Moray."

"Where?"

"At his castle in Scotland."

"It's a bit late, Highness."

"He will be pleased to hear his friend Hamood."

Wilks investigates the number and suggests he drop the zero in the middle.

68

"It rings," Hamood exclaims delightedly, and winks at the contractor. "I told you, Wilikis knows the President." The number rings for fully two minutes, and there ensues an interchange of which, in honour of its sheer oddity, I retail this verbatim account.

"Hello, Fitzroy. Fitzroy? Salaam aleikum. This is Hamood. Shaikh Hamood." Identification at that distance and hour proves a struggle, and the brow puckers, but once achieved a serene amity breaks forth. "How is Al-Fajar?" This induces a fresh element of non-communication. "Fajar, lovely *Fajar*, how is she?" He covers the mouthpiece to explain, "Fitzroy's wife is Down."

"Dawn," Lucy Wilks corrects.

"Yes, yes," the Shaikh cries, as comprehension descends. "The Duchess Khaleej. She is okay? Tell her Hamood says, I love you. We have found a civilization under the ground. You are there, Fitzroy?" He is, but the announcement calls for repetition, being unexpected. "You will take the contract to test the age. Okay? Millions."

The Duke is evidently alerted by the mention of a large figure, though whether of years or *dirhams* calls for oblique clarification never quite achieved until, from a region of darkness, a tiny figure in frilly white rockets into the seated circle to pummel the Shaikh on the chest repeating, "*Ah-ba, Ah-ba*," insisting on her father's attention.

"Okay, Fitzroy. I call back tomorrow. Okay?" He drops the receiver onto the astroturf to cuddle and tenderly restrain his three-year-old.

But the child will not be turned from her intention, and a lean, elderly, black manservant reveals that she has thrown the keys of the Rolls Royce into the swimming pool. The news secures her purpose, for it is in the Rolls that she was to have been returned to her mother. The Shaikh gets to his feet, and stepping round the outsize transistor radio and the telephone, leads the party to the covered pool. Lights are switched on: the keys are visible in eight foot of water, the pool being uniformly eight foot deep throughout. No guest volunteers to dive for them, so the Shaikh himself draws off his *dishdasha* and plunges in, retrieving them at first attempt – a trick surely performed before.

Clambering out, he confides to Wilks, "Whoever marries her, she will fuck his head in four minutes. Watch out."

The interruption procures the release of the Lebanese and the youth. Wilikis is accused of not finishing his whisky. Then – where has his little girl gone?

"Majed took her off. It was time for her bed."

"She fall in the pool?" – eyes rolling in mock-horror. He seizes bottle and suitcase-sized transistor and with *dishdasha* clinging to his wet bulk pads off into the palace by an entrance where servants have made camp, followed by the Wilkses. The air-conditioning is not yet wired up and the air is still heavy from the day's heat. A massive chandelier burns in the main hallway but at floor level electrical sockets gape with tortured wires. A guard, asleep on a pile of plastic sacks, abruptly stands, and grins. There is as yet no furniture except built-in gilt mirrors and verdite consol tables of the style privately classified by the quick-rich decorators as "Louis Squince". They ascend. In great empty chambers cockroaches are the preliminary lords, speckling the marble with excreta and scuttling into the electrical sockets. Lucy Wilks wonders what they feed on.

On the upper floor, Mrs Wilks has at least completed the decor of Hamood's wife's bedroom. A confection of pink and green, it contains a grand quilted bed, on which Hamood himself has made a pile of small, hard cushions, mostly heart-shaped, embroidered "Kiss me" and "YES", with profiles of flaxen girls, mouths ajar. A hesitant portrait in oils tells nothing about this young wife, and this may be providential. She has not moved in yet and it is unreasonable to suppose she ever will. The cushions look to the designer like the turds of some large unclassified mammal that knows by instinct of the premises' likely abandonment. But she is undisturbed at the spoiling of her handiwork.

Through a lordly bathroom they attain Hamood's temporary sanctuary, a small bedroom intended for a child, papered with images of Bambi or Rudolf the Reindeer – the Shaikha's not Lucy Wilks' choice. This chamber too is ruthlessly lit by a suspended chandelier: the original contract required one in every room regardless. A temporary air-conditioner has been implanted into the window. Apart from a single "Louis

70

Squince" dressing table whose chalcedony top supports various pomades and unguents and a pile of Arabic newspapers, there is no furniture – not even a curtain. A mattress and duvet occupy much of the floor.

The Shaikh deposits bottle and radio beside the mattress and re-enters the bathroom, returning with two gold-rimmed tumblers half filled with water; he has draped himself in a towel against the air-conditioning. Passing one tumbler to Wilks, he subsides onto the mattress to top up with Red Label, but, with the tips of his fingers, Wilks lifts the bottle by the neck from his hand, gazing down reproachfully at his master. "Naughty naughty," he chides. He holds out a hand for the bottle-cap, which Hamood surrenders with a wink to Lucy Wilks. Her husband says, "We have some matters of state, Highness." Only then does she withdraw – bottle in hand – to make sketches for the prospective dining room, leaving her husband to step from his sandals and settle onto the floor for the business they came for.

13

Somebody has shunted Alwyn's van so that it blocks the exit from the cottage yard, trapping the Land Rover, closing me off. In the kitchen, I hear Megan and the two children already at high tea.

Alwyn shakes coal onto the living-room fire and settles into a rocking chair. He has the lamb I carried, on a piece of towel on his lap. His brothers each take upright chairs, the game-keeper with his back to the window's untidy gingham curtain. I am left with the only easy chair, under the flounced ceiling light, facing the fire, two Rhyses on one side, one on the other. I can see Dylan the keeper and Alwyn without turning; the middle brother, Dai, is more to one side. In the corner between Dai and Alwyn the television bulges, still soundless: men in uniform are clearing rubble, somewhere east; children in close-up weep hopelessly.

"What is it you want, Mr Goode? And why?"

The questions, like an indictment, come from the keeper, the one I do not know, Dylan Rhys. Maybe a year or so's seniority tells: a touch of grey at the temples. But they are operating by collective instinct: I have felt that from the start, all through the long silences. They are all under threat; a primal atavism is at work with its own code, an entire language . . . "If we're not troubling you."

The English border might be a thousand miles away; the menace if imprecise is unmistakeable. They could make a proper mess of me, three big men to one in this primaeval homestead, stone walls two foot deep, one up from a barrow, whose big lower liths were cannibalised from previous dwell-ings right here over x thousand years, lumps of Cambrian rock barely modified by man's hand, that have dumb-witnessed retribution in every form. But there are children next door. Violence and blood usually insist upon explanation. They can hardly risk a killing. (Even Sophia would enquire in due course, would come to claim the remains of "the man she married".) . . . And surely their fear of what I might know, and how I know it, is a species of life insurance.

I address the keeper directly. "I want what you have to tell me." I clear my throat: "As to *why*, you needn't trouble yourself – yourselves." Turning to the others: "Once I have what you have to tell me, you won't be troubled further." I fold one leg over the other. My socks are the expensive kind, the golfing variety. I have left my wellingtons at the cottage door. The others wear leather boots, primitive weaponry.

"You suppose we have something to tell you," the keeper says, and I nod.

"Why?" Dai this time.

"The prince did not kill himself."

"So you have said." It is Alwyn now, the youngest. "What makes you so sure?" he sneers, believing his retort unanswerable. Yet it is answerable. I have seen it written in the language of the face, not these Welshmen's faces but the English face of their absent squire, Timothy Lunt – a very private language, not easy to translate into words. Lovers know the untranslatable language of touch: I do not refer to a context of love but of shame. I have read Timmy's ineluctable shame and fear even through the medium of a television interview. To me it was a most intimate communication, an involuntary signal interpretable, perhaps, not even by the mother whose milk he sucked nor by his remote patrician father, but only by me, confidant, partner in that furtive amorality which in Timmy's view comprises the soul. Out of that daring, shrouded corruption sprung his confidence. The essential difference he saw between himself and the common run of others was that he acknowledged the vice at the root of the human species and so could turn it to his purpose. As with these very peasants, for instance . . . Yet was the theory as clearcut as Timmy would have himself believe? For if ever that shroud was lifted by the corner, as it sometimes inevitably was in the mere business of living, what his face registered was not boldness, clarity, but an inexplicable shame. A traitorous mouth devilled him, a tell-tale hollowness in the lower lip that the eye confirmed. That was the signal. I have seen it in childhood, we two creeping out from dark woods; in our brothel days, emerging into the deserted small-hours of the lamplit city. Post-coital *shame*. It belonged to such moments and was thus rare and quite brief. I do not think he was ever precisely aware of it. He was surely never aware that this transmitted shame-signal at last stirred in me courage to break his power over me and marry Sophia.

Do I mean break? Then what am I doing in this bleak and dangerous snowbound cottage? Poor Sophia. They should not have named her Wisdom, but Virginia, Innocenta, Snow White.

"And if it were so," Alwyn pursues, "what has it to do with us?"

Indeed, what? Is Mr Tim's vice-power at work in you, too? "That is exactly what I want to know."

The brief pause here is a mistake for the brothers. The keeper fills it, a narrow declaration. "You're barking up the wrong tree, mon."

I say nothing. I have long made silence a speciality. I feel a kind of sorrow for them. But suddenly Dai is on his feet, yanking me up level by my shirt and sweater. " 'Oo the bloody 'ell are you? You come 'ere, out of bloody nowhere, fancy clothes, tailormade overcoat, no bloody labels. In a 'ired bloody Land Rover. Out of some bloody office. You needn't think you're leaving 'ere until we know 'oo you are *exactly*."

I am full of fear. I have got through all this life without being beaten up.

One of the others – perhaps both – calls him off and he lets me go with an expletive. So they have tried to sniff out my identity and so far have failed. Surely this involves Timmy? Yet they neither invoke him nor shelter behind his authority: when they raise him, it's disparagingly.

The kitchen has gone quiet. The showy clock's brass works oscillate, and smoked meat and my own funk make a sour tang.

"I don't think any of you killed him," I say with a wobbly blandness, refraining from smoothing my clothes. "But once I've got proof of that I shall be happier. We shall be more at peace." They can hear me cowering.

"What makes you so sure someone killed him?" Dylan the gamekeeper.

"Please let's not return to that. I *know* he was murdered."

74

This, at least, is becoming less and less of a lie.

"There were nineteen on that shoot." Dai has the figure exactly. "You spoke to all the others, eh?" His sarcasm puffs him.

"Allow me to eliminate you gentlemen first."

"We aren't murderers, I'll 'ave you know." The keeper Dylan again, spokesman for the whole family, living and dead: the forgotten little sister: generations to come.

"Let us accept that, Mr Rhys. Why should a family of Welsh countrymen want to? But someone helped the murderer. Someone planned for him. These things aren't done solo. We all know that. Except by a madman. It always takes more than one. It takes more than one to steal sheep from an estate up the river and sell them at markets down this way, for instance."

This recklessness I address to Dylan – Rhys Uncontaminated – because it is the safest face, contrasting by a deference to the social order or even to a God of love. His response is a quick shadow not of outward anger but inner irritation. The two others exchange rapidly in the argot, then all three are in it, some kind of common hatred becoming defined, and mounting.

Here a child chooses to enter, an exquisite small girl, bearing most carefully in two hands, right up to her father, a saucer of white paste. Taking this offertory, he moistens it at a spigot on the little tank built into the ancient stove. The child's march, to and fro, silences us, allows me to recover kilter.

"I didn't mean to distract us. I only wanted to stress – these things aren't done in isolation. To be more precise. Our prince was surely found where he died. Whoever shot him must have known he was going to be there, more or less at that time. Now how many people knew he was going to be there at that time?"

No one speaks, so I repeat my question and at last goad Alwyn: "The 'ole bloody lot of 'em knew. Anyone can count numbers."

"Yes, yes. We all agree. But is there another peg – would you say – is there any other peg on any stand on the Lunt estate more or less out of sight of the others?"

"Someone 'ad to shoot there," Alwyn replies. He is rocking the lamb in his chair, tenderly or fretfully, and it sucks at his milky teat-finger.

75

"And if it hadn't been the prince on that peg, what a long long way for an assassin to come for no game." Illuminated in the middle of them, I stare into the fire. I must give them time, I know that — time to betray others.

" 'E's from the newspapers," Dai says, " 'e's so bloody clever."

" 'E'll be out of a job," Alwyn concurs.

"What you saying exactly?" the keeper demands, and the other two look at him, questioning the sense of lifting such a hatch. So I answer at once: "What I'm saying is, exactly, someone fixed the draw."

"Bloody 'ell, mon," Alwyn exclaims, and Dai follows, " 'E thinks 'e can play with us. Cat and mouse. Suck your thumb at nights, Mister?"

But the keeper is silent. On the television everyone is in Edwardian dress. Servants galore. One could wonder where the money came from until one remembered how little they were paid. The children have crept in at the back of the room to watch the soundless antics. Or else our little drama. Alwyn calls through to his wife, and her voice summons them back to the unpenetrated quarters. He reaches across to extinguish the picture and the lamb bleats like a baby.

"Where are you from, sir? Please." Keeper Dylan.

Something in his voice touches me. I wish I could tell him. This keeper fears some God, even if a Welsh one. Nor is he a murderer; probably none of them is. The present fear is not quite of that sort. They are accessories to murder — all of them, two of them, one of them, I can't be sure: a trio of Taffies born with sharp wits to a remnant culture and tongue that brand them half-savage. They grew up to extract every fragment of significance, of revenge, of right to a soul as great as an Englishman's. They know about murder on a broader, slower scale than that of any young shaikh with an egg-blown skull; they themselves have been made party to this slow murder by all sorts of sentimentalists playing Canute with history, deluding the natives about the "value" of their Welshness, inflaming the sores with disinfectant, broadcasting their Welsh titbits, Welshifying the schools, fencing the youngsters by language into their picturesque valleys and sodden moors. They know about genocide. Why should they care that some

76

upstart from an Arabian dune dies if they can pocket a quick advantage?

From under fear crawls a Christian sorrow. I turn to the eldest, seeking the puzzled depths of his eyes, frowning my appeal for understanding that his question about me must remain unanswered, watching for a glimpse of recognition – a monkey trust among different primate branches of the same Creator. Then I turn back to the youngest, the maverick. "Alwyn, will you please tell me your life story?"

From Alwyn, "What's this?" and Dai, "Why 'im?" simultaneously.

"You went to the village school. Right? Up to eleven? Then secondary school at Ll – – – ? Right? How did you do? Well?" None of them speaks; Dylan goes wooden, waiting on clarification. I persist: "A pretty good pupil?"

"Came bloody top, Alwyn did," Dai comes out with. "Couldn't stop himself. Top in English, top in Welsh."

"O-Levels, all that kind of thing."

"We all got O-Levels." Dai must chalk them up. "Alwyn's got A-Levels." Defiance in him, too. And I knead it out – he didn't go to the university because he "got pissed and went into the army", three years with the Royal Welsh in Hong Kong, Germany, Northern Ireland, then just when they had got as far as thinking of making Sergeant Alwyn Rhys an officer, they bust him to nothing for insubordination.

" 'E was still to go to college, like," Dai says. *Thick as thieves, those two*, Lady Wynn-Williams reckoned. " 'E went to Swansea for interview. They took 'im but 'e didn't go. 'E went on the building sites."

"McAlpines." Alwyn is smiling to himself, a slow grin. Scorn downing regret.

"We could do with a drink," I propose. They look at me suspiciously. "So you joined the Communist Party," I go on.

Dylan stiffens, at my left.

"YCL," Alwyn corrects.

It was a shot in the dark, but now that he has told me, I see I could hardly have missed. By twenty-one he was handcrafted for the Young Communist League.

"Timothy Lunt know that?"

"Why should 'e care? Your Timothy knows nothing about

anything."

"*My* Timothy?"

"Peas in a pod, you two."

"I don't think I understand . . ."

"I don't suppose you would. That's part of the trouble. You can't see yourselves as others do . . . You and Timothy fell out of the same nest as little boys. You could be brothers."

My blood has turned cold. "I can't quite grasp . . ."

" 'Course you can't. You and Timothy can't grasp nothing about the remaining ninety-nine per cent. You don't bloody notice – it's your type's badge of privilege." Alwyn is generalising.

I follow quickly, "So now you're a regional union rep on the WFTU? Right?"

"They're not Communist," he retorts, and again I sense the whirr of the bat's wing in my dark room, so close to my reach. I ask very gently, "Who brought you into this?"

Now each brother looks at the others in turn: keeper, shepherd, factory hand. They could be managing directors, weathered clerics, at the end of a hike – how have they got stuck with this caste-mark, still drawing water from the well? "It's just about all I want to know." It's the beginning of what I want to know. "After that you won't be bothered. I can really promise you that." I can promise nothing. "Promise you that," I repeat, and like a globule of oil glinting I frown, pleasantly, at each in turn, not knowing which I should be directing myself to, and groping for answers to unspoken questions: how can an outsider know of Alwyn Rhys' connexion with the Lunt estate? Could any Communist register be as meticulous as that? Could *Timmy* be involved with the Reds?

The gamekeeper's pipe provides him phoney occupation. What began as outrage has sunk to sullenness: I have disarrayed his authority. Dai has been rolling one fag after another, and pulls now at his fourth or fifth. Dai's eyes go to Alwyn, with fragments of fear or expectancy, I can't tell. Alwyn feeds the lamb with his forefinger.

My question hangs in the silence, and the little Myfanwy re-enters, a grubby angel in a tiny oilskin apron, carrying a plastic bowl. She puts the bowl on the slate flags up by her father's feet and turns the spigot. A thin stream of hot water cascades into the bowl which she lifts close to its source then returns to the floor with utmost care to shut the spigot off. Nobody speaks, nobody moves. She goes back to the kitchen with her bowl, pink pom-poms quivering on her slippers. I want to pass water: I couldn't do it in the yard like the others because I had the lamb.

Money. There's always a financier, like a sleazy joker whose presence in the pack is unexplained. Timmy? But *why*? "If like you I had children, Alwyn" – so I do, our Frances, single monument to our marriage, a live headstone for an open grave – "I'd want to do my best for them. Give them a better chance. It's natural. Nobody can carp at that. If someone came to me, 'Do this little thing for me – won't harm anyone except some foreigner you've never heard of – do this little thing and I'll see you get enough to give your kids the break they deserve: bright little kids, just like Dad – they deserve the best', I'd say 'Done. What is it, and where's the cheque?' Nobody could blame one."

No response. Are the others standing back for Alwyn, younger by just a bit but always the smartest? I persist, sweetly. "Let's hope you've been rewarded. Don't let anyone short-change you, Alwyn." I pause, sensing vigilance on my left: the eldest one. I want the mood to veer more northerly, colder. "Trouble is, one makes oneself a hostage to fortune. Isn't that the phrase?"

Even as I say it, something slots into place. I feel no joy, only sadness, a nausea at this skulking corruption. The lamb bleats, shakes its tail vigorously, thrusts at Alwyn's finger, and craps onto the old towel.

"I'm not from the law," I assure this keeper. "Trust me that far. I mean, if I was, I'd have had to take action long ago. We wouldn't any of us be meeting here, in absolute private: we'd all be in a court of law. 'Exhibit One. Ivory tags.' All with the same number on. Number what-would-it-have-been? Three? Drives are always taken in the same order – I've never known it otherwise. Point is, you need a craftsman to make tags like that."

Surely the keeper has coloured: Alwyn has glanced across at him, not to warn – too late for that – but to assess something.

"I'm not interested in prosecutions," I press on, "neither

now, nor later. That's why I'm in a position to make a deal: *I am informed how the contact was made, please, you are guaranteed protection.* The information is used in such a way that its source is never given away."

No takers. Nothing.

"After all, I know enough already . . ." The fire smoulders, the woman's voice, reading or reciting, makes a wavering drone. The cottage hunches in the snow.

"What's a guarantee from a bloke like you, anyway?" Dai says narrowly. It seems an age since any has spoken.

"Look at it this way. At least there's a chance I keep my word. The alternative is so . . . disastrous." My head gives a tiny shudder. The glow of the fire has greyed with ash like an old man's face.

After a long silence Alwyn says, "I don't know 'oo made the bloody contact," and I could weep for him.

14

It is as if a fifth has silently joined our quadrille – somebody we each recognise but are too shy to greet. Dylan Rhys tautens, the mouth muscles bunch. Dai's hand goes to his face. I need to re-cross my legs, leaving the damp imprint of my stockinged foot on the unpolished slate. At the point we have reached I feel a sharp buried sorrow. I suppose this fifth to be Timothy Lunt. In our whoring days he used to say, "If you want to deny, Anthony, for God's sake deny completely." Sophia was already pregnant then, and if ever I were to weep again it would be at the memory of her trust in me. For Sophia would give herself to one only; it would be the momentous decision of her life, a blood-pact, soul-pact, an act of faith, admitting no doubt, shadow, reservation; it would be a total gift of body and imagination. If ever she were to allow otherwise, it would occur only through such pain as changes the very lineaments of a person, like the pain-grief that can whiten the hair in a single night. I know that is so, for my innocence was "discovered" by her innocence in that ancient sense which means the revelation of a truth after interminable waiting. I had an image of that innocence as something secretly buried within sound of water, nested under sunlit grasses and ferns so difficult to locate that it had remained curled up there intact . . . until awakened by Sophia's innocence.

It *was* awakened: I have no right to gainsay that now, just because of what time has done to us. Timmy would grouse to me of Sophia's "aggressive innocence". He met her once only, fleetingly, soon after she and I first met, and I contrived thereafter to prevent chance encounters. She has no clear recollection of him; Timmy was the kind of person who could make no impression on her. You could no more easily stain a diamond. Yet *he* remarked *her*: I always found that interesting – how he could not mark her, but she marked him. I think he saw how she could draw me from him even before I admitted to myself that I was in love with her.

And when he learned that she had let me make her pregnant, the complaints began. Young English society had entered the so-called "swinging Sixties", but he had read Sophia's morality with accuracy: it responded to no vogue. This pregnancy belonged no more to an act of the flesh than that which made birth in a Bethlehem stable. She had coupled with the god in me that he denied existed in any man and I had long ago disowned. He referred to her as "your virgin succubus, Anthony", and when he could he avoided her name, or gave his twist to it "Saint Sophia".

If we had been married when she became pregnant, he would have been easier: his worldly wisdom encompassed marriage, and I remember him formulating advices for me accordingly . . . Exploit the gullibility of the enamoured female. "If she finds another lassie in your bed, you've no idea how she came to be there." He knew the last days of his long hold on me had arrived.

I recall no formal break. He did not come to our wedding. My memory of that blanks Timmy out. I shed him like a skin. I do not even recall a guilt. At that time it seemed as if another, truer person had supervened – Sophia's "man I married". Though my job was in Fleet Street, we at once moved our base to the country. I have no recollection of seeing him afterwards or attempting to avoid him, or of him seeking to avoid me. He just fell away, had "gone behind me", like Beelzebub.

Or so I thought.

Alwyn has stopped feeding the lamb. He has looked at none of us since his qualified denial. Expectancy marks our silence: the only movement is the fancy clock.

"You don't know who made the contact?" – the heaviness of my voice surprises me. From a man like Alwyn, such a claim is laughable. Yet I feel no inclination to laugh, no triumph: quite the opposite. A wickedness has entered these simple men; Alwyn's fragment of admission has exposed them, like a slate dislodged from the roof by which the weather will soon play havoc with pretensions of security and warmth.

"You tell us then –" Dai, to me, meaning: If I am so clever . . . So I volunteer, in a throwaway manner, "Timothy Lunt" – at which Alwyn guffaws, disturbing the lamb. It is Dai who gives voice to their response, "Mr Tim is rubbish, mon."

82

My smile masks my astonishment. In the guffaw of the one and the expostulation of the other, scorn resonates. And when Dai persists, "We don't do Mr Tim's bidding," Alwyn caps him: "But 'e'd do ours. Or our friends'. We've got the paintbrush, 'aven't we?"

Now Dai smirks, but Dylan shakes his head quickly and his eyes show outrage. This moment's vignette is lost on me – as they intend. A paintbrush? . . . Yet what is plain is that nothing to do with Timmy Lunt could induce them to take risks – I have caught a similar sound already this night. They could not have brought themselves to act covertly on Timmy Lunt's behalf.

What then?

I am deeply puzzled, have lost my initiative. The other two are glancing again at Alwyn, variously troubled. But Alwyn's gaze is elsewhere. He pushes a hand through heavy hair at the back of his neck. He could remain silent, but this is a man prone to throwing over his advantages. "A bloke came on the telephone. Out the blue. Never knew 'oo 'e was, 'ow 'e knew of me. I still don't."

No, no, that can't be so. Quietly I say: "Just tell me everything you *do* know." And I wait, in our pent circle.

" 'E called me first on a Sunday morning. Wife was at chapel – I 'ad the kids 'ere, I won't let them go. Brainwashing." His derisive grin flickers. " 'E asked 'oo it was. I told him. 'Excuse me,' 'e said, 'is your mother still alive?' I said no, poor soul, she died a few years back now. He said, 'What was her name?' and I said 'Gwynedd Rhys'. I thought it might be an inheritance, something o' that. He talked so proper, very very careful, like 'e 'ad it written out. I thought maybe 'e's a solicitor. I said, ' 'Oo are you then, if I may ask?' an' 'e said, 'George'. So I said 'George 'Oo' an' 'e said 'Mister George'."

I watch the brothers flanking him now, escorts hurrying a comrade from hostile territory whose perils they know. "Go on."

"So I said, 'What's this about my mother' an' 'e said 'It's not about your mother, it's about a chance to earn money in a good cause.' Then 'e began to tell me all about it, what 'e wanted done." Alwyn still will not look at them. He lifts the lamb down to the slate floor, where it pushes to its feet and

83

utters a bleat. He puts the saucer on the range, scrapes the wet excreta, with the flat of his finger, off the towel into the fire, and wipes finger on towel.

"Where d'you suppose he was calling from?" Gently.

" 'Ow can I know?"

"Sometimes one can tell – for example, whether it's from abroad or not – little noises on the line."

"Long distance, my reckoning," he concedes. "Abroad I wouldn't know."

"When was the call?"

"September, maybe. Early October. We 'ad a lot of blackberries."

"And what exactly did he want you to do?"

" 'E said, Did I know the Lunts' estate at Ll – – –, and I said like the back of my 'and, my brother's shepherd there. He seemed to be very very pleased when 'e 'eard that. So then 'e said there would be a shoot at the Lunts' estate in the winter, a particular shoot – 'e didn't know exactly when, and 'ow there would be a particular guest from abroad, 'e'd tell me who later. 'E wanted to know if it was possible to make sure this particular guest shot at a particular peg, you know, on a particular stand, that's all. Though 'e didn't talk about pegs and stands. I said ' 'Ow can anyone arrange that?' and then 'e suggested I work out a way of fixing it and 'e'd call me back some time later and see what I'd thought up."

I regard in silence the last glow in the grate. "Your caller knew the name of the drive, the exact peg?"

" 'E was asking in principle, whether in principle it would be possible. I was to buy an Ordnance map from the District Surveyor's office, six inches a mile, and mark the regular stands on it. 'E'd 'ave one too so we could discuss it in detail. 'E was very concerned we always put the pegs in the same place for each stand. I said, it was Ivor puts the pegs in, but he didn't vary unless Mr Tim instructed him specifically different." He stops, frowning. From the kitchen the woman's voice is still audible.

"Is that all that worried him?"

" 'E was worried they might change places once they'd made the draw. The guns, I mean. I said I couldn't tell about that, once the gentlemen were on the stands, 'oo's to tell what they did? but I could speak to Ivor. Then 'e said, very violent, I'm not to speak a single word to Ivor, nor a single soul except Dai. 'E said if it turned out I'd spoken to as much as a single soul about this except Dai, the 'ole arrangement would be off."

"What arrangement?" I enquire immediately. "How much?"

"Two thousand." He scowls. "But 'e 'adn't told me what 'e wanted then."

"You've collected it already?"

"Maybe."

"Cash, in a hiding place. Yes?"

"Why not."

"No meeting?"

"No meeting."

"You never met anyone?"

"Never met anyone."

"Nor your brothers?"

"None of us."

Dai nods. The keeper's face is still bunched and inward.

"So he telephoned again . . ."

"Twice more 'e phoned. First time, Was I quite sure it was possible? An' I said Yes, an' 'e wanted to know 'ow exactly we would do it? So I told 'im. So then 'e made me tell 'im exactly where them stands were – where one end was and where the other. 'E was filling them in on 'is map very very carefully. Then 'e asked if there was any peg on any stand where one gun would be out of sight of the other guns. I couldn't think of any peg to fit that, so we went through the stands one by one until we came to the Ty-Nant drive. The peg on the end of that stand, number one, is on the other side of the strip of trees there. Now could Number Two see Number One on that stand? I'd 'ave a look. So 'e said, do that, but let's assume the trees are thick enough. They look about twenty-thirty yards of trees on the map: could I make sure a certain guest shot from there? So I said, why not that one, if that's what 'e wanted." The twitching of his foot has been keeping the chair in perpetual motion, but suddenly he quells it.

"You told him all three of you had to be in it?"

"Just me and Dai."

85

"But all three of you *were* in it," I insist. "Or would have to be."

In a new silence the keeper's eyes narrow on his youngest brother. The lamb has found Alwyn's corduroyed thigh and repeatedly thrusts its muzzle from beneath.

Dai leaves it to Alwyn to say what has to be said. "Dylan didn't exactly know 'e was 'elping us – not at that stage." And I interpose my own speculation: "One of you had merely asked him to make a few ivory draw tags for some shoot or other . . . though he would find out sooner or later, surely. I doubt if he's stupid. You're a brainy family."

"We would cut 'im in – Dylan," Alwyn confesses dully; at which his eldest brother requires to insert pipe into mouth and hold it there, although extinguished.

"Is one interested," I say sourly, all trace of sorrow extracted now, "whether you told Dylan before or after, or whether he worked it out himself when he found his unfinished tags had gone missing? Since I'm fairly sure you couldn't have persuaded him to inscribe each of them with the same number." I allow just a moment's pause. "So shall we go on to the next call?"

"What about the next call?"

"When it came, surely. The information imparted. Instructions."

" 'E told me the date of the shoot, 'oo it was exactly: I'd never 'eard of him."

"Is that all?"

" 'Ow we would know 'im, like."

"And where to collect the money."

"Yes, and that."

"And the voice – the same voice? Different voice?"

"Same voice, far as I could judge."

Let him rest there. A moment.

"How long before the actual day?"

"That call, you mean? It was Christmas Day."

"Just about a week before the shoot, then."

"About a week," he assents.

"What if the fixing of the draw didn't work?"

"We 'ad a little plan for that."

"To abort the operation."

86

"Cancel everything. Yes."

"And it was?"

"It makes no difference, mister," he snaps.

But I am back at him instantly. "We have a kind of compact, Alwyn Rhys. Right? You are to tell me about your relationship with your contact, or perhaps contacts. I to ensure you are protected from the consequences of your conduct – all of you."

He scowls again. "We were to stick drawing pins into the telegraph posts by the bridge below Ty-Nant. Dai could 'ave done that in the morning, passing."

"Quite a tricky piece of conjuring for Dai," I speculate aloud. "Two little silver boxes – easy enough to come by something similar. And Dai to be sure to have the Prince draw first. Quite bold, quite tricky. A few rehearsals. No need for the drawing pins of course. The deed was as good as done, unless the shot was botched." They have nothing to volunteer; the others waiting on Alwyn waiting on me. Where do they stand, now, with Alwyn? No double escort any more. No bodyguards. They watch him still, but stalking the narrative. "Everything hung on Dai pulling off that little trick for you, eh? If the –" I grope for the term – "other party didn't pay up, what could you have done? All you ever had was a voice on the telephone."

" 'E'd paid 'alf, anyway," Alwyn says, and Dai smirks.

"Not much these days. Only a thousand to be sure of. Divided among two, perhaps three. Accessory to a murder. You could have got twelve or fifteen years."

Dai says, " 'Oo was to know it was murder?"

"Is that what Alwyn suggested?" – my brows raised – "that what was intended was less than murder? Just a bit of high jinks among the ruling classes?" No response. "Anyway he did pay up. Right? Nobody was silly enough to put the money into a bank. Not, anyway, until the little enquiry was over, the police and all gone back home, a tidy report from the coroner, a regretful little statement in the House of Commons. 'A good friend to this country. Dear-o-dear. But wogs will be wogs. Don't know the form out shooting . . .' And Mister X, who did the deed, without a motive, a man so-to-speak without a body, just a voice on the phone – except he can pull a trigger from a

87

clump of bracken, and crawl away, and stuff banknotes in tobacco pouches up drainpipes – he just disappears without a trace. Vanishes. And that's that." I brush one hand across the other, both ways. "Right, Alwyn?"

He says nothing.

"Until I come along, with a bargain to propose – that I hear the full story of the contact in exchange for not upsetting the Rhys family applecart. And now that's done, too, right? So it's bedtime for all of us?"

Certain orchestral scores build to an energetic "conclusion" whose falsity is given away by a single chord or growl in the bass forewarning a change of key and a whole lot more up the composer's sleeve. Such pauses are brief – a bar, half a bar, which in this cramped, disorderly habitation is brought to an end by at least three of us by way of saying something. One voice prevails, that of a weak man tolerant of mockery too long, exploding with vehemence: "But it's not done. Because I don't bloody well believe you, Mr Alwyn Rhys. It just doesn't go like that." Life, I mean. "You do two things to me, don't you. Perhaps you do them to your brothers. You lie to me with half the truth wrapped up as the whole, and you insult me by taking me as a fool."

"I think we've 'ad enough from 'im," Alwyn resumes quietly. "We don't none of us truly appreciate 'im 'ere, eh?" and he expands in Welsh, Dai concurring, I hunching at prospect of violence, noting in both brothers a common technique of sly threat as with certain habitual drinkers. Yet the older one stays stiff in his upright chair, defunct pipe held from his mouth, intervening in his own tongue with such brevity and effect that I pick up his meaning instantly: "Hear him out."

Which gives me my cue. "Just look at what you would have us believe." I too am *piano*. The lamb bleats. Alwyn has found his own tobacco and rolls a cigarette with powerful hands. "You are an intelligent man," I remind him. "Perhaps we are quite intelligent too. You have created for us a person who intends to commit a murder. Because it must be a murder that appears to be an accident, the killing has to take place in very special and extremely difficult circumstances. In fact, there is only one precise spot, one *stile*, in the entire universe where it

88

can take place. Right?"

No answer is forthcoming. A muffled noise behind me has my head jerking round involuntarily, anticipating assault. But it is only the children standing just beyond the harmonium, staring at their hero, provider, bearer of their little woes and unnameable deeper burdens that the cobwebs above and roughly pulled curtains hint of. I try to resume with composure and precision. "Right? For this person it is an act of exceptional importance. Something very big depends upon it. This man, or someone under his orders, is to put his life at risk by this act. Now what can be so exceptionally important? One does wonder, doesn't one?"

Alwyn pulls at his fag, the other hand vainly restraining the tiny lamb lewdly butting his thigh, umbilicus dangling. At each draw on the thin tobacco he half-closes his eyes – they make such fleeting ease. He cannot but listen.

So I complete the exposition. Somehow this stranger-assassin knows about the drives on the Lunt estate. He knows his victim is a prospective guest. But he cannot do the deed alone. By some extraordinary chance he becomes aware of a potential accomplice, Alwyn Rhys. He *knows* about Alwyn Rhys – that he has access to this particular estate, he's corruptible, smart, won't double-cross him, play him along. But Alwyn Rhys doesn't know him at all. To him he's just a voice on the telephone, a voice entirely unknown to him. Alwyn Rhys can't imagine who it could belong to, who on earth could have put the owner of this voice on to him. The whole remarkable intrusion into his life is a mystery to him. Notwithstanding an inquisitive mind, he hasn't got a clue what or who's behind it. Nor expects a clue. Yet oddly enough, he trusts the owner of the voice. He trusts him first that he won't hash it up and land him and his brothers up to their necks in the shit. And trusts him, second, to pay up the other half of the money even though, if he stood him up, there'd be absolutely nothing he could do about it.

I could do with a pee, but must take my time.

"If it was just yourself, it might be *just* believable. You're a reckless one, aren't you. If you find yourself with an advantage, you hazard it, don't you? Squandering your gifts, your personal opportunities – there's a certain satisfaction in it –

89

that despite all your ability and your promise you aren't on top of the pile. Because your grievance – that's your most precious possession, isn't it? That's the one thing that gets you out of bed in the morning."

"He'd talk through your arse-hole, this bloke." Alwyn at last provoked. "I've never 'eard . . ."

"*Please.*" My hand is raised, fingers spread, trembling ever so slightly. "But it wasn't just yourself, was it. It was the whole clan, that's altogether different. You'd have persuaded one brother into disaster, and tricked the other. You'd have squandered just about everything you ever consisted of. Not even your sense of grievance would have survived that. Oh no" – a tiny shake of the head – "you would never have done that. No, no, no. So what's the explanation?"

I have them all still now. Only the lamb is active, arrogant in its right to survive. Maybe Alwyn tolerates the presence of the children as a kind of ultimate insurance – insurance of one order of reality by another – rather as courts award a sum of money for a child lost in a road accident. A child's love can compensate a criminal conviction. Alwyn is a lot less lonely a man than I.

"The first explanation is that you have reason to trust this voice." I enumerate on my fingers. "The second explanation is, well" – I snuff a laugh – "it flows from the first, doesn't it? You knew how to locate the source of that voice. I doubt if you really knew who that voice belonged to, but quite likely you *thought* you did, that's what matters. Even if you knew you couldn't reach him personally you had a rough idea of how you could apply the frighteners if they stood you up on the money. And the third explanation" – narrowing at him – "is that the source of that voice, at least, knew *you* personally. And the fourth?" – hurrying on – "there is a fourth, isn't there, quite a fundamental one. The fourth explanation is that you knew all along what it was all about. Not about money, was it, because the little prince wasn't in the big money: his Shaikhdom doesn't have so much as a squirt of oil. That's quite easy to find out. So it was about politics, wasn't it, power politics, something very big for Alwyn Rhys up in the hills of Clwyd. And what sort of power politics? Well now – what sort? Just what's your fancy here? Maybe your brothers can fill

90

me in better here." I throw a glance at Dylan, grey and sullen. "Why did you trouble to point out just now that the WFTU was not a Communist organisation? For brother Dylan's sake, perhaps? If so, you misled him, didn't you. Because you know very well, it's Marxist from top to bottom. It sounds very nice and sweet, doesn't it, up in the Welsh hills – the World Federation of Trade Unions, with offices in Geneva, in democratic Switzerland. Very global, very brotherly. Bloody nearly a variety of Christianity. But of course, Marx *is* holy – so holy that you can lie and cheat for righteousness' sake. He teaches you that, doesn't he? Have you got a passport?"

" 'E's been abroad for 'is union, why not?" Dai comes in. " 'E's a regional delegate."

" 'Why not?' Exactly. There's no reason why not. What is your union?"

Here they are all reticent.

"Who cares anyway?" I have to hound him down. "Transport and General? AAW? All sorts send little delegations to the WFTU when they've got a jamboree on – slide 'em in through this or that Liaison Committee. Right? Fraternal gatherings of international socialism, organised by the Czechs, the Hungarians, the East Germans. Sometimes the Russians themselves, with all their free trade unions. Good for the Swiss hotel trade – it can be slack in the spring. When were you last on a delegation, please?"

Alwyn pulls at the last of his cigarette, his sardonic half-smile intensified. Dylan speaks:

"You 'ave to know this for some purpose?"

"We're trying to get to the truth, Mr Rhys. I'm sorry we have to hunt for it so. Both of us sorry, I'd not be surprised."

He enters a brief exchange in Welsh with his brother. And then, sullenly, " 'E went in May, mister. What's it matter?"

Because, I tell him, these international Marxist gatherings have two purposes only: one propaganda, and the other to recruit or to brief agents. Not necessarily professional spies, but people just like his brother who support their aims and could come in handy, say, in their own unions back home.

"Alwyn gave up the Communists years ago," Dylan says, and begins to fill his pipe.

"Is that what he told you?" I have no need to feign derision.

"Then what's he getting himself onto delegations to Communist gatherings for? To cover his telephone bills? I'm only guessing, but I'm a good guesser with half the puzzle done. A WFTU junket in May last year, followed by such a very very odd telephone call in September. Is he telling us there's no connexion? He went through all of that conference – how long was it? – ten days of committees and sub-committees, and little parties and more vodka upstairs in the bedrooms, and nobody said a word about a very special sort of job in Wales? The talent spotters all fast asleep? Or maybe it wasn't Geneva. Maybe London, or Liverpool . . ." What I am tracing under the floor disgusts me – not for the matrix of evil that it is, but that Alwyn's should turn out so banal, so gangsterish a bid for significance.

The mother's voice is audible from the kitchen, again summoning the children.

"You'd better answer 'im," Dylan says quietly in English, pale and tight-mouthed. "Whatever the facts are."

Dai's boots shift and Alwyn leans forward and riddles the fire between the bars. He picks up handfuls of coal from the scuttle and scatters them on the embers. When he has finished wiping his hand on the towel, he sits back in the rocking-chair. "There was a bloke there –" his voice gone flat and muzzy, as if he has something in his mouth, "– 'e kind of took me up. He 'ad good English. We went out on the town, quite a bit. Night clubs an' that. He said he spoke six or seven languages, but not a word of Welsh, so p'raps I'd teach 'im some Welsh. I taught 'im a bit. 'E asked me what I believed in, you know – victory of the proletariat. Then one night we were at this big night-club – pretty terrible it was – women on the stage whippin' each other. 'E said, 'It disgusts you, Alwyn, doesn't it.' 'It just about does,' I said. Then 'e said, would I ever consider for the good of the cause, for the Party like, killing someone? 'To get rid of all this?' 'e said. An' I said, maybe that depended. An' 'e said, 'It'll earn you a lot of money.' So I said ' 'Ow much', an' 'e said 'e might be able to get me twenty grand."

All of this addressed to the floor, or perhaps the lamb, wobbling at his feet.

"This was Mr George?" I wish to know, and I receive a nod, but nothing more, so I continue on his behalf: "By the time you'd got back home and he called you again you'd got cold feet, right? But you'd give him a hand for a rather smaller sum, right? I'm surprised you let him bargain you down to a couple of thousand. And he went on telephoning, until you'd got it all fixed up – except the last call or two it was a different voice on the phone . . ." I peer at him under my brows, and hold him until absence of denial amounts to assent. "Because it was vital there was no possibility of any mistake over the details by talking through third parties. Correct? Now you will tell me please: did you recognise this second voice?"

He turns on me with a scowl. "Of course I didn't bloody recognise it."

"Was it English – an Englishman speaking?"

" 'E 'ad some foreign accent. 'Ow can I tell?"

"A heavy accent?"

"Not much of an accent. Spoke very proper, like I said."

"One wasn't to know which you referred to . . . Now, your friend George: can you reach him?"

" 'E's always called me."

"But can you reach him?"

"I don't know 'is name. No phone or address."

"You must have been able to reach him in Geneva."

" 'E never gave me any identification. 'E was one of the secretariat."

"You knew that?"

"I assumed it."

"What nationality is he, this George?"

"*I* don't know." (I am jostling him into anger.) " 'Ow can I know?"

"Because you're too ignorant to know one foreigner from another, is that right? You who served in Germany and Hong Kong. Top in languages. Can't tell one foreigner from another?" Derision is crossing into exasperation.

But Alwyn is on his feet. "Let's get 'im out," he calls in English to Dai, who looks at Dylan, furrowing, and Dylan doesn't move. "Out!"

I stand to face Alwyn, the uneven ceiling a foot above our heads, and strands of sooty cobweb. "What fucking nationality, Alwyn?" It is a contest of throats, foul mouths, poison-eyes, with the ridiculous five-legged lamb waggling its tail

93

between our feet.

" 'Ow can I tell? You tell me. You're so bloody clever."

I have won his detestation by exposing his pitiable snakes' nest of motive. I repeat with force, "What fucking nationality?" straight into his face.

The lamb staggers to the side of us, and falls, and instinctively he bends to scoop it up one-handed and holds it against his chest. Suddenly I hardly care. What difference is it, this phantom's nationality? It wasn't English . . . neither of the voices was Timmy's. These peasants I have browbeaten into confession would have invoked him hours ago, by name or innuendo, if they had a thread of justification for doing so. Had I come all this way to expose the wrong can of worms? The old-hat ideological melodrama? I am not a journalist any more – another man can have the story. Timmy is surely no "mole"; he does not possess that order of conviction; he is not of that . . . quality.

Megan has joined the children to gape white-faced from where they cluster to sing. I only wish to go. In the end it is Dylan rising and moving just two or three feet to stand beside me that breaks the equilibrium.

" 'E was a Russian, I reckon," Alwyn says, sitting down with the lamb like a shield against all manner of assault, "if you need to know so bloody bad."

15

"So what did you achieve in Wales?" Sophia asks from above as I walk back from the drive entrance with the daily papers. "Or aren't you telling me?" Invariably she looks graceful on a horse, and with her colouring sharpened by the cold and early sun on the snow one could only call her lovely. We were originally introduced at a horsey event: I was on the ground and she was "up", and it was her purity outlined against the sky that caught me unawares. When after two or three months I was conceded her body it was like an absolution from all sin that had gone before.

"I don't know . . . what I achieved."

"I hoped we'd be seeing a big article." It is to be one of her interlocutions in which no outsider could detect the grit in the sweetness. This is the first I have seen her since getting home in the small hours – she left me to sleep on. I had dreamt of her – that we had a child, other than Frances, which was chronically sick because of some congenital flaw. I had come back from abroad with the formula which alone could repair this flaw. The problem was what to do with the formula, whose healing code seemed to apply not just to the child but to the whole home. Sophia was mocking me wildly for claiming to possess a "formula" I could not apply, and of course I knew her mockery was justified. Now she leans down from her mare and her gloved fingers pluck my newspaper from under my arm. She scans the front page perkily. "I mean . . . some big exposé. Wasn't the little prince murdered after all?"

"Oh yes, he was murdered."

"Well, d'you know who did it?"

"Not precisely. It hardly matters who."

"What on earth d'you mean – hardly matters who?"

"It was a Communist thing."

"Oh, them – they can't leave anything alone. What a funny place to do it." She offers the paper back – she never took much interest in current affairs: that was a male field, and she was strict in her division of areas of concern by gender. Anyway there is no news – the weather dominates the front pages: North Wales' late snow has spread south and east, quilting the Home Counties as deep as three inches in places, the nation reeling under this annual cataclysm with customary heroism.

"You mean to say," she resumes, "they just told you that and let you go? It's frightfully hard to believe. Have you thought of the consequences?"

"Consequences?"

"Well. For us. For Frances. If they know you know, they won't just do nothing."

"I'm not sure . . ."

"Oh, Anthony, really. If they know you've uncovered some sort of plot they're not going to sit back hoping you forget all about it."

"If you don't mind my saying so, you don't know what you're talking about."

"I know that Frances will be home in just over three weeks and I really don't think we have the right –"

"Oh *please* . . ." Trickles of animosity swell to torrents with alarming swiftness. Sometimes I suspect there is nothing I can say that will not provoke. And this morning the sight of her English grace disarmed me.

"At least you'll have to report it to your friend Timmy Lunt. Or does he know?"

"I don't know."

"Did they follow you here?"

"Who?"

"Well, whoever . . ."

"Nobody followed, Sophia. Nobody knows who I am."

"At least you needn't have brought that hired Land Rover back here."

"Nobody will trace it." They seem to have tried and failed. It was the one thing I feared when I left the cottage. Dylan had gone to the cottage door first, pulling on his waterproofs, shutting the door quietly, nothing said. Then I, into my wellington boots and coat – no hindrance, no more talk. Out in the yard the snow was falling more densely still; from various points, farther and nearer, tremulous whimpers of

96

new born lambs and the firmer calls of ewes. Alwyn's dog growled and rattled its chain. I tramped to the bottom of the yard: Dylan had shifted Alwyn's van. In the snow I made my inverted yellow funnel. I avalanched the windscreen, and wiped the steam from Gertie's breath within. Only when I reached the highway did I let her out, and she bounced into a snowdrift and played pat-a-cake with her forepaws. Dylan wouldn't have cared much how Dai got home – maybe he and Alwyn were up all night with Alwyn's lambs anyway.

I tell Sophia: "I don't think the people I found it out from will do anything."

"How *can* you be sure?" She heels her mare forward so as to leave herself the advantage.

The editor says, "I can't quite see at this stage, Anthony, you've got any choice. You must go and see Timmy Lunt privately. After all, he's your old friend. You can hardly just dump him in it."

"Don't misunderstand me, I'm perfectly willing . . ."

"No, no, dear boy – I can sympathise with your reluctance. There's a whiff of dynamite in it, of course there is. It could limit one's options a bit, you and he being such pals. Not that we're out to make trouble for the Administration – we're not that kind of newspaper. But we've every entitlement to the facts."

Some hold the view that he has asked to have his knighthood deferred until retirement to forestall accusations of being a Government placeman; others that he is a mere cypher for the proprietor, hunched like a harpy on an upper floor. I need him, and if there are gaps in his fatherliness, I will compensate. He quizzes me across the photograph of himself with the Monarch. "I could let South in on it."

"No Harry. I'd rather we . . ."

"Say no more, say no more. A passing thought. South's perfectly discreet but – you're right – once the News Desk has it, the natural processes take over. So," he continues at once, as one independent of the natural processes to another, "either Timmy knows it was murder or he doesn't. If he does, the reason is plain to see: HMG doesn't want its friends in the Middle East to imagine its security's so lax that assassins can pick off whom they choose at private ministerial house parties.

97

Fair enough. But from what you imply, he's in the dark."

"Or chooses to be."

"You mean, because the little Prince was in his charge, foul play rubs off on him? Or do you suppose he suspects those Welsh brothers . . . I thought you said they were indifferent to him, rather despised him, even?"

"So it seemed."

All at once he looks perturbed. "You're not actually suggesting a cover-up for reasons of guilt? Some involvement by your Timmy?"

I release a half-smile – the defensive reaction of the muddled and weak. "It's hardly possible, is it? . . . He wouldn't want to foul his own nest." Which earns his scrutiny – and then:

"You knew him in early manhood?"

"Well."

"Any flirtation with the works of Marx?"

More like the works of Sade. "He wasn't a political animal at all – political ideas didn't touch him." Least of all the banal insanity of communism. He used to refer to "the proles". I add, "The usual arrogance of wealth . . ."

"Though he threw his hat in the ring."

"It surprised me. I'd lost touch with him then. He had a taste for power – that's the way I read it when I saw he was standing. It was that or sheep farming in Wales."

"So guilt on Timmy's part is hardly a runner."

"Exactly." Yet haven't I read it on his face like a signed confession? What else could it mean? There are those driven to confess crimes they never committed, like virgins that swell with "pregnancies". Is the will to purge as reckless and irrational as the will to mother? Maybe the shame he showed was never more than fear at having miscalculated the come-back: he denied distinction between good and evil: there was only self-interest, in various guises.

The editor says, "Supposing he stumbled on evidence *post facto* and said nothing, just to keep his nose clean, that would be ridiculously short-sighted. Cowardly, too. Would you call that characteristic? – I never quite made him out when I was in the House."

"Not cowardly – canny."

He says suddenly: "You *are* worried about a conflict of

loyalties, aren't you? . . . It's hardly fair on you, after all these years in the peace of the countryside. One forgets that dogs eat dogs in Fleet Street." A note in his voice is telling me: I'm no longer in the scholarship class, I'm superannuated. "It's not fair on you, Anthony," he repeats. "You've given us a splendid lead. Full marks for that. Now it's for one of South's young toughs to follow wherever the threads take him."

"I'll go and see Timmy," I insist at once, trying to steady my gaze. But he persists with a wry face:

"You're interested in the soul of man, Anthony, not his soiled linen. This is about murder, a big mischief, front page – not Why We're Here, Saturday-for-Sunday, but Why Little Prince Saqr Isn't Here as he ought to be." On Saturdays the paper runs 600 words on religion on the Court and Social page – always an uncomfortable mix. Harry wears his paternal frown. "If I dare counsel an old pro: allow me to give the dirty work to a staffer. You'll want to identify. Timmy Lunt's a childhood friend – you'll want him to be your Indian beggar." The crack is meant to be comradely. "Let me chuck it to one of my bloodhounds. He needn't start with your Timmy. He can start by finding out why the Reds should want to put poor young Saqr to sleep. Of course, they love tension, and Saqr was one of us – but all that long-term planning and risk, such a piddling Shaikhdom, without a squirt of oil . . . Have you a view?"

"The old Shaikh's dying. Slowly. They've given him the cobalt bomb at the Wellington. The new heir's a derelict. There's only daughters otherwise. Look Harry." I prepare to rise. "Leave it with me." It's my story, the thread I hold leads out of *my* labyrinth. "I'll take it to Timmy." He can't stop me, but the smile I receive contains that quizzical indulgence which lets me know that if all I have told him turns out invention – a symptom of breakdown – I would still not be beyond the range of his personal sympathy.

16

There are a dozen ways of finding out his private number. Then it is only a matter of raising the telephone and saying *"This is Anthony – Anthony Guise"* – *"Oh Christ . . . Anthony"* – *"Look, I want to come to talk to you."* *"Why not? . . . What about?"* *"Something that affects you politically – something that's come up in my residual newspaper role."* But I choose a different route. I dial the Foreign Office and am put through to his Private Secretary.

"You said your name was?"

"Guise. Anthony Guise."

"And you know Mr Lunt personally. It's a personal matter." His lumpy interpretations invite misunderstanding so as to inflate cause to interpose himself.

"Not exactly."

"Ah."

"It is in connection with Mr Lunt's ministerial role."

"Are you sure it isn't something I could help you with?"

"I don't want help. I want to help Mr Lunt."

"You have some information for Mr Lunt." A further turd.

"I have something to discuss important to him and very probably to the Government."

A silence to smirk in.

"Mr Guise, my purpose is to be helpful. If I could persuade you to indicate what you wish to discuss, I'm sure I could get you together with just the right person."

"It's only Mr Lunt I wish to see."

"He's not actually in the building at the moment . . . I know for a fact that he hasn't got a moment up to the end of next week, and then there's Brussels. I suppose you could try him through the House of Commons. You've spoken to his secretary in the Commons?"

"I've only spoken to you." A distraction intervenes at the official end of the line.

"I'm sorry?"

"I've only spoken to you."

"Why don't you talk to his secretary in the Commons?" His questions became heavy advices, obstructions along the route to the paltry shrine.

The voice from the House of Commons secretary proves to be female and less conceited.

"Are you a constituent of Timmy Lunt?"

"I'm afraid not."

"Might I ask what you want to talk to Mr Lunt about?"

"Prince Saqr."

"Who?"

I repeat it.

"You say his Private Secretary at the Office couldn't help you?"

"He said Mr Lunt was too busy."

"He *is* a very busy man."

So I propose I call her back tomorrow.

Yet when I do so, it is still not the mask of welcome I have anticipated, but a rendezvous in St Stephen's Lobby of the Commons with his Parliamentary Private Secretary, whom I tell at once: It is Lunt I wish to see. "Can you be so absolutely certain?" he challenges bumptiously, the third syllable of "absolutely" rhyming with "newt". "Let's have a noggin and you can tell me *something* of what it's about, that's for sure. One's got to start somewhere, Mr Guise." He confides: "*I'm* out of my depth too. Parliament's my bailiwick, so far as Timmy's concerned, not private customers from beyond the walls like you. But Timmy did specially ask . . ."

We drink at a little table in a mock Gothic chamber overlooking the Thames. He is a piggy, high-pitched man whose stock-in-trade is putting people at their ease. He pats his pockets hopelessly. "I say, I'm awfully sorry! Have you got your own pakitov?"

"Pakitov?"

"Fags."

"I don't smoke."

"Thank God. Neither do I. Normally carry them just in case." He is by turns earnest, jolly, ingratiating, eager to establish points of contact beyond the brotherhood of non-smokers. "You never got yourself caught up in this sort of game?" A hand flicks at interior of the great edifice. "Politics." A modest twitch of a smile. "Knavish tricks."

"No."

"I was Chairman of the Young Conservatives, South-East Region, for my sins. It opened doors for me. Wife was a Vice-Chairman, West Midlands. You never thought of joining?"

"No."

"More's the pity. You *are* one of us, I take it?"

"Socialism doesn't appear to work."

At which I am volubly congratulated. "What more can one ask for!" Suddenly he is grave. A confidential hand lightly clutches my sleeve. "It's not about politics you want to see Timmy? Weren't you a journalist? You see, it's my job to brief him."

"He didn't brief you?"

"I only caught him for a tick. He said he remembers you from school."

" 'Remembers me from school?' "

"Exactly."

"It's about politics."

"Did I hear his secretary mention that little prince?" I nod. "From a domestic angle, so to say? Foreign?"

My arm has frozen to the shoulder. "All I can tell you is that Mr Lunt would be distressed if I discussed it with anyone else."

He draws back coyly, releasing my arm with a suspicion of a thrust. "I'm Timmy's right hand in this place," he smiles. "I shouldn't say it myself, but he's learned to trust me. Anything I'm told stays right here" – he makes a little box for himself with chubby hands – "not one inch further. Half my job's keeping quiet. The other half is protecting Timmy from the slings and arrows of outrageous. So far as this place is concerned."

I have cut short a visit to Frances' school to keep this appointment: Sophia made me promise to put her on guard in case my "cloak and dagger life" jeopardized her safety. It was an absurd precaution, but I was glad to go because sometimes, alone with Frances, away from home, an intimate atavistic recognition would occur like an object unexpectedly unearthed while digging: something would sound on the spade and glancing down we would catch the glint of purest love buried. Precisely this occurred in the afternoon, and I exclaimed inwardly: What terrible interment have I been party to?

The Parliamentary Private Secretary is confiding: "There's an awful lot to do with Timmy's role I can't mention even at home, even though the wife's absol*ew*tly secure. One has to play it by the book."

"Including murder, no doubt."

He draws back as if squirted by a water-pistol. Whatever the havoc to his starched collar he can take a jape in good part.

Frances and I sat in the Land Rover by the school's drive entrance under dripping Oxfordshire beeches, she beginning to unfold to me the fickleness of her friends. Was she ready at last to cling to her father, in the flux of incipient puberty? (Sophia seemed to protect her from me, like some mechanical utensil – an electric mixer, for instance – which only she could be trusted with.) She was playing with the dials on the dashboard, her young nails bearing traces of varnish too pale for the nuns to challenge.

"One can't get more serious than that," the PPS is saying with mock jollity.

I suppose Frances to be the kind of girl to grow up mistaking this pink podge for a man. She said, *"The lucky ones have got older brothers"* and instantly our recognition vanished. *"I wish mine had grown up. I've told my best friend about him."*

"You never really had a brother, Frances."

"It depends how you look at it." She spoke with her mother's voice.

"It's not sensible to try to turn a foetus of five or six months into a person. There was no Death Certificate, no autopsy, nothing. Just one of those unlucky medical things."

"Mummy says there was an autopsy. If he had grown up he'd be at the top of his public school now."

"Of course they had to find out what went wrong. That's quite a different matter – any illness requires that, obstetric or otherwise. They had no right to tell Mummy what sex it was, to allow her to think of it as a person."

"Oh, you obviously can't understand what it is to be a woman, Daddy."

Timmy's PPS is left with his own jollity round the edge of his lips like cream. "Don't suppose you can vouchsafe a little more?" I smile back. He raises his glass and the eyes above the beer are suddenly wary. "One knows your name of course as a journalist," he says. "Is one wrong in imagining that you gave it all up – severed your links with the Street of Ink quite a while back?"

"One can't ever do that entirely, can one." I remember Frances' final wingeing plea as I parted with her in the rain at the school's porch: "*Mummy does so hate you getting involved with these journalist things. You promised her to give them up. You don't do it to bait, do you?*" She has learned from her mother to measure out her "love" for me according to my deserts.

I tell the PPS, "Journalism's like the priesthood, you know, or prostitution. Part vow, part contamination."

"I'm not absol*ew*tly certain I follow you there."

Yet he followed me enough to arrange the meeting. Even then, the rendezvous is chopped and changed – first at Timmy's home in Vincent Square at five, then amid a flurry of telephoned apologies from the PPS at 9.30 p.m. at the House of Commons.

Light on the balls of his moccasined feet, the PPS conducts me along the broad corridors of frock-coated oils and senatorial marbles of forgotten luminaries, sage and forbearing under the burden of self-importance. And if the Right Honourable Timothy Lunt comes to sit for an official artist, how will he fudge him? Like his Whig great-grandfather on the staircase in Wales? I don't recall Timmy having a political thought in his head. There was a formless ambition, certainly, that awaited its repository rather as God's love is supposedly poised for admission when and if time is ripe. For example, his precocity at spotting where others were vulnerable was astounding: when once he left himself open to expulsion from school he knew unerringly how to play on the bewildered housemaster's fear of failure with him. Politics will have taught him to refine exploitation of the common run of sentiment, credulity, laziness, kindness and greed.

I await him in an interview room furnished in parliamentary oak and green leather; the PPS has withdrawn with an assurance the Minister won't be a jiff.

Timmy was not a person of common needs – though it could be said there was a period he needed me as a witch needs her familiar. He seemed devoid of those ineluctable requirements that wring the inmost hearts of other children. I suppose such men are drawn to power: power fills the void. He had not yet obtained a wife, though there was once talk of marriage, I read somewhere . . .

A closed-circuit television displays the name of the Member speaking and the time he started. An ominous electronic chord announces a new speaker. Where is Timmy? It is not a foreign affairs debate: Britain having slid so far down the ranks of principalities and powers, overseas politics take up little of the legislature's time . . . Beyond the trefoil windows I can hear the buses rounding Parliament Square. A pigeon settles momentarily on the precipitous stonework.

All at once I know I should not be here. I must not, *cannot* see him. Not yet. I pull open the heavy door instantly and look both ways. There is no one, but various sounds of adjacent or approaching activity. I return briskly via the corridor by which I came: members, I judge, would approach from the other direction. I dare not be seen actually to hurry to the distant turning in the corridor. I refuse to glance behind me. Would he recognise me from the back, at thirty, forty feet? Surely. My back is tensed for an accosting, "Oi, Anthony!" – like a stiletto.

PART TWO

1

In my room on the ninth floor I raise the telephone, dial 9 for an outside line and then the bank's number. It is past 4.30 p.m.: the staff will be back at work for the afternoon's business.

"D'you have a Mr Proctor?"

"May I know your good name?"

"My name's Guise."

"May I please help you, Mr Guise?"

"You can tell me if you have a Mr Proctor."

"Mr Proctor's line is busy."

"I'll hold."

"You are sure that you require Mr Proctor?"

"I am perfectly sure."

From where I sit on my bed I can view the skyscrapers of the miniature city bunched round the creek. Architects have had a field-day, overturning centuries of hunched earthen defensiveness with a celebration of glass and steel, cement and marble. Thirty years ago it was a walled port, quintessentially Arab: quayside, suk, warren of clay hovels, a few merchants' houses of plastered coral surmounted by wind-towers, and the ruler's fort. Not a yard of tarmac-ed road.

"Proctor here."

"My name's Guise. Forgive my calling out of the blue. I'm just out from England on a visit and have a little problem. I'm new to the Gulf, and one of the letters of introduction I've got is to a Mr Apramian, care of the British Bank. I can't locate him in the telephone directory."

"What's your line of business, Mr Guise?"

"Agricultural économy."

"Fisheries as well?"

"Greening the desert first, I suppose. But a comprehensive plan would include fisheries, yes."

"That would fit," Mr Proctor says. "We do have a Mr Apramian as a client who runs fishing boats in quite a big way."

"Very possibly he. Account with you in Geneva too. My friend . . ."

"Could be your man, Mr Guise."

"How might one reach him?"

"Where are you staying?"

I name my hotel.

"If you have time to drop by here, before six . . . We're down town, Deira-side . . . Five minutes in a taxi."

As Guise was Goode, so Mr S. Abramson of the Ritz, in Mrs Lunt's visitor's book, was registered at the hotel in the Armenian version of the name, Apramian, and had written a cheque there on the Geneva branch of Mr Proctor's bank. Even for a newspaperman recalled from pasture, the delving of this information was a matter of persistence and routine deceit. The harder part — Sophia excepted — was persuading the editor to cover my air fare after I told him Timmy refused to discuss Saqr's death. I think he guessed I lied. I had to agree to cover my own hotel bills, at least until they could be justified by a printable story. As for Timmy himself, I palmed him off with a note pleading some other appointment, dismissing the matter I intended to discuss as of no particular urgency. Timmy, too, will have guessed I lied . . .

Mr Proctor says, "I'm not strictly allowed to dish out telephone numbers." He is a gaunt young man spotted with moles. The photograph on his desk, visible to his callers, shows a diffident group with musical instruments, Proctor himself gripping a cello by the scroll. "Might I see the letter?" The hand held out is broad and clumsy, unsuitable for a cellist.

The unsealed letter purports to have been written by "P. E. Smith" of the Gulf Advisory Service, Welbeck Street, W1 to his acquaintance Mr Apramian introducing his good friend A. V. Guise, agricultural economist, "coming out to your part of the world for a reconnoitre."

"I believe Smith met Apramian on a London visit not so long ago."

"He gets about," Proctor smiles painfully, "if he's the same Apramian. You could attach a note to this letter, giving your hotel and room number and asking Mr Apramian to call you. We could have it delivered to his P.O. box." He hesitates.

"One can't tell how often these people collect their mail. They live by the telex and telephone. You in a hurry?"

"The hotel's expensive. I want to go down to Khor – the last Shaikhdom down the coast I believe."

"This very day?"

"No – soon. No appointments yet. Just a look-see to start with. It's the least developed, isn't it, and all that hinterland must have rather greater agricultural potential than most. I believe there's only fifteen per cent land use, and good underground water . . ."

"It's a trodden path, Mr Guise. And you appreciate they've just buried the old Shaikh. The surviving son's a bit of an unknown quantity. To put it charitably. There's no certainty how he'll choose to spend his money . . . not that there's much of that around in Khor. Not like here." He seems dejected, on a tight salary, handling millions for these Ali Babas.

"I forgot to ask Phil Smith what nationality Apramian was. Armenian, of course, but that's not a nationality."

"I think you'll find he carries an Iranian passport – a lot of the traders on this side are Iranian by origin."

"Good at business," I suggest.

"I'd say," Proctor endorses wanly. "Got a grip here."

"You don't suppose it would be reasonable for me to have Apramian's business number?"

"I imagine your friend Smith could have given it to you." The smile flickers with the same pain. Even in this day and age it is possible to spot a fellow who plays the game.

"Smith it was."

"In that case" – he pivots in his chair and with a display of dexterity punches out an account code on the computer alongside the desk. He reads off six digits which I write on my palm. "That's Dubai of course." His little act of assistance serves as a drop of oil. "If you're off to the Khor, you'll want to see Grover Wilks. Nothing in Khor worth knowing that Grover doesn't know. He was the old Shaikh's tribal adviser – some such title. He advised on everything, really. I hope to hell he'll still stay on now Hamood's Shaikh," he adds daringly. "The GMC would be lost without him. That's him there," he nudges the photograph, "in the centre."

"Gulf Music . . . ?"

III

"Exactly – Circle. Grover's an accomplished harpsichord player. Really super. I knock about on the 'cello. You're not musical by any chance?"

"I sang as a boy." An Indian clerk in flared trousers has entered with papers for initialling.

"My God, if you can sight-read a line" – Proctor is suddenly fired – "Grover would be over the moon. The shortage of tenors is desperate." Under a flap of hair a puckish face looks straight at the camera, the only one not smiling: older than the others, but oddly ageless. "Anything up to 1750, and he's a master. It's a two-hour drive to the Khor, and Grover won't come up here. He does insist on his own instrument – he's a purist of course."

Proctor perfunctorily approves the papers and raises his hands for the clerk to gather up. He is on a higher plane. "Naturally, he's wasted in the Khor. Used to be State Department but you know I think he was really too brilliant for them. He'd have gone straight to the top."

"What brought him to Khor?"

Proctor's need to communicate is undammed. "Oh, he was an Arabist from the start. I happen to know he began in Cairo and then I think Baghdad. He really identified with the Arabs. There's a story about a student mob threatening the American embassy when he was Duty Officer. At the very height of it the young Grover Wilks appeared on the balcony and let fly in *suk* Arabic – called them a bunch of spoiled layabouts and ignorant dupes. You know, in two shakes he had some cheering him on and the rest just slinking away."

"What made him leave the State Department?"

"Oh, there are theories. He came into quite a bit of money, I believe. But it was his wife, mostly, in my view – she's English, you know, very county. He had a London posting – that's when they met. But she's not one to put up with U.S. Embassy compound life out in the field. One of the oil giants snapped him up as Middle East political adviser – he knows the whole thing backwards, and has pull in Washington, I believe. Then he had some sort of a row . . . Been in the Khor a few years now: I imagine he likes the independence of it. They do themselves pretty well," he adds proudly.

"What kind of row?"

Proctor leans forward confidentially. "Grover's not an easy man: you'll see that for yourself. Mind you, I don't know the ins and outs, but someone said the regional bosses weren't following his advice, so he started trying to get at the corporate management in the U.S. through his Washington friends. When the big shots out here got to hear of it – well, you can imagine . . ." The gaunt features work up a painful smile. "I'll give you a note. It's Guise, isn't it? G-U- . . . May I say you sing?"

"I'm not a treble any longer."

The sad face creases again. "You never took it up again?"

"No." In the old days Sophia tried to persuade me – she liked the idea of my singing. I argued that it did not mix with the erratic life of journalism. But I knew it was too late. One could no more re-possess one's innocence than one's treble voice: one could only carry about a casket of purity – rather battered after all these years – which one couldn't open.

Part of Proctor's note reads: "He might be persuaded to sing."

2

A babel of races teem the foyer – Gujeratis, Sindhis, Levantines, North Africans, Thais, Filipinos. The Arab business proprietors will not return till after sundown prayer. A group of four elevators serves the building, and littered stairways of chipped composition stone ascend both sides. According to the notice Orient Sales and Trading is one of five enterprises operating on the eleventh storey.

I enter a lift, just another Western executive with a briefcase. I say to myself, this is quite like old times, but without the coterie of colleagues to mask the isolation. How swiftly the old instinct of pursuit reasserts itself – it is as if the hunt and grubbing are an end in themselves.

OST lies behind a frosted glass door at the end of a corridor which offers no opportunity of concealment. A few yards short of the door the corridor gives access to the stairway, seldom used at this level. On composition stone flooring, leather-soled footfalls approaching from the lift may be heard from the stairway; and the lifts conveniently *ping* on arrival. I station myself at the next half-landing up, where the stairs reverse. Whenever I hear a visitor approach from the lift at either level, I have time to move out of sight. When someone leaves an office, I bend to tie a shoelace. After an hour I repeat this vigil on the half-landing beneath. Several visitors leave the elevator but no one makes the final journey to the door at the end of the corridor, and no one leaves. By a quarter to nine I begin to despair of Apramian coming, unless he's already there, in which case I must not impress my features on him by descending in the lift with him; yet I will never be able to get down eleven storeys' stairs in time to follow him out.

The lift's *ping* is followed by brisk footsteps approaching OST. Leaving the briefcase on the half-landing, I double up six steps silently; then, lighting a cigarette, I saunter the last three steps, turning towards the lifts and further offices in time to be passed by a trim brunette in her thirties, in cotton dress wearing no jewellery. A sportive assurance in the brown eyes and contrived disorder of her full hair mark her as English. She shuts the OST door behind her.

I extinguish my cigarette, remove tie and jacket which I pack into the briefcase, and assume dark glasses. For another twenty-five minutes nobody leaves or enters. Then once again the lift halts at the eleventh, but no footsteps. I promptly adopt the same gambit, and this time am passed by a bull of a man, dressed as for tennis, in white rubber-soled shoes, a muscular weight emphasising the shortness of his flannelled legs. The sallow skin and defiant brush of hair growing in a black line vertically from a narrow forehead declare his origins to be well east of England but not so far south: I take it that my quarry is sighted.

I at once descend a floor by the stairs and take the lift to ground level. Brisk now, I find a space for my rented Mazda a few yards from the exit of the building's underground carport. I return to the lobby and stand to one side of the lifts as if waiting for someone to come out, having re-assumed my dark glasses and tie but leaving my jacket off. Lights over the ground floor lifts tell when the elevator cars stop at the eleventh. Whenever such a lift approaches the ground floor I press the button to ensure that it pauses and opens its doors for me to glimpse any occupants descending to the carport; each time an unoccupied lift stays at ground level I send it on up by pressing a button and stepping out before the doors close. After several minutes I see my quarry and the woman at the back of a lift that empties its other occupants at ground level: they go on down to the carport. I return to my Mazda instantly. A doner-kebab stand casts a light on the occupants of vehicles leaving the underground carport.

As a beige Mercedes slows at the barrier and pulls out, I spot the white roll collar and short sleeves of the man's shirt. He is alone. The Mercedes pauses beyond the exit. Then a pale Volvo reaches the barrier and I recognise the chin and bare throat of the woman. The two cars pull into traffic. I draw in behind, one car separating me from the Volvo. The two cars move up-creek in heavy traffic which does not ease until they peel right at the illuminated clock tower. They take the first bridge over the creek and from there cut through to the coast road, one behind the other.

My little Mazda has weak acceleration but I keep up for four or five miles until the metalled road turns sharply left. Just past the bend I see their lights swing off right into a track between two walls. I shut off my lights. After two hundred yards the walls end and I find myself in dunes and salt flats. Beyond, clusters of palm frond huts are visible in the moonlight. I pull up feeling exposed.

I can see the headlights of the two cars on the dunes as they weave along the track. Both cars are now about eight hundred yards ahead: one halts among a group of huts, the other continues out of sight. The lights of the halted car go out: I see the interior lights go on as its door is opened. From my right, the sound of the sea.

The huts can only belong to fishermen and the track's main function must be to give access to their little community: it is not much used and has been made by the passage of tyres. I pull off beside a rear wall of the compound which flanks the dunes, and lock my trousers and shoes in the car. Tucking shirt into underpants I set off towards the sea at a jog – just an apish Anglo-Saxon in pursuit of fitness, at a late hour. Plausible, except to the dogs: twice I rouse them as the shoreline veers close to huts, and one even gives chase obliging me to arc into the shallow sea. I can make out the bobbins and poles of fish traps, and drawn up on the beach to my left I see other traps like giant lacy leggings. Tarry oil from the great slicks pupped by the interminable conflict up the Gulf gathers between my toes and clings to my soles. A few inshore fishing boats are beached and larger Gulf *boums* ride at anchor without lights. Here and there a cable-drum lies half-buried.

I round a headland and there, white and exquisite some forty foot overall and a furlong or so offshore, a yacht rides at anchor. She has that unattainability of certain women who value their beauty higher than any love it might win them. She too shows no lights, and seems to be crewless.

The dunes rise steeply here. I proceed cautiously, careful not to break the skyline, since the heavenly bodies shine with storybook clarity and I throw a deep moon-shadow. When I spot the two cars ahead, drawn up side by side, I drop and begin to crawl. Two figures are up to their waists in water just beyond the cars: gobs of oil notwithstanding, some ritual is in play, for man and woman holding hands at arms' length circle and duck as if to music. They come together in embrace, and the man grips the woman and flings her into the air: I hear her cry. She is naked. She scampers for the beach, the man charging after her, he also naked, and she squeals like a trapped pig as he brings her down where the waves just reach. There they couple, the moon catching the man's pumping thighs. Even at this distance the obscenity of the act astonishes. Above the waves' hiss and suck I catch her culminating yelp. They lie there in the last of the surf, and first she, then he, crawl back into the contaminated sea.

Shortly afterwards I watch them dress and carry a dinghy to the water's edge. They launch it, and clambering over the stern row out to the motor yacht for the night.

The woman does not leave me. That self-same night I dream of her, in a tableau of confused roles. Borrowed from the choir, I am attending our local country church in the role of priest – "what you always wanted to be" in the words of Sophia who has chosen me to officiate at her marriage with Timmy Lunt. For her bridesmaid she has the woman on the beach. "Will you take this lassie," I say, using Timmy's argot, "to be your lawful wedded wife?" He congratulates me for "picking such a peach" for him, but I can see that Sophia, all in white and radiant with happiness, is utterly saintly and without lust, and it is I in sanctifying Timmy and Sophia's union who experience the ecstasy with the bridesmaid.

3

The following evening I telephone the home of Grover Wilks. It is his wife who answers: here is a lady in whose sprightly nasality I at once detect a recognition of social acceptability: she can tell an English gent even unseen. Within a matter of minutes I am invited to lunch this coming Friday – "if you can face a picnic with a mixed bag of Gulf hands. We're all going up the coast to look for turtles with Billy French – you won't know him. If you can bear to come by eleven, Mr Guise, we'll have time to get there." My acceptance comes with apt diffidence.

Am I the watcher being watched? The dark pudding face of the man waiting in the small car near the carpark entrance the next night is a face seen once too often, even though a head-cloth has been added to the skull-cap. I park some distance behind and remain in my car so that no light falls on my face, feigning sleep. Sure enough, after two or three minutes I see from the corner of an eye the soft black globe right against my window. When at length I enter the hotel and turn to the lifts, the man is at the foot of the marble steps to the foyer.

I know instantly this is Timmy's doing. It can hardly be Apramian's because I remember the dark bulk of this man here from as early as my second day at the hotel, watching disconsolately in his dishdasha at the top of the steps as I returned from the pool. I pitied him even then, for the trick by which life denied him the infinite pleasures of these foreigners, lazing at the waterside with their gold-skinned, moon-bellied consorts. I noticed him fingering his beads furiously, avoiding my eyes . . . As for the Welshmen, they knew me as Mr Goode and I am satisfied did nothing more to have my cover blown. These are my wages for blabbing to Timmy's PPS about Saqr, then scuttling out of our meeting: a simple task for Timmy's intelligence structure – is it MI6? – to have the foreign travel of Anthony Vernon Guise monitored and see that he is under surveillance in a Gulf Shaikhdom that Britain fathered into statehood. To engineer the cancellation of my visa might have exposed him, but to alert his local man to a masquerading journalist who possibly jeopardises Britain's interests – that is a natural precaution.

The discovery spurs me. In the morning, there he is again, back on lounging duty in the busy concourse of the great hotel. I watch him push through the swing door of the gents' lavatory. Without leaving my key at reception I drive across the creek bridge then turn inland, doubling back on a road where the traffic is thin, to confirm I am not followed. I pick up the coast road and find the track between the earth walls and this time follow it across the salt-flats to the palm-frond huts on the skyline. There the track disperses several ways, each to a tiny habitation. Four or five vehicles are scattered among the settlement, including two bulky American cars. One track leads to a flat area strewn with grass mats where the catch is sorted.

As I get out a dog circles warily and two little girls run into a hut. An old woman, unmasked, eyes deeply circled with kohl, pauses over a basin and tweaks her black headcloth across the lower half of her face with a heavily-ringed hand. I call the Arabic greeting of God's peace and extract the obligatory response. I persist in phrase-book Arabic to indicate I have come to buy fish. A youth, slightly crippled, emerges from behind a hut. "No fish," he replies in his own language. "Fish in the *suk*." He points to the town. But I mime a humorous craving: "New fish, from the sea." I can glimpse the sea through the huts: no sign of the yacht – only two or three *boums* visible at anchor.

"Tomorrow," the boy says.

"My friends say, this place for good fish."

"Nothing," the boy repeats indifferently, and stands crookedly, stock still. The sun is nearly at zenith and with no breeze the damp heat is stifling. A man's voice calling from inside a hut is answered by the boy.

I pass my arm across the forehead. "*Qahwa?*"

The boy turns and hobbles towards a hut. I sit on the bonnet of my car: my mistake, I know, is arriving in a cheap car. In a Mazda I have no status among fishermen who drive Buicks and Pontiacs and whose master comes in a Mercedes.

After three minutes the boy re-emerges. "Okay," he says in English. I follow his hobbling figure behind the hut, half of which is open on one side. A water drum covered with palm fronds stands outside. I kick off my shoes and bend to enter. A new carpet is spread across the sand floor of the partition. In the darkest corner an old man in a loin cloth squats with a long-stemmed pipe. In the other corner, its tube sheathed in red nylon velvet, stands a hookah for the evening smoke. The boy motions me to sit, and I clutch my knees awkwardly with my arms, the boy settling opposite. I can hear coffee being prepared behind the cloth partition, and smell it too.

"Good morning. Hallo mister. Fuck you," the boy says suddenly. I respond pleasantly in kind.

"Amriki?"

"Inglisi."

The boy seems disappointed, but the old man nods for several seconds.

Gourds and enamel cups hang from the framework of the roof, and a broad-bladed knife is stuck under the thatch. There are no other chattels except for a prayer mat of dyed grasses rolled up at the old man's feet and a squat lidless wooden packing case with stencilled writing, containing items of clothing.

The boy disappears behind the curtain and returns shortly with a beak-spouted coffee pot and two cups without handles. He pours a half-cup for me and the same for the old man. I sip the thin cardamom-flavoured brew slowly. My eyes are growing accustomed to the gloom and I begin to discern the lettering on the packing-case.

"That box," I commend in my fragmentary Arabic. "Good."

I shift across to run my fingers over the wood. It is strong teak and its joints are reinforced by metal strips. "A R N A", I read across the end panel, but a letter or letters in front missed the stenciller's ink or have been erased. "From the white boat?" I enquire. "*Aiwa*," the boy assents with a grin. Already his teeth are beginning to go. The depth and height of the packing case are the same, and the length double, like a coffin for a fat dwarf. It is quite new.

I hold out my cup for more *qahwa*. At a sound outside the

120

boy and the old man look up sharply. A burly, dark-skinned figure in a sarong blocks the entrance. He is barefoot. A rapid interchange takes place between him and the boy. The newcomer turns to me in English: "Mister – you want?"

"Fish. Fish perhaps?"

"No fish. Now, prayer-time." He picks up my shoes. It is a notice of dismissal. I return the cup to the boy, shaking it to indicate I require no more, and rise, saying my thanks. The burly man conducts me to the Mazda, and watches with folded arms while I back up to turn. "Fish, *suk*?" I query, but get no answer.

Time is running out, and money too at such an hotel. My brief visa has only a week more to run. I have paltry fragments; nothing coheres. There is a Communist conspiracy – or a conspiracy involving Communism: the old story, the ancient paradox, idealism that becomes a fount of evil, the angel of light which, through arrogance, falls from heaven and haunts creation as Lucifer. Now Timmy had no ideals. To engage in a Communist conspiracy – what could it gain him? I knew the boy, I know the man. Yet who else can have had this clumsy tail placed on me in this hotel?

I descend to the main lobby. The man is on his customary settee where the chauffeurs wait. The fellow could be any bigshot's lackey, black, obese, sullenly devoted. But the quality of his laziness is wrong: his is a tormented ease. He glances up from his newspaper, nuzzles a foot back into a sandal.

I approach within a yard or two and stand there undecided. The black foot slides out of its carapace of heavy green and brown leather, and the sole is comforted by a scratch across the welt. Then the big toe, the shaikh toe, asserts its status, its master slot, and this prompts the whole figure to stand and shuffle to the glass-fronted news-stand. The fat at the top of his retreating back above his collarless dishdasha makes a pursed smile at me with the wedge of flesh under his cropped skull.

I cross to where the foyer yields to the atrium. It is the start of the Happy Hour, 6 to 7 p.m., when every guest is allowed a free drink. Guests are scattered at tables in the sunken area surrounding the central fountain, whose water cascades down plastic tubes from far on high. On the little tables nightlights burn in pink wineglasses with gilt stems. The plants are floodlit a vicious green; musak drips from the walls and ceiling like compulsory soup. I approach a desk whose plaque designates the role of the lady seated behind it: *Guest Relations*. "Good evening," I say.

"Good evening, sir."

"I am trying to decide what drink I shall have."

"Oh!" she smiles. "This is the Happy Hour. You can take a free drink with the compliments of the Management." She is a Filipino and wears a badge saying "Sylvia de la Cruz". Her uniform is pink and brown check in nylon tweed, and she is pretty except for her canine teeth which suggest a genetic strain other than human. She produces a glossy card printed with verbose descriptions of fruit concoctions.

"Shall I have Safari Julep or Gulf Pomegranate Surprise?"

"They say that Dubai is the paradise of the Gulf," she says.

"I thought that was Bahrain."

"Maybe Bahrain also a paradise."

"I thought it was Dubai they called 'the Hong Kong of the Middle East'."

"Maybe Hong Kong. You can say Hong Kong."

She is like a composite bird manufactured from the feathers of innumerable species quietly slaughtered for the purpose.

"You know Hong Kong?" she chirrups. "Is it like Dubai?"

"Great places for smuggling, Dubai and Hong Kong."

"Oh – smuggling!" She utters her tinkling childlike laugh, as if I have proposed a game of hide-and-seek all-over-the-world. "You are smuggler?"

"Certainly."

"Oh!" A line exists between amiability and amity that she has been instructed not to cross.

I say, "Not everybody is happy, even in the Happy Hour in the Paradise of the Gulf."

"I think so."

"I think not."

"You are not happy?"

"You see that fellow by the news-stand?"

"He is an Arab."

"Exactly – I don't think he is happy."

"Why not?"

"You should look into his face."

"I think I cannot!" she exclaims, with her mechanical tinkle.

"Who is he?"

"I shall enquire."

"No – don't do that. Have you seen him before?"

"There are many Arabs."

"He works here?"

"Maybe he is security."

"You have seen him before?"

"You have had some trouble with this man? I shall speak to Under-Manager."

"No, don't speak to anyone. Promise?"

I puzzle her. A little frown has touched the emptiness of her oriental face. "You watch," I say: "I shall make him walk right across this hall in front of your desk, without my saying anything to him. Then I shall come back and ask you if you have seen him before."

"You must take your drink with compliments of the Management. In half an hour it will be too late." She taps her wristwatch with a long silver nail.

"And after the Happy Hour, you've finished work?"

"Eight o'clock, I finish," she says, as if her mechanism is known to run down at that moment.

I move on as planned, past the Fitness Centre and Playland into the shopping arcade. I pause to gaze down on the skating rink. Two ginger girls with round shoulders make clumsy circles on the ice. They wear identical T-shirts announcing on the back "We do it in the desert". I enter the darkened Space Galeria, which resounds with interstellar noises. I try to pit my luck in space-war contests on machines called Turbo, Crush Roller and Stratos. I have no idea what I am meant to do. Suddenly I am surrounded by a swarm of small girls in three-quarter length trousers who descend on the machines with cries of rivalry and begin to shoot down enemy space ships with consummate skill. All wear extra-terrestrial antennae which quiver a foot above their heads. But I slot my coins in vain: my machine feeds me no enemy, though I press all the buttons at my command.

I am aware of antennae bobbing at my elbow. "You're doing it all wrong."

"Show me."

The antennae duck in front. Suddenly the machine springs to life and I am engaged in a spatial battle against limitless forces. I inflict terrible casualties, but never enough.

"You're hopeless."

She moves me out, blows up several space ships. All at once the war is finished – never more than a game in the first place.

"Knock-knock," she says.

"Who's there?"

"Dismay."

"Dismay who?"

"Dis may be a bad joke *but* . . ."

"But what?" I ask politely.

"But nuthin'. How does an elephant get down from a tree?"

"I give up."

"Stands on a leaf and waits for the fall. Hey, how can you tell when there's an elephant under the bed?"

I emerge and see the black Arab staring at the window display of a boutique called Mummy and Me. I walk straight past him and he can see my reflection in the window. I re-cross the atrium and see Sylvia de la Cruz talking to a Lebanese in a blue velvet jacket with one buttock propped on her desk, whom I take to be the Under-Manager. I enter the broad corridor which gives access to the Business Men's Service Centre and the conference rooms. A notice outside the first conference room announces *Gulf Overseas Property Exhibition. Choose Your Dream Home Anywhere in the World. Admission Dh.10.* There is a great concourse of people and some kind of reception is under way. Somebody at the door hands me a leaflet shaped like a house which offers Coastal and Mountain Villas, Lakeside Apartments, 16th Century Farmsteads, in Florida, Costa del Sol, Costa Brava and Paphos, and Tax Advice. Nothing is taking place in the second and third rooms. The door of the last room is closed, but a notice outside states simply Movement for Global Reconciliation.

I open the door quietly and shut it behind me. A gathering of about twenty listen to a speaker with fan teeth behind a baize-covered table, evidently responding to questions from his audience. He is saying, " 'How do I see the ethnic composition of the Gulf in, say, the year 2000?' Right? Well, Judy, first I'd like to thank you for asking that question. Communication between peoples is at the root of what we're all trying to do. Right? What we're all trying to do here is promote *communication* . . ." I sit at the back. Every time the speaker says "Right?" he smiles as if to accord his teeth a purpose worthy of their prominence. On the table, arranged in an answering fan, stands a little display of miniature flags of several nations, among which I recognise the Stars and Stripes, the local Shaikhdoms' flag and the Union Jack. Two or three Arabs in dishdashas are present, but most appear to be English or American. At one end of the baize table a woman in charge of a tape recorder preserves the wisdom of the meeting, which is now drawing to a close, for the chairman – an American – is on his feet, thanking those present for their attendance and including a special mention of His Excellency Nigel Fountain CMG (a white head in the audience, of marked nobility even from the back, gives a little bob) who is here, of course, on this occasion not as representative of his country but in his private capacity as a thinking, caring, if one may say, *world* citizen. Cross-cultural understanding, based upon a shared ethical perception to which every nation could subscribe, offered a shrinking world the only chance for civilisation, as we know it, to survive. And he fixes the date of the next meeting, for which the speaker is to fly out from GRPM headquarters in Connecticut Avenue, Washington DC.

I merge with the disbanding gathering. The lady with the tape machine gives me a booklet, and when she reads my card she recognises at once that agricultural economy is directly relevant to the Movement's work. I protect myself from deeper involvement by settling into a corner and studying the booklet with concentrated attention until I am the only one remaining: amid lashings of brotherhood it imparts an obscure anti-Semitism. I move towards the door and push it shut, screening it with a display board behind which I settle with a glass of water from the speaker's table.

I have not long to wait. The door begins to open – first a few inches, then a little wider. At last the whole lumpish figure in *dishdasha* and skullcap emerges from beyond the display board. On catching sight of me the raisin eyes immediately travel on, as if he were looking for another, and he begins to withdraw, but I move swiftly behind the board to kick the door shut.

"*La*," I declare, facing him – No. "No go."

The face does not register alarm so much as despair. It is a large black pudding, heavy pudding, a rather guilty pudding. It sorrows, it sags. It says nothing. The two raisins have lost all their shine. If there is fear it is swallowed up in surrender; if cunning, it is buried by lethargy.

"*Fadhl –*"

"English," I say. "You will speak English." It is after all well known as the language of world brotherhood. From where I stand I pull a chair towards me and sit on it, blocking the door.

"Why you this to me?" the other demands feebly.

I motion him to sit, but no gesture will budge him. The pudding has begun to settle and wait. Waiting and settling comprise much of its time on earth.

I wedge my chair under the doorknob and fetch another, which I place sideways on. Gently but firmly I turn him, handling the dense flesh, and sit him down, shifting my own chair so that we face each other across the doorway. No sooner are we settled than with surprising speed the other dives for the door. I leap to intercept and block its opening with my foot, with the weight of his belly on me. I lightly pull his arm away from the door and propel him backwards, one hand on each shoulder, to his appointed chair. It is a ridiculous mime, solemn, soundless except for the breathing. I see a bolt on the door which I now depress into the floor.

Across the gap between us I offer a brotherly cigarette, and a hand comes out, a lesser pudding, customarily melancholy but touched by a reflex lust now. I light up too. "My friend," I declare, with a phoney smile. We both blow smoke into the air. What we have in common – our distant factor of brotherhood – is Timothy Lunt.

I slip my hand into my breast pocket and the other eyes this movement as if I might be delving for a gun. But it is a visiting card I pass him. He reads the English side first, *in extenso*, turns it over for the Arabic, then reaches forward to hand it back. I decline it – "No, no. Keep it. Show it to your masters. Now, please, what is your name?"

"Ibrahim."

"Are you very busy, Ibrahim?"

"Busy?"

"I wish you to be my guest at dinner."

"Dinner?"

"You speak English?"

"A littel."

"What is your job?"

"I do not take these questions."

"Have you a wife and children?"

"Of course."

"If you do not answer my questions, you will not see your wife and children any more."

"Why?"

"Because you will be dead."

Deep sorrow returns to the pudding. I stub my cigarette, pick up the tumbler at my feet and pour the water out onto the carpet. I lay the tumbler on the floor and stamp on it. Taking hold of the base of the glass and crossing behind him, I catch him in a neck grip with the left arm. With the right hand I hold the jagged edges of glass a few centimetres from the soft plump features by which creation knows him. I feel him go limp.

"First, what is your job?"

A high-pitched moan oozes out like a secretion and the head rocks so that I suppose his eyes to be shut.

"What is your job?"

"I am security," he chokes.

"Who employs you?"

"Hoteli."

"Who do you report to?"

"The management."

"Who? Exactly which man?"

Silence.

"I do not intend to repeat my questions, Ibrahim."

"I speak to the manager."

"Who told you to watch me?"

"I do not watch you, mister."

"Who told you to?"

The moan begins again, and the rocking of the head. I close the spiked glass on his face so that when it moves his cheeks

127

become little balloons under threat. He reeks of cheap scent, manufactured for any sex.

"Who?"

"Manager, Mister."

"Why?"

"How I know?" he wails. He is a slave's son, Nile-black, born to the violent whim of other races.

Still threatening the face with the points of glass, I release the neck and with a hand thus freed feel in the breast pocket of his *dishdasha* for the notebook and in the lower pocket find three or four keys on a ring. I withdraw the jagged glass from the lumps and hollows of cowering flesh. I can smell the urine through the scent. I tread out his lighted cigarette where it has dropped on the carpet.

"Okay, Ibrahim. You go. If you want your keys and your notebook, come to me tomorrow. You know where – I expect you've already had the room searched. Meanwhile, leave me alone. Understand?"

He has got unsteadily to his feet: I can see the stain all down his *dishdasha* from his crutch. He tugs hopelessly at the door, where I notice a bell button which at any time he could have reached for. I release the bolt and he shuffles out, still moaning at the back of his throat. I wrap the splintered glass in sheets from the brochure of the Movement for Global Reconciliation, and am left with the grubby notebook, the meaningless keys, and an overwhelming self-disgust. As I come out past the Business Men's Service Centre, a German is vociferously complaining to the telex operator that, sartainly, sartainly, there *must* be a message.

Sylvia de la Cruz is already gone from Guest Relations. I suppose her to have left early in case I came back for her. The Space Centre is shut, and the ice-rink. A placard offers Zen yoga for Men, Choose any of Three Sessions, and the Beauty Clinic offers 10% on list prices for Facials, Body Massage and Slimming Course. A thickset girl of twelve stares glumly into the window of Mummy and Me, as Ibrahim did, in a garment which complains "My folks went to Bahrain – all they got me was this lousy T-shirt." In the marble foyer I glimpse the velvet jacket of the under-manager disappearing behind a swing door beyond the reception desk and for a moment think of following to ask him where the Miss de la Cruz has gone. *Why?* he would want to know. And was I to say, "Because I have a right to be sure that my old friend Timothy Lunt, the British politician, is having me followed, since I am here to pierce a certain evil, and I need this girl to prove . . ."?

I descend the grand stairway and take myself out through the revolving doors. Darkness is gathering fast and the city clustered at the mouth of the creek is brilliantly illuminated. In the forecourt a Filipino with a face in a perpetual scowl polishes his master's Mercedes as a eunuch prepares a woman for the bedchamber. His worry beads dangle from the mirror and I presume her lord has hit the jackpot in smuggling, the local industry; it is not a beige Mercedes, but he will know the bull-man Apramian. Only I am outside the brotherhood. The forecourt's casuarina trees are hung with coloured bulbs like diseased fruit.

At the reception desk the Pakistani clerk hands me a note: the hotel manager, writing in his own hand, requires I should call him on a certain number. I find it difficult to think through the musak. There is no one to talk to, no one to lay my fragments before. "Why are you doing this?" Sophia demanded, and I told her, "There's something peculiarly evil, Sophia . . . one has a certain obligation." "You're not going back into journalism, for heaven's sake – so what's the point? One doesn't have to go to the ends of the earth to find evil."

Crusading, she meant, can begin at home. "You can't just walk out on the farm for some wild goose chase." The farm came into her family from her mother's side, and like all things connected with her mother was immutably sacrosanct. She frowned at me: "Are you doing this for God?" In the evenings after a drink or two she could grow quite bold in her mockery. I said, "You could say, for truth." "Like your Indian beggars, you mean?" Once I had risked trying to explain to her – somewhere existed a meaning, beyond all the scramble for significance and status: I had wanted to go down through the corruption and degradation to the other side, to find that truth. It was not long after the loss of that first foetus, a bad time, and I thought she understood. "Maybe it's the same sort of compulsion, my dear . . ."

I enter the Coffee Shop and sit at a table. I take out Ibrahim's vile notebook. Its pages have come away from the spine. A portrait of the local Shaikh is printed on the front endpaper and on the back a map of the Gulf from Kuwait to its tortured mouth. The entries are all in Arabic – dates and times. It is valueless to me. I pick up the plastic menu: *Supreme d'Hamour Beaulieu*, it offers, *Poached hamour glaced with our special Beaulieu herb sauce.* I have no appetite. *From our dessert trolley four your choice a daily changing assortement of delicate tarties, mousses, seasonal fruits, selected pastries and gateaux.* I want nothing, only to tell the black man that it was a mistake, I would never have hurt him – more than that: I care for him, I embrace his despair with my own, we are each contaminated by the same source, personified by a Sayyid Lunt of whom he will not even have heard. I have turned those fragments of glass I threw into the bin into splinters of love.

A waiter fills my tumbler with iced water.

I need to lay out my options clearly, subject them to detached scrutiny. Alongside, a single man of about my own age is ordering his dinner. It would be easy to open a conversation, to put to him a hypothetical situation: he looks harmless enough. "I take the brawns," he is telling the waiter, eyeing him keenly from under his brows. "But berry liddle rice." Chubby hands indicate how little: the waiter nods concurrence. "It comes with rice?" "The rice is separate." "Navver mind," he persists. "Berry berry liddle rice." He appears to be Dutch, and has grown bloated, so far from home. Perhaps long ago the formidable belly lost the ability to ingest less than whatever was put within reach. "Now then, what you recommend for the mine gourse?"

I order a cup of coffee which I drink very slowly. From the cash desk each little check inserted sets off a tiny salvo of electronic bubbles surfacing on the hotel chain's profit-and-loss account. Across from me a furtive Saudi is buried in a wine list . . . I sign the check.

In my room the light on my telephone is illuminated. I dial Reception and a Pakistani voice says the manager requests me to call him.

"I already have that message."

"I shall put you through?"

The voice of the manager is mid-Atlantic with Scottish

overtones. "I have been waiting for your call, Mr Guise. If I could ask you to come to my office on the mezzanine . . . McKinnon is the name" – a vouchsafing portending gravity.

At the swing door the musak stops and in an ante-room a clerk bids me wait. A Levantine in a black jacket is paying out paper money with the wheeling movement of certain card dealers. The clerk ushers me in. An upright chair facing the side of the manager's imposing desk makes that end of the room a kind of sanctuary, for lumped into the chair like a sack of grain is Ibrahim.

"Ah, Mr Guise." The manager rises, but offers no hand. "Won't you sit down. It's rather late, but I fear I had to see you tonight." The well cut, vigorous bulk exudes a godless confidence and a chemical tang matched by the sheen of the crisp hair and suit with pockets cut at an angle. Photographs on the wings of his desk show foyer encounters with the celebrated or limitlessly rich in Arab attire and/or dark glasses, and children on a ski slope with a woman with fine teeth and strands of hair blown across her face. These, and various plaques, medallions, awards for proficiency, speak of the international man with access to global perks. Mr McKinnon has come a long way from the academy in Peebles and raw knees in the February sleet.

"I regret having to raise this matter with you, Mr Guise. But I am led to believe you have assaulted a member of my staff and taken from him personal possessions."

"I am sorry."

"I don't quite follow."

I turn to the flaccid figure of Ibrahim, thumb and forefinger working the beads. "I am sorry," I repeat. "*Muta'asif.*"

Ibrahim does not respond. The skull cap has been straightened, but a grey moisture has come to coat his black skin as if the pudding was forgotten in the refrigerator. In two or three hours he seems to have grown a day's beard, like the beginnings of mildew.

"I do not need your explanation, Mr Guise, since I'm afraid you will have to leave this hotel in any case. I have advised this man not to bring charges, unless of course . . . I am bound to say that if he did the consequences for you could be very serious. The foreigner here has very few rights, you will appreciate."

"He is a good man. I would never harm him."

"I do not need your explanation, Mr Guise."

"Perhaps I need yours. He was following me. Presumably you told him to."

The trimmed eyebrows rise. "He is employed here for security purposes. He does not 'follow' anybody. His task is surveillance of guests and their belongings for their own safety. People are coming and going all the time. We are a centre of entertainment and shopping in our own right, Mr Guise."

"Even so . . ." A narrowness has penetrated Ibrahim's resignation. One podgy hand is touching the veneer of the desk as if it were an altar. This is high priest territory; he seldom gets so close.

"He could have no purpose in following you."

"I demonstrated it," I say, "to a member of your staff." But I know all this to be futile.

"You are saying . . . ?"

"You have a lady called Sylvia de la Cruz – at least, that's the name on her badge. She would confirm that this man followed me through to the shopping arcade, and then followed me back. He was looking for me when he came into the conference room."

Mr McKinnon's derision is fainter than his cologne.

"He has a job to do like the rest of us, Mr Guise. His surveillance area is the whole of the lobby level. That includes the conference rooms. He is quite within his rights to go through to the shopping gallery. If I may say so, I do not see that you have a right to discuss the activities of other members of the staff with Miss de la Cruz, or any other employee. I have four hundred people working here, each with his or her assigned role. Miss de la Cruz' is to attend to the special queries and requirements of guests. She is only here on a nine-month contract, extendable," he adds irrelevantly.

"I did not discuss anything with Miss de la Cruz."

"I understood you to say that you did."

"I merely forecast to her that this man would come creeping after me."

"Discussing . . . forecasting . . . Really, Mr Guise, are we

132

not splitting hairs?"

"I was not to know he was a member of your staff."

Mr McKinnon is unmoved. "Either way, it cannot justify your conduct. You subjected him to a dreadful experience. We have been to Conference Room Four and have found the broken tumbler. You will be charged for that. Now, the items that you took from this man? Ibrahim – what are you missing?"

At this shaft of special attention the pudding rises like a dark souffle. "*Kitab*," he mutters. "Small." The hand indicates the size of the book. "Keys. *Thalatta*." He holds up three fat fingers with stained nails.

I deposit notebook and keys on the desk by the onyx penholder. The pudding swells and folds about the raisins, and the raisins themselves, distinctly visible, are now charged with lustre. Nobody touches the surrendered items. McKinnon draws out a gold pen and selects a sheet of paper on which he writes a few words.

"This is the book?" He picks it up. "*Aiwa*," the black man affirms. "And the keys?" "*Aiwa. Aiwa.*" Complex hollows and cracks, betokening the deepest commitment of the heart, appear symmetrically alongside the raisins, and a contra-dictory smile alarms the entire pudding by its rare muscular demand. The slit it makes, intending thankful devotion to this hieratic figure for a glimpse of life in its sheerest meaning, is not an easy slit. It dips in the middle and at each end, and its thin and undulating edges stand out from the surface of the pudding. It is less a smile than a contortion.

McKinnon has completed his writing. "Is that all?"

"*Aiwa, aiwa.*"

He slides the paper towards the black man, offering the pen. The hand comes forth, an infant pudding, its customary melancholy now galvanised by ardour. The paper is signed with the gold pen (that also tells date and time), and as the paltry objects are passed across, consecrated by managerial hands, and the little brownish pips cower and peep from their slit, Timmy's favourite word for members of the coloured races comes back to me. The savages.

McKinnon draws to himself another paper, a photostat. "I see from registration that your visa expires in six days. Do I

133

take it that you intend to stay that time in this country?"

"I have some business still to do." For the bungling exorcist, further bungling.

"I am allowing you to occupy your room tonight, but I must ask you to check out by ten o'clock tomorrow morning. If you are not returning to London-England, I must ask you to alter your entry under 'Destination' on your card. It is a police requirement, you understand. I shall advise Reception on this point. I think that's all, Mr Guise."

4

So Timmy drives me underground, insofar as this is possible amid the Western expatriates of a group of shaikhdoms. I have no plan. I check out of the hotel and write the name of another hotel under Destination on the card. The girl is absent from her desk, but Ibrahim is slumped in a chair in the atrium: a wave of pity goes out to him. I recall my dream the previous night in which I was prawn fishing with the Dutchman, pushing my net on the rippled sand. I found I had caught a big slimy black creature like a squid which I tried to kill by stamping and then by driving the shrimp-net pole into it. But it was unkillable, and just lay on the beach fixing me with baleful incomprehension, while the Dutchman kept calling me back, "Leave it, man, leave it, gum and get the brawns. Why you gilling it? Don't gill, leave it." "It won't tell me the meaning of its name," I protested. "What are you saying, man, 'The meaning of its nime'?" I half weeping drove and drove at the thing mercilessly and futilely.

I turn in my car to the rental company and take to my feet, lugging my suitcase around the modern business area, past the exit where the woman followed Apramian out of the underground car park. I feel my shirt gathering sweat, and seek out one channel of shade after another. I chug across the creek and back again to test if they are tailing me. Droves of gabbling Asians jostle me on the ferryboat. The Arab women are segregated in the stern with their shopping bags – black-shawled, beak-masked robot-harpies whose gender obliterates them: any one could be a watcher.

But what if I am watched? I shall not lead anybody anywhere, I have ceased to be of substance myself, I am only a point of obscure persecution. I do not even possess anything of substance – none of my shards fit . . .

Alwyn Rhys' Russian . . . that box in the fisherman's hut from ARNA.

Something has crept into my mind. I find a bookshop: surely

135

there'll be an atlas or two alongside the dictionaries . . .
Bulgarians export weaponry – even a superannuated foreign
correspondent knows that. But what weapon fits a dwarf's
coffin? And how could any of it bear on Saqr's murder? Or my
desultory surveillance? . . . The whole place is such a mush of
chicanery and intrigue. I am losing faith in my own judgment.
Maybe the hotel manager was telling the truth about the black
man's role: a routine vigil of unrelieved tedium that had
nothing whatever to do with any tendril of the British Foreign
Service or Timothy Lunt.

I regard the sample of mankind surrounding me on the ferry,
each one with his pointless little difference from his fellows,
like a mass of suburban villas – shorter, fatter, blacker, paler;
with marks of past suffering or a moment's violence, sub-
missive, dull-eyed, warted, disfigured, deformed, bald or less
bald. That squat Indian, thickset and ugly, the oiled scalp
stupid and pitted by some forgotten disease – might he be my
watcher? And could the preposterous truth be that his life is as
significant to him – profound and secret and capable of joy – as
mine is to me? "Are not two sparrows sold for a farthing" –
this man and Ibrahim – "and one of them shall not fall to the
ground without your Father?" And I a third sparrow.

Out at sea the fishing boats are returning.

The editor himself was wary, acquainted with the paranoia
which in rare cases besets discarded journalists who once
reached a great public. How wise not to commit himself to my
expenses. Even now I could telephone him in Fleet Street – he
would be getting to the office in an hour – and ask him point
blank: "Can I have a private word, Harry? Have you observed
in me any symptoms of obsession? Unbalance? You see,
Harry, just now I'm so extremely lonely, I rather look to you as
a . . ."

Yet the princeling *was* murdered – a *fact*, however trifling, a
respectable little Fleet Street nugget. And *mine*: nobody can
take it from me. Shall I not permit myself to find out why? And
then, please God, delve beneath to wherever evil split from
good, to the innocent dust life sprang from?

For want of a church I want to slip off my shoes, enter the
cool and silence of a mosque. But these people would not
tolerate an infidel in their sanctuary and I am typecast as of

Western Christendom. I would pray for clarity and the recovery of innocence. For Sophia in whom my innocence once reposed. Last year, clearing the spare wing for the arrival of the trainee farm manager, I happened to open a leather trunk. It contained a packet of my letters to Sophia from foreign places up to the time of her miscarriage: I was still taking great care with my handwriting. Their limpid trust and hope was scarcely bearable to read. She had somehow scoured me with her pure light and the glow of her was in me. And that child that never was, conceived in her chaste body before wedlock, was for Sophia an unsurpassable gesture of trust: she could generate this live soul out of total, unreserved love only once . . . I thrust the letters back in one dust-laden trunk before my grief swamped me.

If there was no church, at least a bank – but not Proctor's. I would make the small ritual of cashing travellers' cheques in a high cool bank. Bankers are priests of a mirror religion that has no god: the same illusion of permanence and universality and authority . . . Across the street in the Gulf Bank, *suk* traders, *boum* skippers, ferrymen, taxi-drivers squat on the marble slabs waiting to collect their deposit slips or wads of dirhams like the halt and the maim waiting their chance to be cleansed. The sandalled feet of a young Levantine official of the bank brushes the canvas bag of an old Arab waiting placidly on a bench for his paltry withdrawal: the official hurries on, then turns back and with the offended foot pushes the canvas bag under the bench. The old man looks up puzzled and penitent.

I am engaged at Foreign Exchange when a voice of jarring familiarity reaches me from an adjacent counter ". . . could I be an awful nuisance? Just a peep at my statement. Are you quite shoo-er?"

The owner of that voice and I must be the only Westerners in the building.

"I say old chap. I say." Beneath the low pink skull the peakish eyes of Offshore Ollie register unqualified delight. "It's Goode, by Jove. Good old Goode," he titters.

"It's Oliver –" I recall only the sobriquet.

"That's *right*! Ollie Mullins. I say, how absolutely marvel-lous." I am suddenly his oldest friend. "What on earth brings you here? You *are* a dark horse, Goode."

"You're agricultural machinery, aren't you?"

"Honestly, you've got a memory like I don't know what," he beams. "I've quite forgotten what *you* do."

"Agricultural economy," I tell him. "Fisheries . . . that kind of thing."

"Look. Hang on a tick – they're just getting my numbers. Then let's go and find a drink. You don't bank here too, by any chance? That would be too absolutely extraordinary."

"I was cashing travellers' cheques."

He steers me out on the balls of his feet, gushing. At a bar overlooking the creek he orders Turkish coffee. "Where d'you put up here, old chap?"

"I've just checked out of one hotel. I'm looking for another."

"You've got to watch the prices here."

"I couldn't stand the musak."

"Really? The musak? You know, old chap, never throw away money on hotels. Short cut to debtor's jail. Where are you operating? No – let me look after this . . ." He pats his breast pocket. "You absolutely shoo-er?"

"There's someone I've got to see in the Khor."

"Nothing happens in Khor, old chap . . . Look, I can get you a bed for practically nothing. A bit primitive. My agent runs a kind of staff dorm at the depot, about twenty miles out of here. Would you mind that awfully? I've only to say you're a colleague, an old friend . . . So you are!" I search his straining hope for duplicity: I am almost sorry not to find it. "How about it, old chap? What time you winding up today?"

"There's something I've to do before sundown prayer-time."

"Meet at the Trade Centre, seven thirty. You can follow me out – you've got wheels?"

"I've been meaning to rent a car."

"You'll have to after the weekend, old chap. No one can survive without wheels here."

It is impossible to think clearly in this heat. I dare not go to an hotel in case I am ensnared in some new surveillance. If I could find a corner to prop my suitcase, and rest and pray . . . and work out how it can be that after half a lifetime Timmy

Lunt, ensconced in the structure of power, has me a half-fugitive wandering the streets of a remote sub-tropical entrepot. Even to rent a car I would have to show my passport and fill in a form that the authorities would have access to.

When the *suk*'s shutters start rattling up I wander the covered alleys of booths that offer bolts of cloth, spices, wristwatches, "perfumes, shoeses, gifts". The proprietors sit crosslegged in their chairs and the strings of the Egyptian ensemble on their transistor radios scramble after one another like a frightened mob. For Frances I buy a packet of incense in resinous globules: at least the nuns will approve.

At sundown prayer I emerge opposite the concrete tower that houses Orient Sales and Trading and take myself straight to the eleventh floor. The Indian behind the desk is extremely fragile and dark in his damask shirt. He seems startled. "Regrettably Mr Apramian is not in."

"Does he perhaps have an assistant?"

"I am Mr Apramian's assistant here."

No sounds come from beyond the partition or the two frosted glass doors. A calendar of hardly credible Swiss mountains hangs beside the Indian's desk, a cactus stands on it, a row of twinlock files backs it. Nothing is given away.

"When is Mr Apramian expected?"

"He will come soon."

"This evening?"

"Maybe this evening."

"Does he normally come in the evening?"

"When he is in Dubai."

"Is he in Dubai?"

"May I know your good name?"

"Goode."

"If Mr Apramian will be here, you can come this evening." Such a statement, it seems to me, is no less a racial characteristic than skin pigment.

"So you don't know when he will be coming to the office?"

"I think you are from England, Mr Goode."

Two can play at tangents. I enquire, "Do you have any sort of prospectus outlining your services?"

"We are import-export. Also for the fishing trade."

"Nothing on paper . . ."

"You can speak with Mr Apramian."

"I have some goods coming from Bulgaria." I watch him carefully. "I would like your company to handle them for me."

"You have no shipping agent, Mr Goode?"

"These are special goods. Mr Apramian was recommended by a friend."

"Which friend?"

"A friend in Switzerland."

"Ah, a friend in Switzerland." Extremely delicate fingers toy with a pen. From somewhere beyond a telex machine jerks into life. "As a rule, we have our own agents for handling goods."

"You've dealt with Bulgarian goods before, surely." I make a little show of impatience. "I haven't been misinformed, have I?"

"I cannot tell." It is like trying to catch the soap in the bath.

His frailty, the twig-like fingers as snappable as the pen, make exasperation easier to summon: "Have I come all this way to be told that Mr Apramian has no dealings with Bulgaria? Am I to tell Mr Apramian I could not be obliged with a simple answer to a simple question?"

"He can take goods from Bulgaria, why not?"

"You mean, 'does'?"

"Also many other countries." He has centuries of the hectoring sahib.

"And you are telling me it is impossible to make an appointment to discuss this consignment with Mr Apramian?"

"How is this possible for me? Tell me!" Damasked arms fly open in a careful puff of temper and I can smell his scent.

I make as to leave. "If people kept regular hours . . ." I pontificate, and declare that I cannot be back for several days.

"You may leave your number," the Indian says testily, knowing he has won. "I will pass it to Mr Apramian."

"I'm staying with friends. I don't have any number with me."

Outside, the petty merchants and shopkeepers are emerging from sundown prayer in the mosques with the inner rightness with the world of those who have had a good crap. Until the next setting of the sun they may accumulate anew an unspirituality worth purging.

Driving into the hinterland Oliver Mullins is saying, "If you do it that way, old chap, they'll never catch up with you." The Chevrolet reeks of insecticide.

"Who?"

"Who what?"

"Who won't catch up with me?"

"Inland Revenue, of course. They've got nothing to get a grip on."

"I suppose not," I concede.

"The whole thing about Liberia, you don't have to file any returns. Nothing on paper anywhere. My directors are both on Sark. Trustees in the Isle of Man. It's a doddle, actually. You don't have anything to do with any of it. Except control the account, ha ha. Nobody knows about that."

"Nobody?"

"Except at the bank, of course." Like the confessional, banks are vowed to secrecy. It could be that this clown is part of no footling conspiracy but his own: unlike Apramian's clerk, Timmy's ripples have not yet reached him. "That's why I bank a bit outlandish, old chap, just to be sure. All banks are a bit of a shambles. Jumped up moneylenders, really. I always give my instructions two ways. Then there's a chance of getting them carried out. Otherwise, no way."

"What makes you do it?" I enquire.

"Meaning?"

"Keep on making money. Dodging tax."

"Oh, the kiddies. Don't you have kiddies?"

"My wife's got our child."

"Separated?"

"You could put it like that."

"Sounds a real balls-up, old chap."

"It is, in a way."

"Except for my kiddies, I doubt if I could stay in this rat race."

"So when they're grown up, they'll have this nice pile of money abroad . . ."

"Look, old chap," Mullins says. "If it wasn't for a few people like me, British industry would be flat on its back, but flat. Three quarters of the goods I sell are British. Half anyway.

141

I'm as patriotic as the next man. Part of one's patriotic duty is to discourage the jolly old Treasury dishing out to layabouts, wouldn't you say? Or perhaps you wouldn't." An aggrieved note has crept in. "You don't say much."

"Sorry?"

"You'll think me an awful cad saying so, Goode, you sound too clean for comfort."

"No, no," I protest. "I'm not clean. Don't mistake me. I wasn't criticising in the least."

5

They will get me over the visa. It has four days to run: I must
renew, or quit the country, otherwise they come looking for
me for contravening immigration law. Easy to find a stray
Englishman in a place like this. And anyway tomorrow,
Friday, I have to break surface in Khor shaikhdom to meet this
Wilks.

Can Offshore Ollie be a watcher? The eyes enquire nothing,
the spent mouth and lurching laugh indicate a clownishness
covering up not duplicity but a sort of futility . . . After an
evening meal decanted from a tin onto Tupperware he takes
me on a tour of his dusty yellow machines in their acreage of
wilderness, extolling them one by one as if together they form
an exotic tree-garden to a perverted god. He introduces me to
bewildered Thai mechanics as the friend from "home" with
whom he shoots birds, and he performs a prolonged mime of
this traditional English blood-bond – "pah! pah!" Pheasants
fall against an Arabian dusk.

Later in the bleak pre-fab mess, alone with me over the
Carlsberg Special Brew, he grows subdued: when he returns
home from these trips abroad, building something up for the
kiddies, his wife seems – how can he put it? – not awfully keen.
Is she having it away with a certain chap? His voice becomes
oddly clipped so that I wonder how much he cares: then the
low balding brow, which has begun to peel where it caught the
sun, puckers fiercely, and suddenly the piggy eyes are wet and
blinking hard.

In the morning he arranges to lend me a Datsun pick-up for
my drive down the coast to the Khor shaikhdom. He worries
about me, a lone compatriot without a contract. "Wish I could
do more, old chap. Good luck. I really mean it. Oh, and I say"
– he dives into his Chevvy parked alongside – "if you have
trouble with the crawlies, get 'em with this johnny." He
thrusts across a purple cannister of Piff-paff. "Watch 'em die,"
he grins, waving me off with globs of unexpended love.

143

Hoardings sprouting in the desert announce each minuscule national identity as one shaikhdom gives way to another: Sanyo, Hush Puppies, English biscuits fresh delicious tasty, Gulfa Healthy Water . . . and all at once on a similar board a green, gold and black flag and in Nashk and English script Khor's peeling motto: *Eternal Values – Dynamic Progress*. A series of signs herald a 100-Bedroom First Class Hotel, but the slip-road off the highway is blocked by rusty oil-drums and the hotel rears beyond with blind windows, a great dun monument to eternal values and dynamic progress abandoned by unpaid contractors amid its dust and sand and *rimth* bushes.

Across a bold bridge spanning the inlet that is the shaikhdom's *raison d'être*, the cramped little town overflows walls built in a previous century when it was a pirate's haven . . . but hesitantly, amid piles of rubble. Unused, unsurfaced roads lead only to a planner's expectation. Goats share the town with their owners, munching through cement bags and packing cases, jumbling the Arabs' hand-me-down Japanese and American cars and the Indians' bicycles. I nose my pick-up through a mesh of alleys and bazaars, shuttered for Friday mosque-time. Nothing is distinguishable . . . Scientechnic, Ali Baba Home Dressers, Yar Mouk Electrical Maker . . . "If you get to the corniche, Mr Guise," Mrs Wilks' classy voice instructed on the telephone, "you'll know you've overshot" – and I do get there, finding only rubble, root-pits for palms in the paving and no palms, and the opaline sea beyond; and where the corniche is abruptly barriered I turn to the nearest large edifice. It proves to be another hotel, this time in operation, quirkily named the Cornish Hotel. In a patch of ferocious sunlight an unmistakeably English drunk rocks on his feet to steady the world.

The Indian receptionist offers several choices as possible residences for Mr Grover Wilks. But one floor up, in the Churchill Bar, Facilities for Club Members Dance Dominoes, where the holy day's devotional boozing has already begun for the local ex-pats on contract, I get my instructions, at the price of accepting liquor. "Grover Wilks," a beer-fisted Geordie in a Bugs Bunny shirt has evidence, "knows more about this Shaikhdom than the Shaikh himself." Loyalty flares with inexplicable swiftness, like a fungoid growth. "This Shaikhdom, may I call you Tony," the Bugs Bunny informant speaks for all present, "this Shaikhdom is the best bloody Shaikhdom in the entire bloody Gulf."

Ahmed the servant admits me by the townside entrance. I follow him up the cool stone stairway, narrow and steep, to the long and elegant *majlis*.

The figure of Lucy Wilks silhouetted against the fretted *mashrabiyya* window – even before she turns about flowers in hand to greet her guest – jolts me with such force that I fear, taking her free hand, she must surely detect it. "You're really perfectly timed, Mr Guise," she drawls. "Which means, Arabia being what it is, that nobody else is ready except you and me." She smiles and her brown eyes dance with fun. "Ahmed – *qahwa* for Mr Guise. We drink Turkish – will that do? Now, you *really* shouldn't have come in a suit. Please take off your jacket and tie. Grover would be horrified. He refuses to wear suits out here – even for the Shaikh . . ."

In her high-necked cotton dress beside the prehistoric earthen vessel between arched windows, she whose voice I first heard as a playful yelp and then a single gull-like mew only sharper, ecstatic, over the moonlit surf, completes the disposal of flowers. "Your arriving on time doesn't mean you're quite new to Arabia?"

"I stopped over once or twice in ancient times."

"Ah well – then we have nothing to surprise you. And you're an agricultural economist, what a mouthful. It sounds immensely learned, and I'm sure we need you here." Her self-command is flawless: her ignorance of what I know instantly valuable. "I once met a young man writing a thesis on the 'political economy of meaning' – definitely that way round. I expect you know him."

"I don't believe I do."

"It's a pity I can't remember who he was because it must be so lonely for him. Perhaps Grover knows all about agricultural economy – it's the sort of thing he would. Where *is* Grover? On Fridays he does everything in slow motion. He's probably conducting the picnic in the kitchen. Are you musical, Mr Guise?"

"J'aime Brahms."

She laughs charmingly. "I somehow thought you would.

145

You see, Grover loves conducting things. Don't tell him you play or sing or anything, or we'll never get away. Now . . ."

I know I have stumbled on something: it is like a little vision given by God to those he chooses. I force myself to keep calm, sit back, admire the fine local artefacts around me, the high graceful Arab room . . .

". . . We're off up the coast for lunch, or down, depending on your point of view – towards the straits, anyway, just where the Shaikhdom meets the Emirate. There's been this awful oil slick: we want to find out if the turtles have survived. We thought we'd go by boat – there's a friend with boats galore. We might cross the line into Emirate territory, so Grover's arranged with a little man he knows from that side to meet us there at lunchtime and make that all right: Wadi Fransi, we call him – Billy French. Did I tell you? It's a bit sensitive on the border. You know the place next door at all?"

"No."

"I'm not surprised. It's difficult to go to and fro, specially for us pinko-greys. Anyway, we've got the Fountains coming with us – d'you know Nigel? – he's our man in Dubai, *ours*, mind, not Grover's (my husband's American, I hope somebody warned you!). And then there's little Ismail Barzakh coming, *if* he arrives – you really never quite know with Arabs, much as I'm devoted to them, though Ismail's quite almost one of us. He was with Reuters in Aden, as he'll tell you himself I'm sure, and now he runs a little magazine in the Emirates which is meant to be radical. They keep threatening to shut it down for running articles about the palm groves going to pot, that kind of thing. It's really quite harmless. You'll be able to talk to him about agricultural economy." Her world seems populated by people smaller than herself, engaged in lesser tasks than comprise her own life. "Now, I do believe, here's somebody else."

In fact it is everybody: first Ismail Barzakh, protestingly ushered ahead by Nigel Fountain with both hands, and then Fountain's tall lady who calls her greeting from the door – "Lucé, this was a too marvellous idea."

"We gathered up Mr Barzakh in your front yard," Fountain says.

Mrs Wilks performs the introductions. Philippa Fountain

moves as if whaleboned. "Now, Ismail, do you know Mr Guise by chance? He is a visiting agricultural economist. Mr Barzakh is our famous journalist, as I was telling you."

"Journalist and author," Barzakh corrects brightly, shaking my hand.

And then Nigel Fountain, silver-haired, distinguished, in a shirt from Lillywhite's: "What was the name?" The negligible smile does not reach his eyes. "Guise? – " The fine head which I know from the back tilts for amplification: I vouchsafe the Christian name. The smile withers. "Another journalist?"

"There used to be a chap who writes," I tell him.

"This one's an agricultural economist," Lucy Wilks confirms, "come to see how we're doing. Grover – where the hell is Grover? It's so *typical*." She moves decisively onto the inner balcony and we hear her calling *Grover – what on earth are you doing? Everybody's here.*

Philippa Fountain is enquiring, So you are staying in the Shaikhdoms, Mr Guise? "It's purely exploratory at this stage." Fountain has asked in a flat voice, what does Mr Guise mean by exploratory? when Wilks enters, mildly distracted, fey, sandals flopping . . . "Hail, plenipotentiary, *ahlan wa sahlan* – and Madame potentiary." Enjoying his late entry. "Hi-ya, Ismail." Wilks crosses to touch Mrs Fountain with the "Common Market kiss" on both cheeks and finds himself beside – "Ah! A stranger in our midst. You must be Mr Guise. I apologise for plunging you into all this" – he indicates the company – "I can't always stop my wife. I'm not enough for her . . . She can't do without an extra man or two. Ismail – I'd have thought you'd be enough. You know Ismail Barzakh, Mr Guise? He's our *enfant terrible*, not so *terrible* really and certainly not *enfant*." He daintily lifts a lock of Barzakh's black hair (with auburn glints) to check on its roots.

"I was asking Mr Guise about his investigations here," Fountain says.

"What investigations?"

"A preliminary survey," I intervene. "Agricultural economy."

"Oh God," Wilks groans. "Not another preliminary survey. This coast is knee deep in preliminary surveys."

"Commissioned?" Fountain enquires.

147

"The initiative was primarily mine."

" 'Primarily'," he echoes, and in the soft mouth I catch the fragmentary smile, another shard just worth bending for.

"You've come ten years too late, Mr Guise," Wilks declares. "There's nothing I can possibly tell you that hasn't already been said. They all come to me for an *aperçu*. God knows why. I'll give it all to you now. Shall I?" He appeals to his little audience.

"Go it, Grover," Barzakh abets.

"This coast is an impossibly dry salty place where the good God intended nobody to live except for a few pirates and smugglers and of course the odd raving Englishman" – a *moue* at Fountain – "until he thought he'd make a joke. So he programmed-in half the world's reserves of petroleum and had a bunch of greedy idiots from my country and yours come and discover it. The local inhabitants get so rich they can't move for the stuff, think the smart thing is have an *agriculture*. For thousands of years they've been content to live off their animals and the sea – except for the odd date palm. The fact is practically nothing ever did or ever will grow here unless you stand over it with a parasol and a watering can three hundred and sixty-five days a year. It's far cheaper and easier to fly the whole diet in from California daily."

An inane grin spreads at applause unsounded.

"There you have it, Mr Guise," Barzakh says and Fountain offers "No comment" with a smirk.

"I promise to ask no questions," I assure Wilks lightly. "I'll just give in my letter and eat my lunch, which your wife impetuously asked me to."

"What letter?"

"A little letter of introduction to you from Mr Proctor of the British Bank."

"Oh, old Presto Procto." Wilks seems relieved. "Don't worry now. Give it me later."

"What *are* you all doing?" Lucy Wilks has returned to stand in the doorway, hands on hips.

"We're putting Mr Guise at his ease," Wilks says.

"Half the day's gone already," his wife declares. "All the turtles will be stone dead by the time we get there. And poor little Wadi Fransi too. Nigel, we take your Range Rover to the quayside, right? We can all fit in if we leave your driver here with Ahmed."

"Both Hadramautis," Wilks puts in. "They can plot the counter-revolution."

"Now Mr Guise, you look strong . . ."

She dispenses states of mind and tasks with equal authority. In twenty minutes she has us all at the jetty beyond the inlet and hampers and canvas chairs disposed beneath an awning for'ard on the convex deck of an Arab *boum*. It has no name, just the Arabic number 97. One dark crewman tends the "diesel" below, the other mans a tiller resembling a gibbet. The thunderbox suspended over the stern inspires predictable wit. A cordial of fresh limes from the mountains is distributed in tumblers and half a mile out slipping northwards at ten knots in a tranquil sea and the mountains' horizon gradually sharpening to our right, our party purveys a shadowless contentment.

"What part of the country d'you come from, Mr Guise?"

"Bucks."

"You mean – sort of Amersham?" she frowns despite her dark glasses.

"More north Bucks."

This adjusts the image.

"Bicester country?"

"Grafton, actually."

"Oh, lovely," she says. "Cousins of mine were Masters of the Grafton for half a century. Right up to after the war. Then they started dying at the wrong time and to all intents and purposes went bust." Soon she has paraded a row of tin-soldier landed acquaintances common to us both whom we rearrange and turn about on their dinky square stands. It is their flaws she knows – social, financial, personal: but what would *they* have to say about that night beach and their Lucy with her swart Armenian involved in assassination and smuggling arms? She exudes an illusion of power, and I suppose that even illusory power is corrupting. Few of those we mention escape reduction to various degrees of littleness, on account of being common or poor or boring or weak. Perhaps it was why she married this surprising American: so few of the available young Englishmen on horseback could

149

have passed muster on all counts. "Doesn't the Grafton have an awful lot of wire fences?" she wants to know.

There are more wire fences every year, I mourn. Sophia foxhunts, not I who (one of the weak, or wet) could no longer hide from myself my dread of the quarry's death.

"We know all about wire," she sympathises. "We've always gone out with the Pytchley. You see, before I married this Wilks" – poking her sunglasses at her husband, in lively conversation with Barzakh – "I was a Willoughby." She says it as if it ought to explain a lot.

It is like a dark stage-set in which by a change of light a central feature is seen to be something quite other than what was supposed: a tree, for instance, a devilish figure that can take action. All at once the sense of active darkness is precise: the very smell of old Mrs Lunt's front hall comes back, where the Visitors' Book lay – the saddlesoap, the yapping corgies. I see the names again . . . Captain St. J. Evans, the Smiths and the Smythes and Schultz and P. Constantinidi, the Hon. E. Browne. It is a marvel what a certain kind of fear can print on the human brain.

I spell it out as I recall it – "O-U-G-H-B-Y?"

"Heavens no, O-W-B-Y."

"Oh," I say, "the Northamptonshire Willowbys." Willoughby/Willowby – a patent deceit of the moment. I see the small and pretty hand that wrote the name: I see it now, bronzed, firm and feminine, clutching her glasses.

"Yes, I told you: Pytchley country." Further out to sea the tankers slide by, tiny too, more toys fetching toy fuel for a toy world. Toy princes from toy palaces dying their little deaths.

I have never heard of the Willowbys – except for her. There was no letter from "L. Willoughby" in the Keeper's batch: it puzzled me. "Useful for monograms," I comment. "You don't have to change your brushes when you get married."

"One really doesn't have monogrammed hairbrushes as a woman," she says. "Your wife doesn't surely?"

"My wife . . ."

"You have a wife?" She has scented a weakness, like her Pytchley hounds.

"Marriage is a dreadfully dangerous business."

"You don't have to tell *me*," she laughs.

I shift the conversation on. "One must have a boat out here," I presume.

"Luckily one has this friend."

"Lends you the boat?"

"Owns lots of these little cargo *boums* and fishing boats. Usually one to spare for us when we want."

"I see it has radio."

"People out here can be quite sophisticated, you know."

"He doesn't come with you?"

"Sonny? Yes, sometimes." She has slipped her glasses on again.

"Not interested in turtles?"

"Oh, he's busy. He likes to think he's a tycoon – cargoes in and out. But I tell him, the Kanoos and the Darwishes could swallow him in a single bite." She makes snap with her jaw: the mouth is what the ladies' journals call sensuous, but determined in the lines that surround it.

"A local Arab?"

"Far from it. Far from it."

"I'm surprised these chaps let an outsider into something like local shipping, import-export, whatever."

"Oh look – dolphins, surely." She strains leeward. I cannot be sure if I detect any disturbance of the water. I let her scan the sea through field glasses undisturbed and I think, Is my amphora taking shape at last? – these fragmentary gifts, from base and lip and shoulder? But what is its function, and from what arcane culture, rooted in corruption?

"Terrible about your young prince here."

"Ghastly," she affirms, not removing the field glasses.

I wonder if it is not arcane after all, but the way of the world writ bold and clear? I remember Timmy's boast about "All's fair in love and war" meaning that wherever morality might count for most man recognised the right to abandon it. If, say, for some tangle of love you need to kill a prince . . .

"We read about it at home, of course," I say.

"Was there much?"

"Not much. Being just an accident."

"Ghastly," she repeats. Is there a tiny movement of the head negating the deed – the merest quiver of heavy hair on freckled shoulders? I remark that it would have been a different matter if Saqr had been Shaikh already . . . or if somebody else had shot him.

"I suppose it would," she says, scanning the mountains now.

"New chap any good?"

"We do the best we can. *Vive le roi*, you know."

According to Timmy it was only "the pathetic obstinacy of the weak" that insisted on seeking God's love in a creation to which He was indifferent. Mankind operated on instinctive urges: self-preservation, the power urge, the reproductive urge (like this woman, he is childless). If certain behaviour was barred, it was only to keep society on the rails, not to satisfy God . . . though sometimes the urges could take the *form* of loving God, "in which there's as much vice," he once riposted, "as lusting for a whore. I'll grant you it's an ecstasy, Anthony – for which man will commit the most outrageous crimes of all." Loving Sophia for her purity, I hid her from him.

"Rough luck on Timothy Lunt," I observe. And mark the pause.

"Why particularly, Mr Guise?"

We have the sea to gaze at, and the closing line of mountains leeward. She is part of my seascape, but I am not of hers. I lower my voice to escape others' attention.

"Saqr dying like that, on his estate."

"The luck of the game," she says.

"Know that part of the world at all?"

"Which?"

"North Wales."

"No."

"They don't hunt there."

"I rather believe they don't," she confirms lazily, as if sleep not exposure might be prowling. It has its own honesty, this amorality – a refinement that seems the reverse of Jesus' sanctity when offered as evidence that men can be angels. Under such delusion a selflessness like Sophia's dries and cakes to domestic martyrdom, loving-kindness to possessiveness. Jesus himself perceived all men as rooted in sin, and always loved the sinner most readily – loved him not only for his repentance but for the honesty that preceded it.

"Timothy Lunt must come out here, I suppose. Part of his

beat, the Shaikhdoms."

"Abu Dhabi," she says, stretching a leg. "Hardly us. We wouldn't signify." She has pretty legs: sockless in her espadrilles, they are innocent like a child's.

In the field of crime these are amateurs, I can see that. Gifted perhaps, brainy; capable of simple errors, like myself. I am aware of a complicity with this lady. Professionals have had roles too, of course, but more distantly – like Alwyn Rhys's Russian contact, standing well clear lest the amateurs bungle the fusee.

I glimpse her eyes from the side, behind her sunglasses. They are lightly closed now. I can pick up fragments of the others' talk over the slap and wash of the bows. Hamood's name is mentioned, and "Emir". Fountain is engaged in a lot of nodding assent with whatever Wilks has to say. Barzakh seems animated like a monkey, and Mrs Fountain regards him with half-humorous condescension as if asked to hold him on a string and not sure which way he might jump.

6

We can see Billy French on the skyline almost before we have swung round to enter the cove. The mountains meet the sea here, and that means our party has sailed beyond the *de facto* territorial line between Shaikhdom and the Emirate – a line the Shaikhdom still disputes even though the British secured ruffianly rulers' consent to it over a century ago. Field glasses are passed from hand to hand and Wilks remarks, "He's got a couple of his tribesmen with him." His wife adds, "Watch out for his handshake, Phil. It's a bone-cracker." And then: "He's really a perfectly harmless little man but he does absolutely love his tribesmen" – a two-part comment whose "but" has me wondering. We can see him descending the precipitous crags to the narrow beach at the creek's head like a mountain goat: his men stay up. "How can he do it in this heat?" Fountain protests, perhaps to excuse his own sweat-patched shirt from Lillywhite's.

We drop anchor thirty yards from shore and are paddled in by the tillerman in a rubber dinghy, three by three, I in the second party with Barzakh and Mrs Fountain. Neither she nor her husband has passed a word to me since we set out two hours earlier. Gobs of emulsified oil float like symptoms of plague. "Billy Fransi," Barzakh volunteers, "is Grover's old friend. Together they keep the border quiet between them. If this part of the world blows up, Mr Guise, run for it. You saw the tankers?"

"Exactly," Mrs Fountain says rigidly.

I haven't arrived naked. I know what the common man has a right to know, from books and newspaper clippings, journals of learned societies, digests of foreign broadcasts. Half the world has an interest in the twisting entrance to this Gulf, and the greatest and local powers especially. The Russians did their damnedest to make something of the peninsula's so-called Independence Movement, with little packets of cash and explosives, until its sparsely educated following took fright

154

and fled along the coast for refuge in the Shaikhdom ten years ago. Washington now fancied to designate the strait an "international waterway", but Moscow, remembering Suez, would have none of that.

Though man-spilled oil has already crept in, human presence on the tiny beach between its ramparts of rock seems an intrusion. French has recced it for us, sussed out the very best flat and shady spot to lay out the picnic, gathered a pile of driftwood and twigs for a fire, found a sand-floored rock chamber where the ladies can sunbathe secluded. He is brisk and active. Lucy wouldn't let him carry her in from the dinghy but jumped out the other side where he couldn't touch her, skipping through the wavelets up the beach. But Mrs Fountain is glad of his strong hand and firm shoulder.

Fountain isn't exactly Curzon, but he is Britain's man from along the coast and insofar as this is Emirate territory Billy French is a kind of host. Perhaps he should have laid on live turtles for his visitors, but there are only shells of past years' eggs like burst ping-pong balls. "If they'd been back here this year, you'd see the flipper marks on the sand," he explains earnestly, as if their absence made a kind of international point that might get back to Whitehall in Fountain's next despatch. "Now sir, how's that for your lady?" He has folded an Arab headcloth on a low rock.

Lucy Wilks says, "Do we really need the fire, Billy? We've got the coffee in a thermos." And he answers at once, "Not to worry, we'll light it another time." He cannot quite bring himself to call her Lucy, though once she had invited him to.

He was not expecting me and mistakes me for some kind of *aide-de-camp* to Fountain until the diplomat brusquely disabuses him over the white wine and prawns: "Up to today, Mr French, Mr Guise and I were not acquainted."

"He came to see *me*, Billy," Wilks puts in. "We're just being kind to him. He says he's an agricultural bod. You tell him about turtles. They're food. He'll put them in his 'preliminary survey'."

"Be nice to Mr Guise, Grover," his wife chides. "He's all alone among strangers."

"There were turtles hereabouts two years ago and no mistake," French insists. "If the gents would like to swim with

155

me round that point of rock after lunch, we can look at the next cove." They are not interested. "I really don't think in all this *oil*," Lucy Wilks demurs, though I recall she could be less fastidious. "What about sharks?" Mrs Fountain asks. French cracks, "They don't eat British subjects, Mrs Fountain," and Grover adds languidly, "Rules me out, Billy."

"I'm not a marine animal," Barzakh declares. "I am land. You know what my name means, Lucy?" She confesses ignorance. "Isthmus," he announces. "I am Mr Ismail Isthmus, Editor *New Age*, Abu Dhabi, late of Reuters News Agency, British Aden Protectorate."

"A spiritual isthmus," Wilks corrects, "surely."

"We have in our midst a true scholar." Barzakh delightedly raises his tumbler. "It means truly 'the way across'. That is, what we take to be the here-and-now, correctly seen according to our divine writings, is no more than a passing from one state of existence to a greater reality."

"What's that meant to mean, Ismail?" Wilks says.

"It's the same in your religion, Grover. You know the inscription that the Moghul Akbar has put across the portal of the mosque, *our* mosque, at Fatehpur?" He looks at each. "No chance," French puts in. "I tell you. 'Thus said Jesus upon whom be peace: The world is a bridge; pass over it, but build no house upon it.' That is your Christian *barzakh*!"

"Not mine," Wilks retorts.

Fountain expresses "relative satisfaction" with the here and now, motioning to the picnic, the cove, the deceptive sea, the skein of tankers on the horizon – and beyond it, presumably, a comfy pension and a sinecure in the bag with his phoney masonry for "Global Reconciliation": the establishment's world on its courses. He accords Lucy a little embrace with his wrist, on account of prawny fingers.

"What do you think, Mrs Ambassador?" Barzakh asks.

"Provided Nigel's happy," she smiles, intending a little joke. Her digestion is quite good now, menopause defeated at last, her children a credit to her. Entering "intellectual" conversations is always a risk.

"Mr Billy Fransi looks for the deeper mysteries," Barzakh says. "Am I right?"

"Well," French replies gravely, "there's the Bermuda

Triangle." No-one responds, but after a pause Barzakh says, "Exactly. And Mr Guise?"

I hesitate, and in the moment's silence they can guess I have a God, like a secret vice.

"Is this your own celery, Lucy?" Philippa Fountain needs to know. "Mine goes so woody."

But Barzakh's eyes are still buttoned on me and at length I quote Victoria Sackville-West, that there can be no fundamental blemish in a creation of such unimaginable magnitude and invention. "Blemish?" Barzakh echoes.

"Corruption . . . evil."

"Really, Mr Guise? You surprise me," Lucy Wilks says. "I would have supposed you'd have thought rather the opposite."

"There was a snake in that very first garden," Wilks observes. "But then the Egyptians made it their symbol of wisdom – put it slap bang in the middle of the Pharaoh's forehead." He tosses back the lemon he has been squeezing. "If you could only hear yourselves. You're all so God-ridden. Most of the troubles of man can be traced to the inability of the human race to be straight with itself. People invent other worlds because they don't have courage enough for this one." It has the ring of Timothy Lunt.

" 'Courage enough'?" I query.

"Courage to accept it and act in it boldly."

"Most people don't have the chance to act in it boldly."

"Don't they, Mr Guise? You can hold up a jumbo jet with a penknife."

Barzakh says, "If everyone did that, we would be short of airlines."

"My point, Ismail, is that only very few are capable of honesty, fewer still act on it."

"You mean capable of lacking morality," I suggest.

"Oh you good *good* man. It's a disease, Mr Guise."

"Our host sounds like a devotee of Nietzsche."

The silence preceding Wilks' lazy retort is distinct. "Look at my poor dear USA, bumbling about in this part of the world with the best of intentions. What does it all produce? An utterly pointless war raging for years at one end of the Gulf, and tension all the way down to here – and beyond." He nods

up the coast, the last fifty miles. "My compatriots' inde-
fatigable *morality*." He shakes his head with the absurdity.

"God save America!" Barzakh says.

"You illustrate my point, Ismail. Why God? America can
save itself, but it won't. There's nobody with the will."

"Is this the British point of view, Ambassador?"

But Wilks takes Barzakh's question. "The British can't
afford a point of view."

French looks expectantly at Fountain, who smiles in his
distinguished way and licks his fingers. The food excels, the
banter stimulates.

"Surely – " French begins, and as they look at him he knows
he is out of his depth.

"In a sensitive area like this," Fountain says, "our policy is
not to rock the boat."

"Oh my God, Nigel."

"Listen to Grover calling on the name of the Maker,"
Barzakh exclaims.

The others have taken a dip – all but Barzakh whose dye would
run: he remains fully clothed, settled under a rock to write.
The rest doze in shade or sun – Lucy a gleaming brown
already. Doesn't her bodily aptness, her zest beside Wilks'
scraggy languor, betray that another man fuels her? But sex
can be so contrary in the partnerships it makes, like God who
picks a disreputable non-entity to show his love. As we
breast-stroke towards the point, French speculates: Wouldn't
I quite fancy a piece of her? And I reply, I wouldn't be the first
to try.

"It'd be the kiss of death," he says unexpectedly. "She'd
bleed you white. She'd feed you up and slaughter you. 'Won't
you have *any* choccy cake, Billy?' " he mimicks through his
nose. "Normally I don't eat lunch . . . You had a go then?"

"I only met her today."

"She was giving you the look."

Exploratory swims take longer than foreseen. He is a
laboured swimmer, and slowed by his khaki shorts – he
brought no swimming garment. I feel I have known him a long
time.

We wade up the next little beach amid evidence of recent
turtles – the laborious pattern of females' flippers to the high

sand hatchery and its detritus of ping-pong balls, the stitched trails of offspring scuttling for the water. "You know their great enemy, Tony? Foxes. The foxes dig up the eggs and eat 'em by the dozen. Some of these made it to the sea, lucky little buggers."

We are squatting at the top of the secluded beach, which the high ground has thrown into shadow. I enquire, "The name Apramian mean anything to you? Runs fishing boats out of Dubai. Other boats too. Owns the *boum* we came on."

"Come again?"

"Apramian. 'Sonny' Apramian."

"I've heard them refer to him, Grover and her. 'Sonny'. Yes. Something between her and him?"

"Why do you say that?"

"Trains of thought."

"How well d'you know the Wilkses?"

"Grover and me are opposite numbers. Except of course, he's much bigger fry, much much bigger fry. He could walk straight in to see the old Shaikh without knocking. You won't catch me doing that with my Emir. He's never heard of Billy French, never will – I'll be lucky if I see him a hundred yards off at the going-home parade."

"What about Grover's new boy?"

"Hamood? A funny one by all accounts. If anyone can handle him, Grover can."

"What makes you say that?"

"One hears things."

"Such as?"

"Hamood has his favourites, you know. Likes to reward them with a bit of land. Services rendered. Grover has to square the locals. One of his chores. It's crown land, mind you – most of the Shaikhdom. But there's always locals with rights. Even this bloody beach. You'd be surprised."

"How long's Grover been doing these 'chores'?"

"Got a bit worse after the old man started going downhill. Since Saqr shot himself, poor silly sod. Hamood's a handful. One of his fancy-boys crashed a beautiful new Mercedes up near my border and the tribesmen found him scraping the broken glass off of him with a wad of hundred-dirham notes." He frowns at the sea. "But what you got to realize, Tony, is the

159

Shaikhdom has access to federal money. The tribes like that. We don't have so much – nothing like, to be honest."

"You don't need much money up in the mountains."

"We don't *need* it – 'course we don't. It'll destroy my tribesmen – look at the Shaikhdoms. But they want it. They want the bright lights, the Toyotas, the grog. Ninety per cent of the mountain tribesmen are mine, but they know all about the Shaikhdoms. There's a special brigade of the federal army supposedly for blokes from Grover's Shaikhdom, but my tribesmen go and join it and find themselves right up on my border facing the wrong way: against their mums and dads. Twelve miles from where we're sitting." His thumb indicates where. "Then they come back to my-side villages on leave and sit up all night telling their nearest and dearest how bloody marvellous the Shaikhdoms are. I love my tribesmen, Tony." He tugs at the tuft on his cheek. "Can't let 'em down whatever. They were somebody's gift to me." He tugs away at his cheek. "Makes me weep to see them sell their souls for a load of breeze blocks and a diesel bloody pump. They go for all the b-s."

"Trouble just now?"

"Get away, Tony. There's *always* trouble. Smouldering, you know, smouldering. One day it could just go *wump!* – can't tell when. Nobody can. I don't like the feel of it just now, since you ask. We had a real set-back, few weeks ago, a real big one and it's been jumpy ever since . . . After five years I persuaded them to fly in a water party from the capital and the third day out they get blown up – wiped out. The *third day.*" Narrating the event he has to stop, to recover, and I think, there's a man who takes his responsibilities too much to heart, a liability in any civil service . . . "Mind you, it'd be a lot worse if it wasn't for Grover. Grover's a brick. If I hadn't gone to see him, and he hadn't gone up the *jebel*, in the shit I'd be, and all my woolly-tops defecting to that piss-artist Hamood. I could do with a drag, Tony."

On our swim back the rock bluff and the bastions of higher rock behind shift fractionally in line of sight with each thrust of legs and arms. Then the figures on the top come into view, head and shoulders silhouetted – French's waiting tribesmen and a third figure with them, Grover Wilks. "He's a sight more agile than you'd credit, is Grover," French comments. "Lord knows where we'd be without him." The sun begins to colour the high rocks subtly.

"Billy – what would you say if Saqr had been murdered?"

"Why? Was he?"

"Supposing you were told he was, what would you think?"

"Anything can happen. Along this bloody coast. Look at us, swimming in oil."

"Seriously."

"If I was told that for a cert, I'd say it was Hamood."

"Hamood up to organising something like that?"

"These funny ones can be dead wily. Saqr was out shooting with the minister, wassername. Right? You reckon somebody picked him off?"

"Before I answer, will you promise something?"

"That depends."

"You'll say nothing to anybody, unless I personally give you permission."

"Not even my old woman? Elaine's tight as a tomb."

"Nobody at all."

"Okay, Tony. Scout's honour."

I tell him just the fact of the murder, nothing more.

7

That evil is at work around me is apparent. But its source – its intention? Often you cannot see the obvious for the looking – cannot recognise God, for instance, for requiring a definition; or because you insist on a rendezvous, he has always gone before you arrive . . .

A genuine sympathy exudes from Offshore Ollie. "You shoo-er you're all right, old chap? You don't look awfully good. You know, I always try not to think about anything on a Friday." He has been at the Carlsberg Special Brew much of the day, killing flies. "There isn't much worth thinking about these days anyway."

The pouchy cheeks and heavy lids of Grover Wilks keep returning through Ollie Mullins' vapourings like a spectre on a foggy moorland. Wilks does not hold together. Spindly and hollow-chested, up the tricky sea-cliffs to seek out French's tribesmen; the fey musician, who according to his wife "can't bear blood", turning back repeatedly to naked force, power by violence, the blade at the pilot's jugular . . . *Let's face it, Nigel, it gets physical* (when the talk touched on the mid-Eastern *Putsch*) – *I mean, when Wadi Fransi's old Emir went, it wasn't done over a cup of tea, old boy*, hamming an English accent, *it was bang-bang all over the palace for a couple of minutes* . . . but relishing the imagination of it. And so sensitive, vigilant a cuckold, regaling his friends with his wife on her lover's boat . . . *Oh, she'd be stuck without Sonny – he fixes all the airfreighting of her fabrics and furniture* . . . and keeps her so damned cute. Complicity is unmistakeable between her and Grover. Years ago I learned through Timmy that evil was the active negation of the natural order, which was full of the glory of God, as the prayer-book had it. The difference in kind between things temporal and things eternal only emerged in elevating the first in defiance of the second.

"Tell you something, old chap," Ollie Mullins is confiding, "when you've a cheque to collect out here: never tell 'em how long you've come for – they just play you along until they know you're about to go, then they just aren't available." Piggy eyes brim with cunning.

Barzakh commented aside, on the return boat journey, "What a loss Grover never entered Congress," as Wilks' complex anti-Semitism became explicit ... *of course, the interests of the really big Arabs and the Hofjuden – your Rothschilds, your Montefiores, your Bronfmans, your Manny Hannies – must become identical.* (A dignified frown clouded Fountain's brow.) *Zionism to the Hofjuden, your court Jews, was never more than a device to stay in the brotherhood. The precarious existence of Israel serves as a power-money nexus for the élite of Jew and Arab alike. Heaven-sent, our godly friend Guise here might say. Or you, Ismail. In the big league of international money and power, it's impossible for the Arabs and Jews not to collude. There's only one bunch of outsiders in today's world.* Philippa Fountain spotted a safe little cue and asked who. *The Russkies, dear, the Russkies.* Her glance of wondering alarm missed her husband. Grover, she chided, turned everything upside-down.

Sometimes clearer the wrong way up, Barzakh commented.

There you are again, Ismail, Wilks returned, *bringing in Mr Wrong and Mr Right. They aren't in the libretto. Mr Power and Mr Money are the leads, perhaps the same role, a doppelganger. I think I'd write the part for a counter-tenor. Very pure, very very experienced. I don't think Phil is with me, Nigel. As soon as there's more money than required for common necessities, my dear, money takes on the attributes of power, and thereafter money and power are interchangeable, even indistinguishable. So far as human motive is concerned. The power-money structures ramify spontaneously.*

But they collapse, Barzakh pointed out.

You get trouble, Ismail, real trouble, that is, only when those with power forget the realities, cease being honest with themselves. When they let the power get into the hands of the mob, that's the only real threat to the structures. Then everything can go ... until such a time as a newcomer has the audacity to consolidate power once more on a basis of honesty – clarity, if you like – get it back from the mob, reassert the will. Good intentions are the prerogative of the weak, my dear old friend.

The echo of Timmy again.

Grover Wilks did not suspect me: or rather, he suspected me only of a risible innocence hung over from childhood, of "still toying with the tortuous improbabilities of the Christian faith. You'd be better off with Islam, Mr Guise. Doesn't put such strain on credulity." But the distance Nigel Fountain set between himself and me stayed fixed all day. At our parting, the peremptory offer of a large soft hand came with a little sneer. "I doubt if I shall have the pleasure again Mr Guise." Fountain knew something that touched on me, but what? Presumably the British maintained some sort of intelligence network here: a brief instruction from Timmy's desk would alert it for me, Fountain would be informed. Yet he disdained to enquire where I was lodging, when I planned to go . . .

I look across at Offshore Ollie: could he be their man? – pink, peeling, damp, drunk, incurious to a fault, buying companionship with petty favours and incontinent confessions . . . yet all the while the master agent, shortwave radio in the Piff-Paff cannister? The coincidence of our encounter bugs me still, but I simply cannot read him as a double man. "Look old chap, you want to get your head down. You look absolutely awful." I can hardly hear over the racket of the Portakabin's air-conditioner. "No good fretting." A moist hand has flopped onto my knee like an ugly, persecuted bird. "It'll all come right in the end."

I remember when we were in love Sophia teaching me the plants in her mother's garden: she made me shut my eyes and thrust a sweet-smelling herb under my nose demanding that I identify it. The smell was ridiculously familiar yet I could not name it – I was ashamed, trying so hard. "Every day you smell it," she taunted. "Open your eyes silly." It was lemon – a sprig of lemon verbena. Now I want this other woman – Lucy Wilks. And she has the smell of blood on her hands, not lemon verbena.

"If I were you," Mullins says, "I wouldn't try for a contract in Khor: they haven't got enough boodle." He lifts his hand to rub fingers and thumb together, then drops it back on my knee. "I wouldn't waste the time." With my knee as his prop he pushes himself into a standing position and makes uncertainly for the plywood door. He turns and for a moment nothing comes. "I say, Guise. D'you mind awfully my telling you that?"

"What?"

"That you're wasting your time, old chap."

"Not at all."

"You absolutely shoo-er?"

"Yes."

"Well, you are, old chap. Goo'nite."

The room is no more than a box separating an occupant from dust and heat – a packing case with a bald light and grinding air-conditioner, domiciliary litter of a culture that admits no metaphysic: at least a *fellahin* hut would return to the earth it was formed from. It contains only its metal and plastic furniture, a single coloured photograph of the bedouin chief who heads the local confederation, and an agricultural machinery magazine which Offshore Ollie has rolled up to swat flies. I cannot be sure if the fever within me is a physical disorder or a wild, impotent confusion. Am I to regard this old desert hawk on the wall as in collusion with Wilks' "Hofjuden"? And even if such were true, where is the power of the lean cat Wilks, or the fat cat Fountain, to affect events?

Is Wilks using his hot little Lucy as a "fulcrum"? He chattered about "leverage" like a blackmailing ponce and I remember Proctor's phrase about him being "really too brilliant" for the State Department.

And for what sacrifice is Billy French being prepared? I catch the whiff of faggots kindling in the coldness in her voice . . . "*a perfectly harmless little man*". Yet somehow a threat to them. All of a sudden I am aware of my own betrayal of French in letting him go – out of reach beyond an international frontier. His "harmlessness" *is* his threat to them: the unfaked innocent, loving his tribesmen, devoid of cunning. One who assists at his own immolation.

An observation of Timmy's, from years ago, comes back – its cynicism impressed me by its daring – how "men use loyalty as a mask for stupidity".

The truth comes down on me like a wave – the high, awful comber breaking over a small boy on the beach at Little-hampton. Instantly the boxed shelter is stifling. I have left the chair. In the bunkroom a shaft of arc-light from the compound falls across Mullins and the Piff-Paff sentinel alongside his snorting head. I stuff my belongings into my canvas grip and scratch Mullins a note. Outside the thin moon is almost flat on its back. But is it for Billy French that tears are across my face as I pull out of the compound? Maybe French's innocence has spurred me to action, but maybe also a man can be drawn to a woman not in spite of but because of the blood on her hands, as if for a man to know God, he is impelled to know God's enemies. Timmy could be beside me with his slow leer.

PART
THREE

1

"You," Barzakh says, "are a man who can understand the international forces, Anthony – I call you Anthony, right? I am surrounded by fools here. These Shaikhdom people live on the brink of a volcano. We Adenis understand it, we have been through it. Some – most of us – were ungulfed, some got out. If I had not got out when I did . . ." He mimes handcuffs round his wrists. "After that, God knows. The East Germans run internal security. Those bastards would love to have the Reuters man by the you-know-whats."

The clock on the apartment wall suddenly rattles and wheezes. Barzakh turns on it with mock vehemence. "That bloody thing!" A mute bird is struggling to escape from a chalet. "It went 'cuckoo' for one day. Twenty years ago. I bought it for my children, but my wife God-rest-her was the only one who heard it. More cornflakes, Anthony?"

Treasures surround us. One table-lamp is a naked lady holding aloft a flaming torch, its pair a gentleman of equal perfection whose parts are a cocoon. An ashtray says Steamer Point. The turquoise carpet is wonderfully deep. At the end of the room an old portable Remington stands on a table amid a siege of papers. When I telephoned him from the Gulf Hilton at 9 a.m. he was still asleep and was still unshaven when I arrived. He gave me coffee and slipped out, returning with the cornflakes. He knows an Anglo-Saxon breakfast.

"Sonny Apramian," I say.

"You tell me you went shooting with him at the country estate of Timothy Lunt and you thought he was acting strangely, okay? Then you hear from your friend in the Conservative Party that the Government know Saqr was murdered and are very afraid it will be found out and they will carry the can. Okay. Now you discover by chance that Lucy Wilks is the lover of Sonny Apramian. Lucy is a dainty lady, too dainty for him. I know Mr Apramian already. That's nothing special. He has fingers in pies like all Armenians –

they're all the same, clever. Look at Gulbenkian. Look at Mikoyan. Look anywhere – under all kinds of stones . . ."

"I heard he's an Iranian citizen."

"Iranian, Iraqi, Syrian, even American. It makes no odds. They belong everywhere and nowhere. The Russians have given them an 'Autonomous Republic'. What does it mean, Anthony? It means they have a place in the valleys to breed spies. The Russians are smart. When the Turks chopped them up in the first War, the Russians said, 'Come here, you're safe. One condition: you spy for us.' I know a lot," Barzakh taps his forehead with a forefinger. His eyes are as wise as an ape's. "I shall dig out more. The whole truth – nothing but. I have certain friends."

What friends, I ask.

"Among the exiles from the Emirate. Friends of friends. I shall soon find what is brewing – if he is supplying them arms. Give me a week."

"Too much can happen in a week, Ismail."

" 'A week in politics is a long time.' You know who said that? Your Harold Wilson, who sold the people of Aden in slavery to the Reds."

"I don't think I've really got a week, Ismail. I've done my business. My visa's about to run out." I picture an odd little figure in khaki shorts with tufts on his cheeks, isolated on a ledge of rock in a barbaric landscape. A designated sacrifice. "Major issues are at stake, Ismail. Could affect the whole region."

"You expect us to *alter* the unrolling of history, not only witness? I already have engagements today. The next *New Age* . . ."

"Listen, Ismail." I am afraid: I seem to divine evil like a dowser. "You know the Emir's water-drilling team that got blown up?"

"It was in our newspapers. An old mine . . ."

"A most convenient, ten-year-old mine, just enough to blow them all up. Even Billy French fell for it. Don't you see? They're cold-blooded. They know what they want."

"What?"

"Power." Passion has the same singleness, the same purity. "God knows, it could affect many, many people, Ismail.

Another Aden . . ."

"People here are fools," he says. "They are living on the slopes of a volcano." It is a kind of refrain. "Grover Wilks is quite a good friend of mine. He's an odd one – that I'll agree. I could see that from the start. Yesterday on the way to find the turtles I thought to myself, 'He is testing us – Fountain and me. He is not telling us something.' He was at the time speculating – about Hamood, about the tribes. 'The tribes were always volatile,' he said, 'and now we've got Hamood. My God! When Hamood was a lad, he went shopping for friends among the exiles' – that's what he said. 'Hamood was always a bit *à côté*' – you know how Grover puts things."

"How well does he know the exiles?"

"This I shall dig for, Anthony. Give me twenty-four hours."

"Was he actually postulating a take-over of the Emirate's peninsula?"

"It was all very very hypothetical, Anthony. He could have been thumb-sucking. Flying kites." He pulls out his Fleet Street metaphors like little plums. "He said the peninsula being a piece of Emirate territory, an enclave in the Pirate Coast, always was an anomaly, a piece of British meddling. He told Fountain, 'You Brits are always doing the wrong things for the right reason.' Maybe he was using Fountain as a sounding board – which way the other Shaikhdoms might jump, how Billy's Emir might react. Didn't you hear him say – I can't recall the context – 'in a nervy world, a *fait accompli* has a ninety per cent chance'? And Fountain said, 'What about the Falklands?' Grover declared it was the exception that proves the rule."

"D'you suppose Fountain realized what Grover was getting at?"

"There was only one thing Nigel Fountain wanted to get out of Grover, Anthony."

"Oh really?"

"I remember Grover confiding it like a state secret – 'Lemon juice.' "

"Lemon juice?"

"How to clean his Gulf chest, Tony."

"Were the Russians mentioned?"

"You can't keep the Russians out of talk like that. Grover

talked about the 'Soviet chimera', and I said, The bastards were only one step away. Half the Palestinians in the civil service here would welcome them tomorrow. Grover said, 'Ismail looks under his bed every night, Nigel'. So I practically do. They dragged my brother-in-law through the streets of Mukalla behind a Bedford truck." He lights a new cigarette from the old one, his hands trembling, and stubs the butt into Steamer Point.

"Why d'you think the Wilkses asked you along?"

"I know the politics," Barzakh answers at once. "I'm a trained man. Look." He jumps up and lifts a picture off the wall – a cartoon drawing of a younger-looking Ismail Barzakh with a wild shock of dark curls, slinking out of a map of the Aden Protectorate with a much-labelled suitcase. It was signed with a dozen or more names, mostly English – "My journalistic colleagues," he explains proudly. I used to know several of them. "The 'last of the few' before they clamped down on Western correspondents altogether. And those" – indicating the labels – "were all my scoops. I'm toothless now, of course. I've no-one to file for. My own magazine: well" – throwing a disparaging glance at copies on the table – "it's censored to the hilt, non-political anyway. I'm a good foil when it comes to floating ideas, not much more. I've had half my stomach out in the Wellington – my Shaikh paid for that, God bless him. I'm compromised."

"Why was *I* there?"

"A mistake, why not? Lucy veering off on her own. She liked you. The human form divine. *Comprenez?*" I recall the quatrain of Blake: "Cruelty has a Human heart/And Jealousy a Human Face,/Terror, the Human Form Divine,/And Secrecy, the Human Dress." He consults his watch. "A week won't do – right? Give me to this time tomorrow – perhaps a bit longer – it's a long drag all the way back to Khor. You go to Immigration, get your visa extended. They'll add a week, why not?"

"I'm not sure they will."

He returns the cartoon to the wall. He says suddenly, "I've always been meaning to ask them to fit a proper toilet here." He seems embarrassed. "If you don't mind squatting . . ." It is the most diffident of invitations.

2

At Immigration the swing door squeaks and bangs all day.

Techniques of official arrogance vary little worldwide – answers given through grilles semi-audibly; inexplicable little delays; sudden absences from the seat behind the counter; an inability to meet the eye, to sustain concentration; the requirement to jiggle the knee beneath the desk, to converse with a colleague on some quite separate topic, to finger through the documents with a modicum of attention, to slap them down before the suppliant. It is as if officialdom has a global motto: *servire est humiliare,* to serve is to humiliate. It breeds a complementary obsequiousness which the applicant before me in the queue has consummately mastered. Even so short a man must bend low to present his request through the slit in the partition. "I am Italy," he tells the clerk apologetically, and his eyes stay shiny. He can smile and speak simultaneously, fattening his already fat cheeks where the smile ends even though the mouth itself is unusually petite. A suit of pale rayon tweed fits most exactly and respectfully, not a centimetre too long – could be a centimetre too short in bending to the horizontal slit, but the effect assists a total compliance. A tiny bob of the tilted, smiling head – a bob that contains both flinch and blink, indicating a most devoted attempt to capture the clerk's meaning – secures the finalisation of the arcane procedure beyond the partition and – in scarcely a few minutes – the return of his passport endorsed for an additional week's sojourn. He does not even omit to turn upon me the smile that successful candidates reserve for those whose marks have still to be announced.

I have no such skills. In my initial bending to submit my passport I grasp that the supervising clerk sits to one side, behind another – unopened – slit. Now upright again, mere fragments of my sports shirt and unrespectful canvas trousers visible from beyond, I hear the matter of my application being referred to the senior clerk, and discussion ensuing. Anxiety stabs. Again I bend, face level with the slit, to lubricate the procedures with obeisant smiles. I do not like my passport long in other hands: it is an ancient professional instinct.

The two clerks have a list of names, I see, in Arabic and Western scripts. A third, beyond, is on the telephone. I try my sincerest Italian smile on the senior clerk whose feet rest on an orange-box cut down to quarter size. His colleague behind the slit raises a hand, and suddenly a little plastic venetian blind obliterates the slit and, indeed, my Italian smile.

And all at once humour has vanished and dread is back like a companion presumed to have been left behind. I remember the moment I glimpsed Timmy after arriving at my new school at thirteen – I had not known he was there: it was years since the dark woods of his Welsh home and its sweet fear . . . but there it was again, the low insidious scent.

The long prefabricated office has no windows in the wall where the swing door bangs. Men in uniform could burst in unseen. I have "no rights" here, as McKinnon reminded me. It matters not if I am guilty of nothing . . . yet, of course, I am: ancient guilt, not yet expiated, is spelled out in the name on the passport they have in their brown fingers behind the miniature venetian blind. Why, Misterr Gweez – why you come to our country as 'agricultural economist' which you are not? Like the snake. What poison you carry, eh, misterr? *To protect you from real evil.* Why you protect us? We have army, police, we have our Arab protectors. Why you? *You are half children in a world grown cunning and cruel.* So if you have something to inform, why you come as this cunning thing yourself? Eh? You creep in, you laugh at us, misterr. Why you laugh at us?

The riff-raff of international humanity is distributed on the benches, wrestling with application forms, awaiting their chance at the horizontal slit. How astonished they would be if one of their number were suddenly to be advanced upon by men in peaked caps and hustled through the door that bangs. How ominous for their own safety. Priorities switch in a trice . . .

I tap submissively on the plastic louvres of the blind. It is parted in the middle by two fingers. An eye sees me.

"Problem?"

"Wait, misterr." The louvres snap together.

Why should I wait, to be haltered and led off to some urinous lock-up and interminable consular wrangle? — a paragraph or two in the national press: Sophia at her suffering best, not saying but looking "I told you so"; and somewhere, behind the little headline, Timmy leering, closing the file . . .

I move to the door and stand looking out into the parking area, watching for the approach of a beaconed vehicle, driven with the arrogant haste of official colours. Am I being fanciful? But if a hitch of any sort has occurred (and it has), what else can it be but that the word has gone out: if Anthony Vernon Guise appears, holder of British passport number so-and-so, report it, detain him . . .

Someone is calling me from within — two or three fellow applicants, hectoring. How swift are citizens of the 'Third World' to side with authority. To gain a miserable advantage they will turn and rend a fellow pawn. Should I duck out and run for it — here, now: set off the hue and cry?

They seem angry in their own right, these cowards. What the hell do they want of me? . . . Oh — ah, standing in the doorway I am letting all the cold air escape.

I take a pace forward, into the violent sun, and the door bangs.

But what next? If I abandon my passport, how will I eventually get out of the place? If I go to Fountain's consulate, it will be the next plane . . .

I cross to Ollie Mullins' Datsun and move it to the entrance of the car park where I can also spy the doorway to Immigration. I wait at the wheel, the engine turning and the air-conditioning on. If the clerks call me back, another applicant will surely open the door and scan for me. They can only ask a further detail, or return the passport stamped: they have no power of arrest.

Twelve minutes later a fat white Pontiac with blue markings and a blue number on the door turns off the slip road towards the car park. The glimpse of the two uniformed men triggers a spasm of accumulated fear. I do not wait to watch them enter the office but draw away slowly and gather speed only when in traffic on the busy sea road and the delusion of safety amid sky-scrapers. I abandon the Datsun at a supermarket.

Two days and nights I lie up in Barzakh's flat. Cornflakes,

luncheon-meat, baked beans, flat bread, coffee, the mute cuckoo. Almost all the reading matter is in Arabic. A notice printed on plastic hangs in the bathroom:

A woman is like the World
At 20 like Africa – semi-explored . . .
At 30 like India – mysterious and mature . . .
At 40 like America – technically perfect . . .
At 50 like Europe – a ruin . . .
At 60 like Siberia – everyone knows where it is but
no one wants to go.

It is a peculiarly sad document and I wonder what Frances would make of it. Would it be passed round the dormitory to be read by torchlight as worldly adult wisdom much more to the point than the platitudes of love taught by the dried-up nuns? "Mummy," she would demand cryptically, "are you still Mysterious and Mature?" and her friends would giggle.

I find the World Service of the BBC and learn on the news that Timothy Lunt, Under-Secretary of State for Foreign Affairs, is to visit various Middle Eastern countries, including the Emirate and the Shaikhdoms. He will know I am here: he will be worried about what I may have learned, that I am still on the loose.

On the Monday at nightfall Barzakh returns – dishevelled, unshaven, greatly excited. For two minutes he tells me nothing, making play with concern for my welfare. Have I eaten? Have I slept well? He is so sorry to have returned later than planned. He warms a piece of flat bread under the grill and makes himself an omelette. I sit on the chintz settee between the naked woman and the ballet man turning the pages of a copy of the *New Age* full of pictures in ill-registered colours. Barzakh brings across his omelette and his warm bread and sits down opposite. "Anthony," he announces, "the balloon is about to go up."

I lay the magazine aside.

"They are planning a *Putsch* and it could be any day." His little brown eyes glitter. He gobbles his meal noisily. "Your business here is done? Your agriculture?"

"I told you, Ismail – yes."

"We shall have to go there. At once."

"Where?"

"Where? To the peninsula! It is the scene of action. We will go to warn our friend Billy Fransi. It is our duty!"

"How?"

"How?"

"I have to tell you: I have no visa – not even a passport any more. Someone's put the finger on me."

"That is the penalty," he declares dramatically, "of grasping at the truth! Your passport is useless anyway, to cross that border. You could not anyway obtain a visa. It is not possible for an Englishman. Anyway, there is no time. I have thought of this, I can cross, to and fro, as I please. I am a citizen of this – volcano." He grins, showing the gold. "You will come with me."

"What d'you mean?"

"As my wife! I am deadly serious."

"Wouldn't it be easier if I took a detour overland – took off into the hills from somewhere short of the frontier post and joined you on the road the other side?"

"You would be asking for trouble. My dear Anthony, you think those Emirate people are quite stupid? They keep watch from look-out posts. They will catch you or shoot you or both. If you are wanted here, maybe they will be watching this side also. So you will come as my wife. My dear wife, God-rest-her, is still on my passport. There are no pictures – that is the way here. You are *sa'ida* Ismail Barzakh, why not? You shall be veiled."

"I'm twice your size, Ismail."

"Not twice. Maybe I prefer a big lady. Leave it to me. They will not ask you to get out of the car. They will not risk interfering, especially if we arrive there at night."

Doubts mount in direct proportion to his confidence. "It's such a familiar trick."

"The trick is familiar because it works."

"The Saudi princess was caught going out as a man."

"Exactly: the other way round. You know how they caught her? Because the security guard at the airport put out his hands to search her – just the routine check for weapons – and she flinched. They will not dare to search my wife. They are only men there. You must trust me, Anthony. I shall wear my *dishdasha* and *ghutra*, the Arab complete with wife."

It becomes a melodrama ringed by absurdity. We rise early. Bigger by far than local Arab women are accustomed to grow, I am done out in black *abaya* and veil. Feet and hands are a problem: we attempt to stain them with a solution of coffee and tea, but the milky expanse of hairy feet is so great that we resort to nylon stockings, which combine uncomfortably with sandals. Items of attire are excavated from drawers and chests. Mrs Barzakh has been gone less than a year, but no qualms intrude. The little man works with a dedicated singleness like the star's dresser on a first night.

The hands, already bronzed, at last take on a deeper stain, and several lumpy rings of faience and opal are forced onto the fourth and fifth fingers, assisted by oil. Long wrists are more obdurate: bracelets are added to their nakedness. The ends of my fingers are stained russet, recollecting some family festivity. I am doused with scent. Barzakh makes me rehearse fluttering of the hands, little spurts of unnecessary movement to portray agitation, and upheavals of travel, clutching at the veil.

"But if I am going to stay in the car?" I protest.

"Just in case, Anthony."

It has become a prank, an incompatibility of intentions, like a circus in a cemetery. I want to pass water, but how, among all this black muslin? I wonder where I fall on the chart – "Like Europe, a ruin"? Getting downstairs and into the Corolla needs careful scouting and is achieved in mid-afternoon, when much of the city rests. Only in the car do Barzakh's findings unfold.

Hamood is at the heart of a plot – he and two cronies from the past, both self-exiled sons of the shaikh of the peninsula's town. The stratagem is for the exiles to return to the Emirate's peninsula with the connivance of various headmen who have been suborned with promises of money. The airstrip will be blocked, the Emirate's little garrison surrounded in barracks, and the leaders of the revolt will request union with the Shaikhdom, to which Hamood will agree, thus justifying an order to "his" section of the federal army to cross the border and consolidate the *Putsch*. The Emirate's distant capital will be faced with a choice between dropping paratroops or abandoning their peninsular enclave. For me it is a familiar scenario of the "Third World": I can remember the assignments. Barzakh played the old trick, posing as a wholehearted supporter who already knew much. His main informant did not know of Apramian – though someone is providing boats. There was talk of a "special weapon" that would swing international opinion behind the take-over. It seems to have occurred to no-one that Saqr was murdered . . . They all know Wilks as Hamood's man, their man, ". . . all things to all men, a *sensitive* man, Anthony. He can't bear blood: I've heard his lady say so."

"You're suggesting it's not he who's masterminding this?"

"Who can tell? Grover's an odd one." It could hardly be Timmy: it could not benefit him. Then who contaminated whom? "Grover should be a big fat ambassador somewhere. He had an exceptional start, from all one hears, right in the middle of things. Cornell, bright star – State Department – good connexions. Instead he swerves off. Finishes up on the slopes of this volcano, like the rest of us except we had no choice. With his snappy little lady – she has push, too." And no fear of blood, either; in at many a kill with the Pytchley from early youth. "I don't know how it happened, Anthony. Maybe Grover's no peace in his life except his music, but some people use music like blue movies. The things of God he does not respect. He was on two months' leave for his honeymoon when his widowed mother died – he was the only child. So he just cabled his lawyers to keep her on ice until the end of his leave. He told me this himself. Can you imagine? – making love with the corpse of his mother waiting? There's no Islam in Grover, no *submission*. My dear wife, God-rest-her, she was very very ill a long time. She was lying in hospital, month after month, with this tube in her nose. She could hardly talk. I used to go there every day and hold her hand. She knew it was me – I could tell that. Grover used to say it was ridiculous. He'd say, You're suffering, she's suffering, she's not getting better, you should let her go, of course you should. Anthony, I wouldn't have missed that suffering, nor would my wife either. Grover called me a fool – it's the only time I've seen him nearly lose his temper. Then he tried to soften me. 'Allah the All-Forgiving,' he said, 'must not be denied things to forgive. You Arabs understand that. It's what I like about you.' Does he think I'm

179

a fool? I know he has no God."

When we stop for petrol I feel absurd and exposed in my *binte*'s weeds.

After the soaring bridge and the hunched town of the Khor itself, the northward road contracts. The sun has disappeared below the horizon but still reaches the rock faces of the peninsula's mountains as they close upon the sea from the east. Human presence thickens here, a string of mud settlements, a quartz quarry, the Union Cement Plant, Al Jahla Ice ... sudden rows of low houses painted white and green, with earthen fretting around the roofs. Something in the road catches the lights – a plastic bag? A tortoiseshell cat, a perfect creature, preening – the car's wheels strike it, thump-thump, cat and driver oblivious. "That was a cat," I say. "Oh," Barzakh replies, "I thought it must be something. Too many cats! You should veil, Anthony, through the village. Keep veiled from now on." The beauty of the cat was like the woman's, and in the path of our righteousness it was destroyed.

"If we reach French, tell him what we know – what then?"

"Events must take their course," Barzakh pronounces. "We shall be in the centre! Nothing will escape us."

"For what purpose, Ismail?"

"What are you asking, 'for what purpose?' You should be sleepy, please. It is only two miles to the frontier post." Thus will farce slide into terror, the mountains closing upon us, and contours of ancient terracing, a civilisation long gone, only discernible at imminent nightfall. "From our position, Anthony, we shall get the complete story. The real exclusive."

"I thought you had given up being a news agency correspondent."

"You cannot give up an instinct!" Is it the fag-end of my reputation or only my life that I am risking on this goose chase? When Sophia referred to my journalistic urge as a disease, a condition to be grown out of, why should I have been aggravated? She is correct; I concur. What right had I to be aggravated at her misunderstanding when I wilfully disguised the nature of my urge? I give her nothing of my true self. For years I have given her nothing. I want to stop, at once, before it is too late, find a telephone and tell her, "I have come here to discover my true self, so that you . . ." I urgently want this. Ahead, a high light. Two little flags – the Shaikhdom's. Three or four long huts. A painted board, "No Photo", repeated in Arabic. A clean white barrier across the road. A sentry box, unmanned. We pull up in an empty macadam-ed bay at the road's edge.

"Sleepy," Barzakh instructs. He sounds his horn and gets out. A man in uniform comes out of one of the huts lazily and re-enters it. Barzakh disappears among the huts. Minutes later he emerges accompanied by a uniformed man with a gun. They come straight towards the car, the soldier slovenly, toes turned out, a bouncing tramp with an evil torch, and the same flooding of the guts occurs as when the police car swung into the city's Immigration compound. I could cut short the charade here and now, before any actual offence, jump out, do a little dance, raise a laugh, go back home with nothing. Harry's editorial budget would only drop the price of an air ticket . . .

Barzakh calls out in Arabic and I stir as if disturbed in slumber. The soldier makes for the boot, throws it open, moves forward, flaps his beam into the car through the shut windows. He remains debating with Barzakh, immediately beside the door: I can view him through the veil – the slack jaw, the persecuted beard, forage cap dumped on the head like a pile of pancakes. His toes still turn out in their cumbling shoes and the tiny slouching movements are of a man impervious to notions of mercy. I remember reading in an account of the soul: "Man stands apart as a creature that can show mercy."

All at once the debate is at an end. Something is called out sharply: an Arabic command. Barzakh jerks open his door, illuminating the interior light. It is all up – a frame-up from the start? Too late for a mock joke now. They will expose such a neutral oddity, without identity, ungendered, between flight and pursuit, and purity and corruption, and tragedy and farce. He has got in, shut the door. He turns the engine on the key, stalls it twice, flooding it. "No pedal," I whisper. "For Christ's sake."

The white barrier into no-man's-land is going up. We jerk forward, under the light and out of it again. Here, the road is unpaved. The name of Christ invoked: the high card, the trump suit. You throw it on a worthless trick, once and for all, like a vow of love. At the next bend we see the lights of the Emirate's post. "No-one is looking for you here," Barzakh says. "But these people can be fussy. Keep sleeping. Cover your wrists. They will shine the torch very very carefully. Put your feet *back*. They will make me take the suitcase from the boot and they will inspect it. Shut your eyes, have no fear." The narrow car reeks of it.

3

When loading a helicopter Billy French is a busy man. Sacks of rice and winter wheat for the tribesmen are to be laid on nets out on the runway, then slung below the helicopters; other nets are to carry bags of cement. In the body of the machine the 48-gallon "burmails" — once Burmah Oil drums — are to be stored with the pumps and solar panels to power them. He has his own loading team of half a dozen Indians. The crew of two are both Emirate airmen, already togged up and smoking against the rules on a bench alongside the hangar.

The sun has just reached the little group, climbing over the last jumble of rock to the east and touching the roofs of the little town and port a few hundred yards northward and the sea of the strait beyond. It is the sweet moment of the day. To the south the mountains soar in a great horseshoe, gaunt, intimidating, belonging to their own world, clamping the little town against the sea on its barren alluvial acreage of level rock and dust. For the Arab world, this is the end place.

Commanding his team, French doesn't see us drive up. We park our dusty Corolla in the long shadow of the hangar beside his own Land Cruiser. It is Barzakh greeting the pilot that alerts him.

"Well, well, well. I do declare," he says, straightening from realigning grain sacks. "And Mr Tony Guise into the bargain. Who the bloody hell let you two into the Emirate?" Good-humouredly; flattered. Barzakh replies with glee, "I smuggled Anthony in as my better half."

"I'm not with you." He shakes hands with customary force. "And what brings you here?"

"You, Billy," I say, and Barzakh adds eagerly, "We have some very very important information for you, Mr French."

"Me Tarzan, you Jane. Me Billy, you Ismail."

He glances at his watch, strapped to his wrist in a complex leather casing. "Mustaq," he calls to a coolie. "Chai-chai. Double quick. Me and my friends."

183

He winks at the pilot and his navigator. He is just as we last saw him – khaki shorts, bush shirt, yellow desert boots, the Edwardo-Mexican moustache recently combed, the frizz of hair round the pate and greying sideburns plumped out a bit. An ill-bred man in Willowby eyes. But this is his ground, his patch of command. Here he makes sense, is all of a piece, not having to mind his p's and q's, to listen out for meanings just beyond him. As we follow him into the hanger he says over his shoulder, "I run this place," meaning the whole peninsula, exaggerating perhaps, but not by all that much – not, at least, as to the town's link with its savage hinterland.

"Sit you down." Two benches flank a metal table in a corner of the hangar. Three more Westland Gazelle helicopters are housed there with no guards apparent.

We tell him how we found his wife giving breakfast to the cat – I had already changed out of fancy dress. Elaine French had taken us in and brewed coffee while I showered off my make-up in the spick-and-span bathroom. She knew he still had to load. We tell him how we got through the frontier. Now the tea comes, and a tin of condensed milk. I say, "Saw your leopard, Billy."

"So what's it all about?" he returns abruptly. He consults his watch again. "I can give you fifteen minutes."

Barzakh does the talking, tells him all he knows, and all that I have told him: fact, misinformation, hearsay, supposition jumbled together. French pulls at the tuft on his cheeks. "Grover," he echoes from time to time. "You can't be right about Grover." And when the blowing up of the water party is mentioned he furrows violently. I say little, biding my time.

" 'Any day', you say," French repeats. "What's that meant to mean? This week? This month? This year? They're always plotting and whispering, those exiles. It's a family pastime."

"I suspect very soon," I say. "A matter of days."

"Which case, sooner I get up into the *jebel* the better. You planning to tell Wof?"

"Wof?"

"Wali's office. Wali won't believe you, of course. He'll spend two days concocting a message to the capital, getting it garbled up, and if you're lucky my capital might get around to asking your capital for reassurance, Ismail, that nothing's brewing. Nice enough bloke, the Wali, but fancies the peaceful life. His policy is, If you see trouble, look the other way. If he believed you, like as not he'd award himself two weeks' leave and get out on the next C-130."

I ask him what he would advise. The furrow remains as if he is bothered by some insect. "Trouble with you two is, no status. I mean, you're a law-breaker straight off, Tony. If my pilot chappie sitting out there knew you'd smuggled yourself into the peninsula without a passport, he'd be on his bike and round to the Wali like a dose of salts. You'd be down there in the dungeon in the fort until Shaikh Hamood and your bloody exiles came and let you out. And you, Ismail, you've only got a 48-hour pass. That doesn't make you a v.i.p. Wait one."

He stands suddenly and seems almost to topple, but recovers, slamming the side of the hangar with his open hand in disgust with himself. Elaine mentioned his dizzy spells. He strides out onto the tarmac and we hear him giving orders to the loaders.

When he comes back he addresses me. "I don't like it. I know what you're thinking, Tony. 'There must be something he can do.' Well, you'd be surprised. I can send a message to Elly, 'If you hear shooting, for Pete's sake keep off the streets.' She's going home Saturday, me old dear. Maybe she'll make it on time." He pauses. "And maybe what you're telling me doesn't add up to a row of beans. Don't take me wrong. I don't know how well you know the Arabs, Tony. Ismail will pardon me saying, it's the breath of life to Arabs – conspiring. Right? We've heard all this before, on and off, from the Khor. Not *quite* like this, mind, but variations on the theme, as Grover would say, variations on the theme."

"This is the real thing, Billy," I say. "It's just a matter of the timing – that's what we don't know."

"What's your next move then?"

"I shall make enquiries," Barzakh announces tamely. "I shall dig."

"Where?"

"Here. The exiles say that certain officials have been squared."

"You've only got today and tomorrow on your pass, Ismail."

185

"Then I shall return." He adds brightly, "If the balloon has not gone up! This is a volcano, you know – the whole coast. They live in a paradise for fools!"

"You've come a long way for a dig."

"I am a professional," Barzakh replies tartly, so that I am prompted to remind French of his having been with Reuters in Aden.

"You remember the decapitating of the British soldiers in Radfan? That was me," Barzakh declares. "My exclusive!" I guess he wants to find a place to sleep.

"What about you, Tony? You seemed to have got yourself into a hole. Do I savvy exactly?"

"Are you going up the *jebel*?"

"I've got no choice, old man. They're waiting for me. They're expecting their grain sacks. I've got cisterns to build. I've promised them. Whatever happens, I'm best up the *jebel*."

"You take me with you? Is that possible?"

" 'Course it's *possible*. I just say the word. You're a pal of mine, that's enough. It's not comfy up there. No mod cons; iron rations. But if you're coming it's got to be now. I mean, now." He stands up. "One thing, though. If there are enquiries – I mean, later – I don't know anything about you smuggling in. You're a bony-fidy agricultural thingumme and I let you go up the *jebel* for your survey to see how the tribesmen live. Quote unquote. Agreed?"

He ushers us out of the hangar. "Age before beauty." He puts out his powerful hand. "Right, Ismail. You dig away. If you're here when I get back, whenever that is, bully for me."

Barzakh looks deflated. "When you get down here again, Anthony, call me up. Yes?" He does not believe any more in the reality of the *Putsch*. I can see the line of white along the roots of his russet-black hair. It is like the dust of cavalry coming over the horizon. I give him Oliver Mullins' telephone number, ask him to tell him where the Datsun is parked. "You say the keys are under the dashboard?" he fusses as the shabby Corolla moves off. His grand international drama seems suddenly to have shrunk to the whereabouts of Offshore Ollie's Datsun keys.

Yet this is no exiles' day-dream.

All morning is spent on the cistern cut into a table-mountain amid the wild *jebel*. Tribesmen mix the cement, I help lay it, French does every job and fixes the water filter and explains how the Diesel mixer works, how to clean it: he habitually brings up water for cement in oily drums, or the tribesmen drink it; even their goats can't stomach oily water, though they thrive on cement bags. He works with relentless vigour.

The men seem diffident and sullen in the heat of the day. Then we descend two hundred feet to the village and I reveal myself to him – a "freelance journalist" who knew Timmy as a child and so "read" his demeanour during the television interview. I tell him of the shooting party, the Visitors' Book, the Rhys brothers, what I know of Soviet involvement. Then of tracing Apramian, the box in the fisherman's hut, of being myself watched, of Lucy Wilks and my mounting suspicions of Grover, of my instinct of impending catastrophe in Mullins' Portakabin. Two things I do not expose: that Lunt has marked my life, and one other, concerning the woman, for neither is explicable to one in whom I find no recognition of evil.

My narrative drains his blood, reduces him to a sweat-patched puppet with clumped hair and fancy wristwatch, starting to get old, brown eyes made round by instant despair. When at last he does speak it is meaningless sound. Christ-alfuckingmighty, so-now-you-tell-me. Then he looks at me with sudden suspicion – so much shattered trust has cut up its own remnants: "What are you doing up here with me?"

He is all I have to pit against the others. "I can't manage this alone, Billy."

"Why not?"

The mud and thatch village suckers to the ledges of the mountainside like a sea-bed organism, its dun polyps occupied by parasites – mankind – including French and me in one of the lower huts, squatting on a rug in its open-sided section. The antiquity of the settlement is given away by knuckles of rock in the pathway which bare feet have worn smooth as shingle. A tiny boy, skullcap tilted forward, replenishes our thin coffee. The aged headman in his *dishdasha* passes by barefoot, springy little axe in hand and crowned by an enamel bowl containing the goat's skinned haunches. In front of him goes his grandson with a pot on his head containing the goat's feet. The old man pretends to ignore the pair of exposed Inglisi

187

feeding on the dates and halwa he has provided.

The helicopter is parked on an abutment beneath. To give the pilot his wind direction a red flag sticks out from the top of a Thorn of Christ tree that sprouts from a crevice alongside. Beneath, the mountains open into a vast bowl. At our height, several thousand feet above the *wadi* bottom, two or three miles separate us from the next wall of mountain, where other villages cling to fissures and knolls wherever a little water may be captured.

I prop my back against an upright, French sits cross-legged, very stiff and straight, with the chargol containing his water dangling beside him. He has taken almost none of the dates and halwa – lunch isn't his meal at the best of times. He mechanically beckons the boy: he has ointment for the eczema the skullcap hides.

The old man has taken up position between huts a tier above us.

He would give his life for these bleedin' people, he says. For weeks there's been something wrong – he'd put it down to the water party. The blood he found there, on a stone about thirty feet away, was a caked puddle. "If it belonged to the bloke who detonated it I hope he crawled away and died." He shakes his head as if still bothered by flies. "*Yallah*," he tells the boy, dismissing him.

He senses the tribes slipping away from him. Three who ought to be here are absent and nobody's telling where, what they're up to. Usually there'd be two or three fellows sitting with him here. With an extra guest, an Inglisi, they'd all be vying with hospitality. They haven't laughed all day, not even the kiddies.

We can hear children's chatter now, goats bleating, a woman churning cream in a bottle close by, somebody pounding henna leaves in a mortar. The old headman has slaughtered a goat, certainly – but in my honour? We cannot yet tell. Between the huts, forty feet above, I see his flank and shoulder: he hones a knife on his palm and every now and then shoots us a troubled glance.

"We've got the helicopter, Billy. We could go back. Then I fly with you at once to the capital."

"You don't understand how this place works. I couldn't get

you onto the C-130 without a document to your name and if I went on me own, I'd be stood in a queue to see the deputy's deputy deputy."

"Surely, somebody down there, in the town, in the peninsula . . ."

"Who'd get the meaning of your story? Tell me who. There's a fisheries bloke – he's German anyway. A cultural bod. A clapped-out quartermaster at detachment h.q: he's on the beer from twelve noon. A brand new little detachment commander from the south. He'd never stir without the Wali. I tell you, I run this place, far as anybody does. The Wali probably thinks he does, but he doesn't belong any more than I do. He never comes up here to the *jebel*, he doesn't speak their real lingo." He tugs at the tuft on his cheek; it's like a permanent tear he's wiping away. "Who are those blokes down there in the town anyway? Rejects from the tribes. They haven't got what it takes to live up here. These people up here are tough and brave and the only people who belong in this peninsula."

He cocks his head listening, and scans the huts and rocks. Only the old man is visible, honing. "So what are we going to do, Tony? Sit here and watch 'em being sold off to Hamood and his . . . his . . ." He breaks off.

It is so peaceful – a coiled peace, like a woman in whose allure one longs to impute a vulnerable goodness. Sophia seems to know when another woman attracts me – there is a certain type to which I suppose she does not belong: while I will be reading something God-given in the other's posture or the lines of her mouth, Sophia will find occasion to label her "hard" or "sluttish" . . . We watch a shoulder of bare mountain glow exquisitely in the final rays. Halfway up that, he tells me, they blew up the water party. He gives a tiny shake of the head and repeats "Grover". I wonder if he should be incanting not the man's name but the woman's, but of course it is faith in the man that he is bereaved of . . . and his tribesmen's faith in him.

This wild sea of precipitous rock that crests at several thousand feet and plunges to the *wadi* bottoms is all Emirate land. Who would believe men live here? – yet they always have, and French knows every settlement, every stab of green in the rock, every minuscule plantation, four trees or five, immemorially nurtured, and how to reach them with laden donkey. Old men and newly born, feuds, alliances, sagas of water sources and fruit trees, the cumulative vision, all are known to him.

No one else comes within accosting distance, except women, to whom we may not speak. The old headman is still visible between the huts above, testing the knife on his thumbnail, keeping us in view. The child brings more dates in an aluminium bowl but not the goat. First thing in the morning we will make fresh cement, set the villagers to completing the lining of the cistern, load the mixer into the helicopter, fly back to the town. We will march into the Wali, say our piece . . .

French says, "These people are behaving like I'd crawled out of a sewer." There is a note of desperation. "You think I'm barmy, admiring these people, liking this place? You want to know why?" He disregards my silence. "There's no corruption here, Tony, corruption of the flesh. This is bone – bone and sinew, no flesh. You know that bit where it says, 'The corruptible shall put on incorruption'?"

" 'In the twinkling of an eye' . . ."

"That's *it*!" he exclaims. "It's in the funeral service. I was in the business as a lad – did I tell you? 'Corruption' means 'rot', of course – that's by-the-by. Point is, there's nothing here to corrupt. That's how it ought to be. No greed, no jealousy, no waste. When I go home, there's too bloody much of every-thing, right? Too much food, too much drink, too much sex, too much bloody soap powder, too much telly, too much thinking about what to do next, what the other feller's got and you haven't. After a week of it I can't wait to get back out here. To the bone. You wouldn't understand that, I don't suppose."

I am thinking: Must I sink myself in French's paltry philosophy and scratching tribesmen to extirpate the darkness of Timothy Lunt?

"Point is, Tony, how you interpret it. If you don't take a little trouble, look a little carefully, you'd call this a wilderness. But these people, they find a bit of a ledge, a crack to hold a patch of soil, it's marvellous – something sprouts! A couple of apricots up here in the *jebel*, tucked away, better than a bloody plantation. All you need, to make sense of it. It's like once a year a bloody good arse, one glorious arse you can't get your hands around . . . make peace with the world, once a year. These people understand that."

But these people keep away from their guests. We can hear murmuring in the huts around us, the prattle and exclamation of children, a gentle clatter of pots. Somebody grinds something in a mortar.

"They put garlic in that stew," he says. "I wonder if the women know."

"Know what?"

"Oh God, what the men know and we don't."

We light the paraffin lamp, but after the moon comes up we douse it. French has his sleeping bag, I take the rug and keep shirt and trousers on at this cool height. Two goats bleat antiphonally each side of the village, and chickens are still muttering. Then they too cease, but the murmuring is not quite extinguished. Small creatures are audible in the thatch, and the chargol precipitates a slow drip. With ridiculous vehemence a donkey brays and is abruptly silent.

The night air is cool and clean. I start wondering what Barzakh has been up to . . .

The whispering can hardly have been enough to wake me, but even before I open my eyes I know a third is present. The moon has gone. Against the starlight two figures – French and a tribesman – squat together, the tribesman with his mouth to French's cupped ear. The silhouette is that of the old man. It must be about 3 a.m.

I do nothing to betray I have woken. The old man creeps off with extreme stealth – melts away.

French rocks across on his haunches. I feel his moustache on my ear. "They mean to kill me. Wilks has paid them."

"When?"

"Dunno. Any time now."

"How?"

"Old man dunno. Coming from another village. I smelled the gardenias –"

The explosion is such that my instantaneous thought is of a cataclysm: thunderbolt, volcano . . . The sheet of flame leaps to the level of our hut and illuminates the whole settlement. French shouts almost at once: "The chopper!"

191

Consternation has erupted – children, women, dogs, chickens, goats, screams, shouts, scurrying.

Standing, we can see, fifty feet below, the shattered machine wildly ablaze on its abutment, and blazing hunks scattering down the mountain. The thorn tree blazes beside it, but no huts are alight: the rock has formed a barrier. French is into his boots in a trice and off down the path. I stumble after, heavier than he, unaccustomed to steep tracks. His familiarity with its twists gives him a fifteen yard start as he turns into the side track to the abutment – so at the new explosion I am untouched: I take it for a spontaneous secondary detonation of fuel and am surprised to see French, well short of the conflagration, pitched into rocks below.

I scramble in pursuit of him: he lies clumsily at the edge of a steep fall, lurid in the blaze.

A hoarse whisper comes to me over the hungry roar, "Forget the crew. They're finished. Get me on my feet."

"Are you hurt?"

"Get me back on the path. Double quick."

I manhandle him back over the rocks. "Double quick," he urges. It takes a full minute, maybe more. Blood webs my fingers. "Get back up to the hut. Get the water, my clothes. Meet you further down."

I scurry back by the steep path the thirty-odd yards to our quarters. Figures clutter the entrances of huts among the tiered rocks right and left. Men descend from further up. Dense smoke hangs over the huts. I surprise a tribesman in our hut, axe in hand: he backs into the inkiness of the closed section. I seize the chargol and French's shirt and shorts, neatly folded.

I do not find him at the junction of tracks, and so go stumbling down the main track, partly illuminated by the blaze. Only at forty or fifty yards below do I catch his voice: "Here. Get down here!"

He is crouched in a steep *nullah* among scrub. "Can't stay on the path. We'll go down here." He has knotted his sarong above his knees. A gash in his back oozes blackness. "They're out to get us."

Clutching his clothes, he sets off again with extraordinary speed, flitting from rock to rock. We keep in the cleft of the *nullah*, precipitous in places, and at several points seeing the blaze above we know we are illuminated. The village itself is capped with smoke.

He halts only after half an hour and several hundred feet of descent. "Can't keep this up." He looks at his watch. "Dawn, one hour. We go on to the next overhang." When we are settled I rip up the sarong and bathe and bind the wound. He upbraids me for wasting water, though I only moisten an end of cloth. It is a complex rent, one side of the spine, and I cannot judge its depth – I probe in vain for rock splinter or bomb shrapnel that caused it. Burns score his back, too: they will fester so quickly in the heat. It is obvious the second bang was meant for us, or at least French: they knew we'd run down there for the crew, soon as the helicopter went up.

He says, "Somebody thought it all out – not anybody in that village. Whoever thought it out couldn't have expected you to turn up. It wasn't a spur-of-the-moment thing, no way. My people don't keep high explosives in their bottom drawers – they have only one job: not to know. Believe you me."

"They could have just shot us."

"Shooting a bloke looks very different, right? Very deliberate, very personal. Choppers blowing up, well – you can invent theories. Cigarette ends, that sort of rubbish."

"They're still being careful."

"If that's what you want to call it."

"If they've already taken over below, they wouldn't bother being careful."

"Something o' that, Tony. Maybe not yet. Maybe today. Maybe tomorrow." He grimaces with pain. "Only thing: far as we're concerned, they didn't time the second bang too well, did they? They only winged us. They won't rest till they've got us."

We have to lie up the entire day. A slow rage rises against this futile man. Why could he not have stayed at the town's airstrip? What was he to me except a means of ridding my life of a contamination beyond his understanding? How could I have got enmeshed in his post-colonial fantasy?

I try, and fail, to sleep. We calculate how long, moving by night, to reach the town. If we risk the last fifteen or twenty miles in daylight, perhaps by next morning but one – providing we can stretch the water, keep up our strength. He knows sources of water along the *wadis*. The first part will be trickiest, descending the several thousand feet to the first *wadi* . . . Meanwhile blood from the wound keeps seeping, like an hourglass.

From time to time distant shouting alerts us.

Now and then he mutters "Grover Wilks" – a kind of obscenity, expressed inwardly. I cannot tell whether the accompanying frown is from his own pain or the other's name. Once he remarks, as much to himself as to me, "Everything fits."

Perhaps hunger keeps sleep away. In early afternoon, crawling back from a crap, he observes, "The body doesn't need much."

I tell him, "The world record for starving is held by a chap called Wafer. I happen to know. Mr Wafer. Eighty-one days, no food."

"You know the bloke who lived on a pillar, Tony? Used to pull up all his food in a basket on the end of a string. If they didn't choose to feed him, he'd die, 'cause there's no way he can get down. No ladder or anything. But I'm not worried, see?" I think, You ought to be: you'll be the finish of us both. He persists: "Get the point, old man? From up here on my pillar I can see everything quite clearly. The whole bit. I can see exactly what's what. What's right, what's wrong, who's bad, who's good. I look all round hundreds of miles. There's Sodom, there's Gomorrah in the distance. The Tower of Babel. Jerusalem the Golden – I can see them all from the top of my pillar. Over there or over there. And up here, the abode of Wotsit, the all-wise, the all-compassionate. You've no need to muck around with religion in a place like this, know what I mean? After all, haven't you noticed?"

What am I meant to have noticed? – he drags me into his fantasies.

"It's a cathedral, right? The biggest cathedral in the universe. They forgot to put the roof on. The roof comes on at night, anyway, like a jolly old planetarium – practically never fails.

"I mean, these people, my tribesmen – they don't need mosques. It's Government makes them build mosques – they want to keep the grippers on them, bastards. My tribesmen'll bob down in the open two or three times a day, do their prayer thing – the old PT. They never miss a sundown one, you know, never. I know exactly what's going on inside them. They're in touch all right." He nods to where we have come from. "If I had to sign on somewhere, I'd sign on for Islam. Only if I could *stay* up here, though, on top of my pillar."

I watch the shadow of our rock creep round, and his blood spreading.

"Simon Stylites was a Christian," I point out.

"Simon who?"

"The holy man on the pillar."

"Oh, I know all about that. Mind you . . ." I shouldn't have started him off again. "Mind you, the Government'll have me out of here next to no time. Put a fancy boy from the capital who'll sit on his bum all day in that little town down there with the a-c full on chatting on the phone. Half-educated, foot-on-the-ladder bloke. I'm an anachronism, anyone can see that. You can't have white-arsed Englishmen running around the *wadis* much longer, can you?" He looks at me with his great penitent eyes. "If I had my way I'd leave my bones out here."

He'll get his wish – wish it on me too. Sophia would in due course start making enquiries. I wonder if she would see my death as a source of tiresome inconvenience, a final action of wilful and typical thoughtlessness.

"And Elaine?" I ask.

There is a long pause. I presume him not to have heard.

"You said?"

"The wife."

"I feared as much, old man." He chuckles. "It's a one-bloke pillar, that's the pity of it."

Later in the afternoon we hear a man shouting quite close. We crawl round to get a glimpse of him – a young tribesman, two hundred yards away, close enough for French to recognise him, his whole body tensed and bowed to fling his shouting to the heights above from his stomach. Has he picked up a scent of us? A minute later we see a companion descending the mountain with amazing agility, bare feet twinkling from rock to rock like a sword dancer's. The two young men continue their descent together more slowly, hounds scouring. We lie very still and quiet till nightfall: at last French stops chattering.

195

When we dare resume our own descent, I see how his blood has formed a large clot in the dust and ants already busy at it.

Before dawn we approach the *wadi* bottom, the nave of his "cathedral", but cannot easily hide ourselves there between one wall of mountain and another. A single massive outcrop of table-rock two hundred feet across rises almost sheer out of the basin. In the starlight primitive stone ruins are visible on top, an up-*wadi* bastion of ancient times which we reckon could provide concealment for the coming day. We begin to climb this forgotten Masada by a steep gulch – according to French the only possible route. Yet he grows hesitant, tiring perhaps, and in obvious pain. We reach a point where we must traverse a ledge of rock: a missed footing will mean a fatal fall. French starts along it, then edges back to the talus where I am waiting. "I don't like it," he says.

"I'll go first."

"I just sit here a minute, right?"

I edge across to a cleft that will take us to the top. He stays put: I have to return to him. "There's a way up," I tell him.

"You go on. I'll wait."

"I can't leave you."

I sit beside him. In the darkness it seems his face has shrunk around his popping eyes. "That Jezebel," he suddenly clutches at the centre of my thoughts. "I never mistook her for anything else."

He shifts his position and his face contorts with pain. "When they go whaling, what they do is fire a harpoon right into their backs. Sometimes they play with them for days."

"We've done the worst," I comfort, without conviction.

So long as he is alive I must stay with him. Anyway I need him for the waterholes: we have only half a chargol left. After a few minutes I persuade him to start crawling across on hands and knees, but he backs up again. "I've taken against, Tony."

I make him stand. I put one arm round his shoulders and facing the rock coax him into the traverse. We inch across with tiny sideways steps. He whispers under his breath and his whole body trembles. At the cleft he says, "I nearly let you down, Tony."

On the top we find several stone structures still with their lintels. One provides perfect cover, from sight and sun alike.

But we are both enfeebled now. He sleeps fitfully; I can no more than doze. Shards of ancient pottery clutter our hide. From our vantage point I can spy the two young tribesmen combing the *wadi* beneath. One man comes through with a donkey and a black umbrella. A donkey could save us.

In late afternoon an aircraft comes over, flying in from the south, and French identifies it as the regular C-130 from the capital. This should mean no *coup* has yet occurred.

As we wait for the sun to go down his chatter begins: it's like a television left on permanently at the end of the living room, as in the Rhyses' cottage. He decides he was unfair to Elaine to talk about the "one man pillar". "What I meant was, if being holy is doing without clobber – nothing between you and Wotsit" – a thick finger points upwards – "then my tribesmen are holy right off, no doubt about it, whether or not they sometimes run a knife through friends and relations. Now, poor little Elly, she's always counting the savings, right? – a new carpet for Sharon (she's the daughter), a piano for Sharon's bambino, God knows what . . . clothes and clutter and gunge. You can stick all that up your anus, Tony. If I had my way, I'd leave my bones out here." It has become a refrain, like Barzakh's volcano. "Before the Holiday Inn sets up here, preferably."

We are propped up, gazing at the last light beneath the lintel that nobody has had cause to look out from for thousands of years. A sweet repulsive smell comes from him.

"Tell me this, Tony. One tuft there, look, another tuft over there. Little bloody bush just there, little bloody bush over there, look. What about the blank spaces in between, eh? If a tuft can grow there, why not there or there?" The thick finger stabs the air. "Just the same ground, same water if any, no bloody shade anywhere."

"Maybe the way the ground drains."

"You're flumming, Tony. You're flumming and flamming. The answer is, *there isn't an answer*. That's the message: you can't take life for granted. It's a gift from Wotsit just where he happens to choose. Here and there" (he is stabbing again) "but not there and there. Trouble with people back home, they're spoilt, the entire lot of them. They think they're alive because they deserve to be alive. They credit it with too much."

"Credit what?"

" 'Credit what?' Life, of course. They pretend they've abolished the other thing, yes? But they're fooling themselves. You know that bit, 'He that loves his life shall lose it, he that hates it – whatever – shall keep it unto eternal life.' They forget that. The whole thing's a whim of Wotsit and we're just part of the whim. Once you get that straight, you've got somewhere. Do I bore you?"

I am watching the moon rise, calculating the cast of its light on the side of the table-rock we must descend. Forty or fifty miles of tortuous *wadi* bed between us and the little town – in a single night I might jog it. But the chargol is all but exhausted.

" 'Course you don't bore me." Maybe I could leave him at the first water-hole.

"You're a church-going man, Tony. I can tell. Right and wrong – you can spot the difference. Most people can't."

"Sometimes evil is so vivid." Vivid as the posture of a woman.

"Grover Wilks," he says. "And the other one . . ."

"You can see it in her?"

"Apramian," he corrects. "Bad."

"We don't know so much about him. I thought you meant Lucy."

"It's different with her."

"Why?"

"If a woman wants to be bad, it's up to the bloke to stop her. She takes her cue from him, that's natural." When he tries to shift his position he grimaces with an intense anguish. "We're meant to turn the other cheek, right? With a hole in your back there's not much left to turn. I used to try to believe all that, a ticket to heaven for good behaviour. If it's true, it's not true in the way they say. That's the trouble with the funeral business: it works the questions into you. You can't not feel the grief when you're burying a littl'un, seven years old. The grief *and* the whim. The tuft question, right?"

The chattering distracts his pain, and the slow leakage of blood induces urgency rather as in a child, inadequately prepared for an exam, cramming at the last moment.

"You see all these people left behind, they're looking over the edge: nothing there. The working classes keep the ashes in the bedroom. By the old photos. Before and after. If my tribesmen did that they'd be called savages."

"The moon's about ready now." I get to my feet but he makes no move. I wonder if he wants to stay here to die. I feel a reluctance to drag him on.

"You learn to fancy the moon like my tribesmen. She's our Virgin Mary. We've got nothing else gentle and delicate at all up these *wadis*. You'd be amazed how quick these girls go off – blown so quick they can't remember when they were young and grown-up at the same time. But the moon, she never lets us down. Right?"

I put out a hand and feel his thick hand trembling in mine as it takes the strain.

"Lead on, McDuff," he declares and follows on like a zombie: where, before, the fear was inordinate, now there is none.

After midnight, the moon gone, we no longer skirt the *wadi* but risk the habitual track along its bed. It seems utterly waterless, parched eroded rocks, and dust and dry sand. At a certain point, in a cluster of large rocks, French swings off and in a hollow no broader than a barrel-top finds pure water. He fills the chargol, and I see his teeth grinning in the darkness. Occasionally we are troubled by dogs from lowland settlements, which have us hastening on for safety; for two or three miles we are plagued by a half-wild dog, barking incessantly, which no hurling of stones and sticks can dissuade. Once we all but stumble over a group of sleeping camels. I notice his pace is slowing; he weaves as he walks as if growing drunk. At about 4 a.m. he stops suddenly, bends forwards and vomits. Tendrils dangle from his mouth, and he stands stock still, bandy legs apart, in a loop of meaningless flesh and sticky bile. I approach to put an arm about him but am roughly thrust aside. He wipes his mouth with bare forearm and resumes walking, not a word said.

Before dawn I know myself to be light-headed. When I pause, my legs begin to tremble uncontrollably. It is I that halt and sit, and French who tries to argue me on, continuing ahead as he speaks. "Five, six miles we pick up a vehicle track. See that *wadi* coming in from the right – that's it." But I can't see it.

"Give me an hour," I plead.

French stops twenty yards on and after a minute walks back. He stands over me stinking of vomit. "We're safe here. Different tribe." So I propose we stop at the next settlement and ask for food. "No villages in this *wadi*, they're all up," he replies, as if to put me in my place. I wonder if it is exactly true.

I settle into a hollow among rocks and gaze at the sky, touched by a glimmer of dawn. A couple of days without food is no record but makes the mind airy. At first he will not sit. "Tonight they'll send a chopper to look for me," he says. "They expect me back today."

I push off my shoes: my feet are a confusion of blisters, some burst. At last he settles alongside. "We mustn't stop properly now. I won't get going again." His voice sounds remote, but he is close enough for me to smell the decay in him. "If Grover's lot found us here . . ."

The dawn mists are clearing from the mountains. He must go on talking. "You see that? Dance of the seven veils, that's what I call it. Not a dance really." I am desperate for a moment's sleep, but his voice comes on and on in little strained bursts. "Just watch her pull the wisps off of her . . . 'Course, they're not real veils, just shreds of chiffon – she keeps 'em last in her cleavages and cracks . . . seductive. Right, Tony?"

My eyes are shut.

"I'm cold, Tony."

"You want me to do your back?"

I get no answer. I hear his teeth chattering and wonder dreamily if he is acting up.

"D'you ever think of the earth as a woman, Tony? Like the real sand desert? Beautiful. Incredibly sexy . . . Like a centre-fold – the whole spread. But no orifice. That's the catch. All those marvellous curves, and no orifice! What a try-on, eh Tony?"

"Why don't you rest, Billy? For God's sake."

This silences him, though his teeth still chatter, and moments later an answer comes, dragging me back from sleep, "Told you already . . . I daren't risk it."

What does he mean? Is talk his last hold on life? – fumbling for a God, or an unattainable sexual fulfilment. Pity for him rouses me and I recall something for him, from long ago: "I screwed the earth once."

"Get away, Tony," he chides, "you're telling me stories."

"Not at all."

"You took out your old man and screwed her?"

"On a hot summer's afternoon. There's a place down below the woods, a secret place, corner of a low field . . . ground's always moist there . . . must be a spring of sorts." I trail off, buying my rest.

"Well?"

"That's all. I was lying there looking at the sky and just rolled over and screwed her. It's sort of clayey there."

"I mean, what made you do it?"

I know exactly. Sophia was pregnant for the first time – our "love child" as she called it. Yet I still felt the corruption on my skin, the contamination of past life. I suppose I was randy – Sophia was terrified of losing the baby, allowed nothing to risk it; the sharp lusts were at me again. I must have been trying to keep myself pure to retain the right to love Sophia. It was an act of ritual cleansing.

"Eh?"

"It was a ritual cleansing, Billy."

I hear his chuckle. "Just a one-night stand, then?"

"It's not the sort of thing one repeats." It was like the time when, answering a reader's overtly Christian letter on something I'd written, I signed myself "Yours in Christ": the very next day I marvelled at my effrontery.

The teeth are chattering again. He shifts his feet, rattles his watch, sighing. I smell him all the time. He says in a firm voice, "If we start now, get a bit of luck on the road, we'd make the town before the Wali gets his head down."

I open my eyes at the paling sky and the last of the gossamer mist on the mountains. "We just burst in on him – looking like this?"

He is standing, hands out to pull me up. I see where he sat and the brown stain of blood left there. I look at him properly for the first time since the previous evening. His face is now puffed and sickly grey: a sheen covers the skin and grizzled bristles and tufted cheeks, the eyes start.

"Bathe your back, Billy?"

"Don't touch it!" he retorts violently, then adds in a lost little voice: " 'S'no good." He goes on holding out his hands

201

while I tighten my laces. "I haven't had one for ten years. *Ten years.*"

"What?"

"A fuck, old man. A fu –" The sudden stab of his wound cuts him short, and his mouth falls open. "Mustn't stop again, Tony, know what I mean?"

He struts ahead, I three or four yards behind because of the smell.

4

The Wali holds office in the old fort overlooking the bay and
strait beyond, and the last tentacles of land to the east. The
little town itself seems at peace. It is now close on the high heat
of the day. Prayer has been called. The stall-holders and
merchants have mostly shut their premises, those few engaged
in the administration of the Emirate's peninsula enclave will
soon be retiring for their afternoon meal and repose. A few
Arab craft swing at anchor in the bay.

The Indian trader's white truck that stopped to pick up two
English derelicts in the final *wadi* draws up in the dust beside
the fort's gatehouse. Both of us are in the open body of the
vehicle. French refused to ride in the cab because his back was
soggy with blood and pus and I think he knew he smelt: I rode
with him to protect him from the bumps and lurches. I hold his
hand not only as a promise of loyalty but a link with reality. He
refused to be taken home or to the town's Health Centre, and
demanded we go straight to 'Wof'. I am too exhausted myself
to counter this stubbornness. I have eaten nothing for nearly
three days. I yearn for a cup of tea, a place to get cool and
clean, ease for my stricken feet, though I too am possessed by
an opaque urgency: we must see this Wali.

The strategy of approach we concocted together has
crumbled away in the *nullahs* and *wadis*. French was to open
by introducing me as a "trusted friend" who had chanced
upon information about an imminent take-over of the
peninsula. Since the Wali had visited England and had
aristocratic connexions, French would present me as a gentleman of status in England, a friend of Mr Timothy Lunt of
whom his Excellency would know. I would then narrate all
that Barzakh had told me, culminating in the final proof: the
bomb attack on the helicopter and French himself. We would
plead for the immediate reinforcing of the garrison, the
blocking of the frontiers, the protection of the airfield . . .

I am the first to climb stiffly down from the truck. French

crawls to the tailboard, which the driver lowers. I lift him to the ground. He stands for a moment, but he suddenly sits in the dust, a ridiculous and repulsive sight — unshaven, swollen, raw-eyed, caked with dust and sweat, swathed with strips from his own sarong that bulge him in front under his bush shirt. Behind, his garments are a mush of brown stinking ooze. Instantly the flies are at him. I still hold his hand, which is hot and dry. I draw him to his feet, and hand in hand like children we enter the darkness of the gatehouse where guards crouch over a primus cooking furiously: they scarcely glance up. We climb by the external stairway of the inner court to the upper floor, then along a corridor to the end door, already ajar.

The Wali is seated at his desk beneath a portrait of the Emir. Opposite, leaning back with his elegant legs stretched out, and buttoned up in a fawn suit and necktie, is Grover Wilks.

Reaching the centre of the small room French hesitates in front of Wilks, who draws up his legs carefully. He regards Wilks like a drunk straining for recognition, then turns stiffly towards the Wali, greets him in a loud thick voice in Arabic. The Wali, a man of middle years in the loose turban and dagger-belt of the Emirate, has stood up out of sheer surprise.

"Excellency, I have come to make a report." This from French.

"Excuse me," the Wali interposes in careful English. "I am having the conference with Mr Grover Wilikis."

French sways so that I need to put out a hand to steady him. The stench must already be apparent.

Wilks begins to say something but French cuts him off in a huge voice, directed at the Wali. "I have to report, your Excellency," he bawls, "that this man Wilks is here and now, selling, betraying this place to the enemies of His Highness the Emir." He points dramatically to the swordfish in a case beside the coloured photograph above the Wali's head. I still grip him by the shoulder. No one seems a match for this situation.

"Wilikis is the first enemy of this peninsula," French bores on stiltedly at a half-shout, like a crier proclaiming a calamity. "He has killed the water-party. He has killed the crew of His Highness' Air Force helicopter. He tried to kill me. He has paid the tribesmen money to support the Shaikh Hamood. He is sending the exiles from Khor to take over this place. With his wife he planned the murder of the Prince Saqr of Khor so that he could control all this through Shaikh Hamood. Excellency, you must send to the capital today for troops. In the name of Allah and in the name of His Highness I beg you, I beg you!"

The Wali has recoiled, bewildered – a soft grandee doing his stint in a remote station. He is not accustomed to unmannerliness, least of all in a Westerner.

An Arab clerk, alerted by the raised voice, hovers anxiously at the door. Wilks, seated again, has his finger-nails to inspect, with an alarmed scrutiny.

"I'm sorry we come to you in this condition," I interpose. "We have walked for three days without food."

The Wali frowns and issues a brief order to the clerk. "I do not quite understand," he adds mildly.

French has started to reel. Wilks' sensitive, musical fingers have now gone to his mouth. He has paled. "Maybe I can explain my friend Mr French's delusion," he offers lazily. "But is he not a very sick man?"

French pivots round. "Quiet!" he roars and collapses across a low table. Wilks tweaks his legs away as glass mugs and saucers scatter to the floor. The Wali motions to a guard, ascended from below, to remove French. I mumble a hurried explanation: "Injured when the helicopter blew up . . . He's developed a fever – blood poisoning . . . Needs immediate treatment. We've been three days . . ."

But French is spontaneously on his feet again, vehemently forbidding anyone to touch him. The guard looks at the Wali, who now instructs that Mr Fransi should be taken to his house and the orderly from the Health Centre be sent to him. French supports himself by the doorposts, heaving as if about to vomit.

"I will go with Mr Fransi, please, your Excellency," I say. "I beg you to believe this place is in danger. There is undoubtedly –"

He cuts me short: "We have not met before."

"My name is Guise."

Wilks says, "I know who this man is, Excellency. A kind of journalist."

"Quiet!" French booms from the doorway. Then, hoarse and stilted as before: "Mr Guise is a friend of this country!"

205

Guard and clerk are trying to prise him from the doorpost, he
clinging on with manic force. I make to withdraw, but the Wali
stays me. "I think – a moment, Mr –"

"Guise."

"Moment please."

Anyway French still blocks the doorway, breathing heavily,
teeth chattering, in mute struggle.

Wilks crosses his legs. "These are the rumours I referred to,
Excellency. That brought me to see you. They are quite
groundless. I suggest this – this recent performance bears out
what I have told you."

"Mr Wilikis is quite well known to me, you understand,
Mr –" The Wali cannot quite recover the name. "He has been
good enough to call on me of his own accord. We have been
enjoying a long talk of the problems of the region. Maybe this
helicopter was an unfortunate accident. All this petroleum
they carry . . ."

The men have detached French and are shuffling him down
the corridor. Wilks re-crosses his elegant legs: he looks filled
out in his buttoned jacket, comfortable. Alone, I am useless.

"Moment please," the Wali says again. "This name?"

"Guise."

He takes a pen and begins to write laboriously. I catch the
derision in Wilks' face, and as I turn towards the corridor I
hear the Wali comment suavely, "Perhaps when Mr Fransi is
recovered, Mr Gweez . . ."

The driver has found newspapers to protect the washable
vinyl seats of the Wali's official car from whatever noxious
substances might exude from the rotting body of Billy French.
But it is no longer only the body in decay: rationality and
delirium are now displacing one another like trough and wave
in an afflicted sea. In the car he clutches at me, repeating with
wild eyes, "Where are you taking me?" accepting no answer,
and then commanding the driver in vehement Arabic to turn
back, turn back – which the man soothingly consents to, and
disobeys.

Elaine French has been writing to Sharon and hopes the
letter will reach her before she does. There is lots she wants to
do this summer – the only thing that worries her: can she rely
on her houseboy Fateh to feed Mercy properly with Dad away

in the *jebel* so much? . . . It is ridiculous, but she is to arrive home without a single present for Sharon's little Janice that originates here. Dad would bait her: "Wrap her up a tribal axe." Typical Billy. Then she thinks – surely there was a pretty sea-shell here not to be found at Southend? There is still a day or two to go down to the shore . . .

But when the crunch of gravel alerts her she is surprised to see from the living room window not Billy's Land Cruiser but a fine car. By the time she has got to the verandah, I am already helping Billy out (the driver stays at the wheel). It is the sheet of newspaper sticking to Billy's back that first makes her think something is not right. Then Billy being helped to his feet, steadying himself on the lump of coral by the verandah steps.

He looks so dreadful!

She puts Mercy down on a wicker chair by the stuffed leopard and hurries forward. "Oh dear, Billy. What can be the matter?"

"I'm dying, Elly dear," he says with perfect clarity.

She doesn't understand that.

The newspaper is still clinging to him when we have entered the bungalow. She and Fateh have cleaned the house top to toe, prior to her departure for home on Saturday, and here is Billy in such a mess, hardly recognisable. He used to talk about "the great unwashed" – look at him now. Music is playing, *The Skaters' Waltz.* "Ah," French says, swaying in the living room doorway, and makes an old joke, "Lez Patinewers and his Ice Men."

In the bedroom we lay him down on towels along the slight hump that is their nightly no-man's land. When I return from the bathroom, he is naked except for the sodden strips of sarong that bind him. Elaine is scissoring off these strips and dropping them on the oatmeal carpet. Most of French's back is a furious landscape of suppuration and livid swellings; and above the rump, the black yawning unhealable cavity of the shrapnel wound. The squat swollen body – thick hairy legs, lilywhite blobs of buttock – is a thing done for, no good any more. He is panting, his teeth rat-tatting. Elaine soothes, "Quiet, Billy, quiet," as if he were her baby.

"That you Elly?" he demands hoarsely.

"Of course it is, silly boy." She is deft with her fingers. "Silly

Billy." Cooing.

"Tony there?"

" 'Course he is, silly." He is wracked with shivers.

"They wouldn't believe us at Wof, Elly. Wali thought we were nutters. Grover Wilks fixed that. He's too smart. You want to get out on the plane tonight. D'you hear that, dearie? It's not safe."

"Don't talk, Billy. Mr Guise will tell me everything."

"You want to get out too, Tony. I'll be all right. I'm leaving my bones here. With my tribesmen."

"Don't talk like that, Billy." Tears have come now, dripping off her thin cheeks onto his back, but the fingers work on, snipping, peeling.

"You'll want to get me under pretty quick. There's no municipal freezer and the Cold Store doesn't take corpses, even the brightest and best of the sons of the morning."

Fateh has woken and hovers at the door wide-eyed. She wipes her eyes carefully so he shouldn't see. French has begun to call "Elly" repeatedly, in a hoarse voice, as if searching for her in the dark, though each time she would answer "Yes Billy", or "Here I am", stroking his temple and his fevered pate, making it beautiful. At length he says "I think I'm cold," and at once she instructs Fateh to switch off the air-conditioning. A period follows in which he seems not lost but hunted; the spasms of shivering run into one another until his whole body is gripped by the rigour and we cannot reach him.

Thus he is when the medical orderly arrives, a Punjabi, making an event of it, bustling and tutting that he was not called earlier, shaking his head over the lesions as if each were a personal insult, so that I feel obliged to propose French should have an antibiotic injection though guessing the poisoning to be beyond reversal. The orderly's response is that the patient should be moved at once to "his" Health Centre, but French suddenly swims into an irascible clarity, shaking his head furiously on the pillow. "I won't bloody go, Shahid."

Elaine mollifies, "Mr Shahid is a very qualified gentleman, Billy. If you're not rude he'll give you an injection to make you better, won't you Mr Shahid?" She finds a smile for him. The orderly's self-esteem has become the central issue, and he now declares he must report to the Wali that he cannot hold himself responsible. He produces a Case Record card and with one of three pens from the breast-pocket of his white coat begins to demand details of the patient – name, birthdate . . . French makes no answer, and when Elaine replies for him he objects foul-mouthed. "Now then, Billy," she scolds, and throws the orderly a humouring look.

Only after inspecting the deep wound with a wooden probe – which makes French's fists clench – does the orderly administer a penicillin injection and a sedative, and begin to apply dressings.

"Tony'd like a cuppa, Elly," French says quite clearly. "Hasn't eaten since Saturday." When she instructs Fateh accordingly, he says at once, "No dear, you get it."

She rises from the bed, catching my eye with a look that is like a precious stone, a diamond-glance of grief and humour and ancient sacrifice: her hour of greatness is upon her, none can deny her. She retreats to the kitchen. There on the dressing-table is the photograph of Curzon being carried ashore in a palanquin.

"Eh – Tony?" The whisper is so conspiratorial I have to bend close, my ear level with the pillow. "Ever had a club sandwich, Tony? The big one on the bottom, right?"

"Sounds nice, Billy."

"The patient must take bed-rest without disturbing," the orderly says.

"Eh, listen." He is gasping, and the whispered words come in short spurts. "You know that sand desert . . . no orifices, no shade – know what it reminds me?"

"You told me, Billy."

"No – something different this is . . . In the service remember? . . . 'And let Light Perpetual shine upon them.' I never could face that . . . Light Perpetual . . . They got that bit wrong . . . Nobody could want that . . . 'Ere, Tony. Do a small thing for me." A fit of panting interrupts.

"What, Billy?"

The panting persists. He gives a little shake of the head. "Can't remember," he whispers.

I can hear Elaine putting out cups and saucers. By the time she has brought them in he has slid into unconsciousness.

The medical orderly drives me back to the Wali's fort. It is nearly 2 p.m., but the Wali's own car is still there. Among the *boums* at anchor I see one bearing the Arabic numerals 97. Under the archway of the gatehouse the meal is almost finished – they are sliding the tips of their fingers round the enamel plates.

This time I knock at the Wali's door: he greets my entry with immediate disapproval. "Perhaps tomorrow, Mr –" the elusive name has scuttled away among the papers on his desk. Wilks is still in his chair.

"Excellency," I begin firmly. "The matter is too urgent and too important." I have shaved, have bathed my feet, wear a clean shirt of French's. I have drunk two cups of sweet tea. An ancient vengeance drives me now, and French's scourged back.

"The office is clos-ed at two o'clock," the Wali says.

I sit, uninvited, in an upholstered chair.

"Excellency, I must ask you to understand. This whole peninsula is in immediate danger."

Wilks says, "Really, Guise. Wadi Fransi has just given us a *mauvais quart d'heure*. We don't want to repeat it, surely."

"Billy French is dying. You will have been responsible for his death."

"This is very wild talk . . ."

The Wali intervenes, "Mr Wilikis our friend, Mister." He has abandoned hope of the name.

"This man's a cheap journalist," Wilks says.

"Mr Wilikis took the trouble to warn me about the rumours. We are grateful to him. We had that fellow here also – Ismail Barzakh. He also made such rumours. When Mr Wilikis heard these things he came to assure me otherwise. Mr Wilikis is a friend of the American President."

"I am a friend of Mr Timothy Lunt. Mr Lunt is not indeed the American President . . . He is expected in your capital this very week."

"Even today," the Wali confirms, and I note the spark of interest. "I know Mr Lunt," he says. "He is often a visitor to our country from London."

"He will be seeing His Highness the Emir?"

"Of course. They must discuss the policy."

"I wish to put it to your Excellency: If this peninsula is taken over by the Khor Shaikhdom and certain friends of theirs, Mr Timothy Lunt will inform His Highness that you were fully warned and took no action. I will have told Mr Lunt. What will His Highness think of you?"

"This is sheer fantasy," Wilks' voice comes from across the room. I do not turn: I have the Wali's attention now.

"Exactly your accusation, Mister?"

I begin to unfold the sequence. I tell it from the deaths of Saqr and the water party much as it has happened except that I represent myself as the servant of the British Government, reporting personally to Lunt. I omit reference to having been watched. I tell, however, of following Apramian and his lady friend, and of seeing them copulate in the surf. "And that woman, Excellency, was Mr Grover Wilks' wife."

"This is too much," Wilks expostulates, but does not move, bunched in his chair. With a show of courtesy, the Wali bids him be patient.

I tell of my suspicions concerning the box in the hut of Apramian's fisherfolk, and reaching here with Barzakh. I bring the narrative up to the present moment.

"Is this all?" the Wali enquires with a nervous smile. He folds his hands. Then he pings a bell on his desk and his clerk comes to the door. "Chai," he orders. "You will take tea, Mister?"

The thick walls of the fort, and its narrow glassed apertures, admit no sound. Except for the air-conditioner, there is complete silence. Wilks remains without moving, fingertips meeting at the mouth in the manner of prayer, but his body tilted back in the chair and an expectancy of humour playing on his face. The Wali looks at his onyx penholder and the miniature Emirate flag beside it. The black plastic material of the arm of my chair has split and a deep ulcerous fissure like the wound in French's back has opened in the sorbo rubber.

Three glass mugs of milkless tea in glass saucers are carried in on a tin tray by an elderly teaboy. Only when he has withdrawn does the Wali speak.

"Mr Grover Wilikis is our good friend. If whatever you say is correct, please, why is Mr Wilikis here?"

I put down my tea carefully.

"Because, Excellency, what is going to take place will take

place tonight. Mr Wilks has come for three purposes. He has come to find out for himself if there is any knowledge here of what he and Hamood and their friends have planned. One. And, second: if there is a little knowledge (and there was, through Barzakh), to disarm you, to convince you of the opposite of the truth – that the Shaikhdom would stop any trouble that might be brewing. And three – to consume your time, Excellency, to make sure that on this critical day you are occupied by him and not by other activities. For you are a hospitable man, Excellency."

The weak smile flickers anxiously. "Mr Wilikis is silent."

"This fellow's a cheap journalist," Wilks repeats, "looking for something to write about: I have it from the British Ambassador. He comes without any proof whatever."

"Someone tried to kill French," I remind.

"So what? The tribesmen think Wadi Fransi is a fool. They have told me so often."

"Billy French is a good man."

"Who the hell are you to decide what is good?"

"You think the tribesmen have the explosives?" the Wali worries.

"Why not? They're everywhere. And anyone can set fire to a helicopter. Even a tribesman. Even a careless pilot."

The Wali falls silent again. He looks trapped and unhappy. He is very late for his meal. His office staff will not be pleased with him, nor perhaps his wife and household.

"Tell me, Mr Wilikis," he says. "Why do you think this gentleman, Mister" – his nod suffices – "has told all these things?"

"He is a liar. Maybe he's mad."

"What makes him to do this?"

"He is jealous of my wife. She has rejected him."

I exclaim, "Oh God." And then. "I have seen Mrs Wilks on the two occasions I have described. I have a wife of my own. Why should I need such a woman?"

"So he has a wife of his own! What does that mean? That he won't grab at my wife, and then turn on her for rejecting him? I can tell when a man wants my wife."

I make a gesture of exasperation. "Do you imagine, Sir, I would bring such a quarrel to your office, that I would invent this? I had no expectation of finding Mr Wilks in your office."

A moment's silence. A marvellous fresh anger is rising in me like a sweet spring – an anger on behalf of French – and I resume, quietly. "We will agree, Excellency, that the kind of operation on which Mr Wilks is engaged cannot be done quite painlessly. Yes?" I produce for the Wali a little smile to invite assent, and pass it across the room to Wilks whose heavy eyes now fixed on me have lost their humour. "Much as we all dislike bloodshed . . . bang-bangs." I sustain the smile a moment longer. "One would not engage in such political adventures without some measure of – how would one term it? – self-protection." The Wali is straining in earnest pursuit of my train of thought.

I rise to my feet, and cross to Wilks. "Up!" I demand. "Stand up!"

Wilks languidly unwinds and stands, as if engaged in a child's make-believe. We face one another, I the bigger.

"Please," the Wali entreats. Perhaps he is frightened for his mean furniture.

I begin to unbutton Wilks' jacket. When Wilks raises his hands mildly to resist, I rip the jacket open, sending two buttons flying. But he sits suddenly, evading my manoeuvre. He begins at once to address the Wali. "Mr Guise thinks he is very clever, Excellency. He has noticed that I carry a revolver in a shoulder holster." He taps his chest. "Yes, I do. I often carry a gun as your Excellency carries a dagger. I am an American. I am a species of diplomat. We are a vulnerable species, Excellency, you will understand that. Even in friendly countries."

"Please may I see this?"

Wilks begins to unhitch the thing under the Wali's curious gaze, a weighted cotton holster like a severed scrotum. I reach out to take it but Wilks deposits it on the Wali's desk. The initiative has slipped from me. "Keep it." Wilks says. The Wali has leaned forward to ping his bell.

I remove the little automatic from the holster and inspect it. "A Biretta," I say. "A present for your Excellency, from Shaikh Hamood of Khor."

The clerk is standing by bewildered. Wilks is straightening his jacket. I release the magazine and empty the rounds. I

213

replace the magazine and pass the automatic to the clerk who meekly hands it to the Wali. I pocket the bullets and offer the empty scrotum to Wilks who is looking with a hopeless derision from clerk to Wali; he will not take it so I let it drop among the glass mugs.

5

I take it as characteristic of the Wali to let Wilks walk out of his
office unhindered and down to the dinghy at the jetty. I
wonder he doesn't provide a thermos of tea to carry with him.
Without any interference whatsoever we board the *boum* 97.
No word has passed between us except when I caught up with
him outside the gatehouse and told him I was coming with
him, all the way.

The same crew man the *boum*, with one extra. The
supercilious Ahmed emerges from below deck and posts
himself silently at the hatchway, eyeing me. Wilks sits on an
upturned box, chin in hand, in his all but buttonless jacket. We
get under way at once, steaming northward into the strait. The
canvas awning has been removed and the deck is without
shade. I find a second box for a seat. In due course Wilks gives
an instruction in Arabic to Ahmed, who is made to repeat it,
and disappears down the hatchway. Shortly after, I hear the
unmistakable bleep of a short-wave radio.

"I do apologise for all this sun," Wilks says suddenly. "I'd
rather be up here. I prefer not to be shut in."

We swing east, towards the humps and islets which are the
last spasms of the land mass. It is unnaturally tranquil and
exquisite and nothing is spoken. For some reason I am
reminded of the hush and expectancy that preceded a public
execution I once witnessed in a neighbouring country as a
foreign correspondent . . . Here are we in the immensity of the
sky and sea, but on sufferance. Billy French can give himself to
his tribesmen wholly because he has no pretension to earthly
power. He appears the opposite of Wilks in his avarice for
power, primed by the conceit of a borrowed ideology, infected
by complicity with Timmy that is still obscure, abetted by his
wife. And where *is* the woman? She cannot be far . . .

In a strained, languid voice Wilks begins to point out this
and that along the barren, ochrous coast – the village at the
head of that creek where Persian, not Arabic, is spoken,

though they've always lived this side of the strait. Round the next headland lies the island where "you Brits stuck your little telegraph station to keep in touch with your substitute emperor in Delhi." He knows the coast intimately from years of study. A finger of land pushes out close to our north-east course, and on its very end squats a domed half-ruin. "No – not a mosque – a shrine, one is led to understand." Visiting sailors have defaced it, in great primitive letters, telling the sea DESH COME HERE. I didn't understand, did I – a half-ass blundering in – what this place could be. Six centuries ago the richest place in the world was the tiny island just across this narrow strait. Only thirty-odd miles of water, only ten of them deep enough for the tankers. If they made it a toll-gate levying one per cent . . . At eight or nine knots the breeze pushes his soft hair boyishly across his brow.

Behind us, where the town lies, two or three helicopters hang about like heavy bees hiving, or lurch off towards the mountains. I do not know if Wilks has seen them.

His face has sunk: even the shape of the head seems narrowed and lengthened, adding to the boyishness. I catch him twisting the gold ring on his little finger furiously. I am witnessing a dreadful haemorrhaging of purpose.

We drop anchor off an islet about three hundred yards long dominated by a high scurr of rock at one end. The empty mainland lies a mere six hundred yards beyond. Wilks says, "I don't exactly know what further purpose you have but I personally am going ashore. I have an assignation here."

"Just one or two points to clear up."

"Oh, are there?" A surprised tone.

Ahmed paddles the dinghy. We land at a sandy cove and settle on the high dry sand under the shadow of a ledge of rock. Ahmed makes a fire. He warms flat bread and beats up eggs in a pan. Though I eat slowly, the pain of first ingestion is so severe I am obliged to stand and walk around. As I resume my seat, Wilks says in a tired voice, "I want you to know I was aware you lied to the Wali."

"But you didn't know in what way. Maybe we have points to trade."

Wilks takes off his jacket at last and folds it carefully, lining side out, on the sand beside him. He glances seawards. We might be two trippers on a sunny afternoon waiting for the children to bring back the ices.

"We are expecting your friend Apramian here?"

"Apramian is not my friend." He winces. "Apramian is a common tough, a hoodlum. Apramian is of no importance. Apramian runs after my wife – you know, of course."

"So he shot Saqr himself?"

"In some societies killing a man is a test of his virility. He is keen on his virility." The grin flowers in all its inanity.

"Hardly a sufficient motive, I daresay."

"Maybe not all by itself. Personally I dislike physical violence. I suppose they could always have found *somebody*." He seems dreamy. I presume "they" to be the familiar demons, Russians. "You were lucky, weren't you, guessing that I had a *pistolet*. How foolish you would have looked . . ."

"I had a tip-off."

"Oh really?"

"Your wife – she mentioned you never wore a suit. Not even for the Shaikh . . . let alone a Wali."

"Ah – did she?" The boyish head nods despondently.

"What makes you so sure I lied?"

He frowns at his watch. Two buttons secure his shirt sleeves, and buttons hold down his collar points. "I have no reason to suppose Mr Lunt would wish to interfere."

"Are you telling me he is a Communist?"

He looks pained. "Surely you are not one of those who ascribe every political event you disapprove of to the Communists? I thought more highly of you."

"We know the Communists are involved." I use the "we" as a protection.

"You presume the Communist system to be inherently evil?"

"One doesn't have to look very deep to make such a presumption." The nub of the matter keeps sliding away.

He says, "Systems of power are neither good nor evil. *You* know that quite well, surely – you're one of those rarities, an intelligent innocent, almost into middle age." Instinctively he invites complicity. "The only morality of power is whether it works or not."

"Both systems work, after a fashion – Marxist, non-

Marxist. You can hardly claim no distinction of morality . . ."

"I suppose one might make a distinction – the Communists institute amorality on a foundation of morality, the West institutes morality on foundations of amoral greed and envy. Take your pick. Power is raised above, of course, though power is the motive for both."

"Marxism is endemically a tyranny."

"And fraudulence is endemic to all democratic politics. A tyranny has the overwhelming merit of honesty."

"Where do you stand?"

"Me? Right now?" he grins stupidly. "Kinda nowhere."

"And this morning?"

"This morning maybe at the pivot. The fulcrum." The grin dissolves into the white sand. Tiny tracks of crabs are visible, lacework laid down at night and erased by the breeze. In the strait beyond two or three tankers are visible ten miles out, and a few smaller craft. The shadow of the rock ledge and of the citadel of rock behind us are lengthening. Southward, Billy French's mountains loom hazily.

"Power is what you want, then, purely and simply?"

"Purity and simplicity don't go easily with power, do they? Power can only be obtained or exercised with a little bang-bang, as you call it, and quite a lot of money. One can leave the appeal of all that to people like Apramian . . . But I'm boring you with the obvious."

"The obvious is often hardest to recognize."

"Wealth and authority have a mutual fascination. You'll have noticed that. In little Britain you must have seen trade union leaders with millionaires. They understand one another instantly . . . rather as men of soaring vision recognise each other across great distances." His voice trails away, the slender fingers interlock round his shins. "Wealth attracts wealth, wealth power, power wealth, power power . . . Where else would the Vatican's money go but to bankroll the Mafia? Poor Mr Calvi – his spoon wasn't quite long enough."

Nor yours either, I reflect.

But it is he that looks at *me* with pity in his disgust. "I suppose you don't notice these things, goddam you. You're too busy mooning around the Garden of Eden with nothing on. With little Wadi Fransi."

"You have it exactly."

"You and Fransi and your mini-Minister, is that right? The last patriots. The Society of St George . . . Ah, *j'arrive* – maybe you *are* a friend of Lunt. He *did* send you."

"In a way that's true. You had something over him, I suppose." He peers at me with remote, pained amusement. "The paintbrush." I offer it like a scorpion in a matchbox. "A powerful paintbrush. Another point of leverage, a mini-fulcrum . . ." I am groping for my truths on Timmy, God knows I have earned them. Pain and derision flicker alternately on his face like someone caught in a signaller's lights. "You didn't require much of Mr Timothy Lunt – only *after* Saqr died, to see that any enquiry came to nothing. A simple accident."

"Such as occurs every hunting season."

" 'Shooting', we say. Not 'hunting'."

"I beg your pardon."

"Enough to destroy a political career," I hazard.

"Do I take it you are adding blackmail to my indictment? Why not?" He flaps his hand. "How convenient for us."

I have a loaf of flat bread in my hand. So he does suppose that Timmy sent me, double-crossing his own set-up. His misapprehension clarifies me, releases my hunger, though I feel an impropriety in feeding myself anew already.

The heat of the afternoon has already diminished. I can see the forms of the two crewmen slumbering on the deck between the boxes. Ahmed squats on the broad ledge of rock above the remains of our fire, scanning the sea with field-glasses. When we hear the sound of aircraft, Ahmed shifts on his haunches and trains the glasses south-west, where the town lies. One aircraft appears – it could be the regular daily C-130 . . . but then another transport aircraft is visible, circling to land at the airstrip six or seven miles away. I realize I have not yet been afraid and I suppose that is the time the fear begins again.

"You could never have carried it through," I say.

"Oh yes we could." He turns on me with contempt. "Certainly we could."

"The other shaikhdoms wouldn't have stood for it, let alone the Emirate. They'd have reversed a coup in the peninsula in forty-eight hours."

"You think you know it all."

The way he says it induces a little spurt of fear: ever since walking out of the Wali's office I have overlooked fear, supposing the serpent to be dying at my feet. Yet here I am self-marooned, adversaries assembling and nothing to lose. For a moment my mind is thrashing about for the logic of this action, like a claustrophobe in a blacked-out room swarming a wall for the door handle.

Wilks says, "Our friends will be disinclined to let us fail completely. Even now." He is deriding me, smelling the fear. "What do you suppose Apramian is up to? Why did we need him? Come, come, Mr Guise. Has your imagination deserted you? You say the shaikhdoms would never let a *coup* stand. How do they survive? Yess? By exporting petroleum. All of them around here. And which way does it go out? There it goes, look!" He waggles his musical fingers at the strait and the dun outline of another land just discernible in the early evening light. "They take no risks with their life-blood. Let us suppose these friends – a pragmatic friendship, of course, no love lost but plenty of common interest – let us suppose they have warships only a day's steaming away. They'd be all tee-ed up to tell the world that *they* will police this little strait on behalf of mankind, yess? To protect one third of the world's petroleum, to ensure the survival of all these countries up the Gulf here. Oh, yes! they'd be acting at the invitation of the little dinky new independent state of this peninsula, big big friends defending the freedom of a tiny heroic fledgling against a reactionary puppet emirate. 'We will clear the famous strait,' our friends declare, 'of its sudden new hazards, and protect the independence of the ancient people whose territory watches over it. We will protect it against all comers!' What may we suppose Timothy Lunt urgently advises Wadi Fransi's Emir? 'Hold it. Hold it!' It's the statesmanly thing."

As he watches the truth dawning on me, his inane leer returns. "Your bright little eyes spotted the box in the fisherman's hut. 'Arms', you exclaimed. 'Shipped by the Bulgars via Varna, too!' How right you were. But what sort of arms? Firearms – we need a few, and a few professionals from the KGB's chicken farm for the disaffected at Birimirtsi. But you can't block a thirty-two mile strait with firearms, can you?

You need eggs, Mr Guise, a string of bobbly eggs." He brings his face round at me like a Hallow's E'en mask. "*Now* we see where Mr Apramian and all his boats are so useful. Yesss? Our Apramian, who loves money and likes to be a big feller, friends in Moscow, friends in Geneva, and stays at the Ritz hotel. Yesss? *Now* we see."

"There can be no purpose in mining the strait now. It would be futile destruction."

"Oh, don't our friends like a little anarchy in the Western sphere? I've no idea what Apramian will decide – he's no creation of mine. He speaks Russian, I don't. He can speak direct from his own yacht. I wouldn't want to interfere, specially now . . . now it hasn't turned out quite . . ." All of a sudden the voice has gone faint and wandering.

"You're mad," I tell him.

I have to wait a long time for him to resume, and when it comes it is in a quiet, rational tone as if he has tried hard to address himself to it. "A few of us are entitled to a little madness. When I was a little boy, my parents used to talk about 'Grover's visitations'. A *petit mal*, I had."

I picture the anxious conferences in the next room, the long maternal vigils, and then the corpse, a month or more gone, on its slab of blue ice.

"Madness is a relative term," he resumes, "wouldn't you say? Yess? Not so long ago – not boring you, I trust? No? – not so long ago I attended a kind of reunion at Cornell with my old classmates. We dined out on the campus – it was summery, you know. We had fireworks and a local orchestra performing Handel's Firework Music. My table was so near the brass we all had to shout, and after we had got beyond the stage of settling who we all used to be, we started asking each other what we had done with our lives. You know, Mr Guise, one can't be falsely modest at a shout. There we all were, a little parade of shouting dolls, straw showing through at the knee" – he taps his palms on his knees – "sawdust trickling out of the shoulders, mouths going ya ya ya, half full of food, trying to construct some sort of edifice of justification for having existed all the intervening years on this planet. Madness?" he giggles. "It was a Grand Guignol of self-delusion!"

The mask comes round at me again.

"But I don't want to take up your time. You're a worshipper of God, I recall. You see us all here *en route* to the skies, like little Ismail Barzakh. The power's all up there, with Allah Akbar, not here at all, yesss?" His voice is trailing again, like a broadcast transmission subject to ethereal forces. Now he is very faint and inward. "It's fair to say, in the power game, this God of yours holds the trump. I don't suppose any of us would dare to play the game if it were not so."

"You mean?"

"The Last Trump," he laughs, and now I perceive the mortal fear in him – but not fear of me. Frightened creatures are dangerous: I have always known that. "Poor little Wadi Fransi – he'd have some sophisticated views on that, I expect?" He looks up. "Where d'you think you're going? You can't get off here."

"I'm going for a crap."

6

The appeal of islets, I am aware, is that they are a paradigm of safety. A man might rule his islet, devote his life to delving all its secrets, name every cove and jut and pinnacle and dell, defy all comers. Islets are beyond the infection of the world.

This one, by contrast, traps the infection.

It is half as broad as long. Towards one end, the rock and dust and parched thorn steepen sharply towards a disorder of massive broken boulders at sixty feet above the sea, surmounted by a scurr that rises another thirty feet. For most of its complex circumference the scurr's cap overhangs, making caves beneath and sand-floored lairs. Nature has imaginatively defended this citadel: only by one fissure is its cap accessible. The cap itself is cracked, like massive crazy paving. The fissures in its surface delve deep into the formation of rock so one can foretell that in the course of hundreds of thousands of years it will crumble away like an old tooth.

As the sun lowers I squat visibly on the scurr's skyline, reassuring them of my presence. There is no reasonable prospect of escape undetected. The sea is still tranquil; but the *boum* is anchored so that the crew views across the third of a mile of water that divides islet from mainland. A tidal race flowing out to sea beyond the last of the land keeps the *boum* broadside to the island on a taut anchor. If I were to risk a swim I must start from the other end, beyond the cove we landed at; but they would shoot me. In any case, I am not yet finished here.

The sun drops into the sea like an orange bladder; on the *boum*'s deck both crewmen engage in prayer. From his low slab of rock Ahmed scans the open sea with field-glasses; beyond its ledge, Wilks lies or sits on the beach, invisible from my scurr. Darkness hurries in towards my citadel like a great crowd for a dreadful proclamation. I stand here, slowly masticating flat bread. A fat moon is already up. The sea sighs and chuckles; in a perfect line it throws a glittering painter at the moon. Waves stir over submerged rocks like the bedclothes of a fretful sleeper. Each man in his station waits.

It is strange how the white yacht comes. Though from my vantage I can view all ways, the slim white hull with its mast and yards seems not so much to have approached from a distance as to have materialized out of the darkness quite close in, two or three hundred yards. I catch the low throb of her engines before I make her out clearly: I have seen her before, beyond the ritual of bodies in the surf. She is without any lights.

I hear the anchor chain run out, and then a skiff is making for the shore – direct for the sandy cove as if it is an old lair revisited, a known haunt for the cauldroning of evil. I can make out two figures, but indistinctly, oarsman and figure in white seated erect. The woman? – my heart gives a little jump. The skiff disappears behind a bluff that fringes the cove from the scurr side. Ahmed has gone from his ledge; and if there is a disembarking or a greeting, these too are masked by the flat of dark rock that barriers the ascending beach.

For a minute there is nothing, then all at once a half-circle of light breaks out on the white sand beyond the ledge at the head of the beach, where I sat with Wilks. I move cautiously to the rim of the scurr's cap, avoiding the skyline both from the motor-yacht and the *boum*, each riding opposite sides of the islet. It requires me to crawl by the hollows and indentations. I find the fissure on the sea side of the scurr by which I attained the cap, and descend by this hand over hand, negotiating the jumble of great rocks at its raised base. I drop towards the sea, seeking cover from small rocks that strew the talus and the thorny shrubs. Once close to the sea, I begin to work round to the southern end where the skiff is beached, by crawling and wriggling through the rocks. I have taken the moonless side, the yacht side, where perhaps the crew are not on the alert for me. Sometimes I drop to the sea itself, sometimes worm up among the rocks for better cover. I am working intensely. My shirt and trousers are paler than the rock, and face and hands paler still: every moment I expect the alarm to be raised for my disappearance from the scurr.

I reach the perimeter of the great slab of flat rough rock, whose furthest edge overlooks the little beach by some eight feet at the upper end. I wriggle across its top foot by foot, then, head down, inch myself forward by my forearms, body and legs dragging like a dummy. As I near the lip of the slab I synchronise each movement with the suck and breaking of the waves. Two feet from the edge I stop. Low voices reach me from no more than fifteen feet. I raise my head with utmost caution; the two figures squatting in the violent splash of white lamplight shake me by their sheer intrusion – a dead-of-night encounter on an islet where none has ever lived, off a barren reach of shore: two men, Wilks and Apramian, oblivious to all else, locked in low talk, the tension between them palpable.

To my right I see the skiff and the *boum*'s dinghy drawn up and the back of Ahmed's head and Apramian's oarsman in profile.

Some thirty feet divide the two pairs. Wilks and Apramian leave no chance of being overheard: their voices, however intense, punctuated by abrupt pauses and flurries of inter-change, are so low than even I can make out nothing. Wilks seems to be pleading a case self-deprecatingly but with a kind of desperation, the other returning again to the same argu-ment. A rock cuts off all but Apramian's profile of heavy brows and black vertical brush crowding the forehead, except when he rocks forwards to force a point and the brutish neck and shoulders are visible. The shifting forelock and pale wild eyes of Wilks belong to another species – a mercurial child, blown about by others' accusations and by inner gusts, mesmerised by the confrontation and meeting its punishment according to the ordination of things. That these two should share the same woman, perhaps waiting on the white yacht . . .

All at once the talk stops. Apramian seems to stiffen, Wilks to slump, head hung and eyes on the white caldera of the gas lamp between them. Apramian stands and I duck, pressing my head into the rock. I hear Apramian summon the two men from the boats. They enter the ring of lamplight: very slightly raising my head, I see their shadows and then the heads of the three men standing. Wilks must have remained seated.

Apramian makes a short Arabic statement – not more than thirty seconds. Then he asks his oarsman for something. As I push up my head a fraction more a shard collected on the table-rock in the *wadi* snaps in my trouser pocket. I instantly drop my head – but they are wholly absorbed. Once more I slowly raise my head. Apramian is emptying the chambers of a revolver, drawing out rounds with his fingernails. He adjusts the position of the magazine before snapping it shut and passing it down: I see Wilks' hand come up and take it. My head comes up a further inch. Wilks holds the pistol, muzzle in his mouth, and the mouth itself an exaggeration of the barmy grin, for the chin is pulled back cretinously to accommodate the barrel.

The explosion is extraordinarily quiet, the popping of a bottle in the ear, but to view it is like an underground detonation that lifts a continent out of the world: the upper cranium opens and scatters in an instant confusion of blood and bone and bright, fine hair.

At the time, I suppose them to have forgotten me. For at that final moment I glimpse the face of Ahmed: his eyes are on Apramian not his master, and are brands of cold hatred. Ahmed is beyond vengeance on me . . . As for the two crews, what business of theirs who stays, who dies, who comes aboard? Only the woman would be certain to remember. My mind feels extraordinarily sharp, though I cannot assess their intentions. I only know for sure that Mr Guise, whatever *his* intentions, has done his damage.

The *boum* is the first to weigh anchor and push out of the channel towards the open sea. Then the white yacht, still lightless, slides away: I bring to mind an old myth about a bird recalled to the living world for a single fatal intervention. Crouched among the sea rocks, I wait ten minutes for either vessel to recollect and swing back to blare the channel with lights. Then I slip into the gentle water just as I am, in Billy French's shirt and my own trousers and suede boots and release the islet to itself.

Swift-footed crabs moving up from the rocks at water-level with their hesitant scampers, will push the frontiers of their nightly scouring up the tilted beach: a complex, haphazard, to-and-fro advance, each spurt of movement a high-speed five-finger exercise or octave scale . . . until one of them chances upon a patch of sand oddly altered – dark, moist, enriched – and then upon some vast convex obstacle, a phenomenon cast down there, fibrous, fleshed, an invitation to collective exploration and an augur of edible putridity.

7

To Elaine French the C-130 military aircraft that carried her each late May on the first leg of her journey home would come out of the sky above the mountain ravines and over the bay like a beautiful arrow of hope. Then when it taxied up she would always be surprised how fat it looked, yet at the same time so welcoming, even cosy.

This is the very day she planned her departure; but this time she does not watch the plane's approach at all, and knows of its being sighted only from the quickening chatter of other prospective passengers seated or squatting along the benches at the other end of the departure hut. She stares at the concrete floor. She wears a plain dress and clip-on platinum earrings Billy gave her when they were courting. Her thin hair is carefully done.

The prefabricated hut is open on three sides, except for a barrier at waist level. A white-skinned officer in Emirate uniform stands on the running board of a Land Rover talking the aircraft down on his portable radio. At the far end of the runway are parked an array of helicopters and military transports. The C-130 taxies up level with the hut, engines are extinguished and the doors push open.

A dark man in an official cap moves along the line gathering from the passengers an armful of cutlasses, daggers and tribal axes, some of which are brass replicas manufactured in India, to be restored on arrival. With orange boarding slips rolled up and stuck behind their ears like carpenters' pencils, they shuffle into a line at a trestle table for security inspection by the man in the cap.

I rise and cross to tell Elaine it is time. She looks up with lost eyes and her hand moves to clutch a corner of the plain deal box laid across three chairs. "Look," I say, "they're coming across now to put it aboard." The rear of the aircraft has opened like the maw of a whale to disgorge vast cargo. It remains open expectantly, and an Arab from the Wali's office is walking over from a car flying the flag to summon a group of Indian loaders.

At the trestle table the man in the cap insists on inspecting the lady's suitcase. I assure her it is only the Emergency that is making them so fussy, though with the case open before him the man's attention is distracted by the coolies lifting the coffin and his hands search through the soft things like a bored lover burrowing for the erogenous parts. I have no baggage; but after the inspection a man with a hole in the cartilage of his ear must needs run a metal detector over each of us, and in an odd reversal of absolution locates only the silver crucifix on Elaine's bosom. The coffin is brought to the aircraft on a forklift. I can see the label pasted on its lid.

Being a military aircraft it is loud with unexpected noises. I sit beside Elaine on canvas seats like rigid hammockers, ranged inwards along the fuselage. Before take-off a member of the crew walks down the gangway fixing seat belts for tribesmen who have not flown before, and has difficulty persuading one old man that he should sit with feet below the seat and not on it. We can see the pale box in the cargo section, through a barrier of webbing.

The flight to the capital is only an hour but several passengers must pass water – it spreads like a miniature epidemic. The old man who would not put his feet below the seat pauses opposite Elaine and addresses her in a bleating Arabic. As he intones his peroration, twitching at his head-cloth, I catch the vocative "Fransi", and when he is done he holds out both gnarled hands like an offering. I have to prompt her to take them and as she does the aircraft jolts so that it is less of a handshake than a steadying of the old man's balance; he will not release her, and his Rip Van Winkle eyes seek hers and hold them too, neither hands nor eyes letting go until a little smile of irritation or shyness creeps into her face and resurrects a long forgotten prettiness.

"You see," I tell her, for she and I have talked long of Billy and all that his love for tribesmen led him into. Her eyes begin to moisten, but shortly she finds her glasses and a scrap of paper and begins to tick off the inventory for crating up for Ockenden. "I really do think," she assures herself, not for the first time, "Billy would want his leopard to stay."

229

At the capital airport the British Consul has come to meet the coffin, a suave, youngish man who is allowed onto the tarmac to attend (in lively Arabic) to its cool storage until the evening flight to London.

In the arrivals hall I introduce myself and the Consul says, "Oh, *Guise*, is it? We had a message from our friends in Interior about a Brit coming in from the peninsula having lost his passport. We couldn't decipher the name. I hope you didn't get swept up in that little non-event up there?"

"Storm in a teacup."

"They're happening all the time. Dust-devils, I call them. What d'you do with yourself?"

"Agricultural economy, one could say."

"Ah." He tilts sideways to confide. "I've just to get that old biddy settled in the lounge place upstairs. She's lost her husband and she's taking him home on tonight's plane."

"I realise."

"He was one of our last remaining tribal chappies the Emirate had on contract. He copped it in some chopper mishap and got septicaemia, poor sod, though his post was to be localised at the end of the year. Still, his lady should collect most of the pension. H.E.'s written her a personal letter." He has pulled it from his pocket. "That's what I call taking trouble. If you'd like to hang on I'll give you a lift to the office and we'll see about a passport."

He moves to Elaine. "I've brought a personal letter to you from the British Ambassador," he says in a kindly tone, and waits for her to open it. The letter is on the smaller embassy stationery and typewritten in very large lettering, composed of two paragraphs each of two sentences. The Ambassador has written *Dear Mrs French* and *Yours sincerely* in his own hand. Ushering me into his car, the Consul apologises for not having introduced me to Elaine French. "She's got enough on her mind, poor soul," he explains. "They really ought to carry antibiotics, those chaps out in the sticks."

"You don't think he might have preferred to be buried out here – up in the peninsula?"

"Odd you should say that. We did get word to that effect. But it's not on, I'm afraid. Simply no Christian burial ground . . ."

"One assumes he was a Christian?"

"You can't just dump a chap in a hole in the ground. Actually, one did hear it said he'd gone a bit bush, but one has to give a chap the benefit."

Driving through the ancient capital's sprawling hinterland of modern apartments and villas, offices and banks, the Consul unveils graver preoccupations. "You've caught us all rather hectic: we've got Sir Timothy Lunt round our necks – I shouldn't say 'round our necks' but you know what these ministerial visits entail. One hundred and eighty, no less, wassailing at the embassy tonight. You can imagine – all those fat cars stuck in that alley."

"I've never been here before."

"How come?"

"I entered the peninsula on a twenty-four-hour pass from the shaikhdoms, then I lost the passport."

"O Lor'. So no entry visa recorded here . . . I wonder they let you in over that border."

"I crossed with an Arab friend who dressed me up as someone quite other than I am, to be absolutely truthful."

"We'll lean on them gently," the Consul says. "Bound to be a little jumpy after that kerfuffle up where you've been. They sent troops up, you know, chasing shadows."

"I heard someone was trying to mine the strait."

"One isn't really meant to know that," he scolds. "How did you pick it up?"

"In the bars."

"I rather thought there weren't any bars up there."

"Oh, on the beach, you know."

"Actually our view for what it's worth is that it was just one of their periodic panics. A mirage. Apparently they sent out their corvette and a few dhows scattered like flies. We don't greatly appreciate rumours about mining the strait. Insurance market goes haywire."

"Who was behind it?"

"If anyone," the Consul says. "Timmy Lunt's asked Political to come up with what he can. Actually it began brewing the day he arrived. You know him at all – ever met him?"

"Who?"

"Timmy Lunt."

"A while ago . . . I didn't know he'd been knighted."

"Oh Lor' yes. Birthday Honours. He's off and away to the shaikhdoms tomorrow, then we can breathe normally again . . . Look, if you've got a suit, I could probably squeeze you an invite for the do at the embassy."

PART
FOUR

1

Harry says from his editorial chair, "It is a remarkable story, dear boy, and I congratulate you." He has a way of quizzing across his desk and the photograph of himself among the Royals which makes the conduct of mankind a comedy in a sense implied by Dante or Balzac. "Oddly enough, though, I don't think we can quite go with it yet, can we – from the point of view of the paper."

It is typical that he should have perceived there might be another extraneous "point of view" . . . and not to *blame* me for it. "You yourself don't want to rush into print at this moment, do you?"

"No."

"Your friend Timmy's involvement puts you in a rather awkward spot. Of course, you might be prepared to sacrifice your by-line. On the other hand, you'd probably rather not be responsible for disgracing him."

"It was not my purpose."

"Absolutely not." I catch his flash of surprise, and wonder if my defensiveness has betrayed anything. "In any case, if he chose to deny any complicity, we're still short of anything to nail him – as I understand it. I doubt if your Mrs Wilks would come tumbling out with a confession – always supposing she doesn't disappear into the bright blue yonder. Where d'you suppose she's got to?"

"I honestly don't know."

"She could come looking for you, you knowing what you know."

"I'd thought of that."

"She damn well ought to be frightened. We can of course suss her out at this end – her connections and all that, her county background. We can be ready to net her."

"I doubt if it'll be necessary, Harry."

"You mean – she's going to find you."

"We established mutual fox-hunting friends." Maybe she

235

had a way of silencing me: she would not be one to leave it untried.

"She ought to know your name as a newspaperman."

"That's nice of you, Harry. Out there I was an agriculturist."

"Meanwhile there's your Timmy Lunt returning from his Middle East jaunt in a few days . . . What did you make of your Welshmen's reference to a paintbrush?"

The light on the internal telephone is flashing. It is the proprietor. The editor draws a pad towards him and makes notes for a leading article for tomorrow's paper: a certain strike called by union leaders without reference to the rank and file has constitutional overtones. As a staffer on the paper I was occasionally roped in to write a leader at short notice. If I was invited to fill a space for tonight's paper I would lament the futility of "significance through power". Power creates an illusion of significance, and by that deception corrupts. Pursuit of significance-through-power thus corrupted Timothy Lunt, Grover Wilks, Alwyn Rhys . . . Its polar opposite is what Jesus taught: significance through love. Love and power negate one another, yet perpetually use one another as to become indistinguishable. Is that perhaps the hidden repulsiveness in the practice of "democracy" – that the pursuit of significance-through-power masquerades as significance-through-love? All the blather about serving the people, fulfilling their will. As a young journalist making my name I used to adjure myself to "love my readers": it was a trick that worked up to a point (I was prevented from becoming an Indian beggar for them). The merit of Timmy is at least that he has known nothing of love: even sex was to him a function of power not of love.

I recall Wilks' phrase about the "fraudulence endemic in all democratic politics", and I even fall to wondering how much icy calculation has gone into the way this urbane and fatherly editor has played his cards.

"Now then," he resumes, lowering the telephone. "The paintbrush."

"I suppose it is something to do with blackmail."

"Would he be having vices, Anthony?"

"I've not seen him for several years."

"Even so . . ." The eyes penetrate with all their good-

236

humoured tolerance of human foible. My deep tan serves as a veil.

"When he was young he was something of a tearaway."

"Girls?"

"By and large."

The pause that ensues is for me to fill: it is my "scoop", it is I who chose to break back into a defunct profession and unaccountably expose myself to bizarre dangers. Every second it persists sharpens the shadow of another "point of view". "You're not wanting me to hand it to the newsroom after all you've achieved? If all this really is to mean his downfall I can very well see that you as an old chum . . ." He is exposing me as a "gentleman" – being a gent never really did go with journalism.

"Leave it with me, Harry." I make to rise. But he will have read the sardonic flicker his word "chum" provoked.

"I suppose there's a chance he'll have heard of your involvement up there in the peninsula. If the embassy are doing a report for him they could have had someone talk to the Wali."

"I don't know, Harry. P'raps I'll find out. I'll keep in touch."

"I'm always here, dear boy." And he puts out a long, bony hand that has sealed many a petty professional loyalty.

2

If Harry knew I had not been home it would have given the game away. Sophia is not even aware I am back in England. It's possible she might call the paper, but she doesn't know the personalities. I cannot bear to go home yet because all that I have risked bears upon Sophia and I still do not know what I am to do with my newly acquired authority over Timmy – my power to destroy. This selfsame, deceptive "power". I am like a dog with a bone which it will not or cannot masticate; it can only slink away and hide it from rivals, and present to those who might love it a mysterious barrier of skulking hostility.

Not that Sophia might love me still. When I telephoned her from the Emirate and carelessly mentioned in the opening sentence that I was "nearly through" I detected a moment of misunderstanding that I meant through *with her*: there was a fragment of bewilderment before her voice clicked back into the statutory coldness she adopted, oh, from several years ago now, on the long-distance line whenever I appeared to be announcing my imminent return. The frost was her attempt to lay an impervious realism across the golden trust and rapture of our partnership's opening phase up to the point – in the words she occasionally flings at me – of "the destruction of our marriage".

And yet . . . she has not chosen to walk out on me, nor I on her for that matter. It is not reasonable to cite the frail figure of Frances, bleached by the beams of two parental suns shining forcibly upon her from two separate points in the sky, as justification for our marriage's endurance. Admittedly, after our early reproductive catastrophe, Frances was allowed to enter the world as a specific attempt to restore credibility to our union. Yet was there not something else? Some bacteriological strain of love that refused to be utterly eradicated? It is a medical fact that despite the supposedly total assault of antibodies the mutational "skill" of certain organisms is such that a tiny percentage will elude destruction and survive to repossess the host, when conditions favour once more. Why has she not burned my ancient love letters? She can hardly have forgotten she concealed them in a trunk in the loft . . .

It is of course the aim of country hotels to pretend to be like "home". But the make-believe of familiar domesticity of the White Bull, dominating the High Street of the little North Wales town nearest to Timothy Lunt's family estate, keeps breaking down: the beds are provided with all-but-inextricable bolsters, the butter on the breakfast table comes in little factory-wrapped portions, and the staff during the late summer season appear to be mostly Portuguese. It is rather like a man in strange company hoping to pass off his mistress as his wife – a situation the White Bull is probably not unfamiliar with.

I have no time to waste. I know my man: he will exploit the least weakness, make a fissure of the tiniest flaw. I need all the facts – yes, facts – at my fingertips when the time comes. Some, I suppose, are what they call of "academic" interest – how Apramian got away after the shooting; others are not. When one or other of the disorderly eyes of Mrs Lunt's cook, Jonesie, first rests on me in the High Street, I see her struggling to place me, but her memory of years ago proves crystal-sharp.

It is the high harvest of the tripper season and caravans abound. My presence along the narrow lanes of the estate and in a chapel graveyard arouses no curiosity.

Lucy Wilks joins me on the third day. It was quite easy locating her – three or four telephone calls to friends around the Northamptonshire border. Instinct told me she had returned almost at once to England, though I suppose I could have worked out why it was bound to be so. She would need to know what I intended, and that doubt alone fixes in her a glittery exhaustion. I need her guilt – not that I shall press her for the details of her role. The management of the White Bull accepts her without demur as Mrs Anthony Goode. We make love that very night: she is wary like an animal at first. I am not in a position to throw her up in the surf – the nearest sea is thirty miles away – but I do very well all the same, indeed all the old skills that the sorrowing embraces of Sophia let wither return with full imaginative vigour. I wake first; her brown head lies in the soft white pillow beside me (the bolster

239

dismissed) like a conker in its shell.

It is only the next day, a Sunday, that we begin to talk. She talks and I talk too – why not? For does not one truth call out another? And yet, concerning Timmy, it seems they kept her in the dark . . . Tomorrow I shall have more of my truth to offer her: meanwhile I allow nothing to interrupt except a visit to the Church of Wales, one of fourteen places of Christian worship in the little town, so I learn. She accompanies me demurely. It is a sung eucharist – I expected better of the Welsh voices, but the congregation is pitifully thin and the vicar's strange impediment blights his spontaneity: he snatches at the ritual phrases as if fearful the devil will make off with them first. After the Collect, as piercing as always, he rehearses his diminutive flock in the Commandments, a practice dropped some while ago by the Church of England but stoutly preserved by its sister church in more fundamentalist Wales. As he grabs at each Commandment and we respond, *Lord have mercy upon us, and incline our hearts to keep this law*, I listen out for Lucy's voice. With the Commandments there is no evasion. "Thou shalt not take the Name of the Lord thy God in vain: for the Lord will not hold him guiltless . . ." *Lord, have mercy* . . . "Honour thy father and thy mother. *Lord, have mercy* . . . "Thou shalt do no murder." I drop my voice to listen and I hear her: "Lord have mercy upon us, and incline our hearts to keep this law."

"Thou shalt not commit adultery." Again, I am silent but not she. The rich hair is heavy on her tanned shoulders. I feel shocked and confused – she need not have come to church with me. I think, I shall fuck her into guilt and penitence for what she has done. It is outrageous. How much more appropriate would it be if I could record a tear swelling in her eye, for it is by no means unknown for a charlatan, a religious dilettante, to secure a conversion or expel an evil spirit. I may be irremediably compromised, even to the point of now being an accessory after the fact of murder; but I cannot help recalling her husband's mocking advice to "build up something" worthy of the pardon of an all-forgiving God. Grover was right – for what use to us is a God if we are to be pure? . . . Only the swank has gone out of her, nothing besides.

"Why did you take me there?" she asks out in the sunlight. I

240

answer that I always go to church on Sundays. Does she expect a proper answer – a woman who can be humbled but is incapable of remorse? Twice in the following hour I catch her referring to Billy French as "little".

As the warm sabbath wears on towards evening the ancient countryside assumes a primal mystery, a soft mist dividing into groves the oak and sycamore that tier the hills. The bleating of sheep reaches us from points not clearly discerned as if our rambling across the half-familiar folds and streams of the Lunt estate is being monitored by means of encoded signals. The panic cry of young pheasants bursting from bracken at our feet is swallowed up with unexpected swiftness by the secret air.

We come across the place where Saqr died without either of us having mentioned it as any kind of objective, and from there we ascend along the perimeter of the wood where the pegs were placed for the guns.

I enquire whether she loves Apramian. She replies gruffly, "You don't understand." I coax her and she says, "I was brought up extremely chaste. When I married Grover I was still a virgin and so just about was he – we neither of us hardly knew what to do. Grover never really discovered, you could say. Perhaps he wasn't interested in discovering. He was very ambitious, and very brilliant and musical: that was enough. But we loved each other, we really loved. Does that mean anything to you? We were like children ... but I knew I couldn't bear to stay a child always. Sonny was completely the opposite. I've had enough of him: he was a beast, and I needed a beast. I think Grover knew I did."

We have reached a point on the hillside from where we can look down on the twist of river half a mile away and the steep slated roofs of the big house, the haha and the cedars, and fragments of drive after it emerges from the clumps of woods and rhododendrons. Even the cottage at the lodge gates where the Rhyses were reared is visible, floating in the thin mist.

"But I longed for Grover's happiness. You know, Grover needed power – that's what I've always wanted for him: that's how I could have brought him happiness. But it's always eluded him – somehow just slips through his fingers. Sonny saw that and would mock him for it, you know, to me. That was unbearable!" Her voice has become hard and nasal and

241

angry at the dissolution of everything. There is still no word or sound or remorse at her own role in the death of good men or even at the hazarding of peace. I perceive in her a sort of moral infantilism and I remember the head on the pillow like a baby in the womb. I am thinking, "You couldn't bear to remain a child but you never grew beyond infancy." Now she shields her eyes with a hand like a steep, tight shade across her forehead. She says, "As soon as I knew what Sonny had done I couldn't bear to touch him – I couldn't bear to be on the same boat with him let alone share a cabin."

The narrow feminine brow furrows wildly behind her cupped hand. I feared she might cry at last: I did not want that – it would be intolerable to have to feel sorry for her. She is looking towards the low fuzzy sun which glows on her cheeks. I do not think she sees the large black limousine, momentarily visible, approaching the house by the drive.

3

Timmy is surprised I have no car – "I left it by the roadside," I explain. "I didn't want to be early." I can hear the dogs' muffled barking – and their mistress' counter-bark silencing them. She had taken them up with her. Timmy had told me on the telephone that "dear old Mama" went to bed after the BBC news. I wanted to be sure her bedroom light was shining before I reached the front door, but has the walk in the very last slate glow beyond the rim of hills cleared my mind? The mist now lies in wads in the hollows.

Here is the smell of saddlesoap: the Visitors' Book and the Game Book.

Timmy had changed into flannel trousers and a pullover, one sleeve turned back a couple of inches. I should not be surprised I am dressed just the same: he and I are from the single cask. I remember Alwyn Rhys' voice: "You and Timmy fell out of the same nest as little boys – you could be brothers." In the drawing room with our port we flank the log fire under the lady Viking in oils expiring on her beach with her dauntless child still too little to raise father's broadsword off the sand. If there are servants in the house, they have retired.

"Well, Anthony, this is a long time. One can't bear to think how long." A concessionary smile crosses the sallow face. "Drink up." He has not altered – people rarely do. The same disdain, the cold humour, the black complicity. Even the same lean, solitary body. With the fuel bills his mother runs up, he wouldn't need to wear his underclothes under his pyjamas on cold nights any more. "What've you been doing with yourself? One used to read your despatches with extraordinary interest – one was proud to say one knew you. I never knew why you gave it up. Maybe you didn't."

"I'm a farmer now."

"Who'd have thought that? I'd rather hoped our paths would cross – we'd have had a bit of fun, you in Fleet Street, oneself at the Foreign Office. I fear it's too late now. You're out of the game, so you tell me; I'm more or less washed up."

"You're doing well, Timmy."

"I've reached my little zenith. The knighthood – you heard about that? – the PM's kiss of death. I'm about to make way for someone else, sure as night follows day. I expect you'll find me joining up as a farmer."

"I'm afraid I haven't come to talk about farming."

"So I rather gather." He trails one fingertip along the surface of the red despatch box on the floor beside his easy chair. "You've come to tell me about what went on in that rather bizarre affair in the Gulf you got yourself mixed up in. Like the very old, dear friend that you are you've come to put me in the picture. You can't imagine how surprised I was that the strange English numero in the middle of that little farrago should turn out to be none other than Anthony Guise, ex-chief chorister of the Treble Block." The smile is back, but the lower lip has altered, that tell-tale throwback to the ancestor on the stairs – *faltered*, I might say, as it did in the television interview.

"No, Timmy." He frowns and waits, as if for a long-delayed joke. "I've come to hear you tell me."

"Dear old lad, surely you know. One's hemmed in by solemn oaths. Why don't you tell me about your part in it? How you got mixed up in the Gulf in the first place . . ."

"You," I say. It is like the moment a weapon is drawn. "The paper discovered you were involved. My old editor asked me to follow it up."

"Follow what up?"

I allow a long, long silence. I suppose him to be looking at me, but I am regarding the fire. I am in no hurry to answer him, but in the end I say, "Saqr's death," and the two words obtrude from the surface of the dark pool of silence like a strangely shaped log or the head of a monster.

I leave it for him to speak next and what he says is, "Why you, particularly, Anthony?"

"He knew we were contemporaries."

"Oh, did he? 'Contemporaries'? How alert of him. And you were quite ready to comply, of course, in pursuit of this . . . fantasy?"

"Yes."

The frown deepens. "One is tempted to wonder why." Here it is – the sardonic pity I expected. But so quietly, quietly.

"It would have been nice to clear your name," I say.

"Ah – but of course. We were very good buddies, you and I. And how did Saqr die?"

"You know very well."

"Yes, I know. Didn't I hear word of your wanting to see me before you took your trip to the Gulf?"

"You know you did. You had a tail put on me."

"A tail? A sort of private eye, you mean?" But I will not be drawn by his mockery. "You flatter our efficiency. All I know is you talked to my PPS and then you stood me up. You funked it. Something's given you courage."

"The truth."

"Oh, the truth?"

"It was too early to see you then."

"Too early to come to a very old friend indeed and discuss a rumour you say your former colleagues had picked up? What d'you suppose I would have done in reverse circumstances? But you always had a bit of a nose for the dirt, Anthony – I sometimes wonder if that wasn't why you went into Fleet Street. Now you're a farmer. It must have been quite a wrench quitting the farm in the middle of the summer, haring off on assignment – a 'positively last appearance', a wild goose chase. It makes me sad for you."

"You connived at the killing of Saqr, Timmy. You went along with the whole plot to take over the peninsula. You took a terrible risk with the peace."

"Now why should I do this?"

"To save your skin, Timmy."

I can see the scene-shift across the dark face, fear displacing sarcasm.

"The port's there." He does not move. His long legs re-cross. He looks at me over the casque formed by his fingertips meeting: one wrist must bend more than the other because of the arm's shortness. I rise to refill my glass.

He says, "What about that little wife of yours? You still together?"

"Why not?"

"She was such a very pure little lassie. I always

wondered . . . And that babba of yours she was carrying – I suppose fully grown up by now." Now he is stalking me. It is the way he always was: he could scent a weakness in anybody – my silence now confirms it. "Was it a little boy or a little girl?"

"It was neither."

He gives a shocked look.

"It was still-born. Sophia aborted at six months." Frances' phantom brother.

"Dear me." A shadow of assumed pain crosses his brow as it must have crossed at innumerable surgeries for constituents' woes. "What caused that?"

"*You* know, Timmy."

"*I* know?"

"I had the clap. I hadn't cleared it by the time she conceived."

"I did warn you, dear lad. You were so quick off the mark." He leers the old complicity. "You talk as if it was I who gave you syphilis. Now that's hardly fair." Suddenly the complicity vanishes. "You blame me, don't you, for the way you are. You've spent a lifetime blaming me. Leading you astray. Now it's touched you in the head." He taps his brow. "Syphilis can do that too. My poor boy. But you'll have cured the clap, surely." His voice is tacky with false sorrow. "You were quite a bad boy, you know. When a bit of mischief was in reach . . ." His eyes are full of lascivious recollection, and the mouth half-open in a down-turned smile. "I knew she was too pure for you, that lassie. She's given you hell, hasn't she, for contaminating her with your rather dubious early life. Aren't we getting to the source of this now? The private impulse behind this latter-day revival of your old profession? All the innuendo, your little bits of fabricated evidence? So sad. Oh, Anthony, what a way to occupy yourself! A grown man. A *religious* man."

A hatred floods me such that I could kill him here, now. My eyes are lost in pulsing caverns of the log fire. I could drag him into hell with me: I would endure all pain to see him burn. My head swims with the wanting. I think of those who have died because of this "old chum" – Billy French, the water party, even Wilks claims a fragment of sympathy. The thoughts race

246

back through the long tunnels of childhood persecution till they encounter the first victim.

"You want me to remind you of the paintbrush, Timmy?"

Now I have silenced him – I have toppled the past back onto him: nothing is audible from him beneath the weight of it.

"I passed Dai Rhys' cottage on the way here," I say. "These things will creep out, of course. Give them time, they creep out. Perhaps the ghost of that poor little girl came to me by night. A visitation of a troubled spirit that couldn't rest until the truth was out."

Now the shame smears across his mouth like custard. It's a melodramatic, clownish shame, as if I have conjured the little long-lost Rhys sister in this very drawing-room, calling her from the darkness of the rhododendrons where they used to meet – she, his exact contemporary, born the same summer, but here now in her ectoplasmic manifestation still a little child of nine or ten. I have not been wasting my time, these past few days . . . They started off together in the same school – high and low, sharing an inkpot, Timmy with his slight deformity of arm and hand. She helped him to learn to hold a pen. A tender friendship took root . . . Then off goes the young master to his prep school, his "gentlemen's school" as Jonesie defined it from beyond the green baize door. The friendship recovers in the holidays, but a secrecy swells around it. They meet there in the rhododendrons, planted to block the serfs' cottage from the big house. Both families are aware of a compelling and childish "secret": it tickles them, but they do not know what it is. The little girl falls mysteriously ill. She will not, or cannot, eat. A fever develops. She admits no particular discomforts. Then they notice – the mother, no doubt – what appear to be signs of precocious menstruation: nothing to be chatted about, of course, or even reported to a doctor. (Peasantry is always slow to call a doctor.) It is understandable why the little girl is off her food. She is a trifle shocked. But she languishes, and when at last they seek medical help it is too late. When they open her up for the autopsy they find the head of a child's paintbrush, for watercolours. The young preppie is back at school by then – a question or two surely asked with a long face but they will have striven to impute no blame. Can one so young be thought of as vicious? . . . It's not the sort of

thing a peasant family likes to breathe a word about, nor yet –
of course – a secret that could be kept from the household,
even the young Jonesie in the kitchen. Nor the brothers ever
forgive. There was leverage there, when the time came. I
remember Grover Wilks in the heat of the afternoon: *The last
thing people will condone is when the primal instincts are seen
to offend. They can't bear to imagine humankind as con-
genitally nasty.*

I say, "It was all the Russians needed to know about you,
Timmy."

"Russians?" His hands part in a gesture of hopelessness.
"Dear me. How you hate me."

"Naturally."

"And your purpose now?"

"I think it's almost fulfilled."

"You intend going into print, I suppose."

"That option is open to me."

"No doubt your editor will be pushing . . ."

"Of course. Harry knows the whole story. But it depends on
me."

"Harry's no fool." I will not respond to his jibes. He asks,
"What d'you want?"

"Nothing . . ." I cannot think of anything.

His eyes too have travelled to the fire. After a while he says,
"You were the best friend I ever had, Anthony."

"I'd better go." I stand: he doesn't move.

"You've given me no chance to find out what it is that you
supposed took place. My people dismissed it, you know."

"I'm going."

"I've not the least notion what you think that burnt-out
helicopter and the death of that wretched contract officer has
to do with Saqr up in the hills here."

So I tell him: I'll show him if I'm mad. I tell him it in outline –
outline only, just enough to show him I know it all, not *how* I
know it – nothing about the brothers Rhys – but *what* I know,
including the tail he put on me in the Gulf, and the way they
blackmailed him into compliance through the little girl's
death. And all he does is look at me with a great fake sorrow
dripping from his eyes.

"I'll walk you to your car."

He pulls the front door shut quietly behind us, and we cut across the lawn. He has a torch – there is no moon.

"I loved you like a brother, Anthony," he complains. "I can't quite grasp how you have let this happen to us . . . You imagine me as the author of a ridiculous plot. It would never have had a chance of coming off."

"It very nearly did."

"I know none of those people, I've never so much as heard of them – Wilks, that Armenian. How can you think I'm a traitor? I've given my life to the wellbeing of this country."

"Oh, come, Timmy. You went into politics because you like power, you always did."

Power compensates for love: I have worked that out. But he retorts: "One's power is negligible. You journalists have more – look at you now, you can destroy me with that incident with the Rhys girl even now. It's the only real muck you've raked. God knows, Anthony, I was only ten at the time."

"They all know in the village."

We have reached the haha at the long ascending paddock. Iron pegs are built into the stonework. He lights me down and when he grips me by the wrist to steady me I can feel him trembling. "You think that's fair," he demands, "to hold a man responsible all his life for what he did at ten?"

"You were saving your political marbles, Timmy."

"No, no," he exclaims. "You're off in your own world again. You're not exactly snow white yourself, you know. Who would have read you in your paper if they knew of you with your knickers down? I've built up something: I've been headed for the cabinet, I could still make it."

"I thought you said you'd reached your zenith."

"One can't be sure in politics . . ."

We are soon among the cedars. The route he is taking me by does not seem to be cutting off the curve of the drive. Clumps of rhododendrons appear. In man's corruptibility lies his salvation – it took the genius of Christ to recognise that; it was the core of his message: the lost sheep, the woman taken in adultery, the boy with the broken paintbrush. "There's a short cut," he says. Every now and then he shines the torch. It is like the beginnings of a maze. "You came here before, surely?"

"Once. Maybe it was twice."

249

"That's what I thought."

Our pace has slowed. The dark leaves billow up like a mock sea. "I was lonely as a little boy," he says suddenly. "Mama was very beautiful and very vain – it's strange to think of it now. I messed her up quite a bit when I arrived – she didn't appreciate that. All that trouble, then a few months later she realized she'd produced a cripple. She didn't appreciate that either. One way and another, the reason father didn't really want her back in his bed again was put down to me. She never thought I was worth the price. Here –" He turns off suddenly into a twisting tunnel of rhododendrons: I follow his torchlight in the blackness. After several yards he says, "You have to crawl here." We emerge abruptly in a glade, banked all round by rhododendrons and shrouded from above by Scots pines. "Remember this? We came here surely ... The doctors bungled me," he resumes, "not much, but enough to allow Mama never to let me forget it. She wouldn't have anything said publicly, but in private she saw to it that I didn't do things with other fellers my own age. There aren't so many families around here anyway."

We have come to a halt in the middle of the tiny sanctuary. I know it to be the place I have recalled all these years. There is no way out, except the low tunnel we entered by. Something prevented the growth of all but ferns and moss and a few brambles in the glade – an intensity of shade, a guilt in the soil. "When you turned up, I took you in as the first real friend I ever had. But of course, you were only visiting some neighbouring relative. I never brought anyone else here, except the Rhys girl. Then you arrived at school three or four years later. I knew I had an ally again. A blood-brother. I needed you like hell, Anthony."

He sits on the ground. I can only just make out the pallor of his sweater and the oval of his face.

"I was in your thrall," I tell him.

"Were you? It didn't feel like that to me ... except sometimes I sensed you pulling away from me. I only wanted to make sure of you, to be certain of – of the loyalty I felt for you. I don't find it easy to make real friends, and when I've discovered someone I don't like losing them. I wanted to commit you to me: did you never understand that?"

Part of me was proud of his protection, I remember that. He generated a wary respect, not only among the boys but among the staff who would give him cold compliments – an "able" boy, "self-sufficient". Even my parents reflected this pride, dropping his name with other parents, occasionally suggesting I ask him over for a few days in the holidays – but I never did. Once he invited me to stay here with him: I remember the private turmoil that invitation cast me into, and the mix of relief and shame when something intervened to prevent it. Somewhere I had my own sanctum, just as Timmy had this black glade. Mine had no precise territorial location: it was shared with Jesus, and sunshine, and belonged to moments such as were captured by the snap that Sophia treasured of myself as a child frowning down at the injured thrush. Each holidays I would recover this inner sanctum – secretly, magically: I could not bear Timmy's sweet blight upon it.

We have fallen into silence and the multifarious fidgetting of nocturnal forest life around us seems to swell to fill it. So Timmy only ever brought two to this place: the little Rhys girl whom indirectly he killed, and me, who have returned to visit him with my unburied hatred. I can feel the pity of it rising in me and all at once I recognise that element of pity for his isolation to which my childish heart instinctively responded. I suppose it is in the nature of love that those who know it are persuaded to carry it forth to those that have never known it – are persuaded, even, to sacrifice it for the deprived ones. For what other purpose shall any fund of love be spent? The unfair advantage is always with us, even unto death.

"I was aware you needed me, Timmy."

"I learned a lot from you," he says. "Sometimes doing my political thing I've thought to myself, what would Anthony have done in this situation? How would he have played it? I used to read you in the paper when I was starting off in Parliament: you were so clever at bringing the issues to life . . . You make me feel very sad now that I had it wrong, all the way through. You helped to humanize me, Anthony: now you've come back to destroy me."

The woods have gone quite silent again: they have no precedent for such a late intrusion.

"I haven't said 'destroy you'."

251

"How many people have you told what you think you know?"

"I've kept Harry in the picture right through. That was unavoidable."

"Including about the Rhys girl?"

"Not that . . ."

"He's bound to act on what he knows, even so. It's an editor's duty. Only if he's sure of it, of course."

"He couldn't easily follow it through without me."

"You've given him independent evidence?"

"Such as?"

"Well, other participants in this – this –" I could hear the caution, "you don't want me to say 'fantasy': we say 'affair'?"

"French is dead. Wilks will say nothing. There's the man who did the murder, Apramian – he won't surface."

"Wilks had an English wife, you said. *She* could surface, I suppose."

"She has. But there's a lot of blood on her hands."

"What are you doing about her?"

I cannot find an answer for him at once, and so he repeats his question.

"I'm screwing her," I reply.

"My God." And for the first time I hear again his cackle laugh: it breaks forth through the secret woods and shrubbery like a little jet of flame in the darkness. "You devil."

"She came here, you know, on a Let Shoot: she reconnoitred the whole site."

"Came here?"

"I can show you her name in your own Visitors' Book – her maiden name, at least."

"Really? What was it?"

I tell him.

"*L.* Willoughby?"

"Exactly."

This quiets him: I take it to be from shock at the intrusion. Then he says, "Dear tragic Anthony. You make me want to weep. What is to be done about you? Larry Willoughby is my neighbour to the north. Ask at the pub, the Post Office. Ask anybody. I've known him all my life. Every year he shoots my pheasants, and I shoot his." He stops. "I beseech you to check.

252

It's only this way there's a chance of your getting better."

"It's a coincidence." I feel winded, without breath. "Besides, she's told me everything."

Again he has gone quiet. And then: "Why don't you let me meet your little woman? She must find something very very special in you if she's prepared to indulge your . . ." He cuts himself off. "Or maybe you've concocted this relationship too."

My throat is dry. L. Willoughby. Larry. Lucy Willowby. A coincidence. He does not deserve this.

"I tell you, she has told me everything." The darkness is stifling me. He belongs to the darkness, and this is his place. "*Everything.*" I will not have him without guilt. I must have him know that he has been found out. Now and for always . . . If I kill him now, I kill his guilt.

He could still be lying: it's his natural element, it always was. He never could distinguish. He is like a man who can see as easily in the dark.

" 'Everything'," he echoes. "So who else is there?"

"Who knows about you – your part in it?"

"That's right: my part in it." The dark presses down, dark and silence in league with him. "Let me meet your little woman. I doubt we'll catch her incriminating herself to others for the sake of zizzipom with an affectionate loony. What is it you fancy about her, eh, Anthony?" I refuse him a reply. "There's only you," he continues. I hear the familiar, forgotten contempt he reserved for those that sought to block him – boys, teachers, brothel-keepers.

He has got to his feet and is shining the torch around the walls of rhododendrons. I cannot immediately locate the tunnel we crawled in by. It occurs to me now that he might suppose if he were to finish me here his problems could be ended – a desperate supposition perhaps, but is not his entire reputation desperately at risk? He has moved to stand over me: his torch shines down on top of my head.

"I'll be going now, Timmy."

"Hold it, old lad. Surely we don't want loose threads among old friends."

All at once I know he *is* afraid. I have stripped off facts and exposed the truth of him, even to himself.

"It was only fair to put you in the picture. I've done that now." But I don't move: I don't know where to move to.

"This lassie of yours . . ."

"Exactly . . ." I hear the fear in his voice. "This 'lassie'." My throat is still dry, but I can get the words out. "You used to like my reporting, didn't you? I developed a few tricks of my own. Interviewing people with a notebook in hand is such a clumsy method. It makes people cautious – they dry up. And one loses the turn of phrase, the vernacular. Everyone has a personal vernacular. Most reporters don't bother about that sort of thing. So I used to record them undetected. A little mike disguised as a wristwatch, a wire-recorder strapped to my tummy. I took the liberty of recording Mrs Wilks' full narrative. For Harry, you know. If and when he wants the story written up. I really must be going now, Timmy."

As I dive for what I suppose to be the tunnel by which we crawled in he extinguishes the torch, and I encounter almost at once a web of stems. "You won't get out that way," I hear him mock, and half expect a hand to grip my ankle. It seems he is wrong, for by trial and error in the total darkness I proceed several yards, wriggling and crawling. Yet it is not the way we entered. Rhododendrons give way to brambles which catch at my sweater and then at my face: they hold me fast, halting me. "You really are making an ass of yourself, Anthony." He must be able to hear my immobility.

With much difficulty I succeed in standing, but am manacled by brambles and one shoot clamps me across the top of the head by the hair.

"You better come back here. I'm not waiting for you and if you stay where you are I'll get you for trespassing."

I give him no answer. I cannot move in any direction.

"What d'you suppose you're doing?"

I still say nothing. I remember Absalom, galloping from the scene of defeat, caught up by his hair in a tree and slain by one of David's loyalists. But I am alarmed and exasperated rather than afraid. And yes, I can see the funny side . . . He must know I am still just a few yards from him: I can see the reflection of his torch beam, but the way it wanders suggests he has not exactly located me through the dense shrubbery. Then he himself begins to crawl out, back to the main pathway – I

254

hear his movements approaching. Surely he cannot reach me without getting similarly snarled himself? I think of joking aloud: "It was a big mistake, remember, the slaying of Absalom – not appreciated at all . . ." but then the crackling and creeping veer away, and next the dancing of his torchlight and then his footsteps on the gravel tell of his return to the house. It will have occurred to him that if he gets a shotgun and shoots me, mistaking me for an intruder, it could seem an acceptable mistake. But will he? I know how he works: he will have swallowed my little lie. He believes the worst of humankind, he perceives ulterior motives where there are none, he reads calculation into acts of spontaneity, deviousness into sheer impulsiveness.

He could return, of course, with a shotgun to taunt me, play with me. That would be Timmy. But if I hurry now I will compound my entanglement. He could surely pick a route which avoids footfalls on the gravel. Ah – he could call up Dai Rhys at the lodge gates cottage on the telephone and delegate the dirty work: "There's somebody trespassing in the woods. Go and get him, would you. Take a dog . . ."

Yet even so it would be a gamble to have me finished off . . . I have these shafts of inspiration – I have heard it said I am good in a crisis.

Perhaps the crisis is past already. I am left to my thicket and the wood – I have begun to see where the trees begin just beyond: it will be clear there. I listen for footfalls, for a sound from the cottage: it cannot be more than two hundred yards distant. Then I hear a twig crack sharply, and every thought and sinew freezes. Is there a nocturnal creature that will make such a twig crack? I wait for the next sound. Yet if he was to have acted would it not have been at once? Let me not be fanciful: he doesn't command the brambles. He could not know how well and truly trapped I am . . . Given time I will extricate myself. If I have time. All my mind is fixed upon the next sharp sound. Is he standing here, close to me, stock-still? Are we engaged in a contest of immobility?

I shall enter no such contest. I have the truth of him, and he knows that. I shan't even trouble to check his "Larry Willoughby".

I wait, and wait. No more sharp sound. I whisper for him.

He has not dared. He skulks in the house.

I am in no hurry now. Did I really imagine I might let him kill me just now in the clearing – I the fit and strong one, he with his ulcer? I did not crawl away in panic: I merely decided not to prolong the confrontation. I did what I came for, did I not? And I have rendered it pointless his making an Absalom of me or anything ridiculous like that. I will take my time in this wood of his. I will call his bluff about "getting me for trespassing". What an odd report that would make in the national press! What a convenient hook by which to draw out the tortuous story of Lunt, TPC, and Guise, AV. I shall take my time picking off the brambles one by one. After all, who has ever heard of anyone perishing through being trapped by brambles? If it comes to it, I can wriggle out of my clothes altogether and worm my way out among the roots. If someone glancing from the Rhys cottage spotted Mr Goode in the buff striding out by the lodge gates, what fuel for the village gossip! And to what bizarre equinoctial masque would the Portuguese staff ascribe Mr Goode's shameless reunion with his "spouse" waiting up in the White Bull's residents' lounge? That wouldn't half bust the make-believe domesticity.

But I am disinclined to speculate further on Lucy Wilks, except to reconfirm my intention not to betray her: I require her unpurged. I also intend to return to my wife and daughter, probably within a very few days. I shall just roll up in a taxi from the station off the early train, picking up the papers at the drive entrance, as if I have come from the airport. I must be careful not to greet Gertie first, before Sophia – at least not too volubly. Sophia will be upset with me – for my sake, of course, or Frances', not on her own behalf – at my inexcusably thoughtless lack of communication over this recent absence, but I shall be patient and loving. It is not as if I could ever love anyone as I loved Sophia. In due course I shall tell her about Billy French and ask her how we can plan a nice surprise for Elaine and her daughter Sharon: she will be really good at thinking something up . . .

Just for the moment, the women can wait. I am at peace both in and with this Welsh woodland, as a theologian might put it, as it is also in and with me. I wouldn't mind having to strip down and slide out among these trees like Adam or a tropical beggar – it's a warmish night. But it won't be necessary. I shall take my time, take my time.

Harry, of course, remains a problem. If in the end I give him no story, not even a story that others can follow up, I will have put paid to my residual role as a newspaperman. He has taken trouble with me, given me the benefits of doubts, laid out a bit of money. He'll think I invented most of it . . . I know I must face up to this – which is why a day later I call him long distance, just to say, at this stage, that I shall be coming back to see him shortly, to talk it all over.

His secretary says immediately, "Ah yes, Mr Guise. The editor was very much hoping you would call. We've been looking for you."

The pips go as quick as that, and I insert another coin. She says: "As you're calling from a box, I'll take your number. I'll call you back and put you through. You won't go away, will you?"

In less than half a minute she is back on the line. "I'll put you through at once, Mr Guise."

I hear the click and say, "Hallo Harry."

"Anthony, dear boy. Where are you? We've been looking all over for you."

I tell him where I am.

"It's about your wife." There is an odd tone in his voice, and I think: it has gone wrong, someone has told her I'm back in the country. I can see Lucy through the glass and say to myself, Damn. He says, "You've not been in touch with your home at all?"

"I think you'll understand, Harry, I wanted to finish this thing off before telling Sophia I was –"

"Yes I understand all that," he breaks in firmly, "but I've some very heavy news for you."

I have seen it at once. "Something went wrong."

"I don't know about wrong, dear boy. Sophia is dead."

When I hear him say "dead" it is like a word out of another language: the language of another species. The phrases that follow float through my head and will come to settle later, I suppose in their own good time. "The day before yesterday." She "misjudged the dosage" of some pills she'd been pre-

257

scribed, so far as he could gather. (But I am not aware she has been taking any pills!) Frances, so it seems, was already staying with relatives "when the tragedy occurred". (She had thought it out.) Harry has the number if I don't happen to have it with me. His condolence is faultless, and if I am aware that such an intrusion is – inescapably – unprofessional, it is no fault of his.

O Rose, thou art sick.
The invisible worm
That flies in the night
In the howling storm
Has found out thy bed
Of crimson joy,
And his dark secret love
Does thy life destroy.